LOW TOR

A New City mystery novel

Frank Eberling

Frank Eberling

©2018 by Frank Eberling. (68.0) All rights reserved
ISBN # 9781796317640
Published by
PALM BEACH FILM GROUP, Inc.
AUTHOR'S NOTE:
This is a work of fiction. Although some historical references are made to real persons, the story is made up. Some liberties have been taken with place names, locations, and the dates of historical events. The Elms Hotel in New City burned down in the late 1960s. What if it hadn't? What if it were still there? When was Lake DeForest dammed and flooded? Other than the obvious references to historical figures or people in the public eye, any resemblance to real people, living or dead, is purely coincidental.
68.0
Photo Credits:

HighTor/Low Tor/Lake DeForest
by Karen Damiani and James Damiani
The Zukor Dells Bridge
from the collection of Frances Eberling Rogers
Author's photograph in The Dells Pumphouse
adjacent to the Zukor Dells Bridge,
by Vincent L. Burns, 1976

LOW TOR

A New City mystery novel by

Frank Eberling

All art is a kind of confession... All artists, if they are to survive, are forced, at last, to tell the whole story; to vomit the anguish

JAMES BALDWIN

Frank Eberling

DEDICATION

To my paternal grandmother,

Elsa Bartels Eberling,

Holder of New City Library Card #1, who introduced me to the works of Charles Dickens, Samuel Clemens, Booth Tarkington, Ann Miller Downes, Agatha Christie, Ngaio Marsh, Upton Sinclair, Sinclair Lewis, Harper Lee, and dozens of other authors she was constantly reading while we grew up at her side.

It has been my experience that many times people do not, or cannot, recognize the influence they have over the lives of others. Thank you, Grandma for the lives you gave all of your grandchildren.

PREFACE:

NEW CITY, NEW YORK, 2016
8 YEARS AFTER THE MURDER

When all is said and done, my father was a difficult, complicated man.

Like the sons of many difficult, complicated men, I grew up bitter, filled with anger and resentment. Was my hostility fueled by his neglect, or the fact that I knew I could never measure up to his accomplishments, his standards, no matter how hard I tried?

I knew that unless I changed my own name, disappeared, I would be forever associated with this difficult, complicated man, unable to climb out from under all the weight his name carried and become my own person.

It was not until the last weeks of his life, when he was accused of murdering a young woman, that I came to understand who he had been, who he was, and how and why he was like the person he had become.

By that time I was twenty years old and thought I had left my father behind forever—the man who had started out as a local high school football hero in New City, New York, went to Florida State University on a football scholarship, was drafted by the New York Giants and was their star for ten years, went on to be a television sports journalist, and eventually a world famous, best-selling author of four works of nonfiction and more than a dozen mystery novels. Is that accomplished enough for you? It was for me.

Growing up, I had only a vague sense of his fame, no concrete details. Just the stuff you could glean from seeing the photographs, news articles, and magazine covers framed on the walls, the trophies in the glass cases, the books on the shelves. It gave me a sense of the big picture without bothering to reveal the specifics of what a person would have to do to earn a place on the cover of both *Sports Illustrated* and the *New York Times Book Review*.

Growing up,

I never watched his game films.

I never watched his broadcasts.

I never read his books.

I remember the last conversation I had had with my father the night before I ran away from home, two years earlier, in 2006, determined never to speak to him again. It was the night of my mother's funeral.

As I stormed out of the house, I turned to face him directly and asked him, "Was it really worth it to lose your wife and your son to write a bunch of second-rate novels? Was it worth all the pain and suffering you caused us by your neglect and lost opportunities, to accomplish *that*?"

The fact that he paused to consider his answer told me volumes. I turned and disappeared into the night. He didn't know where I was for two years.

But then, when he was sixty-two, he was charged with the murder of a poor white-trash woman who had apparently made some stupid decisions and was found buried on a remote piece of property my father owned. I thought about coming back home, despite my desire to never see him again. Could someone who rose from such humble roots and accomplished so much do the horrendous things the police reports described?

By then it was almost too late. I say *almost*, because I made it back just in time to have some long-overdue conversations.

Between what he told me when I returned and what I later learned from his friends, I didn't know what to conclude. Maybe it was time to change my mind about my namesake.

I am not a writer in any real sense of the word. My father was the writer. What you have before you is a more of a book report or journal of what happened to a real novelist gleaned from him, his friends, his colleagues.

To capture the life of a novelist in any sort of prose befitting the subject is an impossibility, I have discovered. In some cases I have made attempts to paraphrase story lines in the interest of efficiency, often to the detriment of what he originally wrote.

Anyone really interested in the quality of his writing needs to go back to the primary source material: the novels he wrote.

Abram Traphagen III
New City, New York
Summer, 2016
Eight years after the murder

CHAPTER 1

THE MURDER
THURSDAY, 3:00 a.m.
OCTOBER 23, 2008
NEW CITY, NEW YORK

My father would later tell authorities that the black SUV pulled up about fifty yards below his campsite on Low Tor, just after 3:00 a.m. on that Thursday morning.

Two men dragged a young woman from the back seat as she pleaded for her life. After a few moments of whimpering, they put a pistol to her head and pulled the trigger.

When Huck, our family dog, the best friend I ever had, raced toward the scene, barking, they shot him through the chest. They looked around hurriedly for any witnesses, but in the darkness, the underbrush and mountain laurel concealed my father's campsite.

They just left the dead woman there like that and backed out down the trail the way they had arrived.

CHAPTER 2

6 DAYS BEFORE THE MURDER
FRIDAY, OCTOBER 17, 2008
NEW CITY, NEW YORK

If you were to fly a helicopter north about thirty miles up the Hudson River from Manhattan on a glorious autumn day, just south of the old brick town known as Haverstraw, you could begin your wide sweep to the west and head over the crest of High Tor.

As you flew over the rocky cliff, if you looked over your left shoulder to the southeast, you would see Trap Rock, a large quarry owned by a company that had dynamited away the west side of the mountain, gouging half of it away for the gravel to pave the streets and reinforce the concrete of a rapidly growing

New York City. To the west of High Tor is a lower ridgeline known as Low Tor. The streams below flow north to South Mountain Road just underneath you, before arcing south to feed into the reservoir. One creek contains the remains of the stone towers of the old Dells Bridge that led to what we called the Dellwood Country Club. Within the bowl of that arcing mountain range, down in the valley below, lies the hamlet of New City.

New City is filled with magnificent trails and vistas, no doubt about it. But much of its beauty was not appreciated by early European settlers. Sailing up the Hudson, they had easier access to the interior on the east bank of the river. The gentle, rolling hills toward the rising sun were more inviting than what they found on the west side. Looking up from the river to the west bank, they saw the steep cliffs of the upper Palisades, almost like a staircase on its side, seemingly inaccessible. But for those who made the effort, on the western face of that imposing ridgeline of rocky ledges, there was a landscape enveloped by breathtaking hills and valleys and crisscrossed with streams that could be dammed up to power their mill wheels. All these uneven landscapes made the area almost inhospitable, difficult to travel, difficult to farm, and the inaccessibility made it late to develop, but develop it eventually did. The original beauty of the New City valley can still be found in the undeveloped areas, if you know where to look.

New City is the county seat of Rockland County, chosen presumably for its central location when Orange County to the north was divided into two counties in 1798. New City lies between Suffern to the west and Nyack to the east, and between Haverstraw to the north and Tappan to the south. Or maybe it was because it was home to The Elms Hotel, where Lafayette is rumored to have spent the night during the Revolutionary War. The sound of horse-drawn carriages carrying important guests was a familiar one to the nearby residents for over 100 years.

Today downtown New City is abustle with the county courthouse complex and a few restaurants across Main Street that serve the lawyers and the jurists and the secretaries and the civil service workers who fill the two municipal buildings every day. A block to the west on Maple Avenue are the firehouse and the Clarkstown Police Department.

To the east of town, heading down Congers Road toward the Lake DeForest reservoir, is Clarkstown High School. Built on the old Carnochan Mansion site in the early 1950s, it is one of the most beautiful high school campuses in the state. Filled with glorious, majestic maples and oaks, for almost fifty years it was one of the best places to get a high school education in the country. In the 1970s the district was divided, and now this campus is known as Clarkstown North. For the old-timers, there will always be only one real Clarkstown High School.

On this autumn Friday afternoon in 2008, the Clarkstown North Rams were on the main football field, getting ready for Saturday's afternoon game with Ramapo High. Walking up and down the field with the players and coaches were alumni from fifty years past. Back in those days a lot of the players left town after their senior year, went off to college, and never returned. Some returned right after college and found themselves back in a New City that was changing radically with the times. Others went off and wandered the world, living their lives, coming back to New City late in life, drawn by its beauty or a desire to somehow recover their earlier, glory days.

On this mid-autumn afternoon, as the sun was starting to drop below the bleachers and the press box on the western sidelines, long shadows crept across the field. The varsity team was going through a light workout without pads. The team was intent, focused, as they worked their way, at three-quarter speed, through the precise movements of the plays designed for the following day. There was a silence from their concentration.

Standing on the sidelines watching the action were two former football players from the class of 1964. When they left the field after that final game against Nyack in early November of 1963, it was the first time Clarkstown High had ever gone undefeated the whole season, capturing the championship. As the alumni watched now, they were remembering days past and their own glory on the field.

Nick Tremontana, age sixty-two, thinning black hair topping his medium height and build, was much more demonstrative in his sideline coaching, or back-seat driving as it were, on this day. Part of that was his personality and the fact that as a halfback during that winning season, he was convinced he knew what was best for the team forty-five years later. Part of it was the fact that he had been drunk since noon. Nick had gone off to college, returned home to New City, and become a high school history teacher at Clarkstown. He spent his days trying to teach disinterested students about the Whiskey Insurrection of 1791 and the Taft-Hartley Act of 1948. He spent his nights sitting at The Elms, nursing beer after beer until the bartender called a cab for him. He was driven home to his empty garage apartment, now run-down and unkempt, another reminder of his two failed marriages, which had destroyed him emotionally and taken all his money. After he retired from teaching, his wives collected most of his monthly pension, and he made ends meet working for Ditto Wyngard, a painting contractor who had graduated in the year before him. Nick and Ditto had been "townies" for most of the forty-plus years since high school.

Also standing on the field that day was my father, Abram "Abby" Traphagen II. While other teammates from that 1963 Rams team had hung up their pads and cleats for the last time after that Nyack game or had played for a few years in college, Abby Traphagen II was the real deal. He left Clarkstown with a full scholarship to Florida State University, and after being a star wide receiver there for four years, he was drafted by the New York Giants. He was 6'4", maintained his rugged good looks, and to the casual observer, was still in good shape. He moved back to New City and bought one of the most expensive cottages on South Mountain Road. For many, he was a hometown hero. For some, he was an arrogant, know-it-all profligate. Either way you saw it, Abby Traphagen was my father, and I was his namesake.

Like Nick, my father was sixty-two years old. Unlike Nick, Abby carried a professional air and was dressed fashionably in expensive sporting gear suitable for the brisk

October weather. A life-long athlete, he was still worked out daily, and showed it with his imposing physique.

Coach Nicholson was the son of one of the assistants to Coach William Morrow, who had led Clarkstown to victory in 1963, so he tolerated the light banter from Nick and Abby and the other townies who showed up as part of the Friday afternoon ritual. After each play, there was some Monday-morning quarterbacking that the coach usually ignored.

But on this day Nick had indulged a little more than usual and so was a little more vocal. "Hey! What's the matter out there? Pay attention! You gotta game tomorrow."

Coach Nicholson stopped and turned. "Nick. You're either gonna have to shut up or leave. You're disturbing my boys."

"Well, if they had a coach out there—"

Coach Nicholson took another step forward. He lifted his open palms in a halting gesture. "Okay, Nick. That's it. Come back when you sober up."

My father stepped in to intercede. "Take it easy, Coach. He's harmless. He's just come down with a bit of the 'old team spirit.' I'm leaving now, anyway. I'll drop him off in town." He turned to Nick. "Come on, Nick. Save it for the game tomorrow."

Coach Nicholson blew his whistle, and the football squad wrapped up its practice with a final huddle. As my father and Nick walked away, my father looked over his shoulder. Behind them, the team all pulled off their helmets and took a knee. The image was one that struck a chord with Abby. As if it were yesterday, he remembered "the last knee" on this field and the long shadows cast in the orange sunset. He waved to the coach and said goodbye to the other townies as he looked down at his watch. His mood suddenly changed as he noticed the lateness of the hour. It was almost five o'clock. He'd have to hurry to make his appointment in town.

In the school parking lot, with Nick in tow, Abby glanced over his shoulder one more time to watch the football squad walking toward the locker room, their cleats clicking in rhythm on the cinder track. Then he hopped into his Range Rover.

Nick was in rare form. "Goddam coach. Can't come close to what Morrow did for us."

"Take it easy, Nick. They're favored to beat Ramapo tomorrow. Let the coaches, coach. We had our chance. You're there to cheer them on."

They drove west on Congers Road to Main Street, across from the County Courthouse, to the old tavern, The Elms. For almost two centuries the wooden structure had housed visitors to the county seat, fed jurors, provided a watering hole for the old-timers of New City.

Out front, Abby pulled to a stop and reached into his pocket. He slipped Nick an envelope filled with cash. "Have one on me. I'll pick you up at noon for the game tomorrow."

Nick took the envelope, and all the baggage that came with it, and walked into The Elms.

My father drove off down South Main Street in the gathering twilight, to the medical complex near the movie theater.

Dr. Ezra Charles, also sixty-two, was another classmate of my father's, dating back to kindergarten.

Doc Charles and Abby had also been teammates on the football squad and had graduated from Clarkstown together. Doc had gone off to Manhattan for pre-med, served as a medic in Vietnam, come back home, and then gone to Columbia medical school before starting an oncology practice in Manhattan that lasted twenty years. After that, he threw in the towel and moved back to New City, where he worked in the county coroner's office for ten years in the 1990s. By his late fifties, he had semi-retired, seeing only patients he had grown up with, turning down most others, spending all his time at Dellwood Country Club, losing golf balls in the deep woods that lined the fairways.

Now, as Abby walked into the office Doc was seated behind his office desk in his white lab coat, holding a file, as his last patient of the week walked out. He stood and locked the door behind him, his mood turning somber as he sat down. Abby sat across the desk from him, awaiting the verdict. He started singing an old Robert Palmer song. " 'Doctor, Doctor, give me the news, I got a bad case of . . .' "

Doc swallowed hard, trying to maintain his composure. Abby looked at him. "You never did like my singing."

Doc took a breath that was more of a sigh. "It's the worst news possible, Abby."

According to what Doc told me later, my father didn't react at first. Then, in keeping with his persona, he tried to laugh it off. "This guy goes to his doctor, and the doctor says 'I've got bad news and bad news.' The patient says 'What?' The doctor says, 'You've got Alzheimer's disease and terminal cancer.' The patient says, 'Thank God it's just Alzheimer's.' "

Doc didn't laugh.

My father decided to try another joke. "This guy goes to his doctor, and the doctor says, 'I've got good news and I've got bad news.' The patient says 'Gimme the bad news first.' The doctor says 'You've got terminal cancer. You've got two months to live.' The patient is bewildered. He says, 'What's the good news?' Doctor says 'You see that beautiful receptionist on your way in? I'm *schtüping* her.' "

Doc, again, did not respond to Abby's joke.

It brought Abby back to reality. "You're not laughing."

Doc opened the file and held an eight-by-ten film up to the light. "This isn't something to laugh about, Abby."

Abby glanced at the negative. "How bad is it?"

"Worst-case scenario. It's very bad, Abby. I've never seen anything progress this fast, despite the treatments."

Silence filled the room as Abby collected his thoughts. On the walls surrounding them were Dr. Charles's diplomas and awards, and in the far corner, a small football trophy from 1963. My father stood and walked to the wall and picked it up. It was from their championship season together at Clarkstown. "So, how long do I have? Will I make it back to my car?"

"You need to get your affairs in order, Abby. Two months. Maybe three, outside. Maybe tomorrow."

The reality he had avoided confronting for the past few visits to Doc's was no longer something Abby could ignore. "So I guess all my workout sessions down at the gym aren't paying off like they promised during their sales pitch?"

"Abby, you're going to have to discontinue chemo and radiation immediately. You're going to have problems. I know the pain's not bad right now. But you're going to have a tremendous amount of fatigue and nausea. Continue to lose your hair. You're going to be in pain around the clock. Severe headaches, maybe even hallucinations. The last few weeks are probably going to be really ugly. I'll do what I can, prescribe what I can."

Doc stopped and closed his eyes. His composure was faltering. His eyes filled with tears and his shoulders heaved, thinking back on all the memories.

As usual, my father tried to lighten the moment. "You're a doctor. You're not supposed to be crying."

"Goddammit, Abby! You've been my best friend for almost sixty years, and I will goddam cry if I feel like it."

Abby was taking the news in his own stoic fashion. There was silence between them as Doc shuffled papers on his desk in an effort to regain his composure.

After a tense silence, Abby interjected. "Give me a week or so to sort this all out, will you? Promise me you won't tell anyone? The press. The public."

Doc tried to compose himself. "You have my promise, Abby. But you have to promise me you have to come by every few days and you'll let me know when the pain gets to be too much. I'll take care of you."

Abby tried to sound convincing. "You got it." He stood to leave.

Doc held his face in his hands, his shoulders slumped. Abby moved behind the desk and put his arm around his old friend. Doc spoke without lifting his head. "I'm so sorry, Abby. So sorry."

"Yeah. So am I." For the first time in a long time, my father didn't know what to say.

CHAPTER 3

NEW CITY, NEW YORK
130 YEARS BEFORE THE MURDER

My father's roots went deep in New City. From the stories I heard growing up, his ancestors had been living in the slums of lower Manhattan until the mid-late 1800s, when two brothers, Horst and Gunther Traphagen, took a barge upriver to work in the brickyards of Haverstraw and later labored as ice harvesters on Rockland Lake.

Both jobs meant living hard lives. In the Haverstraw brickyards, their coworkers proved tough and dangerous, and it was a matter of day-to-day survival. In the winter, the brick ovens provided warmth from the freezing temperatures, but in the summer the heat was exhausting. There was constant dampness from the clay muck. The thick blue clay suitable for brickmaking had been known in the Haverstraw area since the early settler period of the 1600s. At the start, all the bricks were made by hand, packing the clay into forms and baking them in the ovens. There were early attempts to use bricks for other than local housebuilding, but for the first hundred years, the handmade bricks were too labor intensive to be practical for widespread distribution. It wasn't until the mid-1800s that a brickmaking machine was developed, increasing production tenfold, requiring less manual labor, and resulting in a more standard brick shape-and-size. The timing was perfect, as New York City was replacing many of its wooden buildings that had been destroyed by fires in recent years. Haverstraw became prosperous as a result of this invention, and at one point there were more than forty brickyards producing more than one hundred brands of bricks and as many as three hundred million bricks annually.

Later, when the Traphagen brothers tired of the brutality of both the work and their fellow brickmen, they walked up the hill to the west, through the clove between High Tor and Hook Mountain, and toward Rockland Lake. At one point in the late 1800s, natural ice from Rockland Lake was one of the most flourishing businesses in the country. It had started in the 1830s by a small group of entrepreneurs. Rockland Lake's ice, from spring-fed water, was clear and pure.

There, the Traphagen brothers spent three bitter-cold months over three frigid winters, harvesting ice with giant saws and gaffing hooks for the Knickerbocker Ice Company with five hundred other "ice fishers." At 4 a.m. they walked out onto the frozen water in the frigid air, cutting the ice and maneuvering the steamer trunk–size blocks down narrow channels toward the shore.

Some of the ice was stored in warehouses the size of a football fields that were insulated with thick walls filled with sawdust. The ice remained frozen through the spring and into the summer, and when the ice on the Hudson melted and shipping lanes were open, the blocks were loaded onto small, horse-drawn railcars for the trip up Hook Mountain and the block-laden cars slid down the rails through an elaborate pulley system to the barges waiting three hundred feet below. People sailed up the Hudson just to see the transport of the ice. The crystal-clear blocks were taken down to Manhattan on the barges, where they were put into storage and eventually distributed all over the world. "Rockland Lake ice" became known as the best in the world. Meatpacking plants and butcher shops used it. Restaurants and hotels used it to keep food fresh. Lakes near Manhattan were polluted and clouded, and their ice couldn't be used to cool drinks. Rockland

Lake's clear ice could.

To keep the ice fishers employed in the warmer months, a stone crusher was built and the men quarried the nearby trap rock, shipping the stone to Manhattan, where it was used to build the concrete buildings and pave the streets.

In the six years since their arrival in Rockland County, the brothers became as hard as the bricks they made and as cold as the ice they harvested in order to survive the late 1800s. They drank. They stole from everyone they encountered. They extorted money from other workers. They beat up people, including their own wives. It became a family tradition. As the 20th Century approached, three consecutive warm winters nearly destroyed the Knickerbocker Ice Company, and the people of Rockland Lake began to panic. Those winters became known as the "ice famine." With accessibility to electricity and the resultant manufacturing of "artificial ice," Horst and Gunther Traphagen could see the handwriting on the wall, and they decided it was time to move on. As a farewell gesture, they set fire to one of the ice storage warehouses. With insulating walls filled with sawdust, the warehouse burned for more than two days.

The Traphagen brothers, infamous by now, branched into farming, but they didn't want to raise livestock like many of their neighbors. Instead, they cleared acreage and grew vast fields of corn to feed the local livestock. Over the next decade they bought up vast cornfields on both sides of Middletown Road, near what was later called New City Park. They dammed up the Demarest Kill at what is now New City Park Lake and built a sawmill for the lumber they harvested while clearing the land.

Their timing was off. When the railroad came into New City in 1870, local farmers found it easier and cheaper to get their livestock feed and their lumber needs from out of town, via railroad. Dealing with the local Traphagen brothers had become too contentious and sometimes even dangerous. For a short time in the late 1800s, to make ends meet during the cold winter months, they worked at the Eberling Shoe Factory. It was located on New Hempstead Road, adjacent to the Demarest Kill, the stream that runs behind the courthouse. They spent their days cleaning up scraps of leather on the floor and carrying firewood used by the potbelly stoves to keep the cobblers warm.

In the early 1900s, after just a few consecutive seasons of harvests ruined by what can only be described as drunken disorderliness, they sold their land to the Cropsey and Smith families, both of which turned their farm land into family dynasties.

Gunther Traphagen returned to Manhattan, where he was soon killed in a bar room brawl that lasted only seconds. The patriarch of the family, my great-grandfather, Horst Traphagen, became a grounds-keeper at Mountain View Farm at the foot of Low Tor.

When Adolph Zukor, the head of Paramount Pictures, moved to New City in 1918, he bought Mountain View Farm and called it the Dells. My great-grandfather worked on the three-hundred-acre compound, complete with a nine-hole golf course, a pool, and an enormous stone house. Zukor wanted my great-grandfather to help him raise cattle and chickens on the farm.

Two years later, Zukor bought five hundred more acres, expanded the golf course to a championship eighteen-holes, built guesthouses, a screening room to show his movies, and hired more staff.

Zukor had an elaborate stone bridge built across the Dells ravine that gave the area its name. The bridge consisted of a series of towers built from thousands of rocks tilled from the rolling slopes during the golf course expansion. "It's not called Rockland County for nothing," the old joke went among the men who drove the steam-powered machinery that sculpted the newly cleared land into a golf course. The rock towers supported a wooden plank roadbed that was reinforced by huge, arced timbers cut from the local forests. The majestic fantasy of the bridge drew surprised gasps from Zukor's early visitors. It was the talk of the town.

At the age of sixty, my great-grandfather was working full-time for Zukor. He married a much younger Congers girl, who died of cancer in 1918, not long after my grandfather, Abram I, was born. Zukor invited the newly widowed Horst to live in one of the staff cottages, which was not much more than a glorified toolshed, and raise his newborn son. By the time my grandfather was ten, in 1926, he was caddying for movie mogul Adolph Zukor on a regular basis. Then came the Great Depression, and Zukor and Paramount were facing bankruptcy.

My father, Abram "Abby" Traphagen II, was born in 1946, during the post–World War II baby-boom era. His mother was a local New City girl who got tired of being physically and verbally abused by Abram I. In late 1947, when my father was about to turn two years old, she headed out to California at Zukor's invitation, to "make it in Hollywood," and he never saw his mother again. He and his father lived on the Zukor property even after the movie mogul sold it to Bernie Nemeroff in 1948. Nemeroff turned it into the Dellwood Country Club. After the sale, my grandfather and father were invited to stay on, and that's where my father lived in the 1950s and early 1960s, until he went off to college in Florida. He never came home on summer breaks and never moved back to the cottage where he had grown up.

Yes, my father, Abram Traphagen II, born in 1946, grew up on the Dellwood property, watching his father trim the trees and mow the fairways and greens throughout his lonely childhood.

If my father was ashamed of living in a gardener's cottage, a converted toolshed, watching his father and ninety-year-old grandfather mow lawns from dawn to dusk, he never showed it. He would eventually determine that he did not want to live in near poverty like his father and grandfather before him, and he correctly concluded that his escape route was in sports and academics. Close observers knew that something was driving him. He was disciplined and focused, I'll give him that. He excelled in his classwork, was in the Honor Society at Clarkstown High, and lettered in football, wrestling, and track. By the time he graduated in the spring of 1964, he was a local legend, his life filled with friends and promise.

Having come from humble beginnings, he remained humble during this period of time, polite to his teachers, deferential to his friends. Everyone liked him, but everyone wondered what it was that seemed to be bothering him. Was it the near poverty he was trying to overcome? Was he afraid he wouldn't fit in with the more affluent kids? It was as if he had a dark secret he didn't wish to share. Two of his closest friends, Ezra "Doc" Charles and Oswald "Ossie" Hammond, grew up to be a doctor and a lawyer, successful professionals.

The third friend, Nick Tremontana, was the son of another groundsman, who happened to be my grandfather's boss at Dellwood Country Club. Two single fathers raising their two sons in nearby cottages on the grounds. Nick was the closest thing my father had to a brother. Nick did the standard SUNY college route, moving back home to teach at the high school they had all attended. He brought back a drinking problem and a wandering eye. Nick had always been the black sheep in the group, but my father always remained loyal to him. Doc and Ossie could never figure out why my father still hung out with the town drunk from time to time. Others of my father's stature and accomplishment would have moved on, but my father did not. Was it the childhood poverty they shared at Dellwood that had formed the bond? Or was there something more to it?

It wasn't until years later, after my father, the quiet, soft-spoken boy, led his teammates to that 1963

Clarkstown championship football season, after he won the full football scholarship ride to Florida State University, that his personality began to change. Isn't that what happens to all kids who go off to college?

When my father arrived on the Florida State campus in Tallahassee that summer of 1964, he was determined to do everything necessary to fit in and succeed on his scholarship. He majored in both the literature and television broadcasting programs, the latter a course of studies just four years old at the time at that school.

When he wasn't on the field practicing, he was hitting the books or in the television studio. He became an expert at shooting the 16mm cameras, editing the film, and putting together news packages and short documentaries. In the spring of his junior year, a sports anchor called in sick and he was drafted to appear in front of the camera. Old kinescopes I've seen of those early days show an awkward New City boy coming into his own. His friends back home would not have believed it was the shy boy they had known growing up. The confidence he had earned on the football field transferred easily to his on-camera presence. Yes, his friends back home would have certainly been surprised.

In 1968, in the middle of his senior year at FSU, when he was twenty-two, he was drafted by Coach Allie Sherman to play for the New York Giants, and he started making big money. Among his teammates were Fran Tarkenton and Tucker Frederickson. His old friends and classmates from New City, who came to just about every home game the Giants played in those years, say that he seemed to have outgrown his quiet demeanor. By then, after years of accolades, lots of money and attention, and a constant parade of eager women, he started acting the role of big-shot football star. He dated cheerleaders and celebrities. I've even seen a picture of him, taken in the early 1970s, wearing a mink coat and a cowboy hat, trying to "out-Joe Namath" Joe Namath.

Then, after ten years, a serious knee injury put an end to all that living in the celebrity fast lane. His football career was over in 1978, when he was thirty-two. He spent the rest of the season and the following winter and spring wondering what he was going to do with the rest of his life. According to his friends, he was disappointed, but not heartbroken. He knew professional football was a young man's game and recognized that he would have to move on someday, anyway. He had prepared for the eventuality. He and

Doc and Ossie shared the same money-management team, and together their earnings went to work for them, their wealth expanding exponentially over the years.

At the end of the spring season in 1979, the Cable Television Sports Network called, and he started doing training reports from football summer camps and became a color commentator during NFL games. His long success as a player enabled him to make some of the more spontaneous yet astute observations on the air during the games, and the ease he had gained on camera in college came back to him quickly. Once again, he was in the limelight, someone who had worked hard to earn his fame. But for a close observer, the ghosts of his past still seemed to haunt him.

College superstar. NFL superstar. Network commentator. Each step a major milestone and what many would consider an endgame to a successful career, yet he considered them as mere stepping stones for what he really wanted to do. He wanted to become a respected novelist. But his novel writing was still years away back in 1978 when he left the Giants. How does a football player turned sportscaster and documentary filmmaker become a novelist—move out of the fast lane to a quiet, remote area? In retrospect, it was all a natural progression.

His own father, my paternal grandfather, still lived in the tiny cottage on the grounds of Dellwood Country Club, but even though it was only a mile away from my father's cottage, they rarely spoke. I was surprised to find that there had been little communication between them all through his college and pro-football years. I didn't know why. That grandfather died before I was born.

By the end of 1979, my father was thirty-three, a year into his television career, struggling with his writing, when he was reintroduced to my mother, Sandra Schoonmaker. Sandra, five years younger, was the daughter of a former Clarkstown police officer my father had known while growing up. He had spent time with their family. In those days it wasn't unusual for everyone in town to know one another. Chief Schoonmaker knew a lot of the local athletes, and there were community field days and church picnics and Memorial Day parades. Everyone got together at the town's summer carnivals.

Of course my mother was only twelve years old when my father went away to college, but she never forgot about him; never forgot her pre-teen crush on the local high school football hero. She idolized him when he was a seventeen year-old football star and she was just twelve.

They met again as adults at a Clarkstown High School pep rally, where my father, by then a television commentator, was invited to be a guest speaker. My mother had wound up teaching American Literature there. My father didn't recognize her at first and was immediately stricken by her beauty and intrigued by their initial conversation about a literary reference he had made during his inspirational speech. In a "gotcha" moment, she identified the source of the quote he had paraphrased to the students. When she finally introduced herself by name thirty minutes into their conversation, he recognized her and was stunned at how someone he had not seen in more than fifteen years had developed into such an intellectual beauty. He was both shocked and disappointed that she was Chief Schoonmaker's daughter. She told me once when I was older that he looked at her with mixed emotions that confused her. She was unlike any of the women he dated during his decade as a superstar football player.

Not long after, my father decided to pull over from the fast lane of a traveling television commentator and try to keep his assignments local. In 1980 he sold his brownstone in Manhattan and bought a remote cottage off South Mountain Road in New City, near the neighborhood of Centenary, and lived among the elite, less than a mile from where he had spent his childhood in poverty.

An artists' colony in the 1930s and 1940s, this area of New City once housed the likes of the playwright Maxwell Anderson, and the actor Burgess Meredith. Kurt Weill, the composer, and his wife, actress Lotte Lenya, all lived along South Mountain Road. The architect and sculptor Henry Varnum Poor and the Broadway superstar creator of *My Fair Lady*, Alan Lerner, lived nearby.

The cottage in New City allowed my father to court my mother. They would marry within the year, and she moved into his house on South Mountain Road. She was twenty-nine. He was thirty-four.

My father was always polite to my mother's father, but any close observer might have seen that there was unspoken friction between him and Chief Schoonmaker, who could not understand the tension until years later, when he finally suspected what it was.

Over the years, Chief Schoonmaker rose up through the ranks from officer to detective to chief of the Clarkstown Police Department. Later, instead of retiring, he became chief of the newly formed Lower Hudson River Valley Park Police, when it was decided that the state parks in the area should have their own department and jurisdiction.

Was it okay that the Lower Hudson River Valley Park Police had a chief who was in his mid-seventies? They apparently thought that was no problem. How much crime could there be in state parks? With his experience, Chief Schoonmaker was the man they wanted.

CHAPTER 4

DECEMBER 1982
FLORIDA PANHANDLE
26 YEARS BEFORE THE MURDER

In the fall of 1982, a year or so after my parents were married, six years before I was born, their lives were about to change from the marital bliss they had settled into comfortably, but they could not have known that at the time. It happened the night Junior Wiley came into my father's life.

Of course, as a color commentator working NFL games, my father was still on the road a lot during the football season. But when he was home, it seemed from all outward appearances to be a happy marriage.

It happened late that fall of 1982, just as the college football season was about to end in a big rivalry match between the University of Florida Gators and the Florida State Seminoles. The star quarterback of the 'Noles, a shoo-in for the following year's Heisman Trophy, had suddenly disappeared. He would have been the twelfth African-American player to win that trophy. The Gator-'Noles game was traditionally played on the Saturday of Thanksgiving weekend. In 1982 it was bumped to a week later, December 4. In the middle of an already hectic week, my father's life became entangled, and all my mother could do was stand back, powerless, and watch it unfold before her.

Junior Wiley was a black kid from Greenville, Florida, the same town where Ray Charles had grown up, about an hour east of Tallahassee. Tuesday that week, four days before the game, he was at practice. That same night, he disappeared. By Wednesday, when he didn't show up for practice, the fears grew, and by Thursday, the town, the school, the staff, and the team were in a panic. The local police didn't know what to do.

The director of Cable Television Sports Network called my father. As he was a television journalist who made sports documentaries in the off-season and a former football player from Florida State, it made perfect sense for them to choose him to look into the story of the missing football player. My mother told me later when I was older, that he raced out the door that morning without even packing, leaving behind turkey leftovers, a pot of boiling water, and a bowl of unsnapped green beans; he flew to Tallahassee on a special charter and was back and forth to North Florida for the better part of a year.

In the meantime, the network scrambled to find a replacement for that weekend's network broadcast of the Giants–Oilers game. The NFL was coming out of a weeks-long players' strike, and "chaos," "confusion," and "uncertainty" were the operative words at the network and in the league during those November weeks that had just passed.

When my father arrived at Tallahassee airport on a charter flight that Thursday afternoon, December 2, he met up with a pickup crew from the local television station: Cliff, the videographer, MaryAnn, the sound recordist, and a production assistant, a high-energy, petite woman named Robbie. They filled him in with background as they drove to the tiny affiliate station. They were all recent graduates of the broadcast television department at FSU and were eager to work with a guy they perceived as a big-shot network guy from out of town. Since he had gone through the broadcasting program there, they considered him "one of their own."

In the basement of Doak Campbell Stadium, the local news director and the sports director offered him more facts and anecdotes on the career of Junior Wiley, and what possibly could have happened to him.

The following morning, Friday, the legendary coach Bobby Bowden had scheduled a press conference but had also agreed to do an exclusive interview with my father afterward. Bowden had been an assistant coach at FSU the first year my father played there under scholarship in the autumn of '64, and my father was excited about renewing their acquaintance.

Friday morning, as my father and his pickup crew crowded into the press room, other reporters and their crews had arrived from all over the Southeast. Bowden spotted my father from across the packed room and introduced him to the restless press pack as "a former Seminole wide receiver from the FSU Class of 1968. And, oh yes, by the way, he spent ten years on the New York Giants." The press applauded and cheered, which, according to my mother's account of what he later told her, embarrassed my father. He was there to do his current job, not to distract from the frightening uncertainty of a missing young man.

Bowden gave the attendant press the latest updates and introduced Wiley's parents. They cried, solicited information from viewers about their son's whereabouts, and then walked off, still crying. Bowden then introduced the backup quarterback, a cocky white kid from Jupiter High School in South Florida.

Afterward, Bowden approached my father. "Abby. Good to see you. It's been way too long. Looks like they got you a good local crew here. I know these kids. I like your TV stuff, Abby, always did. Let's set up in my office upstairs for the one-on-one. We're gonna have to make it quick. This whole place is going crazy, and I've still got a team to coach."

Upstairs, while Cliff, MaryAnn, and Robbie set up the camera and lights and sound gear, my father and Bobby caught up on old times, trying to keep it casual. Bowden was laughing, but my father could see that he was deeply troubled. During the interview, Bowden talked about what a fine athlete Wiley was and what an asset to his team, gave some highlights of his career, and spoke of how he got along with everyone. Junior Wiley was a soft-spoken gentleman, respected by his teammates. Bowden came just short of saying he was a credit to his race. All the usual football coach PR stuff, but admittedly, more personal than the press conference fluff.

After the standard interview was completed and the camera was moved for re-creations of the cutaway questions, the crew started breaking down the gear. My father walked Bowden out to the balcony overlooking the field.

"Why do I think you're not telling me something, Coach?

Bowden looked across the field. "This has to be off the record, Abby."

My father looked around. The groundsmen were preparing the field for the big game the next day. Memories of Saturdays past filled up my father's head. "Whatever you say, Coach."

"You're back in the Deep South, Abby. Think about it. It may be 1982 somewhere in the world, but not down here. Black kid playing quarterback for the Seminoles? Bound to raise some hackles. Some people don't like change."

"What are you saying?"

"You just heard all I'm going to be saying. Truth is, he could have just gone on a bender and is sleeping it off somewhere."

"Or?"

"You're a big boy. You can figure it out. I don't want that poor kid getting himself killed. In the meantime, if there was foul play involved, that's up to the local authorities. I love that kid, but he's one of fifty kids, and I've got a game to win tomorrow, with or without him."

My father negotiated a follow-up interview with Bowden, scheduled for just before the game the next day, and another just after the game. Another was discussed for the following Monday, if necessary, whether or not the missing Junior Wiley could be found. Bowden also recommended several players to be interviewed by my father after that afternoon's practice.

My father led his crew down the hall to the reception area. He turned to Robbie, the production assistant. "Try to find Wiley's parents. I want to talk to them before they leave town."

Robbie nodded. "They're still downstairs with the local press. I'll run down and hold them up."

"Make sure they know we're here to help with all the Network's resources. And locate his football coach from high school. Madison County. It's just east of here."

"We live here. We know that. We know him. Why him?"

"Because Wiley may have said something to his old coach. Find out if they're still talking on a regular basis."

I've since seen the finished documentary and was able to get a copy of the original A/V script.

From the *WHATEVER HAPPENED TO JUNIOR WILEY?* documentary script:

#	VIDEO	AUDIO
	UP FULL SOT +JUNIOR WILEY'S PARENTS AT PRESS CONFERENCE (S/) EUGENE & NANCY WILEY Parents T/C: 01:04:28– 01:04:45	UP FULL SOT NANCY WILEY: We just want everyone watching this to know that we love you, Junior, and we want you to come back safe. EUGENE: If there is anyone out there who knows something, please call the police. We want our son back.
	ABBY VOICE/OVER	These were Junior Wiley's

		distraught parents at the press conference, trying desperately to retain their composure in public while fearing the worst had happened to their son. Later, we caught up with them.
	UP FULL SOT +JUNIOR WILEY'S MOTHER DURING SIT-DOWN INTERVIEW (S/) NANCY WILEY Mother T/C: 03:02:12- 03:02:30	UP FULL SOT NANCY WILEY: He calls us every night to let us know how his day went. He's never missed a night. So when he didn't call on Tuesday night, I knew

		something was wrong.
	UP FULL SOT +JUNIOR WILEY'S FATHER DURING SIT-DOWN INTERVIEW (S/) EUGENE WILEY Father T/C: 03:02:12– 03:02:30	UP FULL SOT EUGENE WILEY: Having him home for Thanksgiving, well, let's just say it was a very happy Thanksgiving. Then the next week, he's gone. We kept waiting for him to show up at the door.
	UP FULL SOT +CUTAWAY TO ABBY'S QUESTION T/C: 03:25:03– 03:25:10	UP FULL SOT ABBY: What did you do after you suspected something was not right?
	UP FULL SOT	UP FULL SOT

+JUNIOR WILEY'S MOTHER DURING SIT-DOWN INTERVIEW T/C: 03:04:09- 03:04:30	NANCY WILEY: We got on the phone, called three of his friends, and they didn't know anything. The last time they saw him was at practice when he left the locker room.	
UP FULL SOT +JUNIOR WILEY'S FATHER DURING SIT-DOWN INTERVIEW T/C: 03:06:44- 03:07:15	UP FULL SOT EUGENE WILEY: We called his coaches, starting at the bottom, all the way up to Coach Bowden. None of them knew anything. They all got on the phone and started calling the other players.	

		About two hours later they called back and said they still didn't know anything.
	UP FULL SOT +JUNIOR WILEY'S MOTHER DURING SIT-DOWN INTERVIEW T/C: 03:06:24- 03:06:55	UP FULL SOT NANCY WILEY: His teammates spread out around town and started looking for him. His room, the gym, some local bars. They didn't find anything.
	UP FULL SOT +CUTAWAY TO ABBY'S QUESTION T/C: 03:22:16- 03:22:26	UP FULL SOT ABBY: What was going on in your minds during this time?
	UP FULL SOT +JUNIOR WILEY'S	UP FULL SOT NANCY WILEY: A car

	MOTHER DURING SIT-DOWN INTERVIEW T/C: 03:08:21- 03:08:55	accident? We checked the hospitals. A crazy fan? We. . .(crying)

That noon, my father and his crew drove east on I-10 to Madison County High School to interview Wiley's high school coach. According to what my father revealed in both the documentary and the book that followed, that was when he knew that Bowden's earlier hint was probably correct.

When they arrived at Madison High School at one p.m., security guards who were there weren't going to allow them on campus until the principal finally recognized my father. His face was all over the Network in those days. Minutes later, the crew was set up on the bleachers, ready to tape the interview with the head coach of the Madison County Cowboys, who were scheduled to play a game just six hours later.

Coach Jimmy Hobart was nervous, rattled, trying to contain his emotions when he approached the bleachers. He had been a coach at the school for twenty years. He knew the young Tallahassee TV crew from dozens of previous interviews over the past four seasons, and he recognized my father from the Network.

After some preliminary questions about Junior's playing ability at the school, the legacy he left, the kind of kid he was, my father narrowed in on his questions.

From the *WHATEVER HAPPENED TO JUNIOR WILEY?* documentary script:

#	**VIDEO**	**AUDIO**
	UP FULL SOT +JIMMY HOBART INTERVIEW IN BLEACHERS (S/) JIMMY HOBART High School Coach Madison High	UP FULL SOT A.T.: Did you stay in touch after he graduated? HOBART: I've watched him in every home game at FSU since he left high school. A.T.: So you were close?

T/C: 04:02:26- 04:03:55		HOBART: He was the finest young man I ever coached. A.T.: When was the last time you saw him?

There is a deliberate pause by the coach on the tape at this point, until he pointed to the camera and said to Cliff, "You're going to have to turn that thing off."

Cliff glanced toward my father, awaiting his approval. My father nodded, and Cliff turned off the camera. The crew climbed to the top of the bleachers, leaving my father and Coach Hobart alone.

The camera went black at that point on the videotape, but my father kept his mini-cassette recorder rolling in his shirt pocket. He always taped audio versions of interviews, using a mini-cassette audio recorder concurrently with the video coverage, so he could play the audio, take notes, and pick sound bites while he was traveling back to the station, without having to be around a videotape playback deck. This shortcut preserved what the Coach Hobart said next.

From the *WHATEVER HAPPENED TO JUNIOR WILEY?* documentary script:

#	VIDEO	AUDIO
	UP FULL SOT +JIMMY HOBART INTERVIEW **MINI AUDIO CASSETTE ONLY**	UP FULL SOT HOBART: I saw him two Friday nights ago. He used to come to the home games here at the high school whenever it didn't interfere with his practices.
	(S/) Voice of Jimmy Hobart High School Coach	I'm not sure Bowden even knew about it. We would always get together after the game and Junior would critique the game and tell me
	+B-ROLL with HIGH SCHOOL HIGHLIGHT	what he, himself, was up against the next

S. (S/) Junior Wiley High School Archival Footage	day. He could never stay very long, because he had a curfew for his game the next day, but he always came back. That's how loyal he was. A.T.: Did he say anything that would make you think something might be troubling him? HOBART: The last few times he had a girl with him. A white girl. I was surprised, to be honest. He was always so bashful around the girls. A.T.: Do you remember her

name?

HOBART: No, but she spent some time talking to my wife. She might remember.

A.T.: What did he say to you?

HOBART: I came right out and asked him what he was doing with a white girl. He said he was in love with her and they might get married after he graduated. He seemed very assured of that, but he was a little nervous about it.

A.T.: Had anyone

threatened him?

HOBART: He didn't come out and say it at the time, but I thought about what he said later, when he was announced as "missing."

A.T.: What was it?

HOBART: Just some vague references to the girl's family not being too happy about it. I mean he was kind of joking about it, but that may have been to cover up how he really felt. He was always joking.

A.T.: Is it
possible he was
threatened? His
parents didn't
seem to know
anything about
this.

HOBART: There
are a lot of
things young men
don't tell their
parents. His
father was a
long-distance
trucker before
he got injured
on the job.
Wasn't around
much. Don't get
me wrong. He was
always out
trying to earn
an honest buck.
He dragged
Junior to church
with him and the

		Mrs. every Sunday that he was home. Junior used to confide in me a lot. I guess I was kind of a surrogate father to him.

Late that afternoon, my father and his pick-up crew drove back to the stadium in time to interview two of Junior's teammates after practice. They set up in the stadium, the setting sun going down behind the press box.

On the actual documentary itself, you can hear one of Junior's teammates speaking very deliberately, as if afraid to say anything. He was a linebacker from Jacksonville named Nat Franklin, who knew more about life than just playing football.

From the *WHATEVER HAPPENED TO JUNIOR WILEY?* documentary script:

#	VIDEO	AUDIO
	UP FULL SOT/ (S/) NAT FRANKLIN Linebacker Wiley Teammate T/C: 04:02:26- 04:03:55	UP FULL SOT/ (S/) NAT FRANKLIN Linebacker Wiley Teammate T/C: 04:02:26- 04:03:55 UP FULL SOT/ N.F.: He was seeing some white girl on the side. We told him he was crazy, but he was in love. A.T.: You know her name? N.F.: No, I never even met her. A.T.: How do you know it's true?

		N.F.: Scuttlebutt. A.T.: Anybody on the team give him any grief about it? N.F.: Some of the guys teased him about it. Others didn't think it was so funny. We tried to warn him.

After the interview, my father turned to Cliff, MaryAnn, and Robbie on his crew.

"You guys know anything about this? You've only been out of school a few months, right? You ever hear anything?"

Robbie and MaryAnn exchanged looks. Robbie was the first to speak. "He had reputation for flirting with white girls. Don't get me wrong. Joking mostly. Trying to fit in. He was always very polite. But I don't know anyone who responded."

"Did you ever interview him? Come in contact with him?"

Again, they exchanged glances. It was Robbie who spoke again. "Sure, we interviewed him before and after every game for the last three years. That was all part of our coursework here."

"Did he ever flirt with either of you?"

Robbie shook her head. "No, he knew I was dating the camera guy I always worked with back then."

MaryAnn shook her head. "He said something smart to me once, and I told him to knock it off right in the middle of a sound bite. We still have it on the joke reel if you want to see it." The other crew members laughed at the recollection. "It wasn't really malicious stuff. I think he was doing it because he was so bashful, or because he thought it was expected of him. Maybe compensating for that, trying to play the role of 'Big Man on Campus.' It was just innocent stuff. He got embarrassed and really apologetic when I shot him down in front of everyone."

"Anyone around here crazy enough to get mad at him for dating a white girl?"

Cliff, the videographer, laughed. "Just about everyone in the Florida Panhandle and southern Georgia and Alabama."

According to Cliff, whom I talked to later, my father mumbled, "Well, I guess we'll just have to interview all of them."

That weekend of interviews both before and after the big game marked the beginning of a long story that would eventually lead my father to becoming more famous than he already was.

CHAPTER 5

FRIDAY NIGHT, OCTOBER 17, 2008
6 DAYS BEFORE THE MURDER

My father's cottage sits deep in the woods on a compound off South Mountain Road.It was less than a mile away from where he had grown up on the Dellwood Country Club compound. His mountain cottage, where I grew up, was a farmhouse built of local sandstone in the early 1800s, and later additions were built with post-and-beam construction. Before my father bought it, it was occupied by a sculptor who was a part of the local artsy-craftsy coterie. It is quaint, rustic, very expensive, and difficult to find unless you know where to look.

That Friday night in 2008, after my father got word from Doc about his rapidly deteriorating medical condition, he went home and sat behind his computer, reading some files and printing them out.

My dog Huck, a Bluetick coonhound, sat at his feet. My parents had found Huck on one of their hikes along Low Tor when I was just five. He had been abandoned and was starving to death. Huck was the only thing I regretted leaving behind when I left home at the age of eighteen. He had been my best friend for more than twelve years.

My father's den catches both western and northern lights through multi-paned windows in his corner office. He spent hours every day at his desk, working on his novels. As a boy, I would sit patiently outside the door, waiting for him to finish his day's work, but it never seemed to end.

As you walk into his study, your eyes are drawn to an oil-on-canvas painting on the right-hand side wall. Two men, obviously kindred spirits, stand on a rocky outcropping on a misty morning looking out over Kaaterskill Clove, to the stream and two waterfalls below. To their right, in the lower left foreground, the names Bryant and Cole are carved into the bark on a birch tree. I always wondered who the two men were. Just two hikers who happened to be hiking through the woods? Had they been the ones who carved their names into the birch bark?

Behind my father's desk were shelves displaying copies of the sports-related books he had authored, along with his wildly popular, often sports-based mystery novels.

One long shelf at chest height held a special collection of forty-four books, of unmatched size and thickness, by other authors, the names of which would have been familiar to any serious reader, but about which he never spoke until the last days of his life. I never understood, until later, the significance of those books.

Other shelves were lined with football trophies, one identical to the one in Doc's office from their championship 1963 season. Photos in black frames featured my father starring in Clarkstown High School, FSU, and NFL games. It was a shrine to himself. Was it to compensate for a lack of self-confidence? A display of ego? A reminder of his humble roots? All of the above? Or was it something else?

That night, after returning from Doc's office, he gathered legal papers and folders and spread them out, sorting them into piles.

He took a ten-page stack of papers from the printer, signed the last page, and stuffed it all in an 8 ½-by-11-inch manila envelope. It was an important letter, perhaps the most important thing he had ever written in his life, he would tell Ossie, his attorney. He sealed the envelope, turned it over, and with a Sharpie pen wrote "Little Abby," his nickname for me, on the cover. Then, carefully, he placed them all in an accordion file and snapped the elastic band into place.

He picked up a picture from the shelf behind him and looked at it. It was a photograph of him flanked by his deceased wife (my mother), Huck, and me. Taken almost eight years earlier, when I was twelve, I'd like to think it was a symbol of much happier times for all of us. My father and I were having a snowball fight in the front yard one winter night, racing around, pounding and pummeling each other with snowballs for a good half hour, our breath coming in heaves and clouding the space in front of us with each exhalation. Huck kept up the pace, yelping with delight in the frigid air. I never remember laughing so hard as I did that day. It was a moment of sheer joy as I was thinking, *this is what it's like to have a day of fun with your father and your best friend.* The moment was interrupted by my mother, who appeared on the broad front porch balanced my father's Nikon III on the railing, tripped the timer, and ran out to hug her "three boys" in the seconds before the shutter clicked. The shot captured my father in the middle, snuggling my mother and me at his sides, Huck in the center, while we all tried unsuccessfully to contain our laughter. My entire childhood captured in one photograph.

Now my father sat in reverie for a moment before he stuffed the picture into a large duffel bag at his feet.

Reaching into his desk drawer, he pulled out a .25 caliber pistol, considered packing it in the bag. He changed his mind, and put it back in the drawer. Although he wrote about guns constantly in his books, he claimed to have hated them.

He stood in front of his library shelves and lingered over the titles.

Instead of selecting one of his own works, of which there were almost a dozen by that time, he selected *All the King's Men*, by Robert Penn Warren, *The Magus* by John Fowles, and *Sophie's Choice*, by William Styron, and placed them in the duffel bag. They were books he had encouraged me to read all through my high school years, but at that age, taking my father's advice was the last thing I ever wanted to do. By then I had started hating him.

He hesitated a moment, looking at his own body of work sitting before him on the shelves. He pulled out a copy of his breakthrough mystery novel, *The Pits*, one of his most intriguing books, blending his love of local history and the surprising history of filmmaking he had discovered, including some interesting facts about

Thomas Edison and his local connections. He replaced it on the shelf and pulled out *Sweetclover.* He told me once that *Sweetclover* was his favorite of all the novels he had written. Only later would I realize why.

Then he lingered in front of his nonfiction work, *Whatever Happened to Junior Wiley?,* based on his television network sports documentary. His life had changed dramatically after that one book, started him down a new path. Sometimes the simple act of one person has an untold impact on another. He put *Junior Wiley* back on the shelf and then, decisively, cinched the duffel bag and turned from the shelves. Just a few more items, and he would be ready to go.

CHAPTER 6

NOVEMBER, 1982
FLORIDA PANHANDLE
26 YEARS BEFORE THE MURDER

That Saturday, December 4, in the fall of 1982, when Junior Wiley was still a missing person, the Gators beat the Seminoles, 13-10 before a crowd of 57,000 in Doak Campbell Stadium in Tallahassee. So there was a double reason why the town was quiet that night.

It would be another month before the football postseason was over. My father's duties doing color-commentating for the pro games on weekends kept him on the road during those few weeks, well into early January, 1983.

His father, my grandfather, died that February. During my father's football career, my grandfather went to only one home game to watch his son play professional football.

After his father's death, all that winter of '83, my father continued to look for Junior Wiley. It would be another three trips to Tallahassee before he got the lead he'd hoped for. It actually came through his Tallahassee production assistant, Robbie. She called him in New York one night in late February 1983 with information.

Robbie had been out drinking one evening after work and had run into a cop she knew from working in local news. Even though he had asked her out several times and been rejected, he wasn't about to give up, and he engaged her in polite, friendly conversation. They started talking about Junior Wiley, and the young cop had told her there was a young woman, a townie, not a college girl, who, according to friends, went missing around the same time. Her name was Rebecca Samson. Her family denied to the police that anything was wrong, saying that she had no connection whatsoever to Junior Wiley and that Rebecca had probably gone to Michigan to live with some friends. The local police were skeptical and couldn't find her in Michigan. When my father asked Robbie if she had told the Tallahassee news director what she found out, she said, "No. I wanted to tell you first."

When my father asked why, Robbie answered, "Because he can't get me a job in New York, and you can."

My father laughed. "That will be our little secret. I'm flying down tomorrow. Will your cop friend do an interview?"

"Probably not, but he can't hide Rebecca's missing person report from us, can he? Public record, right?"

My father flew to Tallahassee the next morning, and the first stop was the police station to get the name and address of the missing girl. They called Jr. Wiley's high school coach. His wife recognized the name Rebecca Samson.

When my father and Robbie and the rest of the crew showed up at Rebecca Samson's parents' house in a trailer-trash neighborhood and identified who they were, they found themselves at the wrong end of a shotgun barrel.

Her father spit out, "My daughter doesn't date black men. We taught her better than that."

So my father and the crew began asking around, caught up with her old friends from high school. They eventually tracked Rebecca down through an old pal. Lisa Ann Carlin had gone to high school with Rebecca. She was a neighborhood girl who had witnessed a recent altercation between Rebecca and her father. It was Lisa Ann who had later visited the police station to file the missing person report.

At Robbie's invitation, Lisa Ann came to the TV station and started talking even before the camera was rolling.

CHAPTER 7

SATURDAY, OCTOBER 18, 2008
5 DAYS BEFORE THE MURDER
NEW CITY, NY

The Friday evening after my father received his test results from Doc Charles, he had gone home to type a letter and pack his duffel bag.

The next morning, he went to see another old friend, Oswald "Ossie" Hammond. In addition to being a lifelong friend and another teammate of my father, Doc, and Nick, Ossie was also my father's attorney and literary agent.

Ossie had been the only African-American player on my father's high school football team. After graduating, he went to Cornell University where he earned his law degree, and he worked for years in the Civil Rights Movement in the late 1960s, traveling throughout the South before he moved back to New

City to start his practice. Now in his early sixties, Ossie maintained a distinguished air. He was seated at his desk when my father arrived.

When my father told him the news of his cancer, Ossie was shaken.

"Why haven't you told me about this before, Abram? More than fifty years of friendship doesn't qualify me?" He was angry about being left out of the loop and heartbroken by the news of his friend. "What can I do, Abby?"

"You've got to promise. No one can know until I get a chance to sort things through. I don't want the press to get wind of this. A week or two is all I'm asking."

Ossie rubbed his chin and thought out loud. "I can probably hold out a week. But after that, it's going to be difficult. When the press does find out, I'll try to run some interference for you. Like the old days. Maybe we'll set up a press conference, make a preemptive strike at the right time."

My father had placed the thick accordion folder of paperwork on Ossie's desk. He removed the manila envelope from inside and handed it to Ossie.

"Of all the stuff I'm giving you today, this is the most important." It was the letter addressed to me.

Ossie looked at the letter. "Have you heard anything from him?"

"Nothing."

Ossie would later tell me that he saw my father's composure begin to weaken for the very first time as he searched for the right words. He didn't care about dying. All he cared about was seeing me.

"You know, Ossie, I don't even care what happens to me. We all gotta go sometime. The hardest part is knowing I'll never see him again and that he'll probably spend the rest of his life blaming me for what happened to Sandra. Hating me for it."

"He's just a kid, Abby. He doesn't know what goes on in the hearts of two married people. How could he know what really happened?"

"It doesn't make any difference, I guess. It's what he *thinks* happened. Perception is reality."

But from my own perspective, it's not what I *thought* I saw happen between my parents. It's what I actually witnessed. My father must have felt an inkling of that, too, as he continued talking to Ossie.

"The thing is, maybe he is right. Maybe it was my fault. I tried to tell him that in the letter. I told him he should let you read it after he reads it. That is, if you want to."

Ossie tried to be positive. He looked at the envelope in my hand. "You should give it to him yourself."

"It's my dying wish, Ossie. You know firsthand how much it has cost me to try to find him. With no results."

If my father had known at that moment where I was actually living, I don't know how he would have reacted. By that time I had been missing for almost two years, often hiding in plain sight. I traveled around the country, did the Greenwich Village thing, washing dishes, working as a short-order cook in greasy spoons, and drifting in and out of New City, spending nights at the Chief's. Of course my grandfather never told my father that.

Abby continued. "I would gladly pay every penny I have to see him and talk to him again just once. But I guess it's not in the cards."

At that point I didn't care how much he was despairing over my disappearance. As far as I was concerned, everything that had happened to my mother was all his fault, and he deserved the suffering.

"Give him the letter for me, Ossie, after I'm gone. If you ever see him."

"You make it sound as if. . . ." Ossie caught himself with a reality check. "Surely you've got some time. Maybe we can still find him together."

"I'm a realist, Ossie. Just tell him."

"I'll tell him, Abby. But we're going to find him, together."

My father ignored Ossie's optimism. "I want him to be proud of me. I want him to remember the good things about me. I have done some good things in my life, haven't I?"

Ossie was remembering a young, black football player named Junior Wiley from Florida State University, and what my father had done in the aftermath of his disappearance that had probably saved the missing quarterback's life. He tried to place himself in that young man's shoes. "Yes, you have, Abram Traphagen. Yes, you have."

CHAPTER 8

I AM BORN, 1988
20 YEARS BEFORE THE MURDER

In 1988, five years after my father finished his documentary on Junior Wiley and the best-selling nonfiction book that resulted from it, I was born. By that time my father was an even bigger celebrity than anyone could have imagined. Former football star, television commentator, well-known author.

My mother was thirty-seven at the time, my father forty-two.

Was he a good father? I suppose he tried. But between his football commentating, which by that time had become a year-round task, and his working on other books, our time together was limited. I know my mother felt his absences as well.

One of his attempts at bonding was when they found the Bluetick coonhound in 1993, when I was five years old. He named him Huck, after, well, you know.

We lived a typical New City life for that era and I lived a typical New City boyhood for that time. I attended all the schools my father had. New City Elementary, Clarkstown Junior High, and Clarkstown Senior High, which they called Clarkstown High School North, by then. I did all the usual school stuff, but growing up in the shadow of someone like my father is never easy. The deference from teachers who had taught both your parents and had worked with your mother, another teacher in the school who was the daughter of a local cop, is one thing. You can almost accept that. It was the deference from teachers who knew who your father was, that raised other issues and resentment.

The New City my father talked about in books and in the presence of his family and friends was not the New City where I had grown up. That old New City was gone. The small-town character, the innocence, the fact that everyone knew everyone else? The fact that you could leave your doors unlocked? The fact that your neighbor was a childhood friend or the relative of a childhood friend? Your grandparents had been friends with their grandparents. The ministers and the priests and the rabbis knowing the names of all the kids in town regardless of whether or not they were in their congregations? All gone.

The New City I grew up in had lost most of that charm. The locations, or most of the locations, were still there. Lake Lucille was there. South Mountain Road was still there. Conklin's apple orchards were still there. New City Park Lake. The churches and the schools. Yes. But somehow I never got the feeling that they were the same as when my father experienced them forty years earlier. They had lost their small-town luster, and what remained behind for me and my peers was just old memories of what it used to be, "the good old days of New City." What we saw as we grew up never had a personal connection to the past. As kids, my friends and I took it all for granted. It was just a place or a building or a lake where we grew up, with no personal investment, no appreciation for the historical context. Was it because my generation grew up indoors, playing video games, and never spent the time roaming the woods as my father and his friends had?

I've since spoken about this to Nick and Ossie and Doc, and, according to them, they all lived in the woods while growing up. The trails to High Tor and the old, abandoned New Jersey and New York Railroad bed that started at the Vanderbilt lumberyard and went south through town to Bardonia and Nanuet, until the early 1960s, were as familiar to them as walking down Main Street was for me and my friends when we were growing up. It was as if my generation had turned our back on history and refused to bond with the relics of the past that had been so important to my father's generation and those who went before him.

To us, New City was just a place to grow up, generic, and without character; highways and shopping malls and new buildings. It wasn't until I was much older that I realized how much we missed by not having what they had experienced. We grew up without a sense of place, without a sense of belonging, of history, of being welcome. Our youthful haunts could have been anywhere. There was no *there*, there.

The things I did with my friends could never seem to measure up, compared with the stories I heard from my father and his friends: The hikes in the woods, the climbing of the foothills, the swimming across town, pool by pool, lake by lake, like in John Cheever's "The Swimmer." My childhood adventures never quite met the bar. Compared with my father's adventures and what he and his friends experienced, I never felt I had any "glory days." It was all so bland and inconsequential, humdrum suburbia. Had we been cheated? Had we been living a second-hand childhood? It seemed as if the history of the area had been ironed out like the wrinkles in a satin gown, leaving it dull and flat. New City had become a high-profile bedroom community for the nouveau riche, carved out of the rock of history. The kids I went through school with were the spoiled brats of helicopter parents. I suppose, to some degree, I could be counted among that group.

Most of my early years were spent with my mother, as my father was on the road almost constantly. When he was home, he was almost always in his study, working on another book. We rarely did the typical father-son male bonding stuff—fishing, camping. I can count on one hand the times we tossed a football around in the front yard—seems odd for a man who had spent twenty years of his life playing football almost daily. He tried to get me interested in reading his books, but I made it a point to read other stuff instead. And so I became an invisible boy, growing up in the shadow of an immense figure, with no real identity of my own, no real interests. I drifted. Waiting. What was I waiting for? A change of some kind I couldn't really articulate? I knew I couldn't wait to get out of New City.

As for my mother's relationship with my father, it wasn't until I was about ten that I sensed that something wasn't quite right. How was I to know? I had nothing to compare it to. And then she started drinking.

She retired from high school teaching in 2002 after thirty years in the classroom, the same year I started at Clarkstown North. Instead of spending her days with her students, she decided to stay home and get drunk.

She tried to hide her drinking during my teen years. I didn't know what was happening. She just became quiet, non-communicative. We didn't talk for long stretches of time. But I was a teenager, and I had my own issues.

As I got older, my father's road trips were keeping him away even more, as sports on cable television expanded, demanding more programming. When he was home, the arguments between my parents became more frequent. More volatile. She was in pain, and I was not equipped to do anything about it except hate my father even more each time he came home from each road trip. Instead, I started hanging around Lower Hudson River Valley Park Police. I grew closer to my grandfather and his policemen buddies, going out on patrol with them, enjoying their macho banter while riding around on their ATVs, camping out up and down the Lower Hudson River Valley Parks. I tried to adopt their swagger and repartee, but somehow it wasn't very authentic or convincing. I guess I wasn't cut out for law enforcement.

By the time my senior year rolled around, all my friends were talking about college, but I had no idea what I wanted to do. I couldn't talk about it with my mother. Although she was there physically, she wasn't really there mentally. My father wasn't really there either, and I don't recall him ever asking me what I wanted to do after I graduated. Weren't they supposed to be leading the way? Making suggestions?

In 2006, the summer after I graduated from high school, almost by default, I was scheduled to go off to SUNY Albany State, later that fall. But then my mother, Sandra Schoonmaker Traphagen, died of acute alcohol poisoning, a polite way of saying she committed suicide. She was fifty-five. I've always thought she deliberately timed her suicide so it would not ruin or interrupt my senior year in high school or my graduation. Or maybe she finally realized she would never be able to face the empty-nest syndrome by herself when I left for college that fall.

The night of her funeral at Germond's Cemetery, my father drove us back to the house and poured himself a drink. There was absolute silence. And then the argument began. Like a summer thunderstorm, it arrived quickly and with great ferocity, and then ended abruptly. Abruptly because in the two days between her death and the funeral I had decided I was going to leave New City—for college or otherwise. And so I ended the argument with a series of questions for my father. "Do you really think you should be drinking at a time like this?"

He started with the old, "When you're older you'll understand," routine, but I wasn't buying any of it.

As I looked around the room that night, a late June breeze blowing through the screens, I realized that all the pictures on the wall were of him and his accomplishments. It was all about him. One family picture out of dozens.

When I asked the final question. "Was it really worth it to lose your wife and your son to write a bunch of second-rate novels? Was it worth all the pain and suffering you caused us by your neglect and lost opportunities?"

When he couldn't answer, I turned and left the house, vowing never to return. I ran down South Mountain Road to Zukor Road, pumping my fists into the night, crying for my dead mother, my own aimless life. I ran to a friend's house on Phillips Hill Road. I would not see or speak to my father for two years, until early November 2008, two weeks after the murder.

Did I miss New City when I left? Not at all.

CHAPTER 9

SATURDAY MORNING
CLARKSTOWN NORTH
FOOTBALL FIELD
5 DAYS BEFORE THE MURDER

My father picked Nick up at noon. Nick carried a Pabst Blue Ribbon Tall Boy in a brown paper sack as he walked down the staircase of his ramshackle garage apartment.

"Back way or front way?" my father asked.

"Back way."

My father turned east on Old Route #304 and drove to Goebel Road, then headed south, like they had hundreds of times before. As they drove by the reservoir at one point there was a moment of silence. Neither looked at one another. Neither spoke. The reservoir was something they never discussed.

At Congers Road they turned southwest toward the high school.

My father, Nick, and Ossie never sat in the bleachers. They were always on the east side of the field, behind the team bench. Doc Charles stood at the ready on the sidelines, carrying his medical bag, ready to race out onto the field with the trainers in the event of an injury.

A late–October chill was blowing in from High Tor. The next few days would turn cold.

As Nick had predicted, that afternoon Clarkstown North was defeated by Ramapo High.

CHAPTER 10

SUNDAY, OCTOBER 19, 2008
4 DAYS BEFORE THE MURDER

Sunday morning, the day after his visit to Ossie's law office and the afternoon football game with Nick and his friends, my father finished packing up his duffel bag of survival gear. A few books and some notepads, a water purification kit, and a week's worth of freeze-dried food for him and Huck were tucked into place.

He looked again at the .25 pistol in his desk drawer, considered packing it, then closed the drawer without taking it.

He stood in front of his house and gave it what he thought would be one last look. His mind traveled back to growing up on the Dellwood property with his father, the days of caddying and shagging golf balls and mowing lawns that it took to get him to where he was on this day. He got into his Range Rover with Huck and drove away, taking a last glance in the rearview mirror of his 200 year-old sandstone cottage.

Less than an hour later, he arrived at a wooded trail in the shadow of Perkins Memorial Drive, up near Bear Mountain in Harriman State Park. He drove down a service road, cut through some trees, and hid the car in the underbrush. At this time of year it could be weeks before it was found, he knew. He looked over the ravine and threw his car keys into the tangle below. The chill in the air that had started at yesterday's game continued, but he found it invigorating. He had always welcomed the change of seasons and the cold weather it brought. He looked down at the splendor of the valley at his feet. In the distance he could see the craggy peaks to the south, Buckberg Mountain, Dunderberg Mountain, so filled with history of early Dutch settlers, the Revolutionary War, his courtship of my mother.

The beauty of this area always overwhelmed him. Rolling hills filled with burnt umber foliage, craggy peaks filled with so many memories tucked between their jagged edges.

He started hiking—a walk into the woods from which he hoped to never return.

There are close to two hundred miles of hiking trails in the park. Plenty of opportunity to get lost and be alone. His plan was to start there and walk south along the trail ridges back through Harriman State Park, Seven Lakes Drive, and eventually to Low Tor. There, he would end it all. How? Apparently not with his pistol. He would camp until he ran out of food and water for him and Huck. Then he would release Huck, send him home with a familiar command, and drift off into the unknown, reading himself into oblivion, unattached to cables and tubes and the nervous words of comfort attempted by friends and followers that a hospice would offer. He would die alone. He had no doubt that Huck would find his way back to safety just a few miles from home. He had done it more than once. My father once claimed that Huck recognized over fifty words and commands in the English language. One of those was, "Go home!" I had witnessed him follow those orders on several occasions. There was no doubt in my father's mind that Huck would find his way home safely.

Although it's fewer than ten miles from Perkins Memorial Drive to Low Tor, it took my father three days to walk the distance over the craggy, up-and-down mountainous paths. He was in no hurry, and he wanted to take in all the sites. So he took his time, allowing himself and Huck plenty of rest.

On that Sunday, the day he'd arrived for his walk into the woods, my father wandered through the autumn beauty of Harriman State Park, fishing in some remote lakes with a hook-and-line hand reel he had packed.

He hiked his way down the ancient trails to Cypress Pond, better known to locals today as Lake Tiorati, along Seven Lakes Drive in Harriman State Park. It is not unusual for hikers to be out on the trails during the leaf-peeping season, so no one asked him what he was doing when he encountered someone on the trail, or even when he had to hoof it across Seven Lakes Drive.

That first night he pitched his pup-tent, crawled into his sleeping bag with Huck, reminded our dog the tent style was named after him, which made Huck happy, and fell asleep from exhaustion, dreaming of plotlines to novels he would never complete. It was one of the things that saddened him the most, next to never being able to talk to me again.

CHAPTER 11

MONDAY, OCTOBER 20, 2008
3 DAYS BEFORE THE MURDER

On Monday, he walked the northern shore of Lake Tiorati and pulled out his map. It might have appeared as if his hiking were aimless, but he had a preliminary destination in mind even before his final destination of Low Tor.He had been on this trail many times, but it was almost as if he had to reinforce his whereabouts. If this had been four hundred years earlier, he would have happened across another type of wildlife: bears, panthers, wolves, and humans known as *Lenni Lenape*, all at home in their glorious habitat.

He kept circling, coming upon deer and coyote, until he reached a specific crest, left the main trail, and circled around a huge boulder that had been discarded, left behind by the receding glaciers thousands of years ago. The giant rock was familiar to him, as he had been there many times in his past.

The first time was in 1985, after two local spelunkers had climbed down into one of the abandoned iron ore pits that had been mined back in the mid-1700s.

CHAPTER 12

1985–1986
23 YEARS BEFORE THE MURDER
The Pits

After his *Whatever Happened to Junior Wiley?* book was published in 1984, my father wrote a second nonfiction work and became involved in a defamation of character lawsuit that would go on for years. It disheartened him. He decided to stay with fiction to avoid any further lawsuits and to fulfill a lifelong dream and ambition to write novels. It was time.

He also wrote four potboilers in just two years, featuring a former pro football player as the protagonist. They were books he had started over the years but never finished. He wrote them in record time. The hero gets involved with murder mysteries, even though he had no law enforcement background. It was all amateur-sleuth stuff, where the lead character always happens to be at the wrong place at the wrong time. Some readers felt he was crafting his protagonist to be a northern version of Travis McGee, the John D. MacDonald character in twenty-one of the author's Florida novels. Like MacDonald, my father gave his own fictional character a first name derived from the name of a U.S. Air Force base. In this case— "Patrick." MacDonald's Travis McGee lived in Fort Lauderdale on a houseboat that he won in a poker game and berthed in Bahia Mar Marina. It was called the *Busted Flush*. My father's character, Patrick Thomas, lived on an Erie Canal barge boat he salvaged in upstate Lockport, rebuilt it, and docked it at 79th Street pier in downtown Manhattan. He called it *Keat's Folley*, in ironic honor of the boat that John James Audobon sold to the brother of acclaimed British poet, John Keats, sight unseen. Unbeknownst to George Keats, the boat was already at the bottom of the Mississippi River when Audobon sold it to him.

Thoughtful, debonair, philosophical, a ladies' man, the Patrick Thomas character of my father's novels was almost a stereotype. The four books in the series were optioned by Hollywood, but never produced. *Fourth and Goal, First and Ten, Hail Mary,* and *Cross-Body Block* were "too derivative of better works" to make into feature films, the studio concluded. In addition, like MacDonald's series, they were "too philosophical for a television audience at the time," since they contained lots of history about the Lower Hudson River Valley and current environmental threats. Also like MacDonald's Travis McGee, my father's Patrick Thomas, a former running back, leads a heady lifestyle, but in Manhattan, not South Florida, and gets involved with femme fatales, sex, drugs, and rock & roll. The stories were fluff, essentially; formulaic books to be read on an airplane in just a few hours. It was a world he knew, and his publisher capitalized on his name recognition as both an athlete and a television commentator.

It was after the four minor bestsellers in the Patrick Thomas series, but before I was born in 1988, when my father decided that if he wanted to make a name for himself as a serious novelist, he would have to stop writing fiction in such a formulaic manner. He had to write something real. Something original. Something from his gut. He did not have too far to look.

For his fifth novel he wrote about a news event that happened just north of his home in New City. That book was called *The Pits*.

In 1985 two spelunkers had found the bodies of two men deep inside a cluster of abandoned iron ore pits, part of the historical Hasenclever mine system near

Lake Tiorati in Harriman State Park, where my father stood that Monday on his last hike.

When the incident had occurred twenty-three years before this day in the woods, the headlines in the Rockland *Journal News* had read **TWO CAVERS FIND TWO DEAD BODIES.**

The Pits was published in 1986, a murder mystery novel based on the factual evidence my father would discover and then fictionalize.

At first he was going to do the story as fact-based documentary and nonfiction, like the *Junior Wiley* book, but he could not get enough corroboration of his facts, and he was threatened with another lawsuit

The Pits was his breakthrough "literary novel," published when he was forty years old.

For years, these centuries-old mineshafts, or "pits" of the book title, still present around Lake Tiorati, had been explored by climbers and hikers, often with the expedition ending in one sort of injury or another and often requiring rescue operations. But on that day in 1985 the two cavers had taken a passage to an unexplored cavern that apparently had not had previous visitors. At least not for almost seventy years.

What the cavers found in 1985 would eventually keep my father busy with research, travel, and writing for a year.

Now, twenty three years later in 2008, on what my father planned to be his last hike through the area, he approached a small rise in the rocks. He came upon a poured concrete slab platform that served as a secured foundation for an iron gate with a padlock. A sign in the green and yellow park colors offered a warning: RESTRICTED AREA: KEEP OUT. My father gazed down into the empty pit, thinking of the first time he looked into its depths twenty-three years earlier and what had happened as a result.

In 1985, the two cavers had explored the old iron-ore pit on a brisk autumn afternoon, not unlike the one my father was experiencing that day. They took photographs and charted their journey. After dropping down more than sixty feet into the vertical mineshaft using safety cables, the cavers had waded through knee-high standing water from a recent rainfall.

Exploring farther and deeper into the pit, they came to a narrow shelf, about waist level and only two feet high, leading off into the darkness. It was like an empty drawer slot in a bedroom bureau, and from their flashlight beams it looked as if it dead-ended sixty feet ahead. They wanted to make sure. Checking their flashlight batteries and water supply, they stretched out on their stomachs, dragging their backpacks behind them, and skooched their way into the abyss. Halfway to the rear wall, there was barely enough overhead clearance to frog-wriggle their way forward, as the passage arced sharply to their left. After another thirty yards, the narrow tunnel opened into another, smaller cavern.

There, in a chamber room about twelve feet by twelve feet, they found the mummified bodies of two men dressed in business suits, with one derby and one newsboy cap at their respective feet. Their clothing styles were reminiscent of fashionable attire from the post–World War I era into the 1920s. There was no evidence of any food or water containers nearby. Could they have been mining officials who got lost? Could the dead men have been hikers who wandered into the cavern after the era of mining had ended and then become lost? Why were they wearing business attire? Did they die of thirst or starvation? Or fear? How long had their bodies been there? Had the two lengths of rope found beside them been used to tie their hands?

Before leaving that day in 1985, the two cavers looked around and searched the pockets of the men. They took photographs of what would later be classified as a crime scene, albeit from a probable crime committed more than sixty years earlier. The rotted clothing on the two corpses fell apart at their touch. But inside the pockets were several remarkably well-preserved items, preserved owing to the arid and stable temperatures.

One of the items, a round tin five inches in diameter, almost like a biscuit tin, was not surrendered to the investigators at first. The cavers kept it as a souvenir, a novelty, until convinced by one of their wives to turn it in to the authorities. The round tin's contents would eventually provide my father with the information necessary to determine who the dead men were and how they wound up in an iron-ore pit just under a thousand miles from where they worked.

That day in 1985, it took the spelunkers over an hour to get back to the surface and another hour to hike through the woods to the beach house at Lake Tiorati to contact the park police. When the case was investigated by the Lower Hudson River Valley Park Police, my father would actually work with his father-in-law, Chief Schoonmaker, for the second time.

The first case had been a missing persons case when my father was nine years old. He was questioned by Chief Schoonmaker, then the Clarkstown Chief of Police, who would later become both his father-in-law and my maternal grandfather. That first case, in 1956, regarding a missing schoolteacher, had shocked and frightened the small town, and Chief Schoonmaker had eventually questioned all the students.

But in 1985, with the cavers, it was the piece of evidence in the round tin, originally withheld by the climbers and finally turned over to Chief Schoonmaker, that prompted my father to pursue the case, conduct sufficient research, become frustrated by confusing leads, talk to a living eyewitness, and eventually decide to fictionalize what he had found to support his own conclusions.

The results became his novel, *The Pits*, published in 1986.

The history of mining in Rockland County goes back almost four hundred years. Early European explorers combed the area looking for gold and silver. What they found was iron ore.

Over the centuries, dozens of caves, shafts, and pits were dug and drilled and explored, with wide-ranging results.

Even before the Revolutionary War there were mining and smelting operations in the area, manufacturing a variety of products, including farm implements, nails, boat anchors, and chains. The infamous chain, designed to thwart the British ships from sailing farther up the river, and stretched across the Hudson at West Point, was made of eighteen-inch iron links that had been mined close by.

One of the biggest sources of revenue from the iron ore was the manufacture of weapons: swords, sabers, and long rifles.

In an effort to solve the identities of the two corpses, with Chief Schoonmaker's permission, my father began his research and investigation by becoming a spelunker again himself. To hear my mother tell the story later, she was not happy with his research and feared for his safety. But my father had already had a brush with caving from his Florida days. You could say he had a history of caving.

My father hired the two cavers who had found the bodies, and they retraced their trip for him, my father struggling to keep up. He wasn't twenty-one anymore, as he was during his first, earlier caving expedition in Florida.

The bodies had been removed and the scene swept by the crime scene unit. There was nothing left to see, but I guess he wanted to feel the authenticity of the scene before attempting to tell the story, like a method actor preparing for a stage role.

What was he looking for? Answers to who the men were and how they got there? What the mines were used for in recent years? Was there any equipment left behind?

My father then wrote *The Pits* as nonfiction, but was immediately threatened with a lawsuit, once again for yet another book. Not soon after, Rodney Monroe, the primary source witness who had tied the facts of *The Pits* all together, died during my father's writing/revision process. He was ninety. My father could not corroborate conclusively what Rodney had told him. Yes, it was all recorded on video, but the plaintiffs planned to say it was the meanderings of a feeble old man suffering from dementia. The publisher bailed out.

My father quickly fictionalized the entire story.

For the protagonist/first-person narrator of this novel, he chose an old high school friend instead of modeling the character on himself. This friend was a film instructor from Rockland Community College. He called the fictitious character Professor Ivan Heskestad. What inspired my father to choose him was that his old friend was not only a college professor who taught film and made documentaries, but an avid spelunker as well. Everything factual my father had done as a writer/researcher, he attributed to the fictitious Heskestad, who mirrored every step of my father's actual investigative journey in the novel version.

On a subsequent visit to the caves in 1985, a Wednesday morning, my father convinced the two cavers to leave him behind for forty-eight hours with just a few plastic jugs of water. As he followed the men down into the deep, dark shaft and then elbowed his way on his belly across the flat table top crawl- space, his shoulders grew tired and his heart pounded in fear. Maybe this wasn't such a good idea, after all. These were exactly the physical feelings and emotions he was looking for. He wanted to feel what it was like living in the complete dark, not knowing if anyone was ever going to return to lead him back to the top. Would he be overcome with claustrophobia? Would he go insane with fear?

He described those feelings from the point of view of his fictitious protagonist, Ivan Heskestad, in *The Pits.*

The Pits
Pub.1986

It was dank going in. Absolutely silent when my two spelunker friends left. My imagination raced.

What thoughts had gone through the minds of the two men left behind? Assuming they were accompanied in by others, what if the men who had led or forced them into the pit didn't come back? What if those men were killed in a freak accident and hadn't told anyone? What if my own deliverers who had dropped me off forgot about picking me up on Friday evening? How will I be able to tell the passage of time without a watch? If I fall asleep, how will I tell how many hours have passed? Two? Seven? Is it still Wednesday? Thursday? The hours, the darkness, the loneliness, there is no reference to time and space. Complete limbo. Sensory deprivation. What did those two men talk about? How were they brought here? Forced at gunpoint? Drugged and dragged here? When did they realize they were going to die here? How did they accept it? Was there any evidence left behind to indicate how they accepted their fate? Which one died first? What did that death do to the survivor, knowing his own death was imminent?

I knew I wouldn't find out how they got there until I found out who they were and why they were there. Were they being punished? For what? Were they being taught a lesson? Given a warning? Was it an elaborate prank or a practical joke gone awry? Were they meant to be left behind, abandoned, or had it been an accident? An oversight? A miscommunication? Maybe the person who had left them there had forgotten or died?

They were all questions my father intended to try to answer. When the two cavers returned late Friday afternoon to lead him out of the pit, he was shaken, but not broken. He had trust in the men. His only regret was that he had not brought a pad and pencil or a mini tape recorder to document all his thoughts during the ordeal. His imagination was exploding with possibilities. The fictitious Professor Ivan Heskestad would follow in my father's footsteps in the novel. He hadn't slept in two days. His days and nights in the cave led him to one conclusion. Those men had died of uncertainty.

CHAPTER 13

MONDAY, OCTOBER 20, 2008
3 DAYS BEFORE THE MURDER

Now, on this autumn Monday in 2008, my father's second day of hiking after leaving home, he sat on the concrete slab at the site of *The Pits*, reminiscing about his exploration twenty-three years earlier. Did he reflect on how much Rockland County had changed in the past decades? It seemed as if it had everywhere but where he was sitting. He thought of the hours and days he had wrestled with the hidden mysteries and implications of the caving story. What was it like to sit and reflect about the place that had propelled his career forward at a relentless speed? I don't know. One of life's great mysteries.

After sitting on the concrete slab for an hour in the cool air, my father and Huck continued walking through the woods and along Seven Lakes Drive. He walked over to Lake Sebago and visited Baker Camp, where he had attended 4-H camp in the summer of

1954, and later had taken me fishing and overnight camping in my teens. It was a night of silence around the campfire. I guess he had been trying to bond with me.

He walked to Lake Kanawauke, then on to Lake Welch, and later to the border of Harriman State Park. He had spent so much time researching that book in the mid-1980s that he had become enamored with the area. With some of the money he eventually made through the sale of *The Pits* he had purchased a few acres of property adjoining the park, near Call Hollow Road. At one time he planned to build a weekend retreat there as a place to write, but it never came to pass. Now he walked through the property he had not visited in more than two years. Did he leave something behind? Evidence he had been there recently? A granola wrapper? Did it blow away in the breeze?

From there, he and Huck walked along Willow Grove Road, beneath fthe Palisades Parkway through the underpass, and over to Garnerville Reservoir, where he camped out on Monday evening.

CHAPTER 14

TUESDAY, OCTOBER 21, 2008
2 DAYS BEFORE THE MURDER

On Tuesday morning, on his third day of hiking, as he approached the residential districts where there were no woods he could walk through, my father took surface streets. He made his way south through Stony Point and Haverstraw and Garnerville. In Garnerville, he hiked up Central Highway toward New City. It was a steep climb as they made their way to the top, and he and Huck had to stop periodically to catch their breath. He could feel his strength waning even as the sun appeared from behind the cloud cover to warm him up.

At the top of "The Hill," where Central Highway becomes Little Tor Road, he stopped in the small parking lot where all the kids used to go parking and look down over New City on date nights. He, too, had looked down on New City from this height, as he did now, but always alone, dateless back then, when he had done so. He turned east and headed toward the heavy chain designed to prevent civilian vehicle traffic from entering the path that disappeared into the woods along the ridgeline. He stepped over the locked chain, lifted it high enough for Huck to climb under, and hiked toward the Hudson River, to Low Tor. It took about a half an hour, the light on his face changing color as he passed under the thinning canopy of reds, light yellows, burnt siennas. At one point he closed his eyes and walked the trail, using his muscle memory recalled from a thousand hikes. He stopped and listened to the soft whisper of the leaves above. He had chosen the right spot. He walked on.

Anyone seeing this man and his dog walking the crest of Low Tor would have wondered about him; his curious gait. Was anyone watching him? A couple of young boys out exploring the trail of discovery, as he had at their age? Old lovers holding hands for a last walk before their knees and hips would prevent them from making the climb again? A scientist, perhaps, assigned to monitor coyote presence, which had increased in recent years? A chipmunk remembering him from hikes past? Whoever might have seen him would have noticed he walked with an air of confidence, determination, and finality. Confidence in his knowledge of every step of the trail, so much so that he could have literally walked it blindfolded, drawing on recollections of past travels. Determination in his commitment to follow through on the task at hand. Finality in his acceptance of his choice. And so his steps were bold, focused, without regret.

At one point he stopped to listen to the near silence of a slight breeze rustling the remaining leaves overhead. He closed his eyes, straining to hear the sound of bird that might not yet have headed south. As a boy hiking this trail he saw red-tailed hawks, even eagles. At his feet would be the occasional garter snake basking in the summer sunlight. Along the path side would be New England aster, the deep purple of milkweed, brilliant yellows of black-eyed Susan. Off the path one day he had tripped and fallen face down, knocking the wind out of him. When he looked up a soft pink lady slipper was inches from his eyes.

Now, in late October, the falling leaves dropped on turtlehead and white snakeroot, and the dark, shiny green leaves of mountain laurel.

Along the way, he passed a clearing in the woods, an easement for the high-tension power lines that crossed the summit in a north-south axis. When the power lines were first envisioned back in the 1930s, the original plans called for them to cross over a brook and waterfall owned by Maxwell Anderson and his nearby neighbor, Kurt Weill. The power line easement would have ruined their brook and waterfall views, the isolation they needed for their creativity; their solace. They fought to have the power lines cross the summit to the east, where they remain today. Had they taken unfair advantage of the weight of their fame?

My father continued walking another several hundred yards over the rocky pathway. Just beneath the Low Tor summit he stopped abruptly to get his bearings, then turned to the north. About a hundred feet above the path, he dropped off his bedroll and set up his pup tent. He planned to take short hikes away from his campsite during the day, and he wanted to be sure his gear wasn't spotted by other hikers and stolen.

Why had he chosen Low Tor as his final stop, his place to die? What did it mean to him? Why not High Tor? I wouldn't find out until later.

Fatigued, he decided to wait until the next day, Wednesday, to climb to his next destination, High Tor.

He sat looking northward up the Hudson as the sun went down, and he thought about reading for a while, but decided to save his flashlight batteries. The first few nights he had read and written in his journal until late, and he didn't want the batteries to die before he was finished reading and writing on his trip.

Not until some weeks later would I be able to read what he wrote in his journal entries during his days and nights on the trail.

CHAPTER 15

WEDNESDAY, OCTOBER 22, 2008
20 HOURS BEFORE THE MURDER

The next morning, Wednesday, he arose at dawn and prepared for his final hike to High Tor, less than a mile away. He carried his hip-pocket journal, a few pens, and enough food and water for himself and Huck. He left his tent, bedroll, and duffel behind, at his Low Tor campsite. After double-checking to reassure himself his belongings were far enough off the trail not to be seen by other hikers, he started off.

Over the centuries, High Tor has been a lookout post for the Native Americans watching for New World explorers. Over the generations, during their migration east, the Natives picked up seeds and spores on the clothing they wore and carried with them across the vast land. Much of the clothing was hand-me-downs. The fossil remains of plants previously known only to grow in the Rockies have been found on High Tor. How did they get there?

During the Revolutionary War, locals kept watch for the British from its peak, and Benedict Arnold and Major André discussed the terms of the surrender of West Point in its shadow, while a military drum cadence echoed off its face.

During World War II locals climbed its height and they built the High Tor observation tower to watch for invading Nazis flying enemy planes from the north and east, heading toward Manhattan. There are photographs of Kurt Weill and Maxwell Anderson atop that tower, scanning the horizon for enemy aircraft, while dreaming of plots for their new works, perhaps? Some of those veteran volunteers who climbed the High Tor tower every night were still around, traces of their historic footsteps on the rocks now covered with the careless graffiti of teenage climbers.

For generations High Tor has hosted thousands of family hikes and sleepovers and was the site of many a young New City boy's adventures and conquests. Standing at its peak, a viewer is left with the feeling that such a place couldn't really exist in Rockland County.

But there was a time when High Tor's future was placed into uncertainty—the first time in the eons since the glaciers receded. It was in danger of being dynamited and quarried away, like its companion to the southeast, in a quest for roadbuilding materials. By the early 1920s, nearby roads were being paved for widespread automobile use, and the rock and gravel were in high demand.

At the time, the land was owned by Elmer Van Orden, and one day, as he stood on the peak of his High Tor looking to the south, he realized that the nearby quarrymen would someday try to buy his land, and that before long, his beloved mountain would be gone, blasted into smithereens to pave the roads for the onslaught of automobiles. He had spent many years of his life on this mountain, and he claimed that the ghosts of High Tor climbed down into his backyard strawberry patch on some nights.

The playwright, Maxwell Anderson, lived on South Mountain Road during the 1920s and '30s and '40s. He rode his bike to Haverstraw along the dirt road between the ravines and brooks. In the morning, High Tor was over his left shoulder, an ever-present force looking down upon him. In Haverstraw he caught the West Shore commuter train down to Weehawken, New Jersey, (named for the Palisades "rocks that look like trees, or *Wee-Awk-En*, to the *Lenape*), so he could catch the ferry to Manhattan. On his way home in the evenings, as Anderson pedaled uphill, the domineering presence of High Tor again embraced him in its history. Inspired by his daily bicycle rides, the impending loss of his beloved mountain, and by the numerous sightings of ghosts of Dutch sailors, by 1936, Anderson had written his fantastical landmark play, *High Tor*. It's a story inhabited by bank robbers of the Nanuet Bank and the ghosts and spirits of shipwrecked Dutch sailors waiting three hundred years to be rescued. He got his friend and neighbor, Burgess Meredith, to star in the Broadway production. Anderson shared Van Orden's fear for the future of High Tor. In the early days of World War II, Van Orden died, and his property went on the marketplace. High Tor was up for sale for $12,000. Anderson and others went into action, and Anderson eventually became honorary chairman of the Rockland County Conservation Association, raising awareness of the impending threat. Soldiers fighting overseas wrote home sending money and warned, "there had better be a High Tor when I get home." Local kids emptied their piggy banks to the point where High Tor earned the nickname, the *Children's Mountain*.

Efforts were made to buy all the mineral rights to the property around Trap Rock, including the adjoining Little Tor, a relatively inexpensive tactic that would effectively assure that the stone could never be quarried away, no matter who owned the land. Other conservation groups from up and down both sides of the river joined in the effort. By the spring of 1943, three miles of the mountain ridge had been deeded over to the Palisades Interstate Park Commission, in perpetuity.

My father had climbed High Tor dozens of times as a kid, dozens more as an adult. For him it was a pilgrimage to the genesis of his enlightenment. He had taken Huck and me along on some of those trips. For Huck on this day, it was back to familiar territory.

At High Tor's peak, my father searched the rocks for remainders of the steel bolts that held down the spotlight/observation tower that had been torn down in the early 1950s. Rust marks surrounded the surviving supports.

My father looked out over the Hudson River to the north, to Brick-town, and to the southeast beyond Trap Rock and Rockland Ice; south over the valley below, where on a clear day you could see the Manhattan skyline. He turned to the west toward the Ramapo Mountains. He sat down, using his knees as a desk as he wrote in his journal. It was another letter for me.

My Son,

I have come to these foothills for my final resting place. My forefathers arrived on the Hudson docks below in the late 1800s. As a boy I wandered these hills and came to love them. These woods became my own private domain and source of inspiration, as surely as the New England countryside served that purpose for Robert Frost.

Like Frost, I, too became "a swinger of birches"; I stopped by here "on a snowy evening," "mended stone walls," took "the road not taken," and like Frost promised, "it has made all the difference."

As a young man, I fell in love with your mother here, walking these same woods. And as a father I re-explored these hills with you, trying to pass on their infinite joy. I hope my attempts to help you appreciate their beauty were successful.

Now, as I stand on the peak of High Tor, the site of every significant event in my life is within the purview of my outstretched arms. I see the fields and meadows and streams and ponds of my childhood, but somehow, they do not bring the happiness they once did.

As Wordsworth once wrote,

"Where is it now, the glory and the dream?"

LOW TOR

In this valley I was born and raised. On the distant horizon I can see where I grew up in a gardener's toolshed; where I went to school at Clarkstown High, played football. I can see Manhattan, where I achieved riches and fame I never dreamed possible, and where, in the years to come, I achieved my first successes as a broadcast journalist and later a fiction writer.

At my feet, along South Mountain Road, I brought your mother to my home, we started our family, (that's you), and I spent my most productive years as a writer.

So it is on nearby Low Tor that I have chosen to come to die. Not in some sterile hospital room with tubes attached to my arms, in the company of uncaring strangers.

No, if I am to die, let it be here. As painful and protracted as that might be, it is better this way.

I prefer to suffer and die here among the golden leaves, craggy outposts, and rocky soil.

And so I have chosen to take this "final walk into the woods." I accept my fate, whatever these next few days or weeks might hold.

May my final hours be filled with Indian Summer, the nights chilled and clear, while alongside our little pal, Huck.

May my mind remain lucid long enough to write my last few words and say the things I want to leave behind for you.

May I enjoy reading my few favorite books and spending one last time with some old friends between their pages.

My father stopped writing there that late Wednesday afternoon, expecting to write more later in the evening or perhaps the next day as he waited patiently, painfully, to die. How long it would take, he didn't know. He apparently didn't care. His Wordsworth quote, in the middle of the letter, sums up how he was feeling. *"Where is it now, the glory and the dream?"*

He stood and looked down upon the Dells, the Dellwood Country Club, and Lake DeForest. His gazing brought back painful memories of his very first love, as a nine-year-old boy. She was his fourth-grade teacher at New City Grammar School, Ruth Singer. Her disappearance in that spring of 1956 left the town in shock. He reflected on his years of heartbreak, his hidden secrets, and the thinly disguised autobiographical novel he wrote about it all, *Sweetclover.* They all came rushing back to him and took away what little breath he had.

Just the name, *Sweetclover*, conjures up images of happier times, of idyllic summer days, lost forever except in memories, as Wordsworth's "Intimations of Immortality from Recollections of Early Childhood" so profoundly describes.

On reading *Sweetclover* as an adult, as I later would, it was easy to see that he structured the novel on the poet's words. It is all about lost innocence and childhood.

What though the radiance which was once so bright
Be now forever taken from my sight,
Though nothing can bring back the hour
Of splendor in the grass, of glory in the flower;
We will grieve not, rather find
Strength in what remains behind.

After losing his childhood love, was my father ever able to find "strength in what remains behind," or did he continue to grieve? Did it break him? What did, in fact, remain behind? After what he knew about the disappearance of Miss Singer, maybe the only way to purge his pain was to write about it.

It wouldn't be until the publication of his sixth novel in 1988, a few years after his own father passed away in 1983, that people began to suspect what was bothering my father, and for that matter, why he had remained in such close contact with his old friend Nick Tremontana.

CHAPTER 16

The Genesis of Sweetclover, 1955-1956

My father's eighth book, his sixth novel, *Sweetclover*, is a fictionalized account of the strange disappearance of beloved New City schoolteacher.

The central character and narrator is a nine-year-old boy named Aron. Until the very end of my father's life, most readers would not find out with certainty that the character's first-person narration was thinly disguised as fiction, as some locals had suspected. My father had told an *almost true* story through the eyes of his fictitious character, Aron, who, along with his lifelong friend Caleb, or Cal, had witnessed something horrific. The fictitious names my father "borrowed" were from *East of Eden* by John Steinbeck, as a tribute to the two brothers Steinbeck had actually named for Cain and Abel from the book of Genesis. Steinbeck had once been a summer resident of South Mountain Road.

The novel was the story of their fourth-grade teacher, Ruth Singer, who my father fictionalized in the character of Adina Perlman in *Sweetclover*. Most of the story was true, he simply changed the names and intentionally misled the readers—for very specific reasons.

As an adult, the fictitious narrator, Aron, reflects on childhood events from thirty-two years earlier, in 1956.

Sweetclover
Pub. 1988

NEW CITY
Autumn, 1955-Spring,1956

The first time I ever fell in love with a woman I was nine years old.

Her name was Adina Perlman and she was twenty-four years old. After earning her master's degree at City College of New York, she came to town to teach me and the other fourth graders at New City Grammar in the two-story wooden school up on the hill on Old Congers Road.

Miss Perlman was thin, almost athletic in build, and she dressed modestly. "Plain" is what some of the mothers in town would say after their requisite critique of all new teachers. Her brunette hair was cut in a short bob, and she wore no makeup except for a slash of pale red lipstick, almost as a rebellious statement, to defy her otherwise colorless appearance. She was what New City mothers wanted and expected for their children.

Miss Perlman would leave her parents' flat in Manhattan on Sunday afternoons, take a Red & Tan bus into New City, and disembark on the corner of Third and Main. She would walk across the street to where she was boarding in a small room at the top of the stairs in the house of a widow who had rooms to rent. That old widow happened to be the grandmother of one of our classmates, Frank, who lived there with her. That fall, there were no other accommodations in New City that this young teacher could afford on her meager salary. Her front room window overlooked South Main and St. Augustine's Catholic Church.

"A nice Jewish girl from the city," Frank's grandmother had assured all the neighbors and parents when she announced that she was taking in a boarder for the first time since the end of World War II.

As the end of that fourth-grade school year approached for us, Miss Perlman would have stolen my heart and my undying love, taught us about life in the wonders of the Amazon rainforest and Guatemala, taught us fractions, how to diagram sentences to determine subjects and predicates, subjects versus direct objects, and the differences between Rockland County's igneous and sedimentary rocks.

But before the end of that school year, Miss Perlman would go missing. Her sudden disappearance threw our quiet little town into chaos that late spring of 1956, while honeybees danced on the brilliant yellow daffodil blooms, ants crawled on the peony buds, and police and citizens tried to figure out what had happened to this sweet, innocent young woman whom all the students adored. Had she run away? Who could come and finish out the school year for our kids? Were we all safe in our homes at night?

After she disappeared, I couldn't stop crying for days because I was truly in love with her, as only a nine-year-old boy can be.

Of course everyone who knew anything about New City in the mid-1950s knew that the fictitious teacher, Adina Perlman in *Sweetclover*, was based on my father's real-life fourth-grade teacher, Ruth Singer. But no one knew how much of what he wrote was true.

It would only be much later that the world knew the truth of what happened to Miss Singer, a.k.a. Adina Perlman. My father couldn't tell anyone, but he knew. He and his best friend, Nick, called Cal in the novel, had witnessed it all. But they couldn't tell anyone. What difference would it make, anyway? Nothing could bring back this smiling, laughing woman, so full of life, who had stolen his heart.

No, nothing could mend his heart. Certainly not by telling what he knew, what he had witnessed. Not the long summer vacation that followed, not visits to Dr. Cohen, the school doctor, for "little talks," would make his heartache go away. The consequences of telling what they knew would be too great. So when he wrote the novel as an adult, he fictionalized it all.

In 1978, when my father left the Giants, the *Sweetclover* novel was still ten years away. How does a football player turned sportscaster and documentary filmmaker become a novelist? In retrospect, one can see that it was all a natural progression of hard work, obsession, and talent leading to his successes. From *Jr. Wiley* to the Patrick Thomas pulp mysteries to *The Pits* to *Sweetclover*.

But many did not know that, at least in some way, his accomplishments had been driven by guilt and self-loathing.

CHAPTER 17

FEBRUARY 1983
FLORIDA PANHANDLE
25 YEARS BEFORE THE MURDER

Transcript from *Junior Wiley* documentary, 1983:

#	VIDEO	AUDIO
	UP FULL SOT TALKING HEAD- LISA ANN CARLIN (S/) LISA ANN CARLIN Rebecca Samson's Friend	UP FULL SOT LISA ANN: I'm just telling you this stuff because her father is such a jerk. He's always mean to her. The whole time we were growing up he was mean to her and so was her dirt-bag

T/C 12:04:16– 12:05:20	brother. I understand why she run off with Junior. He's the only guy who's ever been nice to her. He makes her laugh.

ABBY: So, are they okay, the two of them?

LISA ANN: Yes. They're okay. That's all I can tell you. I promised her. If I tell you more, Rebecca will never speak to me again.

ABBY: But you *can* assure us that they are

both safe?

LISA ANN: Yes, sir. I spoke to her on the phone the other day. She knows to call when my mom is at work.

ABBY: You know there are people worried about both of them. Especially Junior's parents.

LISA ANN: Just tell his folks they're safe and they plan to stay that way. They'll be back when they feel safe. He

threatened to
kill Junior.
Kill her, too.

ABBY:
Rebecca's
father?

LISA ANN:
Yeah, and her
brother too.

ABBY: Look, I
can't tell you
how to run
your life or
force you to
tell us, but a
lot of people
would like to
know they're
okay.

LISA ANN: Let
me think about
it. I've got
your business
card. Your
phone number.

		ABBY: Well, Thank you, Lisa Ann. We'd like to talk to you again sometime. Maybe you can give us some more news next week. LISA ANN: Sure.

With the interview over, the crew started packing up. Lisa Ann turned to my father. "Is that camera still rolling?"

My father looked to Cliff, and Cliff shook his head. "No. He turned it off."

Cliff walked away from Lisa Ann carrying his camera. He knew the drill. Lisa Ann watched Cliff exit the room and turned to my father.

What my father, Cliff, MaryAnn, and Robbie heard next was preserved by the mini-recorder in my father's shirt pocket. He had not turned it off, and the sound bite would eventually find its way into the finished documentary. He looked to Lisa Ann, who didn't look up from the floor as she spoke.

Transcript from *Junior Wiley* documentary, 1983:

#	VIDEO	AUDIO
	VOICE OF LISA ANN- AUDIO FROM MINI- CASSETTE ONLY, NO VIDEO T/C. +B-ROLL w/HOUSEBOAT	LISA ANN: They're on a houseboat in Apalachicola. My grandfather built it. He named it after me. But you'd better get down there. They're catching a shrimper in the next day or two.
	ABBY OFF- CAMERA, AUDIO ONLY	ABBY: A shrimper?

	LISA ANN- AUDIO ONLY	LISA ANN: Shrimp boat. They're paying the guy to take them to Mexico.

My father didn't ask that last question because he was unfamiliar with the term "shrimper." He asked the question because he was quite familiar with shrimp boats. He knew Apalachicola. He knew shrimp boats.

The Tallahassee police probably could have found the missing kids just as easily, if they had tried. But football season was over by that February, and Junior Wiley and Rebecca Samson had been reduced to just another news cycle about runaway kids.

Transcript from *Junior Wiley* documentary, 1983:

#	VIDEO	AUDIO
	ROAD TO APALA-CHICOA	ABBY VOICE/OVER APALACHICOLA HISTORY

	+B-ROLL VARIOUS SCENIC FOOTAGE, SPANISH MOSS DRAPED ROAD CANOPY +TURN OF THE CENTURY INNS	Want to see what "Old Florida" looks like? Apalachicola has been known as one of the Gulf of Mexico's busiest ports for almost 200 years. Located on Apalachicola Bay on Florida's "Forgotten Coast," much of it looks the same today as it did during the Depression-Era.
	Apalachico la history +B-ROLL; AIR CONDITION-	ABBY VOICE/OVER APALACHICOLA HISTORY Over the years it has gained

	ING MUSEUM +B-ROLL VARIOUS SCENIC FOOTAGE, WATERFRONT -FISHING FLEET- SHRIMPING FLEET	fame for being the "birthplace of air-conditioning" invented to help malaria patients in the mid-1800s, which helped malaria patients, and for its fishing fleet that brings in a bountiful harvest of oysters and shrimp.
	APALACHI- COLA +B-ROLL WATERFRONT /DOCKS, SEARCH FOR BOAT	ABBY VOICE/OVER APALACHICOLA HISTORY It was here, among a collection of ramshackle houseboats, that our search for the missing

		Junior Wiley had led us.
	UP FULL NATSOT: +ROBBIE APPROACHES BOAT OWNER	UP FULL NATSOT: +NATURAL SOUND, ROBBIE APPROACHES HOUSEBOAT OWNER EMMET WILSON
	UP FULL NATSOT: (S/) EMMET WILSON Houseboat Owner +ROBBIE ASKS FOR HOUSEBOAT NAMED "LISA ANN" T/C 13:03:12- 13:04:50	UP FULL NATSOT: EMMET: Am I gonna be on the news tonight? ROBBIE: No. Maybe a few months from now. We're looking for a houseboat named *LISA ANN*. EMMET: That would be Dub's old place. A couple of kids are hanging out there now, from

what I hear.
I've never seen
them myself.
Do I get a
reward or
something?

ROBBIE: The
respect and
admiration of
your friends
and relatives.

EMMET: That
would be a
first. These
kids do
something
wrong?

ROBBIE: Nope,
we're just
filming a
birthday
surprise video
to show at
work.

EMMET: (laughs)

	You know I did fall off the back of a turnip truck, but it wasn't yesterday.
	ROBBIE: True story. It's her birthday next week. Lisa Ann's
+TWENTY DOLLAR BILL IN ABBY'S HAND ENTERS FRAME, EXTENDED TOWARD EMMET. HE TAKES IT.	grandfather hired us to film a joke video.
	EMMET: Her grandfather's been dead for two years.
	ROBBIE: Her other grandfather.
	EMMET: Now I know you're lyin'. (laughs)

		ABBY: We still would like this to be a surprise. Her coworkers will get a laugh out of it. EMMET: I don't see what's so funny about it.
	NAT SOUND ROBBIE KNOCKS ON DOOR OF RAMSHACKLE HOUSEBOAT, LISA ANN. T/C 13:06:18- 13:07:40	NATURAL SOUND:KNOCKING
	REBECCA'S VOICE FROM INSIDE HOUSEBOAT	REB: Who is it? What the hell do you want? Junior, we got trouble. Lisa Ann can't keep

		her mouth shut, as usual.
	+JUNIOR OPENS DOOR, STEPS ONTO DECK	JR.W: It's okay, I know her. "Miss Big Ears" from the Tallahassee TV station I told you about. Hey, Robbie. MaryAnn. Cliff. I should have known if anyone could find me it would be you guys. What's up, Robbie? ROBBIE: Hey, Junior. This is Abby Traphagen, from Cable Television Sports Network.

	We were wondering if you would do an interview with him? JR.W: Why would I do that? ROBBIE: Come on, a lot of people are worried about you, Junior. JR.W: We kinda want to be left alone. ABBY: Hi Junior, I'm Abby Traphagen. I played football for FSU years ago. We can appreciate that you want to be left alone. If
ABBY STEPS INTO FRAME, ADDRESSES JR.W.	

you'll sit down and talk to us, we won't broadcast the interview for at least another thirty days. In the meantime, I'll tell your parents you are safe. They are really worried. I won't tell anyone else. Not even Coach Bowden.

JR.W: I know who you are. I've seen your game films from the '60s. You would do that for me? Embargo this footage?

ABBY: You know that term?

		Embargo?
		JR. W: I was a broadcasting major myself, when I had time to go to classes.
		ABBY: We know you want your privacy. We respect that.
		JR.W: Okay, what do I have to do?
		ABBY: Would Rebecca want to join us on camera?
		JR. W: Nah. We don't need to drag her into it.
	INTERVIEW w/JR.	ABBY: Okay, Junior, we're

WILEY and ABBY TRAPHAGEN. +WIDE SHOT, HOUSEBOAT DECK, SUNSET IN B.G. OVER GENERIC MARSHY WATERWAY AND SABAL PALM ISLAND.	at an undisclosed location. Why are you out here? Why did you miss the Gator game last December?
T/C 13:08:20- 13:09:40 +JR.W.TURN S INTO THE LENS.	JR.W: First off, I just want to say to my parents, I love you, Mom and Daddy, and don't worry, we're going to be all right. I appreciate everything you did for me all those years.

	WIDE-SHOT, HOUSEBOAT, SINKING SUN T/C 13:25:10- 13:25:30	
	CLOSE-UP, JR.WILEY T/C 13:09:50- 13:13:50 +Insert ABBY'S CUTAWAY QUESTIONS, AS NOTED	**JR.W:** Rebecca and I started dating in September, and we kept it a secret for a while. Especially from her folks. A few of my friends knew. Guys on the team. We met a bar in Tallahassee. *LONG-SHOT'S.*
	CLOSE-UP, ABBY TRAPHAGEN T/C	**ABBY:** Why did you keep it a secret?

	13:14:30	
	CLOSE-UP, JR.WILEY	JR.W: Rebecca's father and brother found out about it and threatened to kill both of us if they ever saw us together. We took them seriously.
	CLOSE-UP, ABBY TRAPHAGEN T/C 13:14:45	ABBY: So couldn't you just go to the police?
	CLOSE-UP, JR.WILEY	JR.W: Who do you think they were going to believe? They would have killed us anyway.
	CLOSE-UP,	ABBY:

| ABBY TRAPHAGEN T/C 13:15:20 | But what about football? You have fans. You have a future in professional football. Maybe even become a broadcaster later, like me, if that was your dream? |
| CLOSE-UP, JR.WILEY | JR.W: I don't know. It just doesn't seem important to me anymore. I just want to get out of the limelight. Settle down. Rebecca and I want to get married. Start a family. I want to be a good father like my father was to me. You |

		know, toss the ball around in the backyard.
	CLOSE-UP, ABBY TRAPHAGEN T/C 13:15:55	ABBY: So your football days are over? Even if we could help you find a solution?
	CLOSE-UP, JR.WILEY +JR. POINTS TO REBECCA, OFF- CAMERA.	JR.W: Nah. We decided we want to start a new life. New Place. Clean slate. That celebrity stuff? Let the other guys have it. I have what I want right here, sitting right over there.
	CLOSE-UP, ABBY TRAPHAGEN	ABBY: What about your fans? Your

T/C 13:16:30	coaches? Your teammates?
CLOSE-UP, JR.WILEY	JR.W: I guess I should apologize for letting everyone down. Coach Bowden, my teammates, the fans. I felt real bad about losing that Gator game. So I want to say I'm grateful for all your support over the years and sorry for letting you down, but it's time for me to move on with my life. I have a new life now, and new responsibilitie

		s. We have a baby on the way and I just want to do the right thing.
	CLOSE-UP, ABBY TRAPHAGEN T/C 13:17:10	ABBY: Anything else?
	CLOSE-UP, JR. WILEY, AS HE STARTS TO CRY JR. TURNS FROM ABBY, LOOKS INTO	JR.W: I don't want to be famous anymore. I'm tired of it. We'd just like to be left alone. Disappear. We don't want to do any more interviews like this. We just want to get on with things. Start a new life. Somewhere safe. Somewhere

TO CAMERA LENS JR. STANDS AND EXITS FRAME.	without the hate. Mom and Daddy, someday real soon you'll get to see your grandchild, we promise. That's it.
+DISSOLVE TO NATURAL SOUND SEQUENCE: JUNIOR & REBECCA BOARDING A SHRIMP BOAT AT DAWN. T/C 14:02:10	(:20)
+SHRIMP BOAT LEAVING DOCK, HEADING	(:20)

WEST. +JUNIOR TURNS BACK TOWARD CAMERA ONE LAST TIME, WAVES, SMILES, THEN JOINS REBECCA IN PILOT HOUSE. T/C 14:06:40	
(*)NOTE TO ROBBIE: ONLY USE THIS CLOSING STAND-UP IF WE AREN'T ABLE TO GET ANY FURTHER WITH THE STORY.	ABBY STAND-UP And so it was that Junior Wiley and his sweetheart, Rebecca Samson, left this little paradise from "Old Florida" and fled the country and his

ABBY STAND-UP +ABBY ON CAMERA. +OVER HIS SHOULDER: SHRIMP BOAT HEADS WEST. T/C 14:08:10 +MUSIC UP	past on February 16, 1983, to start a new chapter in their lives. From Apalachicola, Florida, I'm Abby Traphagen reporting for Cable Television Sports Network.
+FADE TO BLACK +MUSIC OUT	

The shrimp boat disappeared over the horizon into the Gulf of Mexico, and my father stood on the dock wondering about the irony. He was filled with *déjà vu*. He had filmed shrimp boats leaving at dawn almost two decades earlier while he was a student at FSU.

After filming a more generic, contingency/backup closing stand-up to cover any unexpected change in the story that might evolve, my father, Cliff, MaryAnn, and Robbie would spend the next seven days waiting for the shrimper to return so they could do a follow-up. In the interim, they returned to Tallahassee to get more interviews, not revealing to others what they actually knew at that point.

They drove to Junior's boyhood home and reassured his parents that their son and Rebecca were safe. They didn't say anything about a baby on the way. My father felt that Junior should be the one to break the good news.

One week later, the shrimp boat returned without Junior and the mother-to-be. The shrimper agreed to do an interview.

Transcript from *Junior Wiley* documentary, 1983:

#	VIDEO	AUDIO
	UP FULL NATSOT +SHRIMPER PULLS UP TO DOCK, STARTS	

UNLOADING CATCH.	
UP FULL SOT +SHRIMPER ON-CAMERA (S/) YULEE THIGPEN Apalachicola Shrimper T/C 15:02:15-15:04:00	UP FULL SOT YULEE THIGPEN: He paid me to take them all the way to the Yucatan, in Mexico. But we stopped to refuel in Galveston and they hopped off on the fishing pier. They paid some Mexican boat captain to take them the rest of the way and I never saw them again.
UP FULL SOT +CLOSE-UP, ABBY, CUTAWAY QUESTION T/C 15:05:00	UP FULL SOT ABBY: What was their demeanor?

UP FULL SOT YULEE THIGPEN	UP FULL SOT YULEE: They looked relieved. They gave me some extra money and thanked me and waved goodbye. I guess they didn't want me to know where they were going. I never saw them again.
UP FULL SOT +CLOSE-UP, ABBY, CUTAWAY QUESTION T/C 15:06:00	UP FULL SOT ABBY: Did you know who they were? That they were considered missing?
UP FULL SOT	UP FULL SOT YULEE: Nope. We mind our own business around here.

That was the end of Junior Wiley, and now that they were gone, safely out of the country and inaccessible to threatening family members, my father was free to show the interview of Junior on television news after the thirty days embargo he had promised. But he didn't show it.

Instead, he kept returning to Tallahassee to get more background interviews with Bobby Bowden, teammates, the police. Again, he never revealed to anyone— except, of course, Junior's parents—that he knew what happened to Junior and Rebecca. Was this ethical? Did Junior's teammates and coaches and friends suffer more anguish because my father didn't tell his story right away?

It took him several months to complete the documentary, going back and forth to Tallahassee. Finally he revealed to Junior's friends what he had found out and showed them Junior's final interview.

Late that spring he even flew down to the Yucatan, and using the information provided by the shrimper about the Mexican boat, he began to search for Junior and Rebecca with the help of a local private detective. But the couple had disappeared, possibly into the interior, some speculated.

At one point he interviewed Rebecca's father and brother.

Transcript from *Junior Wiley* documentary, 1983:

#	VIDEO	AUDIO
	UP FULL SOT +CLOSE UP, REBECCA'S FATHER (S/)JOE SAMSON Rebecca's Father T/C 17:06:19	UP FULL SOT If they ever show their faces again, we'll kill them both, and we don't care who knows it.
	UP FULL SOT +CLOSE UP, REBECCA'S BROTHER (S/)BEN SAMSON Rebecca's Brother T/C	UP FULL SOT I hope they're rotting in some Mexican jungle or prison, like they deserve. He kidnapped her. I tell you he belongs in jail.

17:08:00	
UP FULL SOT	UP FULL SOT
+CLOSE UP, REBECCA'S FATHER	If we find that guy before the cops do, he'll get what's
(S/) JOE SAMSON Rebecca's Father	coming to him. I *guar-an-damn-tee* it.
T/C 17:07:21	

Eventually, with Robbie's help, my father produced the documentary, accomplishing several things: He likely saved the lives of Juniorf Wiley and Rebecca, high ratings for the broadcast due to heavy promotion, and a nonfiction book that pretty much covered the same material plus a behind-the-scenes explanation of how he went about making the documentary. Both the film and the book, *Whatever Happened to Junior Wiley?* were hits in late 1983.

In addition, he continued the affair he had started with Robbie during his second trip to Tallahassee, assuring her an escape from that college town so she could take on the role of a network documentary producer for his team. It was then that my mother discovered that my father's production assistant was now firmly ensconced in a network news job in the number one television market in the country, after coming from the 105th market in the country. That was likely unless she had some sort of help:

The intern affliction: my father could have written the book on it.

When my mother confronted my father with her suspicions, which had been bolstered by his many trips to Tallahassee, he denied it at first. Then he broke down crying and admitted it.

But his thoughts and concerns were elsewhere.

When the book became a surprise hit, it landed my father a publishing contract. He started writing the mystery novels, his longtime passion. And even though my mother later became pregnant with me, my father continued having affairs with Robbie and other television stars and book-author groupies throughout my childhood.

After I was born, in 1988, my father—famous author, former television celebrity, professional football star, college football star, and local high school hero— tried to settle down and become more domesticated. But I guess it just wasn't in his nature.

CHAPTER 18

WEDNESDAY, OCTOBER 22, 2008
10 HOURS BEFORE THE MURDER

What was going on in my father's mind as he gazed down from the heights of High Tor? Below him were the Dells and Lake DeForest and the site of the Sweetclover Bridge, now unseen, covered with ten or more feet of water ever since the reservoir had been filled in the mid-1950s. What memories did those sights trigger? What did it all mean now that he faced imminent death? How much did he reflect on my mother? On me?

As dusk approached, he and Huck climbed slowly down the south face of the mountain. It was a sad time. He was sure it had been his last climb up his beloved peak. But time would prove him wrong.

Walking slowly, he made it back to his campsite on Low Tor, where he climbed to the rocky outcropping and stared down to the mighty Hudson River seven hundred feet below. He looked over to West Haverstraw and north to Stony Point and Tomkins Cove.

As twilight gathered, he stared across the river to the east, to the Hudson Highlands and the twinkling lights of Van Cortlandt Manor, Croton-on-Hudson, and Verplanck.

In the fading light he began to read *All the King's Men*. After reading for a few minutes with his flashlight, he nodded off, and when he awoke, the flashlight batteries had weakened, making the pages turn yellow in the dim glow. With Huck cradled under his right shoulder, he rolled over in his sleeping bag and fell asleep. Soon he would have to issue the order to Huck to "Go home!"

Instead of dreaming of the digressive Cass Mastern story in Robert Penn Warren's novel, he dreamed of the beauty he had just beheld in the Lower Hudson River Valley during the earlier dusk.

CHAPTER 19

LOW TOR THANATOPSIS: HUNDREDS OF YEARS BEFORE THE MURDER

In my father's fitful slumber, facing death, he dreamed that he went out into nature, listened to what the land spoke to him, and took comfort in what he beheld.

Behind him, a hand of comfort from William Cullen Bryant rested on his shoulder, whispering softly in his ear, encouraging him to take the next steps without fear, on life's journey:

Love Nature and hold communion with her visible forms and she will speak to you.

She has a voice of gladness and a smile and eloquence of beauty, and she sympathizes with your fate and will take away its sharpness.

Whenever you are reminded of your last bitter hours, I know it saddens you and makes you grow sick at heart, but you know you have to go forth, under the open sky, and listen to what Nature has to say to you in her still voice.

She will tell you, "You only have days to live before your pale form will be laid in the cold ground near where you were born, to mix forever with the elements.

"You will be in the ground, down with patriarchs of the infant world and with the mighty Lenape in one mighty sepulcher.

"But you will be surrounded by these hills you love, the vales stretching in pensive quietness, the venerable woods and rivers that move in majesty and the brooks that make the meadows green."

He wondered if, "when I withdraw will there be silence from the living and will no friend take note of my departure?"

He knew that everyone that breathed would share his destiny, with no exceptions. They would eventually come and make their bed with him.

And so he was determined to live out his days as he chose to live them, in the bounty of Nature, so when that innumerable caravan, which moves to that mysterious realm where each shall take His chamber in the silent halls of death, he would go willingly.

He was determined to pass on, not like a quarry-slave at night scourged to his dungeon.

Instead, he would go sustained and soothed by an unfaltering trust.

He would approach his grave and lie down to pleasant dreams.

And so he dreamed of the Mighty Hudson and the first people who beheld what Nature offered, and he listened to what she *spake*.

As the first Native Americans marched across the Bering Straits, they cast their eyes eastward toward the rising sun. Generation after generation, they searched, the difficult struggles culling the weak and infirm, resulting in a tribe, strong and tall and handsome and marked with sinewy musculature. They navigated by the stars as their fathers had taught them. They kept walking. They could not stop. They crossed the Rockies and the great American Plains, always heading into the morning sun, and one day, after eons of wandering, the younger generations having followed the marching orders without question, they stood on a sharp palisade not far from where my father now slept, and they gazed down upon the magnificent waterway.

When they surveyed the river, it took their breath away, and they stood in silence, *watching, listening* for what it had to tell them.

The steep palisades on the west side of the river had been formed by glaciers receding, carving gorges out of sandstone like a giant claw, and exposing the igneous rocks that had been formed by volcanoes in eons past. Across the wide water below them to the east, later known as Haverstraw Bay, were the gentle rolling hills of the Taconics.

And as these new arrivals watched, the river itself did a miraculous thing. Something no human had ever witnessed. The river flowed south, down from Lake Tear of the Clouds, and then, as the day progressed, the current slowed in a great swirl and then stopped.

How is that possible? they asked, looking at one another. And then, as they watched in amazement, the water flowed north. *It was a river that flowed two ways.* Surely this was a sign from their gods to settle here and stop their wanderings. It would be a land full of blessings.

They called the river *Shatemuc*, in their native language *Unami*, "The King of the Rivers."

These ancient people would come to be known as the *Iroquois* and the *Algonkins* and the *Lenni Lenape*, the "true people." The *Lenape* celebrated their discovery by painting their faces with the juices of the colorful berries they found and mixing it with the clay from the nearby *Shatemuc*, and they danced in the firelight up and down the shores. Later witnesses called the place the *Devil's Dance Chamber.*

The *Lenape* settled in the area, living off the abundant deer and bears, spearfishing for sturgeon and shad, and wading barefoot in the riverbed to find oysters.

They felled trees and burned and scraped them into canoes so they could travel on this miraculous river. And in my father's dream, while they burned and scraped with excitement, he stood over them with his 16mm film camera to his eye, looking over their shoulders, admiring their handiwork as he filmed.

To claim the territory, they painted rocks with their signs and signals and insignia. They wandered through the Dells in what became New City and left markings on the sandstone walls that would amaze young schoolboy explorers, including my father, for centuries to come.

They broke into smaller tribes, and the *Lenape* settled on the western shore with its rocky promontories left behind by the retreating glaciers. They would further divide into the *Hackensacks*, the *Tappans*, and the *Haverstraws*, while on the eastern shore they became the *Manhattans* and *Wappingers*. To the north were the mighty *Mohicans*.

With abundance for all, they led peaceful lives without want, gave little thought to warring enemies. Men hunted while women tended the maize fields.

And for hundreds of years, life was filled with happiness and contentment, peace and plenty and prosperity for all, and along the banks of the *Shatemuc*, they forgot how to be warriors.

The *Lenape* continued their lives as they had for centuries. Their first roads had originally been deer trails, later traveled for both commerce and socializing, running north and south along the Hudson shoreline. It would eventually become "The King's Highway."

One day, in what would later be determined by white men as 1524, the *Lenape* looked out on the river to see a giant fish, (or was it a bird, with huge wings capturing the wind?) floating up the river. It truly must have been sent by the spirits, for surely no canoe could ever be made so large. These were supernatural beings sent by the river gods for them to worship. In his dream my father put down his 16mm Bolex and tried to warn them, but they wouldn't listen, so mystified were they by what they saw.

Beneath the wings on the back of the giant fish were white men returning their stares. In the front of the boat, *La Dauphine*, was a man from a faraway land whose name was Giovanni da Verrazzano.

The *Lenape*, their hearts racing with excitement, set out in their canoes to meet the gods in the giant bird/fish as my father hastened to the shore to warn them, "No good will come from this." But they ignored him. The giant bird/fish quickly turned south and fled with the receding waters before the *Lenape* could paddle out for a closer look.

It would be another eighty-five years of elders telling tales to their descendants, tales of men who were white, ghostlike, before another great bird/fish covered with white men would sail up the river. This time the elders watched warily. This time it was Henry

Hudson, in 1609, on the *Half Moon*. Again, my father tried to warn them. This time the great bird/fish was successfully met by the *Lenape,* who canoed out to the giant floating miracle and boarded, dressed in deerskin and singing welcoming chants to these white men while my father stood to the side, filming their activities fearfully, in dismay.

Later, Dutch, German, and English settlers arrived, spread throughout the area, and searched the hills for gold. The new community leaders acquired the land from the natives through patents, or were awarded patroonships from the Dutch in exchange for bringing fifty settlers to the land. My father stood by and wept, putting down his wind-up camera. Why wouldn't his *Lenape* friends listen to him? Could they not see the future as he could? He begged them to listen, to resist.

The white men dredged the clay from the hillsides and formed a brick town. Incoming farmers tilled the rich soil the *Lenape* women had used for hundreds of years to grow maize. River traffic brought the settlers' crops to market in the autumn and later, in the early 1800s, ice from Rockland Lake in the wintertime.

Inspired by nature and a swell of Romanticism from Europe, a new form of artistic expression was given birth near where the Hudson and the Catskill Mountains met, where my father now slept.

Washington Irving wrote his *Knickerbocker* tales and James Fennimore Cooper wrote his *Leatherstocking* saga and William Cullen Bryant wrote of Nature's transcendental majesty. Thomas Cole captured the beauty in colorful oils depicting mist-filled mornings, with delicate sun rays peeking from behind Catskill peaks; and explorers, unaware of their own insignificance, trekked down mountain paths, taking in vistas never before seen as they ignored the consequences of unbridled expansion.

Cole's paintings defied the traditional artistic compositions and broke new ground. They depicted steam rising from the rivers and streams, craggy, jagged promontories, falling waters, autumn colors, and places never before seen or imagined. He painted river oxbows and places with names like *Kaaterskill Falls* and *The Clove* and *Schroon Mountain*. He painted scenes from *Last of the Mohicans*. Cole and William Cullen Bryant, *Kindred Spirits*, carved their names into the bark of a nearby birch tree, gazed at waterfalls in a forest glen in the Catskills, admired the rushing stream before being captured in oils in a portrait by Asher Brown Durand.

They were all celebrating the Hudson-Catskill beauty and creating new forms of artistry for a new country. They were trying to preserve the pristine beauty of the area as pioneer settlements encroached. The splendor and tranquility disappeared before their eyes. They knew that their idealized version of the natural landscape would soon be gone and so they sought to preserve it. Some created on scraps of paper, others in books, and others on canvas. In his dream, my father filmed it all on his Bolex in the early 1840s.

What would Natty Bumpo think today? Would Uncas and Chingachgook mourn for what they saw as they trod their ancient deer trails in their soft moccasins that recognized every rock and root their soles/*souls* encountered?

What stories could be told? Stories my father knew he would now never be able to tell himself.

His camera was running out of film, as was his life, and so his dream ended.

CHAPTER 20

THURSDAY, OCTOBER 23, 2008
3:00 a.m.: THE MURDER

It was a combination of Huck licking his face and whimpering while frantically doggy-paddling his way out of the zipped-up confines of the sleeping bag, plus the crash of thunder over near Monsey, that woke my father from his *Thanatopsis Syndrome*.

He shook himself awake, preparing to slide under the cover of the tarp and pup tent, when he heard a car engine. He looked to the west, to the narrow hiking trail that was used periodically as a service road, the one that he, himself, had hiked in on the day before. What looked like a black SUV was approaching, its headlights off, its parking lights turned on. It was difficult for him to see clearly, as he had specifically chosen the elevated site far enough off the trail for his gear to be hidden and safe from other hikers.

The SUV was crawling along the narrow dirt road, edging past the boulders strewn along the path. The trail was rough going even for hikers. Abby had never seen a service vehicle, a mountain bike, or an ATV on the path. All the service workers he knew of always walked to the Tors.

Now, fewer than fifty yards away, the SUV came to a stop. Huck was growing anxious, so my father cradled him closely, muzzling him gently and shoosh-ing in his ear.

In the dim glow of the parking lights, he could see first one man and then another get out of the vehicle. From the rear driver's side they dragged a frightened, murmuring young woman to the front of the car, her wrists bound. One man's hand was over her mouth, almost as my father was then holding Huck.

Then he saw the pistol in the driver's hand, as he swatted it across the young woman's face to silence her. Her blood came quickly. As they scuffled to the ground, all their faces were in silhouette, created by the SUV's parking lights. The two men knelt over her, their knees holding her down, their backs to my father. He could see a young blond woman wearing just a slip. She struggled, frantically pleading.

"I promise. I promise I won't tell anyone. *Swear to God!* I promise, I promise, I promise," she struggled to say through a mouthful of blood and broken teeth.

Huck whimpered and squirmed violently to break free and run to the scene as my father gripped his snout even tighter. At first my father was convinced he was about to witness a rape, but because of the gun, he was helpless to prevent it without jeopardizing his own life. In the split second he even considered taking the risk. Hadn't he come here to die? What difference could it make? Could he talk them out of it? They did that kind of thing in mystery novels, didn't they? But at that moment the driver put what looked like might be a .38 caliber pistol to the woman's head and, without hesitation, shot her point-blank in the left temple. The sound was muffled by what surely had to be a silencer, yet it still echoed in the trees.

The incident that unfolded before him was remarkably similar to what he had experienced once before, as a boy: the abrupt end of a woman's life in the presence of two men and unseen witnesses. He began to wonder if he were beginning the bouts of dementia Doc had warned him about. Was it just a hallucination? What he had seen defied reality.

Shocked by the cold-blooded suddenness of what had just occurred, and fearful of what he was sure to happen if he were to be discovered, he inadvertently allowed Huck to wriggle free. Huck raced to the scene, barking hysterically, trying to be a hero. Or did Huck start barking, forcing my father to release him rather than be discovered himself? No one will ever know.

My father, by this time terrified with fear, could do nothing but watch in horror when the driver turned on Huck as he ran toward the murder scene. The man faced the attacking dog. His first instinct was to shoot Huck point-blank, from a distance of about eight feet. Huck let out a garbled yelp, cut short, a plea for my father's help, and collapsed, twisting to the ground, dead, a bullet passing through the front of his chest cavity.

The two men stood frozen, looking around as the echo of the muffled gunshot faded into the darkness of the autumn night. They looked at each other, scanned the hillside above them and the drop-off below. Where had the dog come from? Was its owner around somewhere? They edged back into their SUV, reversing out of the deep woods slowly but deliberately.

My father waited a moment before struggling in the fading glow of his flashlight to climb down the boulders to Huck's side. He was frightened and angry as he raced to kneel beside his faithful companion, but Huck was dead. My father stroked Huck's snout, scrunched him behind his ears one final time, and stood, heartbroken and enraged. He looked for the lights of the SUV, but they were already hidden by the thick underbrush that lined the trail.

He knelt and cradled his dead friend in his arms, carried him halfway up the hill, and placed him gently in a pile of leaves. He covered him with some fallen branches and twigs, knowing it would only be temporary. There were coyotes in these hills, and he didn't want Huck's corpse to be desecrated. Huck had been more than a dog. He was a loyal, trusted family member. To my father, he represented my childhood and all the emotional weight that carried.

He struggled for breath, composed himself, and walked back to the dead body. In the dimming light of his flashlight he looked down to see the face of a woman in her late twenties. He could see dark bruises on her shoulders and arms that made him assume she had been beaten before her assassination. She wore a thin gold bracelet with the initials *B.O.W.* inscribed. He listened in the darkness. Silence. He checked his watch. It was three a.m.

Abby passed his flashlight over the young woman's body one more time before the beam began to fade to an orange-yellow. On her bare right shoulder, a small jailhouse tattoo: *B.O.W.* He shook his flashlight twice, and it came back on for a second, then faded quickly.

To the west a thunderstorm was moving in. Lightning struck, and thunder exploded overhead just seconds later. Sound traveled at eleven hundred feet per second? He counted to himself. The storm's edge was less than half a mile away. And then came the rain. It started gently, quickly became surprisingly strong, splattering on the few remaining leaves above.

He looked around one last time. Getting his bearings, he began his journey out of the woods. He trod off into the darkness at a slow, even pace, following the hiking trail in the direction of the killer's vehicle. Tire marks were illuminated by the sporadic lightning. The indentations were quickly filling with rainwater from the torrential downpour.

What was he thinking as he tried to figure out what to do next? Why did this have to happen just days before what he assumed would be his last on earth? Why did things always have to be complicated for him? He just wanted to die in peace on this final resting place he had chosen specifically.

Thirty minutes later Abby lumbered slowly through the woods in the blinding rainstorm that swept across the top of the ridge. Visibility was just a few feet. The puddles on the path were two inches deep as he neared Central Highway, obliterating his footsteps and the tire tracks made by the SUV. He was drenched. What had remained of Huck's blood on his jacket was almost gone. He started to worry about hypothermia.

He walked through the pouring rain from Low Tor toward the parking lot on The Hill. His domain had been desecrated. Someone had befouled his childhood playground with a heinous crime, and he was angry. He was soaking wet and shivering, exhausted. He was dying, he knew.

He replayed the murder over and over in his mind like rewinding videotape in a linear editing session, as he had done so many times in the days before digital editing came along with its random-access memory and enabled complex editing with simple keystrokes and mouse clicks. As he walked, he rewound and rewound the tape. What was he missing? What could he identify about the murderers?

When he got to the heavy chain that blocked the trail entrance from public access, it was locked. Had it been stretched between the posts when he first crossed over it from The Hill the day before, or had he stepped over it on the ground? In his rage over Huck's senseless death, he couldn't remember clearly. Was he losing his memory, as Doc had recently suggested would happen?

My father crossed over from the trail onto the roadway blacktop, jogged slowly to the count of one hundred, then speed-walked for the next hundred counts to catch his breath, alternating between the slow run and walk into the downhill darkness. There were no cars to flag down in the predawn deluge as he maneuvered the steep switchbacks of the descending highway toward South Mountain Road. He had to stop, sit down in the empty cornfields in the heavy rain.

The rain began to diminish an hour later, after Abby had struggled through the storm that had felt as if someone were whip-cracking a fire hose in his face. He arrived on the front porch of his father-in-law, my grandfather, Chief Walter Schoonmaker, off Little Tor Road, near Camp Jawonio.

Schoonmaker had been a member of the Clarkstown Police Department for most of his adult life. In the 1990s, the Lower Hudson River Valley Park Police was formed, taking jurisdiction of all state land on both sides of the Hudson from Kingston on south. Schoonmaker had been hired as chief, despite his postretirement age. Now, in 2008, he had attained a powerful voice in all that happened in the parks system. He wasn't anyone you would want to mess with.

My father pounded on the door, covered with mud and the diluted remains of Huck's blood, wearing a maniacal look on his face. About to collapse, his breathing was labored. My grandfather opened the door in his bathrobe. In his late seventies, he looked like a distinguished, by-the-book cop, still in great health, or sufficiently great to keep his official position. Some say it had become an honorary title, something to keep him busy while other men were long retired. How had he managed to keep his job well past the time when most other officers had been put out to pasture?

It was five in the morning when the Chief saw his son-in-law standing before him, drenched to the skin, looking like he was on the verge of collapse.

"Jesus Christ, Abby, what happened to you?"

My father was gasping for breath. "Someone shot Huck."

At first my grandfather was angry. "What? What are you talking about? You woke me up at five o'clock in the morning to tell me someone shot your dog? What happened to you?"

"I told you. Someone shot Huck . . . and some young woman . . . Out in the woods near the Low Tor lookout."

"Come on in here. A young woman? Shot? You're not making sense. When?"

Abby continued to gasp for air as he entered the house.

"About two hours ago."

"What the hell were you doing out there?"

"Camping. I was camping with Huck. Two guys pulled up in a SUV, dragged a girl out, and shot her in the head. I saw the whole thing from my campsite. Huck ran to them, and they shot him, too."

"Why didn't they shoot you? They didn't know you were there? They didn't see you?"

"No, too dark. I kept hidden until they were gone."

Despite their many differences over the years, both public and private, my grandfather jumped into action. He tried to be comforting, taking charge, consoling my father.

"Okay, hang on, Abby. I'm gonna call the team. Can you show us where this all happened?

"Sure, sure."

My grandfather moved to the phone on his kitchen wall and dialed his office.

"Sergeant? Chief Schoonmaker. My son-in-law just woke me up. It seems we have a murder on our hands. Get everyone we have and the Crime Scene Unit and meet me on the Little Tor overpass parking lot in an hour. It might still be dark up there even after daybreak, so bring all the lights you have."

The Chief hung up and turned to Abby.

"Come on, we're going to get some coffee in you and a shower and some dry clothes. Where's your car, by the way? I didn't see it in the driveway."

"It's up near there. I couldn't find my keys."

"You couldn't find your keys? You walked here? You picked a hell of a time to get Alzheimer's."

My father stopped cold at the odd reference to his own earlier joke with Doc Charles, but of course my grandfather was unaware of the significance of his attempt at humor at that time.

Just about everything I've related about my father so far, I learned later, after talking to him and his friends and other witnesses. But I heard firsthand what just transpired between him and my grandfather. The ironic part of the conversation between these two men, by now mortal enemies because of what had happened to my mother, is the fact that I was upstairs, hiding in a bedroom. As they pulled out of the driveway, I pulled back a curtain and watched them disappear into the night as they drove to my house.

My only thoughts at that moment were for poor Huck and what he had meant to me as a boy. When my father first said it, as he staggered in through the doorway, I wasn't sure I'd heard him correctly. I had been half asleep upstairs, and I froze in place when I heard his voice. My immediate fear was that he'd discovered that I was there visiting, and he was storming in to retrieve me and force me to come home. I couldn't reveal myself and ask him to repeat what he said about Huck. I started to cry quietly with grief and uncertainty. What was going on? I wouldn't be able to find out anything, without blowing my cover, until my grandfather returned at the end of his workday.

I wouldn't find out about my father's terminal medical condition until later.

CHAPTER 21

THURSDAY MORNING, OCTOBER 23, 2008 3 HOURS AFTER THE MURDER

At my father's cottage, he unlocked the door with a key from under the front porch geranium pot. He took a shower as Chief Schoonmaker stayed on the handheld, two-way radio talking with his office. His proficiency, professionalism, and leadership were apparent as he gave orders.

Twenty minutes later Abby stepped out of the bedroom clean and dry, near total exhaustion. To my grandfather, he looked disoriented, confused. The Chief put down the two-way and offered Abby a cup of coffee from the Mr. Coffee urn. "I made myself at home here. Something tells me we're going to need this." He handed my father a mug and poured the remains into his own thermos. He looked curiously at

Abby's labored breathing. "Are you okay? You're acting strange."

"I'm okay. Just tired."

"Are you sure you're all right? You sound like you've been running for days."

My father ignored the question.

Another thirty minutes later, dawn was about to break over the Hudson. The rain had slowed, and my father and grandfather met the Lower Hudson River Valley Park Police Crime Scene Investigation Team at the maintenance road entrance on The Hill. The chain between the posts was down on the ground.

Detective Terrence Mays, my grandfather's deputy, was wearing a yellow slicker. He approached my grandfather and began his summary. "This rain has probably covered up a lot." He turned to give my father an accusatory look. "We should have been in there two hours ago."

My grandfather cut him off. "We needed Abby, here, to pinpoint the spot. You could have been wandering around for days, trampling the evidence. Okay, let's head 'em out, boys."

My grandfather led the police convoy as they drove slowly down the narrow, rutted road, squeezing past tree trunks and boulders that encroached the pathway.

The coroner's vehicle stayed behind in the parking lot, awaiting the summons to carry out the body. Abby rode point with the Chief and Mays. "Don't let us get too close, Abby. We don't want to destroy any evidence or tracks." But as everyone could readily see, the tracks had already been washed out by the rain.

Abby looked around, trying to get his bearings. They drove slowly past the power line right-of-way that crossed over the Tor. My father kept glancing over his shoulder until he was sure they were close to the scene. "Okay, it's just up ahead."

My grandfather picked up his radio mic. "Hold up, everybody. And watch where you step."

Behind them, vehicles filled with officers stopped where they were, and the Crime Scene Investigation team got out. Abby, still in a state of semi-shock, was reluctant to walk forward.

Finally he turned to my grandfather. "Right up there in that clearing."

Mays and the other officers walked slowly forward in the dawn light, their flashlights sweeping the ground. Abby squinted in the light to see anything of what he remembered. "Her body should be right up there. Another twenty yards."

But then, as they walked, he didn't see a body where he remembered it, so he inched forward, continuing to check his bearings. The Chief and the officers scanned the crime scene, looking back to Abby for confirmation of the location. It went on for five minutes, rainwater dripping from the leaves and branches above.

Finally, the Chief caught up with Abby. "Are you sure this is the spot?"

Abby glanced up the rocky hill to where his sleeping bag was.

"Hold on a minute."

Abby climbed the steep incline as the officers watched him. He found his rain-soaked, soggy sleeping bag and duffel bag where he had left them. He turned back and looked down to the crime scene, confused, trying to align the trees across his field of view with what he'd witnessed only hours earlier.

From below, the Chief yelled up to him. "What?"

Abby scanned his field of view again. "Five yards in front of where you're standing. You should see tire tracks and blood, if the rain hasn't washed them all away. That's where her body was."

The Chief and the officers exchanged quizzical glances as Abby came down the hill carrying his sleeping bag and duffel. Soaked with rain, they weighed easily twenty pounds. He looked around, concerned and confused.

The Chief turned to him. "Okay, Abby. Walk us through it and tell us what you saw. I want all the details."

My father repeated the information to the group, of what he had seen in the middle of the night, just three hours before. He could tell by their looks that they all thought he was crazy. Lost in one of his own murder mysteries, they wondered? Were they snickering behind his back?

A half hour later, after a thorough search of the area by the Crime Scene team, they turned up no evidence: no tire tracks, no blood, no footprints. No evidence. Nothing.

My father was frustrated with disbelief. He could tell that the Chief and his men were starting to believe he might have imagined the whole thing.

"You're absolutely sure about this, Abby?"

"I know what I saw, Chief. I didn't hallucinate, and I'm not doing drugs. Not those kinds of drugs, anyway."

"What kind of pistol was it?"

Abby hesitated. "I couldn't say with absolute certainty."

"Abby, I know you've been under a lot of strain lately."

"Don't start. I know what I saw. Someone killed my dog."

He walked abruptly halfway up the hill to the pile of leaves and branches where he had hidden Huck's body and tossed away the dead limbs that had been covering Huck's corpse. The Chief and the officers again exchanged quizzical glances, as if Abby had lost his mind. "I didn't want the coyotes getting him." Abby carefully brushed the leaves aside and pulled Huck's bloody body into an embrace. For the officers it was a confusing yet sobering moment. He walked over to them, determined.

"Someone killed that woman in cold blood. Huck went after them. They cut him down, shot him like they shot her. Just like I've been telling you."

Mays turned to him. "Mr. Traphagen, with all due respect, a dead dog is not a dead woman. Did you cover her body with twigs to protect it?"

Then my father turned angry. "I don't give a good goddam about her. She's your problem, not mine. But I will tell you one thing. I'm going to find out who killed my dog."

My grandfather interrupted. "That' crazy talk, Abby."

"I am crazy. They just made me crazy."

"Abby, I'm sorry to have to tell you this. We're going to have to take Huck's body as evidence. We're going to have to perform an autopsy and ballistics tests. If what you say is true, we're going to have to match the bullets to a weapon. You said it was the same gun that shot them both?"

Abby nodded affirmatively, then reluctantly attempted to pass Huck's body to Mays, who in turn stepped back and pointed to a lab-tech assistant, who put it in a body bag designed for human remains.

"The same gun."

"You're going to have to leave this up to us, Abby."

Abby seemed far away, yet determined. Was he contemplating years of companionship, thinking of how he'd played with Huck and me? "I'm going to find out who killed my dog."

The Chief turned back to his men. "Okay, boys. Let's spread out. You know the drill. We'll start all over again."

He turned to my father. "Let' go home, Abby. You need to dry off. Get some rest. There's nothing more we can do here."

They drove back slowly along the service road to the Little Tor Road parking lot. The rain had started again. My grandfather pulled up to the coroner's vehicle that had stayed behind in the lot. He rolled down his window. "You guys can go back. We can't find the victim's body."

The coroner's drivers exchanged puzzled glances.

My grandfather watched them back out of the parking lot. He looked down into New City and then back to my father seated next to him. "I thought you couldn't find your keys. Isn't this where you parked your car?"

"No."

"Where is your car?"

"Up near Perkins Memorial Drive."

"You and Huck hiked from Perkins Memorial Drive?"

"I told you, I was camping. It took us three days. Just a few miles per day."

My grandfather looked at him skeptically. "Something's not adding up here, Abby."

My father didn't answer him. Instead, he looked over his shoulder. Who has a key to that chain, he wondered? He tried again to remember if it had been locked when he first arrived Tuesday morning, and again, when he had left just hours before.

CHAPTER 22

MAY, 1956
52 YEARS BEFORE THE MURDER

Yes, it was in the fourth grade that my father fell in love with Miss Singer, just as every boy in the class, including his three friends, Nick, Doc, and Ossie. But it was with Nick alone that he shared the secret that would bond them for life.

Growing up, Nick and my father lived on the Dellwood Country Club compound, just as their own fathers had a generation earlier. Tiny cottages and toolsheds behind the maintenance barn provided the living quarters, and so Nick and my father grew up like brothers, sharing adjacent cramped quarters as shadows working for the powerful men who belonged to the club.

Nick's father, Nick Tremontana, Sr., was my grandfather's supervisor, but Nick never rubbed that fact in my father's nose. They spent their child-hoods together, tobogganing down the golf course's first fairway hillside in the winter wonderland that New City became each December. When the air turned warm, they spent their days caddying and shagging balls through the spring and summer, swimming in the pool at night when the members were gone.

In this environment Nick and my father came to witness the influence and behavior of powerful men, some who took their wealth in stride, others who spent hours on the golf course, in the company of their caddies, bragging about their riches, their influence, their power. Most of them were from Manhattan and came to the country club only on weekends. In that pre–Palisades Parkway era, some stayed in the guest rooms. Others stayed in nearby rooming houses rather than take the drive down Route 9W back to Manhattan in the middle of the night after bouts of heavy drinking. Some drove fancy cars; others were chauffeured in limousines. Some even flew from Teterboro and landed at Christie's Airport, a grass strip just a few hundred yards south of the country club's entrance, where Zukor Road meets North Main. There, they were picked up by a club limousine.

My father came to hate these men for their wealth, their fancy clothes and their bragging, their dismissive attitudes, their self-perceived specialness.

He saw them as destroying the New City he had grown to love. Weren't these the men who were cutting down the woods to build the new housing developments in town?

What he didn't know as a nine-year-old boy, but would soon find out, was that some of these men were encroaching on more than his beloved territory. They were competing for the affections of his teacher, who would become the inspiration for the fictionalized version of Ruth Singer, the character my father called Adina Perlman in *Sweetclover*.

My father told that story mostly from the point of view of the nine-year-old protagonist, Aron, as recollected thirty-two years later by the adult Aron. Part of the story Aron tells is from my father's own recollections. Part of the story Aron tells is what my father learned about the investigation, incrementally, as he grew older. He chose to fictionalize a lot, including what had really happened.

With some minor exceptions, the story is narrated in the voice of Aron.

Sweetclover
Pub. 1988

NEW CITY, NEW YORK
LABOR DAY WEEKEND, 1955

It was the beginning of Labor Day weekend. Cal and Frank and I were playing in Frank's barn on the second floor. Frank's grandfather's mail wagon from the early part of the century had been stored there since just after World War I, after he started delivering the mail in a motor car. We used that mail wagon as our stagecoach in the television western reenactments that we performed in the barn, tales of bravery we hoped to appear in one day on real television.

When Frank's grandmother called, we walked down the sidewalk, which was flanked and shaded by rows of broad-leafed catalpa trees, and sat on the back porch of the old Victorian-style house. She served us homemade lemonade, and she was all excited because her new boarder was about to arrive on the one o'clock Red & Tan bus.

Moments later, after the sound of the bus shifting gears, there was a knock on the front door. We put down our lemonade and ran past the grape arbor and down the side driveway to the front porch to get a glimpse of this boarder, who we knew was going to be our fourth-grade teacher the following week. School always started on the first Wednesday after Labor Day, just days away. As we rounded the corner, Miss Perlman, who was dressed in a late-summer outfit and holding a small satchel and suit hangar, looked at me and smiled down from that porch railing, and I fell in love instantly.

She stood looking at Cal and Frank and me, dressed in a late summer outfit and holding a small satchel and suit hanger. "Hi, Frank. Is your grandmother in? Who are your two friends? Will they be in my class, too?"

Just then Frank's grandmother opened the door. "Miss Singer. So glad to see you. How was the bus? Lots of holiday passengers? Come on in, make yourself at home."

Miss Perlman turned, looked directly at me, and smiled. "Hope to see you boys on Wednesday."

She walked through the front door, and my life would never be the same again.

When the school year started, Adina Perlman was bashful and hesitant in front of the class. Her shyness made the boys even more enamored by her, and that smile carried her through the first several weeks.

But as the trees turned muted reds and golds and the chilled air filled with the smell of burning leaves, she found her stride, and her class lectures became even more interesting, sometimes even humorous, to the delight of the entire class. Most of all, she lived up to the origins of her name—"gentleness." She was a gentle soul to all her students. Didn't understand a math problem or falling behind on reading assignments? Miss Perlman was there to help with a gentle touch on the shoulder. Some of the boys even pretended not to understand just so they would get her extra attention.

Those fall days in 1955 brought a glorious color to our world. How could life possibly be better for this nine-year-old boy, in love with his teacher as she paced the front of the classroom, squeaking her chalk across the board, recalling facts and figures meant to inspire and entertain us? Was this what it meant to be in love? My heart was full as we approached the Christmas break.

Cal and I spent a lot of time hanging around the boardinghouse owned by Frank's grandmother, hoping to catch a glimpse of Miss Perlman when she wasn't at school. What did she do in her off-hours, we wondered, beside grade our papers, those poorly written compositions in scrawling cursive penmanship?

With the help of a friend whose dad worked in Manhattan, I bought her a book at Brentano's, and it arrived just before the break. I wrapped it in holiday paper with a red bow. It was *East of Eden*, by John Steinbeck. I read it before wrapping it, taking care not to crinkle the pages or crack the spine so she would not be able to tell it had been read before. I just knew she would like it.

The Christmas break was uneventful but for my quiet longing to return to school to see Miss Perlman again. I was actually glad when the vacation was over, and I looked forward to seeing her every day as the long days of silent, gentle snowfall were upon us.

What we didn't know was that Miss Perlman had met someone.

The novel, *Sweetclover*, closely parallels the "official version" of the real murder investigation. Unbeknownst to some readers, even to her friends, Ruth Singer/Adina Perlman had met a young man. He cleaned out the mouse cages at a place in New City called Carworth Farms. At the time, Carworth Farms was a well-known rodent-breeding facility, located across the street from the brand-new Clarkstown Central High School on Congers Road. Carworth Farms provided thousands of laboratory mice and rats to the medical experimentation and pharmaceutical industries. Someone had to clean the rodents' cages.

The young man's name was Douglas Knapp, and he was an army veteran who had served in World War II and Korea. One night when school had reconvened following the Christmas break, Miss Perlman met Douglas after work at the New City Library. At that time, it was on the corner of Maple and Demarest Avenues, across from Gunnar Pedersen's Sporting Goods store that had once been the original New City firehouse.

The library had been built just a few years earlier, constructed of cinder blocks bought by the local children. For one dollar, you could buy a cinder block and paint your initials on it. There are pictures of the building, taken just before the volunteer masons put on the brick façade, which shows all the cinder blocks with the children's initials on them. My father's cinder block was just above ground level on the southwest corner. In one of the surviving snapshots you can see *A.T. II* in white paint brushstrokes. The library itself was a small structure with a decent collection of classic books and popular fiction. All the bestsellers were there. The basement was filled with children's fare and the magazine archive. Copies of *National Geographic* dated back to the 1930s.

Miss Singer went there on a regular basis to find recent books she had read about but could not afford to buy and to seek out recommendations for her students to read.

Sweetclover:
Pub. 1988

NEW CITY, NEW YORK
SPRING, 1956

After the schoolteacher's disappearance, Miss Van Houten, the librarian, told Chief Eckerson that she had seen Adina Perlman talking to veteran Randall Simmons in the library. She was surprised by this because the two were so different.

The new year, 1956, had just started, and classes were back to normal. The first time Miss Perlman met the veteran, Miss Van Houten told the Chief, his hair was slicked back and he was wearing khakis, a blue shirt, and a friendly smile. Like Miss Perlman, he was mostly alone in the world, nearly destitute, and like her, he lived in a small room. His room was on the Carworth Farms property.

The two loners began to see each other at the library several nights during the week. He was definitely not her type, but Miss Perlman seemed to lack the confidence to attract someone more educated and refined. He told her what he did, cleaning rat cages, and she laughed. It embarrassed him, and she caught herself, apologized. He spent his evenings in the library trying to improve himself and complete his education so he could get a college degree, or so he claimed. He actually had no place to go, no money to spend, no hope of ever going to college, even on the G.I. Bill.

After their third meeting in the library, and the halting first conversations, Randall Simmons gathered his courage, as he had before the invasion of the Iwo Jima and climbing Pork Chop Hill, and offered to walk Miss Perlman home. Asking her was the most difficult challenge of the three.

"May I walk you home? It seems to have become colder. Might even snow, I heard."

Shy, but eager to meet new friends, Miss Perlman agreed to let him walk her home, or at least part of the way.

That chill January night in 1956, according to the librarian, they left the library together. It was getting colder, and they pulled up their collars. Adina

Perlman was curious about this young man who appeared to show an interest in her. What would it be like to be held in his arms to fight off the freezing temperatures?

They walked south on Maple Avenue, in silence except for the muffled hiss of wet tires on wintry streets. A light snow began to fall, softening the glow of the streetlights. They walked past the Methodist Church, where her fourth-grade students had attended kindergarten in the basement just a few years earlier. They walked past the shoe repair shop and the Boy Scout office and Miller Dairy, and the vacant lot where Eberling's Market would soon be relocated. They walked past the Episcopal Church rectory and the Little League field, and finally they arrived at the rectory behind St. Augustine Catholic Church. There, she turned to say good night. She didn't want anyone to see Randall walking her home, and she was reluctant to let him know where she actually lived so early in their friendship. He pulled his gloved hand from his coat pocket and extended it. She smiled and did the same. They shook hands briefly and she turned away.

"Stay warm," he said to her back as she walked to Third Street. She waved over her shoulder. Anyone watching would have seen a small smile of hope cross her face.

A week after Randall walked Adina at least partway home, her life changed again. One Friday night in late January, she was invited to a birthday party of another teacher, to be held at Jerry Carnegie's Tavern on Congers Road, right near the school.

Usually on Friday afternoons after classes, she gathered her bag in her small room at the boardinghouse, walked across the street past the state trooper's headquarters, and hopped on a Red & Tan bus to bring her back to her parents' flat in Manhattan for the weekend.

The northbound bus would stop at Third Street in front of St. Augustine's, on its way into New City, the end of the line. A few hundred yards north, next to The Elms at Congers and Main, the bus would turn around in the strip-mall parking lot and head south toward the Port Authority Terminal on Forty-Second Street in Manhattan. A quick subway ride would bring her a block from her home, and she would join her parents for dinner every Friday night at seven.

On that January night, Miss Perlman decided to go to the teacher's birthday party. After checking with her landlady to see if it would be all right to spend

Friday and Saturday nights in her room, and after notifying her parents, her plans were set.

Later, during the cocktail hour, Jerry's Tavern was packed with teachers from New City Grammar, from Street School on North Main, and from Bardonia School to the south and Congers Elementary to the east. They all knew the birthday celebrant. There was a cake, silly cards, the singing of "Happy Birthday" over and over again.

But then, just as the party was winding down, half a dozen business executives who had driven in from Manhattan enroute to the country club, walked brashly through the door. It was their tradition to stop in for a few martinis to get their weekend party started. At least three of them approached and asked Miss Perlman for a dance, but there was no dancing at Jerry's Tavern. As she looked around, she realized that she was the butt of a joke, and so they laughingly offered to buy her a martini to apologize.

Miss Perlman's original plan had been to walk home from Jerry's to her boardinghouse after the party, just a few short blocks. How could one martini hurt? At first she said no, continuing to hang out with the other teachers. But as the teacher party's momentum slowed, the men were back with another offer of a martini. No man had ever paid much attention to her before, certainly not the boys in college. She agreed to a drink. These were successful businessmen in gray flannel suits. Country club men. What could go wrong?

And then, one by one, as the teachers left, saying good night to Miss Perlman at the bar, she stood there with a martini glass in hand, trying to look sophisticated, surrounded by these men.

By that time, Adina Perlman had become drunk for the first time in her life.

She was finally able to excuse herself from the Dellwood gentlemen, feeling more fearful as they became more insistent in their intentions.

That birthday party night, after refusing a ride back to her boardinghouse by the last Dellwood swell, she waited until they all left. Jerry offered to call Whooley's for a cab, but Miss Perlman refused.

She staggered out and walked from Jerry's Tavern down Congers Road toward Carworth Farms by the high school. It started to snow. She pulled her collar up close to her face so no one would recognize her. Drunk teachers, she knew, would not be tolerated at New City Grammar School. At Carworth Farms, she staggered around in the blustery snow until she saw the bunkhouse with a light on.

She knocked on the door. Randall answered, surprised and confused. "Why, hello, Miss Perlman. This is certainly a surprise."

"I went to a birthday party for one of my teacher friends at Jerry's Tavern. I think I've had too much to drink. Too much to go back to my own room. I'm not used to drinking."

Much to his surprise, she let herself in, walking past him into the tiny room, which was sparsely furnished with a twin bed and a small dresser. Everything was in perfect order, military style.

On the nightstand was a gooseneck reading lamp that he could swing over when he was reading in the tattered armchair that had lace doilies on the armrests. He had checked out a few children's books from the library; easy reading. *The Black Stallion*, by Walter Farley, *Old Yeller*, by Fred Gipson, *The Lion's Paw*, by Robb White. An *Argosy* magazine was placed neatly under a windup alarm clock.

She smiled wanly by way of explanation. "I don't want my landlady to see me drunk."

Randall invited her to sit on the tattered armchair in the corner. He started to heat some water on a hot plate to make Postum. A few minutes later, as he approached to serve her, she stood to accept the mug, put it on the nightstand and then pushed to embrace him. She collapsed in his arms and began weeping. "May I stay here tonight?"

He looked around his tiny room, embarrassed. "Sure. You can take the bed. I'll sleep in the chair."

"No. I want you to sleep with me in the bed."

Randall wasn't sure what she meant. "What? What do you mean? Keep you warm? I've got an extra blanket."

"I'm a virgin. I'm almost twenty-four years old. I don't want to be a virgin anymore."

He started to tremble. "Oh, I couldn't do that. It wouldn't be right."

"What's the matter? Are you a virgin, too? Don't you know what to do?"

"No. It's just that . . . you're drunk."

"I don't care."

"I wouldn't be right. Anyway, I don't think I can. Since the war. Since Korea, I . . ."

"What?"

"I don't know. I just don't—"

"You don't find me attractive?"

"No, that's not it. I think you are beautiful."

"Are you one of those . . . *homosexual* people?"

"No, no. Not at all. I just can't seem to . . . concentrate or focus on. . ."

"You think I'm ugly?"

"No, I think you're beautiful. I can't explain it. I'm just—"

"Randall, I want you to. I'm asking you to. You wouldn't be taking advantage."

"No, no. I could never do that."

His refusal only made Miss Perlman even more sad. By then she was weeping for herself and for him. It made him petrified.

She sank onto his narrow bed, and when she wasn't vomiting violently in the bathroom, she spent the night there. The room never stopped spinning in wild ellipses. He slept in the chair. She was still sick the next morning, hung over. The room continued to spin.

That same day, Saturday, when her landlady realized that Miss Perlman had not come home to her room on Friday night, she assumed that she had changed her mind about spending the night in New City and had caught a late bus home. Miss Perlman's parents never thought anything of it, as Adina had told them she would not be home that weekend.

Adina stayed in bed all day and then spent Saturday night on Randall's bed again. He walked to Keinke's next to The Elms and bought Alka-Seltzer and some

Coca-Colas to help settle her stomach. She couldn't seem to stop dry-heaving.

By Sunday night she was feeling better, and she thought about walking back to her room, but she and Randall spent the night talking. To see if she could keep something down, he fed her saltines and chicken broth that he made from a bouillon cube on the hot plate in his room.

Miss Perlman showed up at school that following Monday morning, wearing the same clothes she had been wearing at Jerry's Tavern the preceding Friday. The students didn't notice it, but her friend who taught second grade did. Nothing was said.

Weeks went by, and Miss Perlman became a regular at Jerry's Tavern on Friday nights. She told her parents she was spending the weekends in New City at her boardinghouse. Frank's grandmother watched her get on the bus on Friday afternoons and assumed that she was going home. But Miss Perlman apparently had other plans. Instead, just a few blocks north of where she boarded, she climbed down from the northbound bus at the turnaround at Main Street and Congers Road and walked down the hill past the cemetery that dated back to the Revolutionary War. Cater-cornered across the street was Jerry's Tavern, where she mingled with the Friday-night crowd. Her friends on the faculty didn't seem to know where she was sleeping on those Friday and Saturday nights.

One Saturday night in February, Miss Perlman's mother called unexpectedly from Manhattan to speak to her daughter. Of course she wasn't there. Frank's grandmother thought quickly. Hadn't she seen Miss Perlman boarding the bus? Then she lied to the teacher's mother and told her that Miss Perlman was spending the night at a pajama party with the other single women schoolteachers, and no, she did not know the phone number, had no way of finding it, but would deliver the message personally the next time she saw Miss Perlman.

Weekend after weekend went by, and the deceit continued.

The winter passed, and my classmates and I noticed a change in Miss Perlman, but at the age of nine we were unable to articulate just what it was that was so different. She didn't smile as much as she did when she first arrived, and she didn't seem as patient. An adult might say she was distracted. The odd thing was that she was dressing differently. Her clothes seemed *nicer.* More expensive. Certainly more expensive than a teacher could afford.

One Monday on a rainy, late spring morning in May 1956, she didn't show up for class. The principal, Jeff Cameron, arranged for a last-minute substitute teacher. Then, fearing the worst, he drove over to the boardinghouse and made a discreet inquiry as to whether Miss Perlman had missed the bus into town from Manhattan the night before or had overslept that morning. Her landlady shook her head in dismay, confided in Mr. Cannon that Miss Perlman had not slept there the evening before, or any Friday or Saturday night in recent memory. She referred to a small calendar on her kitchen wall, pointing to the dates that were checked off. The principal took the calendar with him. Their eyes met briefly, both reluctant to address what the calendar might mean. She told Mr. Cameron of the missed phone call from her mother.

Mr. Cameron drove back to school, interrupted Miss Perlman's friend, the second-grade teacher, Miss Cosgrove, and led her out into the hallway.

"Do you know where Miss Perlman might be?"

Miss Cosgrove started crying. "I don't know anything about it."

"Did you know that Miss Perlman was not going home on the weekends?"

"Yes, but I don't know where she was staying."

"You didn't ask?"

"It was none of my business. I thought she might have a boyfriend, but I don't know who."

Later, when Miss Cosgrove spoke to the police, she would remember some more details. It was unclear to her where Miss Perlman was spending her weekends because every time she had asked her, Miss Perlman's story would change, as if to purposely confuse her.

Mr. Cannon walked back to his office and made what he would later describe as the most difficult phone call he would ever make as an educator. He called Miss Perlman's parents in Manhattan and asked them if she was sick or had overslept.

Of course they didn't know where she was, had thought she was spending the weekends at the boardinghouse. They immediately got on a bus to New City.

Our beloved Miss Perlman was now officially missing.

Meanwhile, in the fourth-grade classroom, the students sensed that something was amiss. Miss Perlman had never been absent or late. The substitute teacher was trying to keep us occupied by showing us slides from her recent trip to the Grand Canyon. But like the photographer who was showing her pictures, the students couldn't seem to focus either. The whispering had become constant.

Cal and I sat in the back of the room, silent, looking down at the floor, not able to look at each other.

During the actual investigation of the real disappearance of Miss Singer, when a Clarkstown police officer showed up to talk to the students, it was, ironically, Chief Schoonmaker. He would become my father's father-in-law in another twenty-four years, and eventually, my grandfather. In my father's novels, *The Pits* and *Sweetclover*, the fictionalized investigator is named Chief Eckerson. Chief Schoonmaker/Chief Eckerson asked the fourth grade students questions. Did anyone know where Miss Perlman was? All the students tried to be helpful.

All the students, that is, except for the two boys in the back of room who sat in silence, not daring to make eye contact with anyone. Nick and my father were trembling in fear.

The real fate of the real schoolteacher named Ruth Singer, called Adina Perlman in my father's mystery novel, would not be known for years, even after he wrote the novelized version of her disappearance. What happened to Adina Perlman in the novel was a completely fictionalized, fabricated version of the real events.

As in real life, the novel's investigators deliberately framed the wrong man. At first the deceit was difficult. But as the days and weeks went by, it became easier.

What really happened to Ruth Singer would go unknown for years to all but a few. As suggested in the novel, they may have arrested the wrong man. Was it intentional and deliberate? Had they simply jumped to the wrong conclusion, or were they looking for a scapegoat? Nothing would be known for a long time.

Not until after my father had produced an award-winning documentary and published the nonfiction book based on the disappearance of an FSU star quarterback named Junior Wiley.

Not until after he had published other works of fiction and cut back on his broadcasting schedule to pursue his full-time ambition as a mystery writer.

Not until he wrote the four potboilers and then published his first serious novel, *The Pits*, in 1986.

Not until his father and Nick's father were both dead.

Not even after the publication of *Sweetclover* in 1988.

By then, it had been thirty-two years since Miss Singer's disappearance, few were around who remembered, and the new local residents didn't care. Time marches on.

In real life, Douglas Knapp, the man they eventually blamed for Ruth Singer's death, had an arrest record in some small town in Pennsylvania, where he was falsely accused of assaulting two women and beating them. Douglas had spent a year in jail and had since been drifting from job to job. In today's world, he probably would have been diagnosed as mildly autistic to begin with, and suffering from post-traumatic stress disorder. During World War II he had seen action on Iwo Jima, and later, in Korea, more horrors. What little mental capacity he might have had to begin with became even more diminished. In those days it was called shell shock, and he was on his own.

But all this wasn't made public until Chief Schoonmaker found out about Douglas Knapp from Miss Elsa Bartels, the librarian, and used the information to convince the district attorney that he was guilty of Ruth Singer's disappearance. My father's fictionalized version followed the so-called investigation closely, changing the names. He changed but few of what were perceived as the factual details at that time. Douglas Knapp became Randall Simmons.

Sweetclover:
Pub. 1988

Winter, 1956

Over a period of a month, Miss Perlman met with Randall in his room several weeknights that January and February, after their library visits. It was just to talk. Other nights, they took long walks for entertainment and walked over to Congers to the Last Chance Saloon, where there was less of an opportunity of being seen together by someone she knew. Numerous times they walked over the roads where the floodplain of the Upper Hackensack River would soon be submerged under the new reservoir.

Randall asked to see her on the weekends, but she told him that she went home to Manhattan every Friday night. Randall didn't know that she was lying to him.

After that first Friday night birthday party at Jerry's Tavern and that first weekend sleeping on Randall's bed, Miss Perlman had gone back to the tavern on subsequent Friday evenings despite her overindulgence the first time and despite her newfound friendship with Randall. There was something exciting about being around those powerful men at the bar. Her blood would roil with the taboo feeling it gave her. There was another feeling. Was it hope, maybe? She felt they had the answers that held the key to her future. Somehow, she wanted access to that key.

After the second Friday night at Jerry's Tavern, at the invitation of one of the Dellwood wives, she went back to Dellwood to join the partying, as she had hoped would happen.

One of those weekend wives gave her a more formal dress to wear for the parties and a place to sleep. Over the course of several weeks she became friendlier, more outgoing in front of the group. She was continuing to attract the attention of the men who started flirting with her that first night at Jerry's. She had apparently become bored with her somewhat static social life, and her new friend wasn't any help. He was both helpless and hopeless. How would she be able to let him down without hurting his feelings? What would he do? How would he react?

At this point Miss Perlman was leading a triple life; one at school, one with the oblivious, harmless Randall, with whom she felt some sort of a kinship; and a third, more clandestine life at weekend parties at the Dellwood. Things became decadent rather quickly when the men found out that she was sleeping at an apartment of one of the weekend guest couples. Some might even say that things got out of hand.

One warm spring weekday afternoon when there was no school, Randall Simmons and Adina Perlman went swimming at a favorite local swimming hole. It was a wide part of the Demarest Kill/Upper Hackensack River Watershed. The creek was known to locals as Sweetclover. There, they spent the day swimming, drying off on the nearby rocks, having a picnic lunch she had prepared in her boardinghouse kitchen.

"I saw some of the books you checked out of the library," Adina said.

"Stuff that wouldn't interest you, I'm sure."

"I like them. I use some of them in my classes. What else have you read?"

"Boys' stuff mostly. *Lassie,* the Hardy Boys series. Do you know those books?"

"Oh, yes. I've read all of them, and the Nancy Drew books as well. Some of those two series were written by the same author, under a pseudonym."

"A what?"

"A pen name."

Randall was disappointed. He had hoped to meet the author one day. "I like those Hardy Boys. They remind me of growing up in a little hometown. Almost like this one."

"You might like this book." She pulled a green leatherette hardback with an embossed silhouette of Mark Twain on the spine from her carry bag.

"This book was written by a man named Samuel Clemens. But he wrote it using a pen name, Mark Twain."

On a blanket spread out in the shade Miss Perlman read aloud from *The Adventures of Huckleberry Finn*. Randall had heard of it, but had never read it, and he asked her about the Mississippi River, about slavery, about why it was illegal for Huck to run away with Jim, because he was another man's property. "How can one man own another man?" he wondered.

According to Randall's later interrogation, Miss Perlman told him that this day at Sweetclover had been "the happiest day of my entire life." The dappled sun on the water, the contentment on his face, his laughter as she read to him about the con men Huck and Jim meet. It moved Randall deeply that she felt that way about being with him. Just before they packed up to leave that day, when she told him how happy he made her, he cried, and he cried again

when he related the story of that day to the interrogation team. That day at Sweetclover had been the happiest day of his life, as well.

After Miss Singer's death, Miss Bartels had brought the friendship of Miss Singer and Douglas Knapp to the attention of Chief Schoonmaker, just as Miss Van Houten had informed Chief Eckerson in the novel. Both librarians told the chiefs that they had seen the two talking and thought it was an odd friendship, a teacher and a man so socially awkward and clumsy and obviously upset. Chief Schoonmaker/Chief Eckerson pounced on the information, convinced that they had found the answer to Miss Singer's/Miss Perlman's disappearance. Or at least *an* answer. Didn't the librarian tell him she watched them leave the library together at least half a dozen times?

The real veteran, Douglas Knapp—eventually charged with Ruth Singer's murder by Chief Schoonmaker and the model for my father's fictional character, Randall Simmons—wasn't a murderer. He was just some American war veteran, considered collateral damage, who was lost, drifting through life, hired to clean out the mouse cages of the world. Defenseless.

Sweetclover
Pub. 1988

NEW CITY, NEW YORK
SPRING, 1956

Just days later, after Miss Van Houten spoke to the Chief, Eckerson paid Randall a surprise visit at Carworth Farms. He was cleaning the rat cages when the Chief walked in acting nonchalant. He followed Randall from cage to cage during the interrogation that followed.

"Just a few questions, Randall. Nothing serious. We're still trying to determine what happened. You have nothing to worry about. We understand that you knew Miss Perlman."

It was then that Randall told Chief Eckerson a story that sealed his fate.

According to Chief Eckerson, one night in the late spring Miss Singer had shown up on Randall's doorstep again.

He was surprised and happy to see her. "Are you okay?"

She started crying, and it confused Randall. "I'm pregnant," she said.

She didn't think he could really help her, but she was so distraught and confused, she needed a friendly ear to talk to. She didn't wish to share anything with the gossipy teachers at school, and she certainly couldn't tell her parents. Mr. Cannon would have no choice but to fire her.

"I don't understand. I thought you liked me. Aren't you my girl?" Randall had asked.

Randall explained to Chief Eckerson that he had started crying that night because he misunderstood what she was saying. He thought she was telling him about her pregnancy because she was implying that it was his fault, and he couldn't figure out how something like that could ever happen.

The crying was all Chief Eckerson needed to hear to make Randall his number one suspect.

At this point in the investigation Randall's admissions and Chief Eckerson's accusations began to veer off in different directions.

Never mind that Randall told the Chief that Miss Perlman had tried to comfort him and had told him that she became pregnant from a man she had met somewhere else.

According to Chief Eckerson, Randall confessed that when he found out that she was pregnant, he was confused and became hysterical, thinking she was somehow telling him that he was the father.

According to what Chief Schoonmaker would later claim in public and the corresponding story that my father told in the novel, the veteran flew into an angry rage over the announced pregnancy, and when Miss Singer tried to calm him down, he pushed her away and she fell down and hit her head. He took her for dead.

Sweetclover.
Pub. 1988

NEW CITY, NEW YORK
SPRING, 1956

According to Chief Eckerson, Randall waited until the middle of the night, and in a panic, he carried Adina's body over his shoulder. He was surprised at how light she felt. He carried her across Congers Road to Cairnsmuir Lane and then behind the Carnochan Mansion. Down the hill behind the site of the new Clarkstown High School, he carried her to the football practice field. Kids would be practicing football and playing field hockey there for decades.

He marched on through the woods, across Strawtown Road, and down to where the land had been cleared for the new reservoir, and there he dumped her into the swampy streambed.

According to Chief Eckerson's account, Randall admitted all this in the weeks that followed Miss Perlman's disappearance, but Adina Perlman's body was never found. Had it washed away?

At the time, it was one of the few instances in American jurisprudence where a murder charge was filed against someone without a *corpus delicti*, or dead body. Another murder, just a year earlier in Florida, involved the kidnapping of Judge Curtis Chillingworth and his wife, Marjorie, who were taken out to sea off the coast of Palm Beach in June, 1955. They were dumped overboard and then clubbed over the head until they drowned. Five years later, charges were eventually filed against the hired killers, despite the fact that the victims' bodies were never found.

From Chief Eckerson's perspective, Randall had confessed to everything. But Randall denied ever saying those things about Adina Perlman's falling. He claimed that he told Chief Eckerson that after she told him about being pregnant, she hugged him good night, left him, telling him she was going to walk back to her boardinghouse.

Like in John Steinbeck's, *The Winter of our Discontent*, or William Faulkner's, *As I Lay Dying*, the narrative point of view changes during some of the chapters. A small section of the novel *Sweetclover* is told in the first person, through the eyes of the fictitious grammar school principal, who also had a crush on Adina Perlman and was determined to find out what happened to her. The fictitious principal, Jeff Cameron, suspected that Chief Eckerson knew something and was not acting on it. Not everything made sense to him. It was too pat. The principal figured that since Chief Eckerson already had a patsy under arrest for the murder, all interest in the disappearance would be dropped. So Principal Cameron pursued his own leads.

Just as in real life, the fictitious principal Cameron in the novel suspected the Chief was covering up something, so he went to visit the veteran in jail and told his story in the first person.

Sweetclover.
Pub.1988

1956 NEW CITY, NEW YORK
ROCKLAND COUNTY COURTHOUSE

It was after hours when I went to the jail behind the courthouse. I walked down the alleyway to the entrance. I could hear prisoners singing in their jail cells, their voices echoing down the narrow corridor. The jailer was a neighborhood kid, now grown, and half asleep on this night. He recognized me from his own school days.

"Hello, Mr. Cameron."

"I'm here to see Randall Simmons."

"I'm not sure he's allowed visitors, sir."

"I'm here to give him a message from his mother."

"I'm not sure—"

"I'll only be five minutes."

"I should really check with Chief Eckerson."

"I already told him. We're good."

The jailer hesitated, not sure what to do. Finally, the fact that I had been his school principal, an authority figure, convinced him. I was led into the visitation room and told to sit behind a table. A minute later Randall Simmons was walked into the room by a guard. He was in handcuffs, chained to his waist. The guard, another former student of mine, left the room when I nodded toward the door.

"Randall, I'm Jeff Cameron, the principal at the school where Miss Perlman taught. I'm trying to find out what happened to her. Is what Chief Eckerson saying about you true?"

"No, sir. I don't know why I'm here. After Miss Perlman told me she was pregnant, I was confused. I couldn't understand what she meant. I thought I was her boyfriend."

"So you had nothing to do with her being injured or hitting her head?"

"No, sir. She never hit her head. I don't know where Chief Eckerson came up with that. Me and her just both cried for a while and then she got up and left without saying anything. She just hugged me goodbye."

"Did you speak to her after that?"

"No, sir. I never saw or heard from her again. I didn't know what happened to her until Chief Eckerson showed up at work and arrested me for murdering her."

"So you didn't tell him that you knocked her down and later carried her dead body to the new reservoir?"

"No, sir. I would never do anything like that."

"Randall, you have a police record for being violent against women when you lived in Pennsylvania. You even served jail time."

"I didn't do that either. I never understood why those two women would make up such a story."

I decided to pull out all the stops. "So you're telling me right now, in all honesty, from one decorated military veteran to another, that you had nothing to do with Miss Perlman's disappearance?"

Randall did a double take at the "decorated military veteran reference." He stood and saluted me.

"Yes, sir. That's what I'm telling you. No, sir. I would never do anything like that to her or any other woman. My mother and father taught me to be respectful to women. Always. I thought she was my girlfriend. I don't understand what's going on."

We were interrupted when the jailer burst into the room followed by the guard. "I just called Chief Eckerson. He said you never talked to him and you had no business being here. You're going to have to leave now." He was frightened.

I turned to Randall. "Hang on, Randall. I'll see what I can do."

The next morning, Randall Simmons was found dead in his cell. From what was reported by the Chief, he had apparently hanged himself from the cell bars with strips of torn and tattered bedsheets. Chief Eckerson said that Simmons simply "committed suicide" in the jailhouse behind the New City Courthouse, within days after being charged with the murder. It was a common thing with confessed murderers, he assured the townsfolk. The coroner agreed. The case was closed.

My father would interview the real retired principal, Murray Cannon, in 1987, while he was writing the fictionalized account of the teacher's disappearance. Murray Cannon had been thirty in 1956, and was, in 1987, sixty-one years old. The principal confessed to my father that he suspected something was not right with the investigation, but he could not prove anything. He assumed that Chief Schoonmaker was protecting someone, but he wasn't sure who. Murray Cannon knew about the birthday party and the weeks that followed, from talking to Miss Singer's colleagues. He suspected that some of the Dellwood Country Club members might be involved. According to Mr. Cannon, the real Chief was pinning it on the real veteran because it was so easy. So convenient. Case closed. My father fictionalized it all to soften the effect, make it more believable.

With the introduction of a second narrator, *Sweetclover* became an amateur sleuth-style mystery, well-told but, some would say, mainly of interest to local people.

With the publication of *Sweetclover* in 1988 the real principal told my father that he was flattered, confused, and even a little frightened by the portrayal in the novel. Some of his friends even started calling him Jeff, after the fictional character. Would it ruin his relationship with the real Chief Schoonmaker? Would Chief Schoonmaker try to silence him? Despite the highly focused local angle, *Sweetclover* did well with both the critics and the book buyers, owing to my father's sense of place in depicting what New City was like back in the glory days of the 1950s. Film rights were optioned.

The fictionalized account followed what Chief Schoonmaker wanted everyone to think: the rat-cage cleaner was responsible for the schoolteacher's disappearance. According to the Chief, the veteran's plea to Principal Cannon was just an excuse for the murder. The plot was uncannily close to what really happened. Up to a point. How, readers wondered, could the nine-year-old boys in the novel know so much about what happened? Nick and my father were not surprised about Miss Singer's disappearance.

Sweetclover.
Pub.1988

NEW CITY, NEW YORK
DELLWOOD COUNTRY CLUB

WINTER–SPRING, 1956

Cal and I were not surprised about Miss Perlman's disappearance. We suspected what happened because we were eyewitnesses to some of the events.

In the weeks that followed her birthday party at Jerry's Tavern, Miss Perlman went back for happy-hour cocktails and had accepted the invitation of the Manhattan businessmen to accompany them to the Friday and Saturday night "serious" cocktail parties at Dellwood Country Club.

On those nights, Cal and I would sneak up to the clubhouse, peek through the curtains, and watch what was going on. The windows were closed to keep the cold out and the heat in, but we could hear what was being said. Later, in the springtime, we listened through the screens of the open windows.

Cal and I watched and worried. We watched because we were curious. We watched because we were in love with our teacher.

One such night, having already had one martini at the tavern and a second martini at the country club, Miss Perlman had danced with all the men and was feeling dizzy.

One of the wives of another member had come to her rescue after the third martini, and we watched them half-carry her to their nearby guest apartment on the country club grounds, where she spent the night of that second weekend.

She was hung over all day Saturday again, like that first night at Randall's, but recovered enough to attend a more private soiree on Saturday night in an evening dress borrowed from the host wife. There, the men were relentless in their flirting, and she hardly knew how to handle all the attention.

The third weekend started out the same, but this time Miss Perlman had prepared for it with another evening dress borrowed from the wife who had become friendly and a promise not to drink too much. Another Friday and Saturday night went by with more martinis, more open flirting, more lies to her parents about what she was doing, and more lies to her boardinghouse landlady about where she was staying on those nights.

Before long, a few of the men offered to buy her party dresses, which she awkwardly accepted and kept in her new friend's apartment. Cal and I honed our surveillance skills.

The lies continued, even to her friends and colleagues at school. Her classroom demeanor changed, her wardrobe improved, and her weekend partying became more raucous. Cal and I knew about it because we were eyewitnesses to it all as we watched through the windows of the country club ballroom and the apartments of her newfound friends.

Cal and I witnessed it all.

CHAPTER 23

MAY, 1956
52 YEARS BEFORE THE MURDER

The weeks in the late spring of 1956, after Miss Singer's disappearance, were difficult for my father and Nick. He expressed their sorrow through the voice of Aron, his fictional protagonist.

Sweetclover:
Pub.1988

JUNE 1956
NEW CITY LIBRARY

For me it was mostly all about Miss Perlman and my love for her. Can a nine-year-old boy really be in love with an older woman the way I claimed to be? Ask any nine-year-old boy that question. Ask any man

who's ever been a nine-year-old boy, and you will find that the answer is an emphatic, resounding yes. Can they articulate the feelings it causes to race through their bodies? No.

The way it manifested itself in me was that I wanted to know everything about Adina Perlman. Somehow, I knew, by knowing as much about her as I could, it would help me heal. Of course, in those pre-computer days, finding out about people was a lot easier said than done. I actually developed the idea from our friend, Frank's grandmother, the landlady who owned the boardinghouse across from St. Augustine Church, where Miss Perlman stayed and where we had first seen her in the days leading up to the opening of the school year right after Labor Day.

When it was finally accepted that she was dead and that she wasn't coming back, the landlady and Adina Perlman's parents were tasked with cleaning out her sparsely furnished room. The landlady asked her grandson, Frank, our classmate, along with Cal and me, to help carry her things down the steep, narrow staircase.

Upstairs, there was an eerie silence as her parents, Frank and his grandmother, and Cal and I stood looking around the room. On Miss Perlman's quilted bedspread, hand sewn by Frank's grandmother, was an Irish novel Miss Perlman had been reading when she disappeared. It lay open, facedown, next to her pillow, half read. Her mother picked it up and looked at the title and started weeping.

One of the tasks was to decide the disposition of the forty-four books she had stacked on the closet shelf. Miss Perlman's mother glanced at the spines and shook her head. "That's where all her money went. She couldn't stop buying books. She was a voracious reader. Give them away to the library or throw them out. I can't bear to look at them."

The landlady asked Frank who might like them, and he remembered that I had given one of the books on the shelf, East of Eden, by John Steinbeck, to Miss Singer as a gift before winter break. He suggested to his grandmother that I would want the other books. Of course I jumped at the offer.

Cal, Frank, and I packed up the books in six brown paper A&P shopping bags. We lugged the bags to the front baskets of our three bikes and pedaled up Main Street to my cottage on the Dellwood property. As we rode through downtown New City, past the courthouse, Squadron A Farm, Senator Buckley's weekend estate, and Christie's Airport, my heart was filled with sorrow, yet also with hope, owing to my newfound treasure. Sorrow for Miss Perlman, whose dreams may have lived somewhere in these books. Hope for myself that someday, by reading her favorite books, I would come to know her better, understand her, and somehow determine what it was that made me feel the way I did about her.

At the cottage, with the help of my two friends, I hid the forty-four books under the tiny cot in my tiny bedroom, out of sight of my father's watchful eye. They were my secret.

With money I had saved shagging balls and caddying, I bought myself a flashlight and some batteries at Moore's Hardware Store on Main Street, so I could secretly read Miss Perlman's books after my father went to bed at night.

The first Friday night, when I knew for certain that my father had fallen asleep from drinking, I pulled the books from beneath the bed. Using my new flashlight for illumination, I made a list on my composition pad of all the books Miss Perlman had kept on the top shelf of her room.

The Naked and the Dead, Barbary Shore, The Deer Park,
 by Norman Mailer
The Natural, by Bernard Malamud
Dangling Man, The Victim,
The Adventures of Augie March, and *Seize the Day,*

by Saul Bellow

Call It Sleep, by Henry Roth

Young Lonigan, The Young Manhood of Studs Lonigan, Judgment Day, the trilogy by James T. Farrell.

The 42nd Parallel, 1919, The Big Money, the trilogy by Jon Dos Passos

Winesburg, Ohio, by Sherwood Anderson

From Here to Eternity, by James Jones

Something of Value, by Robert Ruark

Lolita, by Vladimir Nabokov (published as two green paperbacks by Olympia Press in 1955, but not generally available to the American public until later, due to obscenity laws. How did Miss Perlman acquire them?).

The Talented Mr. Ripley, by Patricia Highsmith

Soldier of Fortune, by Ernest K. Gann

The Catcher in the Rye, Nine Stories, by J. D. Salinger

Andersonville, by MacKinlay Kantor

Notes of a Native Son, by James Baldwin

Main Street, by Sinclair Lewis

The Magnificent Ambersons, by Booth Tarkington

The Caine Mutiny and

Marjorie Morningstar, by Herman Wouk

The Big Sleep, by Raymond Chandler

The Great Gatsby, by F. Scott Fitzgerald

Lord of the Flies, by William Golding

The Ginger Man, by J. P. Donleavy
(Paris edition, 1955).
Selected Poems, by Robert Frost
A Good Man Is Hard to Find, by Flannery O'Connor.
After Dark, My Sweet, by Jim Thompson
High Tor, by Maxwell Anderson
The Fellowship of the Ring, The Two Towers, the Return of the King, a trilogy by J.R.R. Tolkien.
Border Town Girl, by John D. MacDonald
East of Eden, by John Steinbeck
All the King's Men, by Robert Penn Warren

The last book I picked up was the book that had been found near Miss Perlman's pillow, unfinished. It was *The Lonely Passion of Judith Hearne* by Brian Moore, a novelist born in Belfast, Northern Ireland. I read the summary inside the book jacket, and it became clear to me why Miss Perlman's mother had started weeping when she picked it up off the bed. Did she know that her daughter had a lonely passion? I added the title to the list. Forty-four books in all. A treasure beyond counting.

The next Saturday morning, instead of shagging balls on the driving range, I rode my bicycle to the corner of Demarest and Maple avenues and went into the library with my list. Miss Van Houten was just finishing up her Saturday-morning reading of kids' stories, so I wandered around the small room, examining the spines of the books on the shelves. Eventually the library cleared out, and it was just the two of us. The silence of the room was forever linked to that day, the musty smell of books, aging paper with sticky fingerprints.

When Miss Van Houten was finished with her paperwork and was pulling out a long narrow drawer of her card catalogue, I walked over to her and cleared my throat. "I was wondering if you could help me."

Miss Van Houten looked over the top of her reading specs and smiled at me. "Are you looking for a book? The children's books are in the basement with the magazines." She pointed to the staircase.

"Not exactly." I pulled out of my pocket the list I had torn from my composition book and carefully unfolded it. "I was wondering if you could tell me, from looking at this list, if there is any common denominator here."

She gazed at me a long time without looking at the list in my hand. She blinked rapidly before speaking.

" 'Common denominator'? What grade are you in?"

"Just finished fourth." I handed her the list, and she nudged her reading glasses higher on the bridge of her nose. I followed her eyes as they moved slowly down the list, as if absorbing and computing facts and formulas from a calculus I would never understand. Finally she closed her eyes tightly to hold back her tears, pursed her lips, and hung her head in recognition.

I kept looking at her, and she quickly recovered. "Miss Perlman wanted to be a writer. A novelist."

I wasn't sure what that meant. "How did you know this was a list of Miss Perlman's books? These books are all different. Some are British. Some are Irish. A lot of the writers are Jewish. There's some poetry. And a play. How can you be so sure?"

Instead of answering my question, Miss Van Houten looked over the list again, to see where Miss Perlman's reading had taken her. The World War II battlefields in the South Pacific. New England autumns. Chicago and Mexico. Manhattan. Exotic islands. The truck farms of California. Summer stock theater in the Catskills. Irish pubs. Gothic towns of the Deep South. The mind of a perverted college professor as he lusted after a twelve-year-old girl. The Midwest. A Tex-Mex border town. A Louisiana bayou. Dark mysteries of Los Angeles.

"These are books you would read if you wanted to be a writer in today's world. They represent some of the best writing out there. Two of them have not even been published in this country yet due to obscenity laws. Do you know what that means? Who else in this town . . . Wait a minute. Ernest K. Gann? He used to barnstorm out of Christie's Airport. He's on this list. And Maxwell Anderson, the playwright? He lived down the street from you."

A famous playwright lived down the street from me? How could that be possible, I wondered?

"He's on this list, too. But who else in this town—" She didn't finish the question. She didn't want me to see her fighting back tears. She handed the list back to me. "And besides, Miss Perlman told me she wanted to be a novelist."

I reexamined the list. A thousand questions raced through my head. "I'd like to find out more about that, becoming a novelist. Do you think you could talk to me about it some time?"

Miss VanHouten changed the subject and started talking about something I personally knew was a lie. "What that soldier did to her was horrible. Somehow I feel responsible, since this is where they met. He used to come in here and try to read books. Simple stuff. I told Chief Eckerson the man wasn't really capable of reading a book. He couldn't concentrate.

And then he goes and kills that lovely woman, your teacher. It's just horrible."

My eyes fell to the book list, unable to look her in the eye. Everyone in town apparently believed Chief Eckerson's story that Randall Simmons had killed Miss Perlman.

I looked at her and made a decision. "I'm going to be a writer, too," I told her.

Miss Van Houten patted me on my head and dismissed me. "Good for you." She turned back to her card catalog.

Starting that summer break, having just finished the fourth grade, I started reading Miss Perlman's books. It took me two years to get through the forty-four books, and by the time I was starting seventh grade, my worldview was transformed and my life's course was set. Someday I would be a novelist. I was going to make it happen.

My father's friends would later tell me that whenever my father wasn't practicing with the teams or competing on the playing fields, he had his nose in a book. Since the scene in the library between Aron and Miss Van Houten was based on an actual conversation between my father and the real librarian, Elsa Bartels,

I wasn't surprised. He was visiting the worlds Miss Singer had visited, hoping to find some evidence that she had traveled there. Hoping to form some connection. Her literary tastes would begin to shape his own worldview, even as they began to inform the world of the fictitious boy, Aron, in Sweetclover.

CHAPTER 24

Sweetclover:
Pub. 1988

JUNE 1958
NEW CITY LIBRARY

To say that I merely read Miss Perlman's books would be an understatement. I absorbed them.

From the very first day after my visit to the library, I read them with one thought in mind. What discoveries will I find in this book that will open the door for me to become a novelist? At first it wasn't clear how this would work. Weren't the writers telling us stories for our entertainment? Was there more to it than that? But then, as I worked my way through *Winesburg, Ohio; From Here to Eternity; The Great Gatsby; Lord of the Flies;* **and** *Andersonville* **at the rate of about one every two weeks, I began to understand what the novelists were doing.**

How they created the worlds that would not let you leave when the book was finished. Like the prisoners of war in the MacKinlay Kantor novel, there was simply no escape.

How they introduced you to characters who would remain lifelong friends.

How they made you wonder what happened to them when the story was finished. Would there be sequels to these lives?

And then I started thinking about how each one of these books changed me in some way. Changed my understanding of myself, of humanity. Changed my understanding of good and evil. Changed my understanding of my own feelings.

It wasn't long before I came to a startling conclusion. With every book I read, I became *a different person*. My physical appearance didn't change, but I was a different person. Forty-four times in a row during fifth and sixth grades, I became a different person.

Like Miss Perlman, I experienced the loneliness of a young Ohio boy during the World War I era.

I walked through a fantasy world in a place called Middle Earth.

I was shipped out to an island in the South Pacific to witness horrors during World War II.

I witnessed the crumbling of a mid-western family dynasty.

I saw the depths of human depravity as an isolated civilization of a group, comprised of adolescent boys stranded on a deserted island, began to unravel.

I traveled through Harlem and read reviews of *Native Son* and *The Invisible Man,* which made me curious and encouraged me to put those books on a new list I had started.

I followed another lonely boy, like myself, through Manhattan as he complained about the shallowness and phoniness of it, all while wearing a deerstalker cap.

The books took me away. But most important of all, I was taken out of New City. It was no longer the center of the universe for me. There was something else out there in the world.

By the summer of 1958 I had finished the fifth and sixth grades and had read all forty-four of Miss Perlman's books. The sights, the sounds, the friends I made in those pages both exhausted me and stimulated my imagination. I felt as if my head weighed one hundred pounds, my neck no longer strong enough to support it. My mind raced. My brain was exhausted. It only made me hungry for more.

This was when, my father would later tell me, his life got really complicated.

Sweetclover.
Pub.1988

JUNE 1958
NEW CITY LIBRARY

I went to Miss Van Houten for advice in the opening days of summer vacation after sixth grade. I rode my bike to the library, timing it so my arrival would come after the Children's Reading Hour in the basement on Saturday morning.

She tried to ignore me at first, but I walked right up to her desk. She turned. "Yes, Aron?"

"I've read all of Miss Perlman's books. What should I read next?"

Once again, as was her wont, she closed her eyes and breathed deeply in exasperation before she answered. "You read all those books?"

"Yes."

"All of them." It wasn't a question.

"Yes. All forty-four."

She cleared her throat discreetly. "Do you have your notebook?"

I reached into my backpack and pulled out my composition book and a pencil. She waited while I sharpened the point with the small plastic pencil sharpener in the shape of a frog that I carried in my pocket. I collected the wood and graphite shavings in the palm of my hand and stuffed them in my jeans' pocket.

She rubbed her eyes, hesitated, as if she were not sure that what she was about to do was the correct thing. Finally she looked at me. "These are some of the best from the last few years. 1957 to 1958, mostly, but not all."

Then she proceeded to dictate the list to me off the top of her head, her eyes remaining closed. "Here we go.

Dandelion Wine, by Ray Bradbury
Dr. Zhivago, by Boris Pasternak
On the Beach, by Nevil Shute
A Death in the Family, by James Agee
From Russia with Love, by Ian Fleming
The Assistant, by Bernard Malamud
On the Road, by Jack Kerouac
The Wapshot Chronicle, by John Cheever
A Rage in Harlem, by Chester Himes

Eye in the Sky, by Philip K. Dick
Sonny's Blues, by James Baldwin
The Many Loves of Dobie Gillis, by Max Shulman
Night, by Elie Wiesel
Breakfast at Tiffany's, by Truman Capote
Exodus, by Leon Uris
Our Man in Havana, by Graham Greene
Dr. No, by Ian Fleming
A Coney Island of the Mind,
by Lawrence Ferlinghetti
The Executioners, by John D. MacDonald
The Getaway, by Jim Thompson
Suddenly Last Summer, by Tennessee Williams
The Darling Buds of May, by H. E. Bates
Lady Killer, by Ed McBain."

I reviewed the list, trying to categorize them.

Miss Van Houten read my mind. "We have all these here in the library. Some may be checked out when you look for them, but I'll put you on the waiting list. I hope you like poetry, too. A book of poems in there. Beatnik stuff. You know what a Beatnik is?"

"I think so."

She stopped and made me look up at her. "You must promise me you will never tell anyone I gave you this list."

I looked at her, confused. "Okay, but why?"

She put her hand on my notebook, as if to hold it down in place or yank it out of my hands. "*Do. You. Promise?*"

"Yes," I said, not knowing why.

She stood and turned to the card catalog. "I would start with *Dandelion Wine*. Or if you want a few laughs, go for *The Darling Buds of May*."

That was the last conversation Miss Van Houten and I would have for another year.

CHAPTER 25

THURSDAY, OCTOBER 23, 2008
THE AFTERNOON FOLLOWING THE
MURDER

That afternoon in the police station tech lab, after a fitful sleep of just six hours, my father described the face of the murder victim to a police sketch artist. As they sat at the computer and the session progressed, he saw a remarkable likeness evolve.

The Chief bent over for a closer look. "That's her? You're sure?"

"Absolutely amazing. It's her. Even more accurate than in one of my novels."

"I hope it's that good. This is the real world, Ab. Right now we have absolutely nothing else to go on. No tire marks, no physical evidence, no body, no bloodstains."

"No bloodstains? Come on. There was blood all over."

"That was a pretty heavy rainstorm. Two rainstorms. Enough to wash away blood, leaves, tire tracks, DNA, anything they might have left behind. No missing persons reports to fit this description yet."

He turned to face my father. "Abby, come on into my office for a minute."

The Chief led my father into his office and closed the door. They both sat down. My father looked over his father-in-law's shoulder to the parking lot. My grandfather tried his best to be patient and show concern, but his patience was being tried. My grandfather couldn't help but remember what my father's behavior had done to my mother, how it had caused her death.

"Are you sure you haven't left anything out? People are beginning to ask questions."

"What kind of questions?"

"Lots of questions. Like maybe there was no young woman. Like maybe you've flipped out, got lost in one of your own mysteries and don't know how to get out."

My father thought about that. "You're saying I made up the whole thing? Why would I kill my own dog?"

"I'm not saying you did. I'm just saying that being my son-in-law is only going to buy you so much."

"What do you mean?"

"I mean, filing a false crime report is a crime in and of itself. Or, maybe if there really is a dead woman, maybe you have something to do with it."

"That's crazy."

"You said yourself you were crazy."

"I just want to find out who killed my dog."

"Look, I know you've been under a great deal of strain these last two years. First Sandra, then Little Abby disappearing. But you've got to take it easy and let these things play out their course."

Abby remained silent.

My grandfather put out a feeler. "Have you heard from him?" He was referring to me. He knew full well where I was—back at his house, hiding in the upstairs bedroom.

My father thought back over the past two years, how painful they had been for him. He stood and walked to the window. "No. Have you?"

My grandfather lied. "No. You know you'd be the first to know. I've got every available resource looking for him. If he can be found, my guys can find him. It may take a few more months."

It was my father's turn to be cryptic. "I don't have a few more months."

"You've got to be patient."

"I've run out of patience."

"We're doing everything we can. In the meantime, you just need to go home and try to remember anything else about what happened last night. Any little detail. Our guys haven't found anything yet, but they're good and they're going to keep looking."

Of course, they hadn't looked for me at all. My grandfather knew where I was every day for the entire two years after I left my father's house.

My father reflected. "I'll think about it. Huck was with us for almost fifteen years."

"I remember. You found him when Little Abby was, what, three?"

"Five. Huck was all I had left. I want to find out what happened to him."

"Abby, I'll make you a promise. I won't try to write any mystery novels if you promise not to get involved with this. Just let my guys do their jobs. We'll find who did this. I can't promise you you'll get any justice, but we'll find out who did this."

When my father didn't respond, the Chief continued. "Go live your life, Abby. Let me clean up this mess."

Abby stared out the window into the parking lot that was carved into the nearby woodsy hillside, turned golden in the autumn light. He wanted to say, *What life is that?* but he remained silent.

After a moment he thought back to the composite on the computer screen. "Can I get a copy of that composite sketch?"

My grandfather was skeptical. "What for?"

"I don't know. It may spark a memory."

My grandfather glanced to the doorway, pondering my father's question. Finally he nodded. "Sure. Tell that techy I said you could have a copy."

When I had left home that night two years earlier, I walked to the house of a Clarkstown High classmate. He drove me into Manhattan, where I slept on the sofa of another high school friend who was already attending NYU. I worked in a trendy restaurant in Greenwich Village owned by the parents of another classmate. I worked off the books, got paid under the table, didn't use any credit cards, and virtually disappeared.

I became a Village kid and, by association, an NYU student. I had hoped to go to college someday, maybe become a computer engineer. But for two years I washed dishes, bussed tables, and eventually worked my way up to being a waiter. I even drove a gypsy cab for a while. All cash. No records, no way to find me even if the police had been looking for me, which, at my grandfather's orders, they weren't. Even the private investigating agency my father hired wasn't up to the task. I had disappeared in an effort to punish my father.

CHAPTER 26

The fictionalized account of my father's first heartbreak continued as each milestone was passed in the late 1950s.

Sweetclover.
Pub. 1988

JUNE 1959
NEW CITY LIBRARY

Following the first day of summer vacation after seventh grade, I returned to talk to Miss Van Houten. All the other times I had just checked out the books on her list, two or three at a time, from the assistant librarian, who always eyed me skeptically.

This time, Miss Van Houten handed me a new list from under her desk blotter that she had, apparently, prepared earlier, in anticipation of my early-summer arrival. How did she know I would return?

A Separate Peace, by John Knowles

The Sirens of Titan, by Kurt Vonnegut, Jr.

A Raisin in the Sun, by Lorraine Hansberry

Alas, Babylon, by Pat Frank

Goldfinger, by Ian Fleming

Goodbye, Columbus, by Philip Roth

The Apprenticeship of Duddy Kravitz, by Mordecai Richler

The Loneliness of the Long-Distance Runner, by Alan Sillitoe

Hiroshima, Mon Amour, by Marguerite Duras

Groucho and Me, by Grouch Marx

The Hustler, by Walter Tevis

I looked at the list. "There's only eleven books on the list. One of them is by Groucho Marx, the television guy?"

"He's more than the television guy. Read it. Learn from it. It will make you laugh. You need to laugh."

"But there's only ten besides that one."

"That will get you through the summer."

She reached into her top drawer and handed me a folded copy of the most recent New York Times Book Review. "I want to see you in here every Monday afternoon when school begins in the fall to pick up a copy of this. I want you to sit over in the corner by the window and read this every week from cover to cover. You pick your own stuff from now on."

"I have football practice after school every day."

"You have whether decide if you want to be a football player or a novelist. You can't be both."

"Why not?"

"You just can't."

"Can I pick it up on Saturdays the following week?"

She thought for a moment. "Every Saturday. It will be almost a week old by then, but I'll save it for you. If I'm not here it will be in this tray." She pointed.

I picked up the Book Review she had just given me, unfolded it, and began to leaf through its pages. I had stumbled upon a treasure map, a marked pathway. All I had to do was follow the pathway.

"Sit over there." She gestured toward the south window facing Demarest Avenue.

"The next time you come in here I want to see something you have written yourself. You want to be a writer? Prove it. Write."

But I didn't know how to write. I couldn't think of what to write.

Sweetclover.
Pub. 1988

NEW CITY LIBRARY
July, 1960

That would all begin to change, like a wave that has been building up in intensity for miles off the coast from an encroaching storm as it nears the shore, and then finally crests, pauses briefly, before crashing onto the beach. It happened in July of 1960, after I had finished the eighth grade.

On the morning of Monday, July 11, 1960, I rode my bike to the New City Library, planning to read The New York Times Book Review, as I had been doing regularly, since the summer before. Each week I shoe-horned more invaluable information into my brain. Would I be able to remember it all?

When I opened the door there was the usual buzz of students looking for ways to pass their lazy, hazy, crazy days of summer with their noses in a book.

But this time when Miss VanHouten saw me enter, she stopped what she was doing, reached into her top desk drawer and pulled out the Book Review from the Sunday before. She extended it to me as I approached her desk, folded back to a specific review with a large paperclip to mark its place.

"This is the moment you've been waiting for."

I didn't know what she was talking about, but I was to find out in the next few minutes of reading. I took the Review from her hands and started reading.

TO KILL A MOCKINGBIRD. By Harper Lee. 296 pp. Philadelphia and New York: J. B. Lippincott Company. $3.95.

By FRANK H. LYELL

IN her first novel, Harper Lee writes with gentle affection, rich humor and deep understanding of small-town family life in Alabama. The setting is Maycomb, a one-taxi village, "awkwardly inland," where "a day was twenty-four hours long but seemed longer," and nobody hurried because there was nowhere to go; where a snowstorm was a big event, and in the scorching summer heat ladies "bathed before noon, after their three o'clock naps, and by nightfall were like soft teacakes with frostings of sweat and sweet talcum."

It is an easy-going but narrow-minded community, whose foot-washing Baptists feel perfectly free to denounce Miss Maudie Atkinson, a passionate garden-lover (for whom the scent of mimosa is "angels' breath"), because "anything that's pleasure is a sin." At the other extreme stand men like Atticus Finch, a highly esteemed lawyer and legislator and the embodiment of fearless integrity, magnanimity and common sense. In the novel's chief public event, Atticus ignores all the harsh criticism of his "lawing for niggers and trash" to defend a worthy young Negro falsely accused of raping a girl from the town's most disreputable white family.

It went on.

I finished reading the review and looked up at Miss VanHouten, who was standing there, looking at me, with her hands on her hips. "It's time for you to get to work," she told me.

"Can I check out this book? Do you have a copy yet?"

"We have two copies, but they were already checked out and as soon as they come back in they'll get checked out by the people on the waiting list. It will be weeks. You don't want to wait that long."

That very afternoon I gave my friend's mother a ten-dollar bill and she asked her husband to buy it for me at Brentano's near his Manhattan office, as she had done for me with *East of Eden* almost five years earlier. My friend's father arrived home from work the next night with two copies of *To Kill a Mockingbird*. One for me and one for himself. He gave me back my ten-dollar bill.

I got to work, and as I read, I walked the streets of Maycomb, Alabama, during the Great Depression, arm-in-arm with my beloved Miss Perlman, as we turned our heads in wonderment.

CHAPTER 27

THURSDAY NIGHT, OCTOBER 23, 2008
15 HOURS AFTER THE MURDER

My father sat in the living room of his cottage, watching the news.

On the screen in front of him the anchorwoman addressed the camera, much as he himself had done for so many years.

"It's a bizarre murder straight out of the pages of one of his best-selling mystery novels. Sportscaster and NFL Giants' football star Abram Traphagen claims to have witnessed a murder during a night of camping near High Tor, in New City, just north of Manhattan in Rockland County. For more on the story we go to Ronnie Leeds at the crime scene."

The television screen switched to a live shot, broadcast from the parking space on The Hill, revealing the woodsy pathway toward Low Tor behind her.

The reporter, a businesslike woman in her forties with short-cropped blond hair, dressed in slacks and a herringbone tweed blazer, stood in front of yellow plastic crime scene tape, took her cue from her earpiece, and spoke to the camera lens.

"According to police reports, Abram Traphagen, known to close friends, football fans, and millions of mystery novel readers around the world as 'Abby,' was camping near the base of the historic High Tor promontory."

The reporter turned and gestured over her shoulder.

"It was here, he later told police, that he witnessed a gangland-style slaying of a young woman at approximately three a.m. this morning."

The screen filled with an interview with my grandfather that had been videotaped earlier. The Chief spoke to the off-screen reporter who held a microphone at his chest. "Traphagen told us that two men pulled up in a dark SUV, dragged a young woman from the back seat, and shot her point-blank in the head. He could not see the men's faces, but he reported that the woman was a blonde Caucasian in her mid-to-late-twenties. The assailants then shot Traphagen's dog when it attacked them, as Traphagen watched from his campsite up the hill, about fifty yards away. The alleged shooters apparently did not realize he was there." The Chief's interview was very official sounding.

The footage then showed Ronnie Leeds talking to my grandfather as they walked the pathway toward the crime scene, the videographer backpedaling in front of them while the reporter voice-over narration was heard. "Chief Schoonmaker is, ironically, the father of Traphagen's late wife, Sandra, who died two years ago.

"When the Hudson River Valley Park Police and Chief Schoonmaker scoured the area with their crime scene unit, no evidence of a murder could be found. Only the body of Traphagen's dog, shot through the chest, was retrieved."

Chief Schoonmaker appeared in another on-camera interview. "By the time we arrived, shortly before dawn, the heavy overnight rains in the area had washed away just about any chance that we could find any forensic information."

The reporter appeared in a closing stand-up, talking to the camera, yellow crime scene tape across the path in the background. "According to Chief Schoonmaker, every available officer in the department is working the case, looking for possible leads and scouring the crime scene. No woman fitting the description has been reported missing, the Chief told us. Reporting from Low Tor in New City, in Rockland County, I'm Ronnie Leeds."

There was no mention of a composite sketch. Did the Chief not want it known that a composite existed of the victim, or was it a delaying tactic?

CHAPTER 28

FRIDAY, OCTOBER 24, 2008
30 HOURS AFTER THE MURDER
FIRST TRIP BACK TO THE CRIME SCENE

The next morning, Ossie drove my father up the winding road to the trail near Perkins Memorial Drive where he had covered his Range Rover in the brush.

"Jesus, Abby. How could you ever find this place?"

"Just have to know where to look."

Using his spare set of keys, my father headed south on the Palisades Parkway to the Route 45 exit, followed by Ossie. From there, Ossie headed south down 45 into Spring Valley. My father turned east on South Mountain Road, turned left at Little Tor and drove up and parked on The Hill. A cooler breeze was blowing in from the north, and there was a rustle of the few remaining leaves as he crossed over the chain and took the trail. Forty minutes later, out of breath, he approached the Low Tor encampment. There was nothing there but more yellow crime scene tape and silence. No follow-up forensics. But something kept drawing him back.

He circled around the tape and looked for any remains of his drenched belongings up above. The duffel bag had been taken as evidence. Inside were his journal, his paperbacks, his clothes. He gathered up his pup tent and folded it. It was a soggy lump under his arm as he walked back to the Range Rover.

Abby went home, stepped into the laundry room, and cleaned up the dog bowl, dog mat, dog toys, dog memories, memories of happier days with Huck and me.

CHAPTER 29

HUCK
1993
15 YEARS BEFORE THE MURDER

I do remember the day my father brought Huck home when I was just five years old.

He was tiny, speckled with black spots, his tail between his legs and a sad look on his face. My mother and father had found him on the Low Tor trail. The story goes that he had been obviously abused, then abandoned by his owner, probably because he was a runt. Huck was skittish at first but soon came to realize he had come to a good home. He would later become my best friend, and for the next dozen years we were inseparable.

CHAPTER 30

SATURDAY, OCTOBER 25, 2008
2 DAYS AFTER THE MURDER

That Saturday, my grandfather was seated behind his desk at the Lower Hudson River Valley Park Police station house, watching my frustrated father pace the floor, speaking his thoughts out loud, as if noodling his way through a novel plot instead of his own, real life.

"Why was her body left behind and then, less than three hours later, removed from the scene? Why did they come back for her body? Did they have second thoughts? Because of Huck, did they suspect there was a witness they hadn't counted on being there?"

The Chief swiveled slowly in his chair. "That's a very good question. That's what we're trying to figure out. Emphasis on *we*, not you. My guess? To clean up any evidence they thought they might have left behind. They were not counting on anyone being there to witness the whole thing. The presence of Huck probably spooked them."

My father continued to pace. Was he losing his grasp of reality? "Could they have waited up on The Hill, thinking someone may have followed them out? Then, when they saw me run past, did they go back and remove her body just to be safe? They went back to cover their trail? Is that something that might have happened?"

My grandfather shook his head. "Abby, we can speculate all day. This is not one of your mystery novels. This is, according to you anyway, a real murder. Although we have no body, no weapon, no evidence.

"Correction. You have a dead dog. My dead dog. With a bullet hole in his chest."

My grandfather looked at my father, shaking his head.

Later that day, my father went to the hospital with Doc Charles for another follow-up exam. According to what Doc told me later, it was demoralizing for my father. Was he finally accepting his own mortality? His time was up, he knew, but he didn't want to leave this vale of tears without having a conversation with me.

CHAPTER 31

1985
23 YEARS BEFORE THE MURDER

The Pits
Pub. 1986

My father had spent the better part of his precious time off in 1985 researching *The Pits*. What he discovered fascinated him and would fascinate the public, he was sure.

The novel was born in 1986, and written in record time, thanks in part to my father's continuous taking of copious notes, his organizational skills, and his rapid, manic writing regimen.

Those who wanted to think of it as fact were free to do so. Those who were threatening lawsuits were reminded that it was fiction, that, as the familiar disclaimer clearly stated, *Any resemblance to any persons, living or dead, is purely coincidental.*

The right to privacy cannot be passed on to heirs. This is especially true for people in the public eye. When you become a celebrity, you essentially give up the right to privacy, like it or not. The mixture of fact and fiction caught the reading audience's attention, and it became a best-seller. The public liked the character of Professor Ivan Heskestad, modeled after my father's friend at Rockland Community College. A college professor who taught documentary filmmaking solving crimes? Maybe he was destined to become the next Indiana Jones?

The evidence was there for those who chose to look for it. Inside the five-inch tin can found by the Harriman State Park, Lake Tiorati cavers, in the jacket pocket of one of the dead men, was the roll of 35mm motion picture film. It was remarkably well preserved by the stable, cave environment. When Chief Schoonmaker first inspected it, he immediately thought of showing it to my father, the television star. Who better to identify it and get it transferred to a watchable image than Mr. Television himself, my father? In the novel, the fictionalized Lower Hudson River Valley Park Police Ranger, Chief Eckerson, gives the film footage to Professor Heskestad to analyze.

Fictional Ivan Heskestad's fictional queries mirrored in the novel what my father had done in his real-life research.

My father took the film to a lab in Manhattan, and an old-timer technician examined it. It was nitrate-based film stock, which meant that it was likely made before 1948, when safety film became widely used. This 1948 date corroborated that the wardrobe on the dead men predated that era.

Prior to 1948, cellulose nitrate-based motion-picture film was highly unstable, and if not stored under the proper conditions, it would melt down to jelly. Or worse, being highly flammable, it could burst into flames through spontaneous combustion. Apparently the stable temperature and low humidity in the iron ore pit had preserved the film for what the technician would later confirm was almost seventy years.

It was determined that the film from the canister was what is known as a "work print," the original positive-print struck from the camera-original negative. Work prints are reviewed by editors to decide what to keep and what to cut, and how to arrange the shots, without having to constantly touch the delicate, original negative until later, after all the editing decisions are made.   Once those decisions are approved, editors then go back and, under surgical conditions, conform the fragile, vulnerable negative to match the edit from the producer-approved work print.

The lab technicians told my father that running the seventy-year-old work print through a projector would surely have damaged it. They had to figure out a safer way.

The first step the lab took when my father delivered the ancient work print was to carefully clean it. They then put it through a contact printer and reproduced it onto a new inter-negative, one frame at a time. They then ran the inter-negative through a Rank Cintel Flying Spot Scanner and were able to digitally reproduce a black-and-white positive print. They transferred the print to the brand-new Betacam SP format for a videotape master. From that video master they made several VHS copies for my father to return to my grandfather, to be examined as evidence. They placed all the workflow materials in a vault, isolating the original, unstable nitrate print in a special safe container designed for that use.

What the film on VHS copies revealed was remarkable. At the beginning of the footage was a chalkboard, a forerunner of the modern movie slate so familiar to film audiences. There was no striped clapstick along the top, which is explained by the date on the slate, **February 5, 1920**. This meant it was six to eight years prior to the advent of widespread film sound. As film sound had not been perfected by 1920, no striped clapsticks were used at the beginning of each take to help synchronize the sound with the picture during the editing process. After the mid-1920s, sound would have been recorded on a separate recording device. Later, in the editing room, they would synchronize, or "sync-up," the film frame of the sticks coming together with the "clap" on the separate sound track, and lock the two sources "in-sync." No clapsticks to sync picture with sound meant no sound recording, so the pre-sound date on the slate appeared to be accurate.

Also scribbled on the chalkboard was the name of the film, **"DELIVERY BOY,"** the roll number, the names of the camera operator, **PHIL**, and the director, **MO**.

Then there was the production company name. In barely discernible smeared chalk on the board, you could make out the letters **EdStu/Fl.**

What followed was just over four minutes of what appeared to be a very early pornographic film. The plot was simple. An actor disguised with grotesque makeup, looking like a Chinese delivery boy complete with a pigtail, knocks on an apartment door with a bag of groceries. A woman, dressed in a flimsy bathrobe, opens the door to allow him in. She gestures to an empty pocketbook to indicate that she has discovered she has no cash to pay for the groceries. She shrugs her shoulders, then coyly offers herself in payment. In her bedroom, with a light breeze blowing through the curtains, the woman seduces the delivery boy.

And so my father's investigation continued. For days he watched the stag film over and over again, looking for clues. He started piecing them together from the footage itself.

Many films at that time were made in studios in New York City or Fort Lee, New Jersey, often on sets with retractable roofs, allowing bright daylight to expose the film without having to use a lot of artificial electric lighting. If the date on the slate was correct; if it was, indeed, shot on February 5, 1920, why wasn't the man wearing an overcoat? How could the woman be in a flimsy bathrobe? Why is the bedroom window open? Why is bright sunshine coming in, the curtains on the open windows blowing during winter months? Wouldn't it have been freezing for the performers up north in February with the roof pulled back to allow in the sunlight?

At one of the editing bays at work, my father, and later the fictional Professor Heskestad in the novel, froze a frame of the window and digitally zoomed in. Although the outdoor background was overexposed, or "blown out," he could darken it enough digitally to make out a tree just outside the window. It was not the kind of deciduous tree found in New York or New Jersey on a February day.

Easy, he thought. The film wasn't shot in the New York area, but perhaps in Los Angeles, where more and more films were being made by then. But the more he looked, he realized that it wasn't the kind of tree found in southern California either. He recognized it from his Florida days, a tree commonly found in northern Florida. It was a live oak, with Spanish moss hanging from the outstretched branches.

He started doing research. Who was making films in 1920? Who was making films in Florida? Who owned the Rockland County land containing the pits where the film was found in the early part of the 20th Century? What was the connection between all of this?

In the novel *The Pits,* the fictional Professor Ivan Heskestad continued in my father's investigative footsteps.

That summer of 1985, my father spent his time researching in the George Eastman Museum in

Rochester, taking prodigious notes. He would use these notes to outline, and then write as he went along, the nonfiction book he was planning to publish, regardless of the outcome of his research. He was, he knew, as tenacious as a pit bull, and something would come out of it one way or another. It was only a matter of time. He wrote the nonfiction version in record speed. When it came time to convert it to fiction for legal reasons, it was just a matter of changing the point of view and a few other narrative elements. By this time, these types of tasks had become something he could do quickly.

With just a few frames of film and stills printed of the slate, technicians in Rochester were able to hypothesize that the film had likely been developed in the Edison film processing laboratories in West Orange, New Jersey, site of the Edison studio and his laboratories during that era.

How did they determine this?

The process of elimination.

The work print had scratches running parallel to the film's edges. Where had these scratches originated? Had the original negative been scratched as it rolled through the camera? Had the processing equipment scratched the negative during processing? Had the contact printer scratched it making the work print?

The technicians cross-referenced other extant films known to have been made during the fall of 1919 and early winter of 1920.

From the surviving films of that era, they found a match.

It was from a period costume drama, *Pioneer Ramble*, filmed near Jacksonville in the pine and palmetto forests of north Florida in the days leading up to February 5, 1920. Like a ballistics test, where striations on a bullet can identify the gun from which a bullet has been fired, the scratches on the film demonstrated conclusively that the early porno short had been shot by the same camera as the costume drama filmed earlier that same week in 1920.

Jacksonville, my father wondered? Who was making films in Jacksonville on this scale at that time? He knew from his days in Florida that Jacksonville had plenty of live oaks draped with Spanish moss.

But filming a relatively complex costume drama set in early Florida?

With a simple premise of a costume drama/ pornographic film shot in 1920 and developed in the Edison laboratory, my father had made an important discovery that raised more questions than it answered. Did Edison know about this porn film? Were there more? Did he condone such activity? Who were the two dead men in the cave? Were they connected to Edison? Was there a Florida-Edison-Hasenclever Mine connection?

Using the porno film as evidence, my father started researching the evolution of the filmmaking business. He started at the beginning, narrating in the voice of the fictional protagonist, Professor Ivan Heskestad.

The Pits:
Pub. 1986

By the late 1880s, Thomas Alva Edison, who was widely known by every schoolchild for inventing the electric lightbulb, was on to new and different things. The most recent was his entrée into the world that would become the motion picture industry. He had already invented the recording device that would evolve into the phonograph. Edison was familiar with the railroad magnate Leland Stanford, who had made a wager with the artist Eadweard Muybridge about whether or not all four of a horse's hooves were ever completely off the ground when running at a full gallop.

To prove his theory, Muybridge developed a fast shutter system on a series of still cameras, enabling the cameras to make exposures at 1/500th of a

second, thereby freezing the motion, un-blurred. His photographic sequences of a horse running past his cameras, passing through trip wires that triggered the exposures on twenty-four separate cameras, proved that Muybridge was correct and provided the groundwork for Edison. Persistence of vision in the human eye enabled the series of still photographs of the horse to appear to move when those pictures were viewed in quick succession like flip cards.

Edison pondered, What if I could build a device that does for pictures what the phonograph did for sound recording? Working with the engineer W.K.L. Dickson, he invented the Kinetoscope in 1891, providing solo viewers with a means to view fascinating material while bending over and peering into an eyepiece at the top of a wooden box nicknamed a "peep show." Dickson would later work with Edison on many filmmaking ventures and would be one of the first Americans ever to appear on a motion picture film, but Edison would eventually fire him.

Thus in the late 1800s the peep show phenomenon evolved, enabling just one person at a time to view a succession of photos printed on postcard-size pictures. The viewer would peer into the eyepiece, using his right hand to turn a crank attached to a rolling drum, like a giant Rolodex® Rotary Card File. The effect was like using your thumb to "flip" through a stack of cards—"moving pictures" on a rolling drum seen through the peep-show eyepiece, giving the appearance that the subjects on the flip cards were actually moving.

Edison eventually asked his friend George Eastman to develop a strip of photographic material—"film" that could be run through a camera and, later, used in the next evolutionary step of the peep show.

The old story goes that Eastman asked Edison how wide he wanted the strip of film to be. According to legend, Edison held his thumb and forefinger about an inch apart, or 35mm, and said, "This wide." Eastman did his job and invented a strip made of cellulose nitrate to run through the Kinetoscope.

At the Paris Exposition of 1900, as Edison was touting his electric lights, at a nearby venue another exhibit was getting a lot more attention. It was the work of Georges Méliès, and he was displaying his own invention, the forerunner of what would be a motion picture projector.

Edison's work would evolve into both a motion picture camera and later a movie projector. Edison and Dickson found and financed an invention by another tinkerer. When they bought the patent from the unsuspecting inventor they insisted on taking credit for it. The "Vitascope projector" enabled films to be seen by more than one person at a time. As with Georges Méliès's machine in Paris, auditoriums could be filled with paying customers, the films projected to hundreds of viewers at once. When one audience left, another hundred people paid to fill up the auditorium.

As their work progressed, Edison kept tight control of his patents. He recognized a gold mine when he saw one and would eventually become this country's first movie mogul. Cameramen such as Billy Bitzer went out into the field to film what were called "actualities; three-to-five-minute, lockdown shots of an event or a scenic location. Guys like Bitzer, working for one of Edison's competitors, went around the country and filmed what we might today call tourism films.

Two actualities were filmed in Palm Beach in early February 1905 by Billy Bitzer. The first was a boat parade on Lake Worth, with Henry Morrison Flagler's railroad bridge over the Intracoastal Waterway leading up to the Royal Poinciana Hotel in the background. The next day the cinematographer filmed a pool party in Palm Beach, the men in black wool, knee-length swimsuits diving into the pool and showing off for the camera and the women on the pool deck.

There were no live oaks draped in Spanish moss in any of Bitzer's South Florida footage.

Altogether, Bitzer filmed some three hundred of these short film travelogues around the country, and they became enormously popular in the early 1900s. Thousands of movie houses opened. Thousands of people saw Bitzer's experiences in Palm Beach and wanted to go there in the wintertime.

By the first decade of the twentieth century, audiences demanded more than just boring lockdown shots of events and what were essentially travelogues of Niagara Falls and the Grand Canyon, or streetcars in San Francisco, more than shots of a train that looked like it was coming through the screen and into the theater.

Bitzer and his colleagues started filming short, ten-to- fourteen-minute melodramas and comedies called one-reelers.

In 1893 Edison had built a studio for the Kinetoscope in Menlo Park, New Jersey, and eventually had his staff start cranking out one-reeler narrative stories, with actors acting out roles. The studio, called the Black Maria, was a big tar-paper shack with a roof that could be retracted to allow sunlight to illuminate the scenes. During this time it wasn't just Edison who realized that fortunes could be made in the movie industry.

By 1909, dramas and comedies started pouring out of New York and Fort Lee. Many of the films were written and directed by the soon-to-be-famous D. W. Griffith and filmed by Billy Bitzer.

Thousands of films were shot and distributed, but few have survived the past century, owing to the unstable cellulose nitrate base of the film stock.

But hundreds of these early films have survived. How, you might ask? The answer: a fluke.

During the early years of filmmaking, 1894 to 1912, copyright laws did not protect filmmakers' rights of ownership. Copyright laws were strictly for printed material. This loophole in the law allowed anyone to make pirated copies of films in circulation, sell them, and thereby profit from the work of others.

This potential loss of revenue from theft angered Edison and Dickson, who shrewdly concluded that in order to copyright their films and legally protect their work, they would have to turn their films into printed books. So they undertook to print every frame of a given film on paper spools, or bind the paper photographs into books, and copyright the paper spools or printed books. When you consider that these cameras recorded at 18 to 24 frames per second, you realize that every minute of film involved printing over fourteen hundred separate photographs.

Later, after World War II and the advent of "safety film" stock, the Library of Congress initiated an effort known as the "Paper Print Collection," to re-create these films, which had been thought forever lost due to the chemical instability. Technicians re-photographed these picture books, one shot at a time, on film. The registration was shaky owing to the almost impossible task of precisely aligning each shot with the former shot in the sequence. But the new film prints reproduced accurately whatever was in the still photographs, including negative scratches on the film and silhouettes of occasional stray hairs in the camera's gate.

Other prints survived the cellulose nitrate danger from that early era in odd, often surprising ways. In the late 1970s construction work on a building in Dawson City, Canada, uncovered an entire abandoned swimming pool filled with boxes of film tins that had been buried decades earlier. The pool was adjacent to an old movie theater that at one time showed silent films.

The Dawson City theater was at the end of the distribution line for these films. After a week or two of screening, the projectionist decided it was cheaper to store them in the abandoned swimming pool next door than to send them back to the distributor. In 1929, for safety reasons, the film cans were buried under a layer of dirt that had been dumped in and over the swimming pool. There they sat, in an inert environment, temperature-and humidity-controlled by the Canadian permafrost line. More than five hundred films from the pre–World War I era, once thought lost forever, were rediscovered in that Dawson City swimming pool in various states of restorable condition. Works by D. W. Griffith and Billy Bitzer, Sam Goldwyn, and Mack Sennett were preserved.

It was through this Paper Print Collection, stored in the Library of Congress, that the Rochester technicians working with me were able to find a match to the film found in the iron ore pit. The costume drama, Pioneer Ramble, filmed in the Jacksonville area, was shot on the same camera and probably sent to the same film processing laboratory in Menlo Park at the same time as the pornographic film recently discovered in the pocket of one of the two dead men in the iron ore pit.

Had the "Phil" and "Mo" listed in white chalk on the slateboard tried to sneak their porno film through the laboratory without it being detected, as part of Pioneer Ramble, the legitimate costume drama? The technicians showed me a reproduction of that featurette, reconstructed from still photos during the Paper Print initiative and subsequently stored in the Library of Congress.

The film story, Pioneer Ramble, is based on a true Florida event. A group of settlers was traveling on Florida's west coast in the late 1880s to homestead some land. In the middle of the dense pine and palmetto forest they were attacked by a group of renegade Seminoles who didn't want white settlers encroaching on their land. As the frightened settlers fought off their attackers, what made the scene somewhat surrealistic and even more frightening was that the Seminole warriors were not wearing traditional regalia and war paint, but clothing out of Elizabethan-era England. How could something like that be possible? Were the pioneers hallucinating from fear of imminent death? It was later determined that this same band of renegade Seminoles had earlier attacked a Shakespearean theater troupe that was touring through the west coast area of Florida with trunk loads of theatrical costumes. The attackers had frightened off the troupe and stolen all their stage wardrobe. The filmmakers had captured on film a perfect re-creation of one of Florida's most bizarre Seminole attacks from that era.

As fascinating as Pioneer Ramble was, the scratches that matched the pornographic film, were clearly evident and distracted me.

But the Jacksonville connection still confused me.

By the early 1900s, other people realized the fortunes possible from making, distributing, and exhibiting motion pictures. Insisting on total control, Edison tried to prevent any competition, by enforcing newly-minted patent restrictions on his cameras and projection equipment.

Whoever wanted to make and project movies had to use Edison's technology and his patents, resulting in royalties for him. By 1908 he was suing anyone in the motion picture business who was using the equipment that he held patents on, and were not paying him his royalties.

He sued anyone who did not belong to his newly formed Motion Picture Patents Company, also known as the Edison Trust, a consortium of about ten production studios that were making films at the time. Film companies not in his group were forced to use European equipment and/or film, or faced constant lawsuits from the MPPC for failure to pay royalties for using Edison's equipment. He was trying to shut down the European film market in this country, keep films to their one-reeler length, control costs, and control who could invest in films.

The "patent wars" were under way.

If the lawsuits did not work, Edison would send out enforcers, who arrived on set with billy clubs, knocking down scenery, chasing away the cast and crew, destroying the sets, stealing the cameras and stopping production. Work by these thugs became notorious and frightened off a lot of filmmakers.

Edison's "patent wars" had an impact on production up and down the northeast coast for a decade.

Filmmakers who were working in the New York boroughs and Fort Lee, New Jersey, had a diversity of landscapes, all in close proximity to Manhattan.

Partially in response to Edison's enforcement, partly because of the quest for evermore exotic locations, filmmakers started looking for other places to make films, somewhere out of Edison's immediate reach. Somewhere that offered a variety of backdrops aside from the streets of New York or the farm fields and rocky crags of northern New Jersey. Weren't there other people making films somewhere else?

Someplace that was sunny year round and wasn't cold in the wintertime?

I soon discovered the Jacksonville connection.

In 1901 a fire had started near a mattress factory in Jacksonville. The dried Spanish moss used to stuff mattresses was extremely flammable. North Florida was in the middle of a prolonged drought, and most of the buildings in the city were wooden structures with wooden roofs. One day, sparks from a nearby chimney landed on a pile of Spanish moss outside a mattress factory. A fire broke out and eventually burned to the ground 150 blocks in the downtown area. Some twenty-five hundred buildings were destroyed in a fire that would become the third largest city fire in U.S. history, behind Chicago and San Francisco.

During the planning for rebuilding the city fathers invited architects from all over the country to give the new downtown a distinctive look. The architects chose to copy the masters and duplicate the looks of the great American Prairie and some other, more exotic locales. Some say that many of the new buildings even looked like the Parthenon in Greece. Others copied Roman temples and architecture found in France, Germany, and England.

In the aftermath of the fire, you could stand in the downtown area of Jacksonville and at every turn it was as if you were in a different city. It was like standing in the middle of a. . . giant movie set.

Word quickly spread, and for the first two decades of the twentieth century, Jacksonville became a filmmaking center, partially because of the diversity of its locations. American landmarks and international destinations could be imitated. They were all there. Within a few miles were prehistoric jungles and pristine beaches. It was sunny all year round and warm. Edison's goons weren't lurking about, ready to tear down your set.

What made it even better was that it was a day and a half train ride up Henry Morrison Flagler's Florida East Coast Railway to New York, where the film developing labs were. Flagler's railroad would eventually extend south from Jacksonville to Key West, but that destination could not be reached by rail until 1912.

Careers were born in Jacksonville. Oliver Hardy was a movie projectionist in Georgia when he decided to try his hand at acting in this new movie capital just across the Florida state line. Eventually, hundreds of movies were made there, mostly one-reelers, running from ten to fourteen minutes.

They made biblical epics, comedies, melodramas, and mysteries set in exotic locations and earlier eras, all filmed without leaving the Jacksonville area. The film negative was shipped overnight to the film labs in New York on Flagler's railroad.

In the meantime, by 1908, Billy Bitzer had teamed up with an actor turned director for a kidnapping melodrama, The Adventures of Dollie. The director's name was D. W. Griffith. Between 1908 and 1913, writing, directing, and filming, they churned out four hundred of these ten-minute stories, using actors, sets, props. That's three or four films a week, four hundred times in a row, in just four years. The film industry was flourishing. The audiences demanded more. New York and Jacksonville responded.

For the first decade or so of the new century, the city fathers of Jacksonville had welcomed the legitimate motion picture industry, but by the end of World War I the novelty was beginning to wear off. A new political regime came into power, one that concluded that movie people were crazy, even immoral, and they didn't like those crazy sinners doing crazy things in their town.

You say you need a shot of a fire truck racing toward a fire? That's going to cost money, unless . . . you call in a false alarm and simply film the fire truck when it races past the camera enroute to what they think is a burning building. Oooops! False alarm! But the filmmakers got their shot, for free.

Down south, some of the group of Jacksonville filmmakers continued to ignore Edison's threats, where the year-round temperature and sunny days made it more hospitable to be filmmakers.

It was in this out-of-town filming location in Jacksonville where Edison eventually forged informal partnerships with such studios as Kalem and others.

By using intermediaries, filmmakers found Jacksonville a perfect spot for their growth of early pornographic films. There was no front office oversight, and it was possible to make clandestine, arm's-length arrangements with legitimate filmmakers for the use of sets, props, and wardrobe. There were plenty of bathing beauties on the beach, and there were plenty of exotic locations for erotic tales.

CHAPTER 32

MONDAY, OCTOBER 27, 2008
4 DAYS AFTER THE MURDER

Abby went back to the crime scene on Low Tor yet again. It was his second visit in two days.

He paced the scene and the nearby areas even more closely, getting down on his hands and knees, the sharp rocks of the hillside trail cutting into his skin. He crawled up and down over a hundred yards on knees weakened by thousands of hits on the playing fields, knees raw and painful and worn out. Finally he found something he was looking for on a sharp-edged tree branch at fender level. Was it what he thought it was, a minute paint scraping from the SUV? Using a pair of tweezers, he scraped it into a plastic bag and placed it in his pocket.

CHAPTER 33

TUESDAY, OCTOBER 28, 2008
5 DAYS AFTER THE MURDER

The next day, Abby headed over to the Chief's office. The headquarters were built into the side of a steep rise on South Mountain Road, near where it meets Haverstraw Road.

It was a gusty day, with a strong northeaster trying to blow in, spreading leaves all over the parking lot. The lot seemed empty for this time of the day, and then he noticed a paint crew unloading tarps and scaffolding gear from two trucks. It looked like Ditto's crew, and my father looked for Nick, but didn't see him. He could catch up later. Now he was late for his appointment.

Inside, the receptionist gave him a neutral nod and waved him toward the Chief's office.

Chief Schoonmaker shuffled folders on his desk. "Have a seat, Abby. Still no news. We're working on it. That's all I can tell you."

Detective Mays moved into the open doorway and stood in silence, ignoring my father. A second officer stood behind him, Charlie Trask. "Sorry, Chief. The pressure-cleaning guys are finally here. They got to clean the building. Gonna spray paint it later this week when the wind dies down. We gotta move your car to the side parking lot, otherwise it'll be covered by old paint flecks and debris. You can move it back later this afternoon."

The Chief tossed his car keys to Trask. "You take care of it. We're kind of busy here. Abby, where are you parked?"

"Close to you.Here." He threw his keys to Mays without giving it a second thought.

My grandfather turned back to my father. "So what you gotta do, Abby, is just sit tight and let us do our jobs."

The Chief moved to the window and gazed out. He watched the painting crew put down traffic cones and spread tarps all around as they prepared the pressure-cleaner compressor.

The officer moved the Chief's car first and then drove my father's car around the corner to the side lot, upwind from the pressure-cleaner spray and protected by the building's wall.

Behind the Chief, my father started to stand up. The Chief turned, approached him. "Hold on just a minute." His familial tone had changed. Now it was business.

My father remained seated, wondering what was going on. He didn't have long to wait. My grandfather's tone seemed to change. "Do you own a handgun?"

My father was startled. "What? Why?"

"I'll ask the questions. Do you own a handgun?"

"Yes."

"Did you have it with you on your camping trip?"

"No."

"Why not?"

"Why would I need it?"

"What kind is it?"

"Twenty-five caliber semiautomatic. "

"What kind did the alleged killer have?"

And this is where my father told a lie about the case. "I told you. I couldn't see it clearly. Why? What does ballistics say killed Huck?"

"Report's not in yet. Where do you keep it?"

"I keep it in my office desk drawer at home. What difference does it make? I don't like these questions."

"Abby, I'm on your side. But like I said, being your father-in-law only goes so far.

CHAPTER 34

MARCH 1964
NEW CITY
44 YEARS BEFORE THE MURDER

When my father first heard word in the spring of 1964 that he had been awarded a full scholarship to play football at Florida State University, it was the talk of the town. His coaches were proud. His teachers nodded their heads as if to say, *Of course, we knew he could do it.* Doc, Ossie, Nick, and the rest of the guys wanted to get him drunk and celebrate all weekend. He declined.

That night at the kitchen table, when he told his father the news, his father simply said, "I guess that means you think you're too good to do any work around here anymore," and stood and poured himself a drink.

My father looked at his father's back. He wondered, is that the only reaction I get from him on the happiest night of my life? He turned and walked outside. Alone.

He hopped on his bike and rode off into the early spring dusk. At that time in New City, seventeen-year-olds didn't ride bikes. It was considered beneath their dignity. They drove their parents' cars. My father didn't have a car to borrow. He didn't care about the social stigma of riding a bike. He was heading into the future, he knew. He headed south on Zukor Road to North Main and then into New City. He couldn't understand why his father would treat him the way he did. But it didn't make any difference anymore. He was going to escape soon, and he didn't know whether to be joyous or frightened. He would celebrate without his father.

He parked his bike outside the library and walked in. The librarian, Elsa Bartels, who would later be immortalized in *Sweetclover* as Miss Van Houten, was alone in her domain this soon after the dinner hour.

She reached under her desk, pulled out a gift-wrapped package, and extended it to him.

"What's this?"

"This is a small town. I heard a celebration was in order."

"You heard?"

"Everyone in town knows."

He took the package from her and unwrapped four books. *Cat's Cradle* by Kurt Vonnegut, Jr., *The Spy Who*

Came in from the Cold by John LeCarre, *The Collector* by John Fowles, and *V.* by Thomas Pynchon.

"You might have a tough time getting into that last one. It's a little. . . *obscure.*"

"I don't know how to thank you for all you've done for me."

"I do."

"What?"

"Give me an autographed copy of your first novel."

"I don't know when that might be."

"When it's time. You'll know."

She reached under the desk again and pulled out a gray box with a snap latch and a handle and offered it to him.

"What's this?"

"A portable typewriter. You can't write a novel without a typewriter."

"You bought this for me?"

"No, I bought it for me. But I'm not using it, so you can keep the dust off it for me."

With his thumbs, my father squeezed the chrome latches that sprang open with a crackle. He lifted the top of the case, pivoting on its rear hinges. Inside was a barely used Smith Corona manual typewriter. The smell of ribbon ink filled his head and his imagination. He inhaled deeply, reaching out and touching the keyboard, and his fingers shook. With his left pinky he typed an *a*. The key jumped to attention, followed his marching orders, and hit the platen with a sharp snap.

"You do know how to type, don't you?"

"Yes, Mrs. McCarthy at Clarkstown taught me how."

"She taught me how to type thirty years ago at Congers High School. Lot of good it did me."

"Were you a classmate of my father's?"

"I was until he dropped out in the tenth grade."

"I need to talk to you about Miss Singer's books."

"What about them?"

"I need a safe place to store them until I can afford to have them shipped to Tallahassee."

"Bring them in. I'll see that you get them in a few weeks."

"I don't know how to thank you, Miss Bartels."

"I already told you how. Oh, and you can send me a postcard with a Florida beach on it next winter."

"I don't think they have any beaches in Tallahassee."

"Wakulla Springs. Thirty miles south, on the Gulf. That will suffice."

"Wakulla Springs?"

"They filmed *Creature from the Black Lagoon* there in 1953. It was supposed to be the Amazon jungle. A postcard. Send me one."

CHAPTER 35

JULY 1964
44 YEARS BEFORE THE MURDER

At dawn on the day of his departure for Tallahassee, just two weeks after high school graduation, my grandfather drove my father from Dellwood to the bus stop on the corner of Congers Road and Main Street. The Elms Hotel *watched* from the southeast corner. They were riding in the same pickup truck in which Miss Singer had taken her last ride, but you, dear reader, don't know about that just yet.

On this occasion, the truck bed contained two battered suitcases that had been given to Abby by Ossie's mom. Miss Bartel's gray typewriter case with the Smith Corona inside was sandwiched between them.

In the parking lot in front of Whitey's Luncheonette, my father's father got out of the cab and smoked a cigarette in silence as they waited for the bus. As my father pulled his luggage from the pick-up, he gave the rusty truck bed one last glance that lasted but a second. He hadn't wanted to look even that long.

Before long, Coach Morrow and Coach D'Innocenzo pulled up in a station wagon with a carload of my father's teammates to say goodbye and wish him well. They were all there, Nick, Ossie, Doc, and four other players in a second car, whooping it up in the rising sun. They, themselves, wouldn't leave for college for another six weeks, as none of them would be playing football on their college teams, so they didn't have to show up early for preseason practice.

As the Red & Tan approached the parking lot turnaround from the south, Abby's father stuck out his hand for a handshake, his elbow straight, to keep his son at a distance. "Do a good job. You don't want to wind up old and stupid like me."

My father shook his father's hand without making eye contact. My father wanted to say, "There's no chance of that ever happening." Instead, he just nodded and said, "Thanks, Dad."

He stashed the two borrowed suitcases in the wheel-well compartment of the bus and gripped the typewriter handle in his left hand. He squeezed the handle hard, as if to make sure the gift inside was really there and what it meant for his future. He turned, gave a final wave to his coaches and his friends, and got on the near-empty bus. He was met with smiles from a few commuters who recognized him as the hometown hero and knew they were witnessing an historic event. He sat in the front seat, behind the steps, for the best view of the road ahead, the typewriter on his lap.

As the bus pulled away, he turned to look out the rear window and saw my grandfather taking a last drag of his cigarette. He gave his son a little wave and stepped back into the pickup's cab. My father was convinced that his old man had a look of relief on his face, as his school friends continued to whoop and wave. He was leaving them all behind and sailing off into the great unknown. They were really the only family he had.

The bus rode south on Main to the first stop at Third Street to pick up some morning commuters. As the bus idled there for a brief moment, one of the last things my father remembered seeing in New City was Father Carrick, out in front of St. Augustine church, sweeping off the front steps in time for seven a.m. Mass. My father had not been to mass in years.

He shifted in his seat, turned to the west, and gazed out at the upstairs bedroom window of the boardinghouse where Miss Singer had roomed. He could almost see her standing there, waving goodbye to him from behind the white lace curtains. In his vision she mouthed something to him, a fond adieu or some sort of well-wishing, perhaps, but he could not read her lips as she blew him a kiss. What would she think of him now, the little boy who had idolized her from the back of the fourth grade class eight years ago, he wondered? He wanted to make her proud.

From there it was on to Penn Station for an overnight train ride to Jacksonville and then a Trailways Bus west along Highway 90 to Tallahassee.

He would not return home to New City or see his father for four years.

CHAPTER 36

1964–1968
FLORIDA
44–40 YEARS BEFORE THE MURDER

What happened to my father at Florida State University in Tallahassee? Simple. He became another person.

When he arrived for preseason training on the full football scholarship to FSU in the summer of 1964, he was almost overwhelmed, for one thing, by the intense heat. It was oppressive all day and all night, except when it was raining, which was every afternoon. The changing of the seasons, what little there was, was gradual. He was in the Deep South. Some people even called it L.A., for Lower Alabama, because of the way the people behaved and spoke and thought.

He was almost overwhelmed by the enormity of the FSU campus. It was as big as the entire town of New

City. The Strozier Library could have held a hundred New City Libraries.

He was almost overwhelmed by the sheer number of students. His high school graduating class at Clarkstown High was 264, out of a student body of fewer than 900. FSU had just over 12,000 students enrolled that fall.

He was almost overwhelmed by the sheer talent of his fellow football players. Most were on scholarship, which they had all worked hard to deserve. It wasn't like high school, where some of the guys were there just for the fun and the friendship. These guys were all serious competitors in their new cutthroat world. It was like a business. But my father didn't have to worry about his chances. Even among these competitors, his innate abilities left him untouchable, irreplaceable, indispensable.

He was almost overwhelmed by the number of beautiful women classmates. He had never had time for a girlfriend in high school. Or maybe that was just his rationalization. He was too embarrassed to ask out any girl. He knew he could never bring them to his home, the tiny cottage toolshed on the Dellwood grounds. He could never introduce a girl to his father. Here, the playing field wasn't just leveled. It was tilted in his favor. He was on a football scholarship, and he was a campus celebrity.

But most of all, he was almost overwhelmed when he realized that what little family he had once had, was now gone. There were all leaving to pursue their own destinies. He was going to have to face the future alone. He became determined.

Although he was almost overwhelmed by the opportunity FSU presented, one thing helped. It had a superior department of literature, his chosen major.

He was almost overwhelmed by the rich world of Southern literature, of which, until his arrival in the South, he was only remotely aware. Yes, Miss Singer's collection had included Flannery O'Connor's *A Good Man Is Hard to Find*, and a book by some guy from Florida's west coast who was writing pulp fiction starting in the early 1950s, and yes, he had read *To Kill a Mockingbird*. But he didn't know that those books were the tip of the iceberg, an iceberg that went very deep in the Deep South.

In his freshman year he was required to read a book, *The Moviegoer*, by an author he had never heard of, Walker Percy. He was surprised. More than surprised. Harper Lee and Flannery O'Connor notwithstanding, he had been unaware of the literary movement that was now, both literally and figuratively, within arm's reach.

He made an appointment with the professor who had assigned the book and told him what he was looking for in the way of novels to emulate. The professor was more than willing to help. To Abby's surprise, the first reading recommendation he made was not a novel, but a nonfiction work from the early 1940s, *The Mind of the South*, by Wilbur J. Cash.

"In order to truly understand any of these works of Southern literature, it is essential that you read this book first," the professor told him.

And so he did read it. And just as the professor had claimed, he came to understand the mind of the South and how different it was from what he had experienced growing up in New City. It opened an entire new world.

He made weekly pilgrimages to the professor's office, and there he came to be acquainted with the canon of William Faulkner and explored Mississippi. And then he gained another perspective toward Mississippi with Eudora Welty. He headed, figuratively, to Louisiana, to re-read *All the King's Men*, by Robert Penn Warren, a book he'd read from Miss Singer's collection when he was in the sixth grade. But when he read it this time, he realized that he was reading more than great prose. He was reading lyrical, melodious poetry in the form of rarefied prose few writers could ever hope to duplicate.

He headed east to Alabama and, upon re-reading *To Kill a Mockingbird* and then seeing the movie not long afterward, he recommitted to becoming a novelist, so powerful was its impact. Even more so than in the days following his reading of *The New York Times Book Review*. Was Harper Lee working on a follow-up novel?

He moved on to Georgia and read more of the Flannery O'Connor works that he had started in fifth grade. And then he started reading Carson McCullers. Why had none of his teachers at Clarkstown High ever told him about this marvelous writer, who, although she had been born in Georgia and spent her life writing about Georgia, had been living in nearby Nyack since 1945? He could have bicycled to her front porch just to catch a glimpse of this literary giant, if only he had known she was living so close.

He got caught up with the Florida pulp writer John D. MacDonald and started reading his new series about Travis McGee, a salvage consultant living on a houseboat in a Fort Lauderdale marina. He couldn't wait for the proposed follow-up novels in the series.

He continued his journey in William Attaway's Kentucky as he followed three brothers north to a

Pittsburgh steel mill, in *Blood on the Forge*. He began to *understand*.

Instead of being overwhelmed by this new world he was living in at FSU and letting it wear him down, he thrived in the imaginary worlds Tallahassee's program had introduced. He sensed something moving forward in his life. His imagination, simmering for years now with the countless words from the books of Miss Singer and Elsa Bartels, was coming close to the boiling point. Every event he witnessed, every conversation he overheard, was turning into story he would write. He found it difficult to focus on football, but knew what was expected of him and was committed to delivering. He would get the job done.

He made a pledge to himself. He would not go back to New City until he graduated, and, in fact, he did not return until he was drafted by the Giants in 1968, during his senior year at FSU.

The journeys he took in his imagination, more recently stimulated by the writers from the South, would change his perspective forever. No longer was he the ethnocentric boy from New City. He had been introduced to *the mind of the south*.

And so it was, he came to identify himself as a New City boy by origin, who had been tempered and forged into something much larger, more well-rounded, more *informed*. While others looked down at their shoes as they plodded through their everyday, hum-drum lives, his gaze was lifted upward toward the future.

But he was having trouble with the writing. He had promised Miss Bartels that he would show her something he had written, but in the five years since she'd challenged him, he had nothing that he could be proud of to show, nothing to say, *this is what I am capable of doing.*

And then one day when he was wandering around Doak Campbell Stadium after practice, another life-changing event blind-sided him.

He discovered the campus television station, and his entire life would change once again. There, in the bowels of the stadium, was the fledgling four-year-old television station and its accompanying Broadcasting Major Department. It wasn't long before my father had two majors: literature and broadcasting. As he never planned to go home over summer break anyway, taking on a second major allowed him the opportunity to tell stories with more than just words on paper and earn two degrees simultaneously.

That winter semester of his freshman year, after the football season and its accompanying obligations were on hiatus, he learned how to shoot and edit 16mm news film. The head of the department was not about to say no to the request of a football star, albeit a freshman. As a result, my father learned to tell more elaborate and complicated stories as time went on. Some people thought it odd that a football star on a full athletic scholarship should be treating that fact with indifference, almost taking it for granted while becoming more obsessed with having his stories broadcast on the school's television station.

Just as it had in high school, his football prowess had become a means to an end. He'd known it would be his ticket out of the New City of his father. Now, in Tallahassee, he was using football as a means to study filmmaking. Later, during his career with the Giants, it was never about the game or the season, but always about where it was leading when his football career inevitably ended. He would capitalize on his fame and fortune and become a storyteller. If that meant telling his stories on television before an audience of millions, he would do it, as long as it led to a life of writing novels that would have made Miss Singer proud.

And so in the off-season he lived at the television station when he wasn't out shooting film, traveling around Florida on a great treasure hunt.

He mastered the use of a light meter and a windup *Bolex* 16mm camera for shooting support footage. For interviews he taught himself how to use an *Auricon Pro-600*, which could record sound on a magnetic stripe on the film's edge, as well as images on four-hundred-foot film magazines. Ten minutes of images and sound per reel. The camera, power supply and recording device were heavy and cumbersome and had to be plugged into an electrical wall outlet, but he made it work for what he was doing. He was motivated more than he had ever been.

That first winter, he started out doing sports features about FSU's basketball team and then started researching nearby locations that held intriguing human interest stories; stories about Florida's history, Florida's environment. Every direction he drove on his treasure hunt led to gold nuggets.

On Valentine's Day in February 1965 he traveled to Daytona Beach to film the Daytona 500 and interview the race winner, Fred Lorenzen.

During Spring Break, while other college students were getting drunk on Florida's beaches in Ft. Lauderdale, Daytona, and Pensacola, my father hopped in the one of the Campus News vans, and with a map and itinerary, he shot almost a dozen documentary featurettes in two weeks on twenty locations, all by himself.

Apalachicola Fishing Fleet: (9:30)

A look at the historic shrimp and oyster industries, with interviews with several fisher-folk who discuss environmental concerns and the future of their livelihood in Florida. He spent the night filming on a shrimper out in the Gulf of Mexico, his camera wrapped in a plastic bag to keep the salt spray from the shrimp nets away.

Falling Waters State Park: (6:00)

A look at Florida's tallest waterfall at seventy-nine feet, and the nearby oil drilling industry from the early 20th Century within the State Park property.

Civil War Reenactment of the Battle of Natural Bridge: (10:00)

Over 400 Civil War buffs gathered to re-enact one of only two major Florida Civil War battles. In 1865, at Natural Bridge on the St. Mark's River south of Tallahassee, twelve-year-old boys kept the Union Army at bay, preventing them from taking over Florida. He filmed interviews with reenactors from the Union and Confederate armies, both "officers" and "enlisted soldiers", and B-rolled it all with battle footage he shot on his wind-up *Bolex*.

Devil's Millhopper. (6:00)

An exploration of Florida's most infamous, prehistoric 120-foot deep sink-hole near Gainesville, where archeologists have found the prehistoric remains of sharks and eight million year-old camel bones.

Yankeetown. (10:00)

A visit to the small town on Florida's Nature Coast, where the Elvis Presley movie, *Follow That Dream* had been filmed in July of 1961. He interviewed Florida novelist Richard Powell, whose book *Pioneer, Go Home,* was the source material for the film. Other interviews include two women who claim to have dated Elvis during his stay, and how that changed their lives. He also interviewed a boy from nearby Gainesville, by then aged fourteen. His name was Tom Petty, and he had taken up the guitar four years earlier, inspired by his meeting Elvis during the filming of *Follow That Dream,*.

Ray Charles' Birthplace: (7:00)

A retrospective biography including footage of his home in nearby Greenville, and interviews with friends and neighbors who knew him as a young boy.

Florida's Tallest, Oldest Tree: (5:00)

A 3,000 year-old bald cypress tree near Orlando that was 125 feet tall. (This tree was burned down by an addict smoking crystal meth in 2012).

Ichetucknee Springs: (7:30)

A four-mile trip down the crystal clear waters of Florida's favorite river, filmed while sitting in a floating inner tube. Tubing the Ichetucknee was a rite-of-passage for Florida's college students in those days.

Tarpon Springs Sponge Diving: (10:00)

A visit to this Greek settlement on Florida's west coast, with footage of sponge divers on boats preparing to harvest. Underwater footage was taken by my father, by placing a camera in an aquarium he had brought along and dipping it a few inches into the water, with the lens below the water's surface, to capture on film the hard-hat divers' harvesting of sponges.

Ma Barker's House: (6:00)

In January, 1935, Ma Barker and her son were killed in an hours-long shoot-out with Federal Agents in Ocklawaha. Nearby residents staged a reenactment for my father's camera thirty years later.

Cross Creek: (10:00)

The homestead of Marjorie Kinnan Rawlings in Cross Creek had been left to the University of Florida in her will when Rawlings died in 1953, but it was not open to the public until 1970. My father had to get special permission to film on the property and tell the story of this Pulitzer Prize-winning novelist who was, over the years, thrilled, inspired, nurtured, and eventually heartbroken, by what she found in this quiet spot between Lake Orange and Lake Lochloosa, south of Gainesville.

Zora Neale Hurston: (10:00)

The story of a young black girl, who grew up in Eatonville, Florida, near Orlando. In this town founded by former slaves, she listened to the stories and folk tales she heard while hiding under the front porch of the general store, eavesdropping on the elders who gathered there. She evolved into a member of the Harlem Renaissance in the 1930, working with other literati like Langston Hughes. After writing stage plays, several novels, two autobiographies and numerous short stories, she fell into obscurity, her books went out of print, and she became a housemaid in Central Florida. By 1960, she was living in a Fort Pierce welfare home, where she died penniless and alone. She was buried in a pauper's grave. By 1965, she was long forgotten by all but a few scholars. My father couldn't even find her burial plot when he tried to film it. He interviewed several Eatonville residents who remembered her. It would another eight years before Alice Walker (who would later write *The Color Purple*) would find Zora's burial site, write about her, and bring her to the attention of the world once again. Her books are now back in print and *Their Eyes Were Watching God* is required reading on many a college campus. It was made into a film by Oprah Winfrey). My father's short documentary went relatively unnoticed that spring of 1965.

When my father brought the footage back to school after Spring Break and told his instructors what he had accomplished, they were dumbfounded. From that point on he was given *carte blanche* to film whatever stories he wanted to. He took every advantage that he could of their generosity, on every break from the classroom and the football field.

Twelfth Annual Florida Folk Festival: (54:00)

That May weekend of the 7th, 8th, and 9th in 1965, he filmed the *Twelfth Annual Florida Folk Festival*, capturing performances by whip-crackers, cloggers, gospel singers, banjo strummers, thimbles on washboard players, and legendary folk-singer/ songwriters Will McLean and Gamble Rogers. He also shot an interview with longtime festival director, Cousin Thelma Boltin.

Over the next three years, before his graduation from FSU in the spring of 1968, he filmed dozens more stories, while other students and his teammates were just getting on with their regular college work and getting drunk on weekends.

John D. Macdonald: (12:00)

An interview with the reclusive author about his remarkable work habits, his concern for the Florida environment, and his new Travis McGee Series. When my father first approached MacDonald through his New York agent, MacDonald was not interested in doing a television interview. When he found out my father was under twenty years old at the time, he reconsidered. It was one of only three television interviews MacDonald did in his lifetime.

Wakulla Springs: (6:00)

Travelogue of beautiful site where *Creature from the Black Lagoon* had been filmed, in 1953, doubling for the Amazon River, as the New City librarian had told him. He took the time to send a postcard to Miss Bartels, as she had requested. It was a photo of the beach beneath St. Mark's Lighthouse.

St. Mark's Lighthouse (6:00)

Thirty miles south of Tallahassee is St. Mark's Lighthouse on Apalachee Bay. Built in the 1830s to help boats avoid the treacherous shoals and oyster beds, it's light can be seen for over twelve miles away from its eighty-foot tower. The flame has only been out once, and that was during its short occupation by the Union Army during the Civil War, when they burned the staircase to prevent access to the kerosene lantern above.

Florida Caverns, Marianna: (6:00)

A look inside one of Florida's most accessible caves and a little-known tourist attraction. It was discovered in the late 1930s by a geologist who crawled into a sinkhole underneath a fallen tree. During the late Depression, over 200 workers from the Civilian Conservation Corps worked for a dollar a day to map it out, string up lights, and make it accessible to visitors. It opened to the public five years later.

Ocala Cow Pasture Cave (10:00)

So intrigued was he with the Marianna Caverns, my father started looking around for more caves to explore. He didn't have to look far. Within a fifty-mile radius of Gainesville, home to the University of Florida, there are over 200 caves. North Central Florida has a foundation of porous limestone, and the results of years of flowing water are caves and waterways that run for miles underground. Some that are close to the surface result in Florida's notorious sinkholes, known to swallow up entire houses.

He convinced the television station to buy an underwater housing for his 16mm *Bolex* and some diving lights. Based on his track record, they didn't hesitate.

With the help of a local spelunker club, he chose a cave thirty miles south, in the middle of an Ocala cow pasture. He left Tallahassee at dawn and drove to Gainesville, about 150 miles to the southeast, hoping to get an early start. What the spelunkers didn't tell him was that they would have to wait until after dark to sneak onto the cow pasture. It was on private property and they did not have permission from the rancher.

By nightfall, the two locals got rip-roaring drunk in a nearby tavern, at first hiding their lack of sobriety from my father, then just twenty-one at the time. It wasn't until they had parked on a right-of-way, climbed over barbed wire fence, and dropped themselves on a steel-cable ladder straight down into a sixty-foot hole in the ground the dimensions of a street man-hole, did my father realize how wasted his two guides were.

The first cavern opened up into an underground lake, about forty feet square. Due to heavy rains, the crystal-clear water level was higher than the spelunkers had ever seen it before. So high that the water level blocked access to the adjoining cavern. One guy had to dive down into the water and swim under the limestone portal to the next cavern. As excited as my father was, he was more afraid than he had ever been in his life.

The lead caver bobbed up in the next chamber and swam to the nearby shore. He waved his light underwater and yelled for them to dive in and follow the light. My father and the second caver swam under water from one chamber toward the next, following the light beam. As a joke, the first guy turned off the beam and within seconds they were disoriented, holding their breaths with nowhere to surface in the pitch black. The light came on, and they both quickly followed it to the lead caver. And then to my father's dismay, the two guides both passed out, drunk.

He turned off all three of their lights and spent the night shivering in total darkness, knowing he could never find his way out without his two guides. He wasn't sure how this film story was going to end.

By morning, they had sobered up, and apologetically led the way back to the surface, where they were met by the rancher and two sheriff's deputies and escorted off the property. Film gear in his hands, he was issued a warning from a deputy who happened to be an FSU Seminole fan and recognized him. The two cavers were cited for trespassing. My father was somewhat claustrophobic after the incident, but he had to ignore it during his research for *The Pits*.

Cedar Key. *(8:00)*

Status of the Florida Fishing industry, including early experiments with clam farming by the University of Florida.

Rosewood: (8:00)

A visit to one of Florida's first African-American towns, originally settled by former slaves and site of the infamous lynch mob that burned it down in 1923. Interviews with two survivors of that horrific event from Florida's violent history.

Hemingway House, Key West: (8:00)

Just six years after Hemingway's suicide in 1961 in Ketchum, Idaho, my father gave Tallahassee viewers a glimpse of the place where the Nobel Prize-winning author had spent his most productive writing years from 1928-1940.

My father eventually visited dozens of places in Florida, making a name for himself behind the camera, as well as on the playing field. He was obsessive, filming the more popular tourist destinations, as well as stories off the beaten path.

The Edison Winter Home, Ft. Myers: (10:00)

One of his favorite stories was a ten-minute feature he filmed in 1967, at Thomas Edison's winter home, *Seminole Lodge* in Fort Myers. There, he interviewed a man, Rodney Monroe, who while he was a young man, right after WW I, had been Thomas Edison's laboratory helper. It made such an impression on that young man, he remained after Edison's death in 1931, and was still working as a groundskeeper, more than thirty-five years later. My father wondered what that would be like. As the son of a groundskeeper himself, he envisioned himself playing on the Edison estate as a young boy in the early part of the 20th Century. *The Edison Winter Home* was one of my father's favorite documentaries that he produced as an FSU student. Little did he know he would return in 1985 for some follow-up questions for that same Edison grounds keeper. By then, Rodney Monroe would be in his early nineties.

What impact did all this travel and exposure to Florida's history and lifestyles have on him? With some notable exceptions, he was falling out of love with New City and its history, and that love was easily transferred to Florida, its history and environment. Would he continue his television work if he ever moved back to New City? He didn't know. But for every story he filmed, he also had to write the script, and writing the scripts on deadline was what taught him the discipline.

There was no time to wait for a muse, as John D. MacDonald had told him when he had the chance to interview the reclusive author on film.

"It's a job. You just write."

CHAPTER 37

The Pits
Pub. 1986

1920
88 YEARS BEFORE THE MURDER

My father continued to tell the story of *The Pits* in the voice of Ivan Heskestad.

Just as pornography had evolved in the early days of still photography, so it did in the early days of filmmaking.

At first it was just teaser films, showing various stages of nudity or long kisses and fondling. Each successive film became more daring, more provocative.

These films were originally shot and shown in brothels, first in Europe and then later in the United States.

As demand increased, more explicit films were made and shown. Filmmakers could earn lots of money for just a few hours' work, but there was always the threat of imprisonment.

And then, in the United States, there was the threat of Edison's oversight, which may have been far worse than prison.

World War I had several lasting impacts on filmmaking. First, filmmakers in the United States no longer had easy access to cameras and film stock made in Europe. Only Edison's cameras and Eastman's Kodak film were readily available. Second, there was little access to legitimate films made in Europe, with their longer, more engaging plots. Demand for lengthier, more complex American-made films grew even stronger. Edison resisted this demand at first.

During the war, few, if any, pornographic films were shipped to the United States from Europe. Later, American soldiers returned from Europe, where they had seen some of them. Demand became stronger. Some filmmakers tried to fill that growing audience demand, and the small pornographic film industry that had started in the United States before the war, began to expand.

When rumors spread that pornography was being filmed in Jacksonville, the local politicians became concerned.

During the World War I years, a lot of the film industry both in New York and Jacksonville had begun to look for a new home where the land was cheap and it was sunny all year round. By 1920, many had moved west, to Hollywood. Some packed up and headed out in the middle of the night. People disappeared without a trace and were never heard from again.

The Jacksonville film industry slowly faded into obscurity, with a few stubborn holdouts still trying to get by. The few filmmakers and film labs that hadn't already gone out of business shuttered and moved to follow the industry money trail.

Any remaining Jacksonville filmmakers still shooting films once again had to send their exposed negatives back to New York on the northbound train and wait a few days for it to be processed. Later, the negative and a work print would be shipped back down for editing. If you were filming something you didn't want anyone to know about, it was tough and risky to keep it a secret. If you were doing something in defiance of Edison's patent wars or in defiance of

Edison's public reputation, you could expect trouble.

Some filmmakers apparently shipped pornographic negatives mixed in with negatives from legitimate films to the labs, in hopes that they would not be discovered during the processing and printing process. Or some, perhaps, even worked with a paid accomplice in the laboratory. With the volume of work being pushed through the labs, sometimes they got lucky.

Sometimes they didn't. Such was the case with the filmmakers behind *Pioneer Ramble* and the footage from *The Delivery Boy.*

They got caught.

CHAPTER 38

TUESDAY, OCTOBER 28, 2008
5 DAYS AFTER THE MURDER

Later that day, not long after my father had departed, Chief Schoonmaker addressed six of his officers in the meeting room of the LHRVPP. "Okay. Anybody have anything new?"

The men's faces were blank.

The Chief held up a folder and spoke to Detective Mays. "We know Traphagen owns a couple of wooded lots up off Call Hollow Road, near Cheesecote Pond. Somewhat secluded. It would be a perfect place for a suspect to bury a body, hide stuff if he was going to."

He pointed to Mays. "Why don't you go up with Trask and take a look? Nose around. See what you can find."

The officers took the bait.

CHAPTER 39

TUESDAY, OCTOBER 28, 2008
5 DAYS AFTER THE MURDER

After leaving the Chief's office and the interrogation about his handgun, my father drove into downtown Manhattan. The question about a weapon had rattled him.

Driving across the George Washington Bridge, he looked south down the majestic Hudson. Was the tide going in or out? He was confused. Was dementia a symptom Doc should have warned him about more thoroughly? He would call and ask as soon as he finished the task at hand.

Driving down the Westside Highway, he exited to the surface streets and drove into midtown. He pulled up near a Manhattan N.Y.P.D. precinct house and parked his car. He had called ahead.

My father had met Captain William Tremer twenty years earlier. It was at a guest-speaking engagement my father, still a recognizable football hero, attended to benefit kids in the Police Athletic League. The two men had struck up a conversation, and a friendship began. My father started consulting with Captain Tremer in order to fact-check his procedural mystery novels. They had shared many a meal, and war stories, at the most expensive steak joints in Manhattan. Anyone listening might have concluded that Tremer wanted to be the football player my father had been, and my father wanted to be the investigator Tremer was. They formed a mutual admiration and respect society.

Now, inside the police station, Captain Tremer met my father in the lobby and walked him back through the busy precinct room to his small private office.

Abby reached into his briefcase and took out two plastic bags. One was a copy of the composite sketch of the dead woman. The other held the tree branch with the minute paint scraping he had found at the crime scene. He handed the items to the captain.

Looking at my father suspiciously, Tremer held up the plastic bag with the branch and paint scraping. In his other hand he held the computer printout of the illustration. "This *is* research for another book you're doing, Right? *Right?* Procedural information for another one of your mystery novels? *Right?*"

My father shrugged, transparently, as far as Tremer was concerned. "You're correct. I'm testing the limits of modern scientific evidence gathering and forensics. I want to make sure it reflects today's advanced crime scene technology. Can't fool the readers these days. Too many episodes of *C.S.I.* on TV. That's my story and I'm sticking to it."

Tremer smiled as he examined the two items. "I saw your story on the news the other night. You wanna talk about this?"

"Maybe the less you know, the better."

"What is it exactly that you want me to do?"

"Someone's got to be looking for a thirty-year-old woman somewhere. A missing person's report? Find out who she was. A name. A background. What does B.O.W. on her bracelet and shoulder tattoo stand for? Was it her name? A boyfriend's initials? It could lead to something."

"Let me see what I can do."

"How long on the paint sample?"

"A few days, maybe. That's a lot easier nowadays. Belong to someone you know? A test, perhaps?"

"You never know. And, Captain? The Chief doesn't have to know anything about this."

"Your Chief or mine?"

"Chief Schoonmaker."

"He probably already sent out the composite on the Internet. He's going to find out any leads on the woman the same time I do. *If* I do."

"Is there any way you can exclude his jurisdiction from your broadcast of the picture?"

"Sure."

"Same payment plan?"

"Dinner at The Palm and an acknowledgment in the next book?"

"Sounds good to me." Abby didn't like lying to the captain. He knew there wasn't going to be another book.

"Thanks, Captain."

"Our little secret, Abby."

Both men rose from their seats and shook hands. It was a done deal.

At the very moment my father was sitting in the office of the homicide investigator in Manhattan, a 2004 black Ford Explorer SUV pulled into my father's driveway off South Mountain Road and parked. There was silence in the empty woods. The driver got out and walked to the vehicle's hatchback, pulling a shovel and a knapsack from the trunk.

Inside my father's barn, afternoon sun slanted through the windows, lighting shafts of dust almost two centuries old. The driver propped up the shovel in the corner behind some ancient gardening tools my mother had used in her garden, turned, and left. There was fresh dirt drying on the shovel blade.

The driver then used a key and entered my father's house. A moment later, he stepped out onto the back patio and looked around at the silent woods surrounding him. Holding a thick, padded sheathlike device that he pulled from his knapsack, he took my father's handgun, loaded it with four bullets, inserted the gun into the muffler, aimed it toward the ground at his feet, and pulled the trigger four times. There were four soft *whumps*, as the .25-caliber bullets were fired. There was not an echo in the woods. He dug through the leaves and dirt and pulled the spent bullets from the dried grass and dirt in front of him and put them in four separate evidence bags. He put the muffling device into his knapsack and returned to the house with the handgun.

Back in his cottage later that evening, my father sat at his roll-top desk, thinking. He pulled out his handgun from the top drawer, examined it closely, and sniffed the barrel. It was unmistakable. It had been fired recently. He couldn't remember when he last fired it. Could the smell have lingered so long?

There was a knock on his front door. He replaced the gun in the drawer.

The Chief and Detective Mays stood on Abby's front porch along with Charlie Trask, the same officer who had moved the cars earlier that day to prevent spray from the pressure cleaner from getting on them. Behind them, a patrol car sat in the driveway.

The Chief walked past him and entered the foyer. Mays and Trask followed.

"Came by earlier and you weren't here."

Abby didn't know what to make of their intrusion. "Had to go into the city. Publishing stuff."

"That handgun you told me you had this morning? I need to see it."

Abby stared at his father-in-law for a moment, led them to the den, opened the drawer, and pulled out the pistol. He handed it to my grandfather.

"Why are you doing this?"

"We have to examine all of our options."

"Come on. I'm one of your options?"

"You know the drill. It's just a routine check to exclude you from the list. The process of elimination. You said you didn't have it with you."

"Even if I did, I wouldn't use my own gun to murder someone with it and then tell you about it. I wouldn't kill my own dog with it and then put it back in my drawer."

"How old was Huck, again?"

"Fifteen. Why?"

"Old for a dog. In good health?"

"You mean did I intentionally put him down?"

"I have to ask these questions. If I don't, someone else will."

"I told you. Huck ran toward the woman, and they shot him point-

blank, just like they shot her."

"When was the last time you fired this gun?"

"I don't know. Maybe a year ago. Target practicing."

"When was the last time you cleaned it?"

"I don't know. After the target practice, I guess."

"You don't seem sure."

"I can't remember. Maybe a year ago. Could be two years."

My grandfather passed the pistol to the Mays, who examined it and then sniffed the barrel.

He turned to his boss. "This gun has been fired recently."

My grandfather turned to my father. "Mind if we run this in?"

My father was growing more skeptical and annoyed by the second. "Don't you need a search warrant?"

"Not if you give us permission. It's just a matter of routine. If you have nothing to worry about . . ."

My father shrugged in annoyance.

Mays put the pistol in an evidence bag as the Chief spoke to his assistants. "Why don't you leave us alone for a few minutes, guys."

When the officers left, my grandfather started in. "Listen, Abby, I told you my being your father-in-law only travels so far. You gotta be straight with me on this. Absolutely straight."

"If I did it, why would I report it? Why not just bury the body where it was shot and be done with it, or throw it over the Tor? A sheer drop of several hundred feet to where no one has access? Another few weeks and it would have been covered in snow. Who would ever find it way out there?"

"A guilty conscience? Panic? Fear? You tell me, Ab."

My father was beginning to lose his temper. "But why hide the body and clean up the evidence and then come into town and tell you? It's not logical on the face of it."

"Calm down, Abby, lower your voice. No one is accusing you. I just have to cover the bases." He glanced out the window. "Logic's got nothing to do with it. You're not trying to convince a reader of some plot contrivance."

"I get it. I'm not mapping out a book, here." He turned abruptly to face my grandfather and changed the subject. "What have you heard about Little Abby? You haven't done anything to find him, have you?"

My grandfather suddenly grew furious over the accusation. He leaned into my father's face.

"Listen, you stupid twit, I'm trying to protect you here and I'm a little short on sympathy right now. It <u>was</u> *your* fault Sandra killed herself and *your* fault Little Abby ran away.

"You wanna know why? Sandra fell in love with her childhood sweetheart and wanted you to be that same, stand-up guy all your life. But you changed. You became a football star in college and in the pros. That was hard enough, but she probably would have survived it.

"But you had to keep going. You weren't content just to retire, step out of the limelight, and take it easy. It wasn't enough. You had to become a big-shot broadcaster and a best-selling writer, and on and on. Instead of all your time on the road just during the football season, you were on the road all year. Away from your wife. Away from your son.

"You wanted all the money and the fame and all the women that came with it. And you got it."

"I gave Sandra everything."

"Everything 'money could buy,' right? She wasn't interested in that. I watched her being heartbroken for over twenty-five years before she finally drank herself to death right before my eyes. All she wanted was that boy she fell in love with back when she was a little girl. She mourned for that young man."

"And Little Abby knew all that?"

"Does he look stupid to you? Of course he knew it. As soon as he was old enough, he saw what it was doing to her."

"Why didn't someone tell me?"

"It's tough to tell something to someone who's convinced he knows all the answers. You're not a good listener. We all told you, every day, in our own way. You just weren't interested enough to pay attention. You're pigheaded. No good deed goes unpunished."

"What?"

"I'm trying to help you and you're giving me a raft of shit. I deserve better than this."

My grandfather turned suddenly, angrily, and left.

It put my father on the defensive. It confused him. Was he losing it, as Doc had predicted?

CHAPTER 40

JUNE 2006
2 YEARS BEFORE THE MURDER

During my last two years of high school, my mother became very quiet. She had been retired for two years by that time, after thirty years of teaching. She spent her days listening to classical music, working in the garden and potting shed next to the barn, and reading Walt Whitman. She wanted my father to do a documentary about the poet, the time he spent in hospitals with wounded Civil War soldiers, but my father never got around to it.

During my elementary and middle school years my mother and I were very close, together every afternoon and evening doing something. We became buddies as we hiked the nearby trails, always with Huck, went swimming or ice-skating at Lake Lucille, fishing on the shores of Lake DeForest, and biking. We picked apples in Conklin's orchard, and grapes on the High Tor vineyards. What we were really doing was waiting. Waiting for my father to come home and pay some attention to us.

Some days she would drop me off with my grandfather and I would spend the afternoon with the Chief and his officers, doing whatever they were doing. But as I got older and started to spread my wings and hang out with some of the guys from school, she was spending more time alone. She spent her days and nights waiting for my father to get home from whatever he was doing—sportscasting, book tours, book signings, just about anything to keep him away from home. I rarely saw him.

At one point she was going to convert the two-hundred-year-old post-and-beam barn into a sixty-seat theater for plays and readings. Many of the Drama Club students she taught at Clarkstown High were looking for a place to have showcases. She had started writing one-act plays and was planning to have them performed several times a year, but her dream was never to be. I followed her around the barn with a broom one day, sweeping up debris and holding the end of a long tape measure as she measured out the stage size. She even had an architect friend draw up a few preliminary sketches, and I watched as they paced out the plans on the rough floorboards. Stage *there*, dressing rooms *here*, public restrooms *over there*. Pave the empty field for parking. But as time wore on and her drinking grew worse, her vision became a fanciful diversion, coping with her unhappiness. One day I found her sitting in a director's chair near what would have been the apron of the stage, a script folded open on her lap. Her eyes closed, she was mouthing the words of the actors, trying to envision it all; the blocking, the line readings. When she heard me, she opened her eyes and closed the script, taking my arm and leading me back to the kitchen. "Someday," is all she said with a wan smile. The play she held in her hands was *High Tor*, by Maxwell Anderson.

Within a month we got caught up in planning for my high school graduation. Two weeks after that, she was gone. She didn't leave a note, but I can only assume she got tired of waiting for my father. With me heading off to SUNY Albany in the fall, I wouldn't be around anymore to wait with her. She couldn't face her own empty nest.

CHAPTER 41

WEDNESDAY,
OCTOBER 29, 2008
6 DAYS AFTER THE MURDER

The next day, my father went in for a follow-up examination. That night, he and Doc and Ossie made plans to have dinner at Jack's Steak House in Stony Point. Jack had been another teammate from their Championship Season of 1963. The other guys were surprised when my father pulled up in his Range Rover with Nick sitting beside him. They exchanged glances, raised their eyebrows.

At first, when they sat down in the restaurant, my father was besieged with autograph seekers. With the recent TV news reports, it seemed my father's stock was up.

After the meal Nick excused himself and moved to the bar. Apparently the waiter wasn't bringing the drinks quickly enough. Jack, the proprietor, pulled up a chair to the dining table and joined the group. He leaned into my father. "Why are you still hanging out with the town drunk, Abby?"

My father was upset with the question. "Friendships are important to me, Jack. Nick and I go way back. You know, just like we all do."

On the way out the door, Abby vomited up his meal. Doc had told him that brain-related therapy caused the highest incidence of nausea. Abby understood now why it had been discontinued.

He didn't want people to think he was drunk. Worse, he certainly didn't want people to think he was throwing up because he'd recently been undergoing therapy treatments.

CHAPTER 42

FRIDAY MORNING,
OCTOBER 31, 2008
8 DAYS AFTER THE MURDER

Three days had passed since Chief Schoonmaker and his deputy showed up to question my father about his pistol. My father drove to Manhattan to meet with Captain Tremer a second time.

The Manhattan detective didn't waste any time when my father sat down in his office. "It's paint from a 2004 model Ford Explorer. But something tells me you already knew that, didn't you? You saw a black SUV that night in the woods, according to the TV news reports I saw. So what does it mean to you?"

My father looked over the report. "It proves I wasn't hallucinating. How difficult would it be to find out who has a black 2004 Ford Explorer in the North Rockland area?"

"It's one of the most common vehicles out there. I know six guys who own them. You probably know more in Rockland. We could probably narrow it down to a few hundred owners. Computer cross-referencing has come a long way. But it's allocating the manpower to follow up and then justifying it somehow to my captain."

My father nodded. He understood.

CHAPTER 43

EDISON ESTATE, FORT MYERS, FLORIDA 1985

My father wanted to find out more about Thomas Edison, his film works from that era, and his policy on pornography. He contacted the Edison Estate in Fort Myers, Florida, thinking back to the ten-minute television feature he had filmed there almost twenty years earlier, when he was at FSU. He knew the property. He told the management there about that piece he had filmed in the summer of 1967, and told them he wanted to do a follow-up. The Edison property managers, excited for the publicity, agreed to let my father come down with his crew.

Edison had moved to Fort Myers in 1885 to build his rubber laboratory and experiment with the bamboo plants he grew on the property that were being studied as a possible alternative filament for his electric lightbulbs.

During that 1967 FSU piece, my father had interviewed the man who worked the grounds. Rodney Monroe had actually worked side by side with Edison. And yes, the old caretaker was still alive, according to the management. As an honorary docent, he even led tours around the property still. My father figured that he would have to be in his early nineties. Perhaps he could shed some light on the information my father was seeking.

In *The Pits*, again, we hear the story unfold from the point of view of my father's fictitious protagonist, Professor Ivan Heskestad, as he interviewed the ancient gardener, who was assigned the fictitious name, Richard Langford.

The Pits:
Pub. 1986

FORT MYERS, FLORIDA

The Thomas Edison winter home, Seminole Lodge, was designed and built in modules in Maine in 1885, as a New England–style house. Some say it was the first prefabricated house in the country.

It was shipped to Fort Myers on four schooners.

They sailed from Fairfield down the coast, around the tip of Key West, and into the Gulf of Mexico. They finally reached their destination on the shores of the Caloosahatchee River.

The interview I had requested with the Fort Myers group was ostensibly to do a feature about Edison's home and the laboratory. Both still exist. Today, it looks almost as if Edison had walked out the door yesterday. The staff assumed that my feature piece would be used as a positive, enlightening travelogue to promote tourism. In an attempt to add human interest to the story, I told the staff I wanted to interview the oldest surviving Edison employee, and I was stunned when they told me about Richard Langford. I did not know of such a person, I claimed. A primary source witness was still living? How old must he be in 1985?"

"He's almost ninety years old, but he's still very spry. He loves giving special tours. He takes his mentorship with Mr. Edison very personally. Richard started working for Mr. Edison when he was in his late teens."

"Yes, I'd love to interview him."

In real life, my father flew from New York to Fort Myers with Robbie, the producer, who by that time had been working with him in New York for almost three years. They met up with MaryAnn and Cliff, his Florida crew from Tallahassee. It had been more than two years since they had first worked together on the Junior Wiley story.

Did the real caretaker remember being interviewed by my father twenty years earlier? If he did, he never let on, and my father didn't remind him.

In the novel, *The Pits*, my father played with the truth. He had Professor Heskestad operate his own documentary camera, with just a sound recordist he called Nita.

The Pits:
Pub. 1986

The ninety year-old man at the Edison house was Richard Langford, who had been a laboratory assistant for Edison during the World War I years.

Langford, still spry, just as the staff had described to me, walked us around the grounds. He was tall, thin, and self-assured in his khakis, blue Oxford shirt, and thirty-year-old necktie, as he led us across the estate.

According to Langford, it was during the Gilded Age that Edison started looking for a winter home and a

place to work. He traveled to Saint Augustine on Henry Flagler's railroad and took a horse and buggy to Jacksonville. There he took a train across the state to Cedar Key on Henry Plant's railroad, and then a small boat to nearby Sanibel Island. A realtor took him on another boat up the Caloosahatchee River to Fort Myers and showed him a thirteen-acre estate owned by a cattleman. Soon after he sketched out plans for a house, a laboratory, and an enormous garden containing thousands of plant specimens. Edison's family spent its winters boating, camping, and fishing for tarpon off the dock on the river. By the early 1900s his friend Henry Ford bought the adjoining property.

Edison's laboratory was a long, narrow clapboard structure with multi-paned windows. A number of mismatched laboratory tables and workbenches ran along the interior walls and a dozen tables ran down the center of the open room. Filled with glass beakers, machinery, tools, and gadgets from long ago, it was maintained in the same disarray as when Edison last walked out the door, in 1931.

My sound recordist, Nita, had fitted a wireless mic on Richard before we started walking, threading the lavalier mic inside his shirt to his necktie and hiding the transmitter on his beltline. Langford appeared excited. We had picked up a local grip, Ray, who followed with the tripod at the ready as I held the camera for the walk-and-talk interview. Richard spoke enthusiastically on the guided tour. Did we know there were six thousand plants in the botanical garden on the dozen-plus acres, including goldenrod for rubber production and a stand of bamboo? Did we know about Mr. Edison collecting beeswax? Richard laughed. Surely we knew about Edison's infamous naps?

I listened politely as I filmed and Nita recorded sound of Richard's tour. It was all the nice folksy stuff that served as a delaying tactic before I started asking the hard questions. I was waiting for an entrée, and Richard provided one without realizing it.

It happened while Richard led us through a thirty-feet-high stand of bamboo. I would later say I could feel the hair on the back of my neck prickle with the unexpected revelation from Langford, who revealed to us on camera, pointing as we walked, that bamboo was one of Edison's favorite plants. The sinewy strands could be carbonized and used as filaments in lightbulbs, which was one of the reasons for growing the bamboo. "He wanted a cheaper element than tungsten, one where he could control the production."

I nodded politely before Richard continued. "The tough stalks were also used by Mr. Edison to build the swimming pool here on the property in Fort Myers in the early 1900s."

I was confused. "Bamboo was used to build a swimming pool?" I asked. I was trying to picture that.

Richard responded, facing screen left while I continued rolling the camera, keeping him framed to camera right, filling up the rest of the frame with the bamboo stalks behind him. "The pool had been made out of Edison Portland cement, using a formula Edison perfected."

Richard laughed at this, and I asked him why he was laughing. He replied, "Ironic, really, using bamboo reinforcing rods in the Edison concrete instead of the usual iron rebar reinforcing rods."

"Why is that ironic?"

"Actually, it's ironic twice over. Edison cement and Edison bamboo instead of iron rebar. Mr. Edison had been in the iron-ore business. At one time he had his own iron-ore mines."

I restrained my double take. "Wait. What? Edison was involved in iron-ore mining? Where? When?"

"North Jersey, Bergen County, not too far from his West Orange laboratory. It extended just north over the New York State line."

"In Rockland County? That's where I grew up. That's where I teach."

Richard hesitated, suddenly turning wary. "Yes." He walked ahead, stepping quickly for a ninety-year-old, as if to change the subject.

I feigned indifference, but I knew we had taken a giant step forward in our discovery process. We had established a connection.

I glanced at Nita—who had been warned earlier of a possible ambush interview—to make sure she was still rolling sound. Nita nodded back.

The story Richard then told us made my heart race. I'm paraphrasing here:

It seems that by the 1880s America's most prolific inventor was thinking of more ways to make money. Edison and his partner, W.K.L. Dickson, were working on a device that would make it easy to separate iron ore from otherwise unusable, low-grade ores and rock, through the use of magnets. They called it the "magnetic iron ore separator."

Edison started buying up tracts of mountaintops in northern New Jersey, about forty miles north of his Menlo Park laboratory. These giant mine projects consumed huge amounts of money as experimentation plodded forward.

Through an intermediary, he eventually bought a huge tract of property near Cypress Pond, later known as part of Lake Tiorati, in what would become Harriman State Park in northern Rockland County.

The rocky, mountainous terrain is still filled with once-active digging sites, holes bored one hundred feet deep into the rock and later left abandoned, Richard told us.

The price of iron ore eventually dropped when vast deposits were found in the Mesabi Range up by the Great Lakes in Minnesota.

Eventually Edison became fed up with the proposition that had lost him so much money. He would later be quoted as saying "but we had a lot of fun spending it."

Not one to be outsmarted or to allow his misfortune to get him down, he used his rock grinding equipment to create the Edison Portland Cement Company, and the cement would later be used to build the original Yankee Stadium and his own Fort Myers swimming pool.

When the iron ore idea didn't pan out and it started to bore him, he began to expend most of his energies on inventions that would change the world of entertainment. Along with friends like Dickson and George Eastman, he would invent the movie industry.

The iron ore shafts were abandoned. The Hasenclever Mine was mostly forgotten by all except those miners who had worked there and the adventurous hikers and cavers who explored them.

I asked Richard, "Were you ever a part of the iron mine experiment?"

"No. it all happened before I was born . . ."

I proceeded cautiously, not wanting to spook him. "Have you ever seen the mines?" I asked, feigning mild curiosity.

Richard paused, looked around, and found a seat on a park bench in the middle of the bamboo grove. "Yes."

"Did you hear about the two bodies that were recently discovered there?"

After a moment of reflection, he started weeping.

I exchanged glances with Nita. It takes a lot to make a ninety-year-old man weep. They've usually seen it all. I regretted having made him cry, misleading him, gaining his trust, all for a story. I felt my own treachery. Richard was an old, gentle soul. The highlight of his life had occurred when he was twenty years old, working with a genius, his mentor and hero, and he had been living on those fond memories for the next seventy years as head groundskeeper and honorary docent. He had thrived on the excitement and vicarious fame, the ability for bragging rights, to be able to say, "I worked with the famous inventor, Thomas Alva Edison, and helped him in his laboratory."

I motioned to Ray, who spread the tripod legs, took the camera from my shoulder, and mounted it on the tripod head, leveling it up, all while Richard tried to regain his composure. I attempted to comfort him, put him at ease.

Finally he was ready. "I knew this would come back to haunt me. I didn't know it would take almost seventy years."

He continued sobbing quietly and began his story as I stood behind the camera and quickly reframed into a tighter shot. He looked into the lens.

"Okay, Richard. Don't look into the camera lens. Just talk to me over here. Have a conversation with me. Forget the camera is here."

Richard collected his thoughts, wiped his eyes before continuing. "Mr. Edison was a good man, you know, despite any stories you might have heard. It pains me to have to tell you this, but now I know I must." He struggled to compose himself.

"You see, there were two brothers, always troublemakers, really. Their names were Phil and Mo. They were first beaten and chased out of New York by

Mr. Edison's accomplices for violation of the patent laws. I'm assuming you know about those patent laws that Mr. Edison had Congress pass to protect his inventions. These men took refuge making films in Jacksonville and tried to patch things up with Mr. Edison. Sometimes they made legitimate films during the day, but at night, using the same sets and wardrobe, they started making other kinds of films that were shown in . . . houses of ill-repute."

I looked at Nita.

"I'm sorry to use such language in front of a lady," Richard said. "You may have to explain to her later what that outdated term refers to."

Nita didn't smile. She leaned forward and patted his shoulder in an attempt to comfort him, and Richard continued. "One day I was working with Mr. Edison in the laboratory here and we had some visitors. Four men. Two of them I recognized. They were Mr. Edison's employees, Mickey and Hank from up in Menlo Park, up north.

"Apparently they had traveled from New Jersey to Jacksonville to find these two independent filmmakers, Phil and Mo, who, like I say, were earning money making one-reelers. They were usually dramas or comedies, but they were also making another kind of film when only crew members they trusted were around nights and weekends. They had to be careful who knew about these films.

"Mr. Edison had become aware of what Phil and Mo were doing. Someone in the lab in New Jersey found some footage by accident after those two tried to sneak it through during the film processing of one of their period dramas. One was about Florida's pioneer days. Something about Seminole Indians wearing Shakespeare-era costumes while attacking some settlers. Mr. Edison had apparently become very angry when he found out about the other film. He sent Mickey and Hank, those heavies from New Jersey, to bring Phil and Mo to Fort Myers. Mr. Edison wanted to send them a strong message."

I interjected. "Did Edison want to sue them, or to convince them to stop making porno films? Or stop making them without him being paid royalties? Did he object to pornography?"

"I'm not sure why he wanted them to stop. If it could make him money, I'm not sure if he would have objected. He was a businessman. A good man. A moral man," Richard said. Was he trying to convince us or himself?.

Richard was silent as he reflected back more than sixty years. Then he continued. "Some of this I found out about later. Some I saw myself. One night in the winter of 1920 Phil and Mo were in Jacksonville filming another one of their pornographic films. It was on a set that a bunch of the guys used. They had used it earlier in the day during the filming of some costume drama set in France. King Louis-the-something-or-other. On the night in question, they had gone to a local brothel and hired a prostitute with the exotic name of Flamingo. She was slowly peeling down her black stockings in preparation for being ravished by some Simon Legree–type character, complete with a fake oily mustache.

"At that moment, Mickey and Hank, the two employees of Mr. Edison, arrived on the set wielding Louisville Sluggers.

"They later told me that at first the hooker was angry. She started to scream. 'I told you guys, no spectators without me getting extra.' Mickey and Hank started laughing at her.

"Of course Mickey and Hank hadn't been invited by Phil and Mo to gawk, or anything else. The brothers recognized Mickey and Hank immediately as Mr. Edison's enforcers. They had crossed paths more than once. They stopped cranking the camera and held up their hands.

"Mickey and Hank sent the hooker on her way with

a dollar tip. Sensing trouble, Simon Legree ran off without saying goodbye. Then Mickey and Hank carefully removed the film from the camera magazine, unspooling it onto the floor, exposing it to the light, ruining it.

"They looked around the set to see if there was any more film. Mo and Phil backpedaled around the room, looking for an opportunity to escape. Mickey and Hank did a thorough check of the room, the nearby worktable, and a film changing bag and couldn't find anything else. No other 'works in progress.'

"Finally Mickey spoke up." Richard started doing impressions of the players, jumping back and forth between the characters and his own narrative voice. He took on a terrible version of a New York accent. 'Didn't Mr. Edison warn you'se about this sort of thing?'

"Phil tried to take the offensive. 'What's with you'se guys? We got permission from the old man to use this equipment. We pay our royalties on time.'

"Mickey was dismissive. 'What have we told ya's about making this kind of film without our permission? Eh? How many times?'

"Phil pleaded, 'You can't blame a guy for trying to make an honest buck.'

" 'You call this junk honest? This is garbage.'

" 'What are you talking about? Other guys do it all the time.'

"Hank stepped forward with a blackjack and, with an uppercut motion, smashed Phil's testicles. Mo cowered in fear and knelt to the floor. Mickey tied their hands together, and knotted ropes were tied in their mouths. They were led to a car outside.

"Twenty minutes later, blindfolded, Phil and Mo huddled in fear as Mickey and Hank's automobile pulled into the Jacksonville railroad yard and made its way slowly toward Edison's private railroad car.

"The railroad car took them through the night from Jacksonville to a spur near Fort Myers. There they boarded Mr. Edison's battery-powered pleasure yacht on the Caloosahatchee River. They docked here out on the river."

Richard pointed toward the waterway. I glanced at Nita, a signal to be sure to remind me to film some B-roll of the dock and the battery-powered yacht that was still berthed there almost seventy years later.

"Mickey and Hank took Phil and Mo to where I was helping Mr. Edison working in his laboratory that day," Richard continued. "Their hands were untied and the knots taken from their mouths.

"There, in front of me, Mr. Edison interrogated the

men in a threatening way. I had never seen him talk to anyone like that. Apparently he had warned them twice before never to make dirty films on his equipment.

"Edison circled the men as he spoke, his hands behind his back. Like I say, I had never seen him like this. He seemed more disappointed than angry. But he kept it all inside as he spoke to them."

At this point Richard took on the imperious voice of Thomas Alva Edison. " 'And then I receive this by courier.' Mr. Edison said to Phil and Mo."

Richard imitated Edison's hand motions as he spoke. "He took a can of film from his roll-top desk and extended it to the porno producers. 'Here, you can take this with you on your trip. As a reminder.'

"Mr. Edison put the canister into Phil's jacket pocket.

"Mo asked Mr. Edison, 'What is that?'

" 'A little something that you tacked on the end of *Florida Ramble.* I think you called it *The Delivery Boy.* I guess you didn't think we would notice. Our lab guys caught it.'

"That's when Phil interjected. 'Wait a minute. What trip?'

"Mr. Edison turned to his two henchmen. 'Mickey, Hank, Why don't you show these gentlemen one of our other business enterprises?'

"Then Mr. Edison turned to me. 'Richard, I think it is time you see what the outside world has to offer. I'll tell your dear mother I sent you on an adventure to see my lab in West Orange, up in New Jersey. You've been after me to send you up to Menlo Park, haven't you?'

" 'Yes, sir,' I said. I had never been out of Fort Myers, except on Mr. Edison's boat on the river and the Gulf of Mexico. I was really excited about going.

"Mr. Edison put his arm around my shoulders. 'Well, why don't you accompany my two colleagues up north on a train while they show these two *filmmakers* here what mining for iron ore is all about? I think you'll enjoy the trip, and you'll get a chance to see my laboratories in Menlo Park and some of my properties up in the Ramapos.'

" 'Where, sir?' I said. I had never heard that term.

" 'The Ramapos. A mountain range north of New York City where we did some iron-ore mining thirty years ago, or so. You can get to see the pits.'

"Phil and Mo were blindfolded again. Their hands were tied behind their backs for the remainder of the trip.

"I tell you, I was so excited. I had never been on a train before, and now I was going to see the famous laboratory where Mr. Edison had accomplished so much."

Richard stopped for a brief moment, recollecting before continuing his story. "We took Phil and Mo by boat up the Caloosahatchee to the dock in Fort Myers where Mr. Edison's thugs had us wait, making sure no one was around to witness the transfer.

"One of the bad guys, Phil, said, 'What if I have to take a leak?'

"Hank laughed. 'Do it in your pants.'

We loaded the captives into Mr. Edison's private railroad car and we headed out to Jacksonville. In Jacksonville, we hooked onto a train out of Miami and headed north.

"We rode the rails through the night, and I watched the sun come up over South Carolina. Overnight, as they filled me in, I learned about Mickey and Hank's earlier encounter with Phil and Mo in Jacksonville, the night before.

"Another twenty or so hours later Edison's office-on- wheels pulled up to a loading platform in Menlo Park, New Jersey. The temperature was in the thirties. I had never been so cold.

"We had time to kill, waiting for nightfall. Mickey and Hank locked Phil and Mo in a room, and found me a winter coat to wear while they gave me a tour. I was thrilled to wander around the laboratories, fascinated by all that I beheld. Imagine, I was standing in a place where all this history had been created. It was sacred ground for me. I wanted to stay, but Mr. Edison's colleagues were anxious to move on.

"Late that night, after dark, the two troublemakers were again transferred into a waiting automobile, and we drove off into the night, north, up Route 17, through the top of New Jersey and into northwestern Rockland County, through Suffern. I've looked it up on a map, since."

As Richard continued his story, I realized that his destination had taken place not far from where I taught classes at Rockland Community College. I knew the area well from my own hiking and spelunking trips and from taking my cinematography classes out into the hills to witness the autumn colors. They are brilliant in that area. (The leaves, not the students).

"Another few miles, near Sloatsburg, on what would eventually be known as Arden Valley Road, we turned into a wooded area and drove a few miles to Cedar Pond. On the new maps it shows where the area was eventually preserved by the State of New York as Harriman State Park, and Cedar Pond would become known as Lake Tiorati.

"But on that late night in 1920, Cedar Pond was a dense woodland and swampy area, formerly owned by an associate of Mr. Edison's, purchased thirty years earlier during Edison's time of interest in low-grade iron-ore extraction."

Langford told us that Edison's crews would bore holes a hundred feet into the rock in search of the ore. In 1920, many of the boreholes still anchored iron ladders that disappeared into the blackness and led to natural caverns and tunnels of various shapes and sizes. The boreholes were perfect for the easy extraction of the low-grade ore. Perfect for holding two men, two men considered recalcitrant, considered a dangerous liability, considered a threat to Edison's reputation. Perfect to teach them a lesson.

Langford continued with his story. "I waited in the car with Phil and Mo while the two other men walked ahead. Moments later, when they returned, Mickey and Hank removed the blindfolds from their captives and led us all down a narrow path to a nearby borehole.

"They looked around. 'Where are we? I wanna talk to the old man again. We thought we had a special deal with him.'

"Mickey tried to take control of the situation. 'Shaddup!' Hank pulled his blackjack from his hip pocket and slapped it against his open palm in a warning gesture.

"Mickey put on a miner's cap and strapped a battery to his belt. From the trunk of the car he pulled a spool of rope woven into a ladder. We walked another twenty yards in near darkness. He tied the rope ladder off to a nearby tree and dropped the other end into the back hole. When I saw the open pit, I began to wonder what was going to happen. I became frightened.

"Using the rope ladder, Mickey climbed down into the circular abyss in front of us and disappeared into the blackness. A moment later he reappeared.

" 'I ain't going down there,' Phil said.

"Hank laughed. 'You'se both going down here, whether you like it or not. You can climb down hand-over-hand, like my friend Mickey just did, or take the *express route*.' He turned to Mickey and quickly flipped his wrist upside down, as if he were playing slapjack, and they both laughed. 'The boss just wants to offer you'se a little cooling-off period. You'll get used to it in a few hours. The old man just wants to spook ya's. Give you'se a chance to think about what you are doing. Maybe do a little convincing. Think about a career change.'

"With dawn just hours away, I watched as Edison's

men forced Phil and Mo into the pit. Mickey tossed me a miner's cap and I put it on, following the four men who descended before me. At the bottom, my heart raced as we walked through a labyrinth, a maze-like hike up and down over boulders. Finally, we belly-crawled our way through a low-ceilinged passage toward a cavern. I've never been so frightened. But I didn't want them to know that. They seemed to know where they were. Maybe been there before a time or two.

Once in the chamber, the brothers pleaded not to be left alone. To my shock, the thugs left them in the vault-like room, blindfolded, their hands tied loosely. They wanted the knots tight, but loose enough to guarantee their release from the ropes with some time-consuming effort. They spun the men around in circles, first one way, then the next, as they themselves moved in erratic circles around them. They lost their bearings, and, now disoriented, Phil and Mo's escape from the actual abyss would not be possible in the complete darkness."

Richard stopped speaking and stared into the distance for a moment. "I remember what Mickey said to them as we crawled out. 'We'll be back tomorrow with some food and water for ya's. This will make you start the correct thinking process.'

"Mickey and Hank giggled as we crawled our way out. At the top of the bore hole, they pulled up the rope ladder and threw it into the trunk of the car."

Richard leaned forward, lost in reflection.

I pulled out to a wide shot. Camera still rolling, I sat next to Richard, my arm on his shoulder. "That was where their bodies were found a few months back, Richard," I told him. "In the pocket of one of the men was the canned spool of 35mm film depicting a pornographic act. The scene slate said, *The Delivery Boy*. I've held it in my own hands. I've seen it with my own eyes."

Richard turned to me. "Imagine, they had filmed that just two weeks earlier. I watched Mr. Edison slip the canister into Phil's pocket that night in Fort Myers.

"The next morning, I was dropped off at the train depot in New Jersey for my trip back to Fort Myers. I was told by Mickey and Hank that they would return in a day or two and lead Phil and Mo out of the pits." Richard shook his head in disbelief over Mr. Edison's betrayal.

"I was reassured by Mickey, 'Don't worry, kid, we're just trying to scare them,' as my train pulled out of the station."

It wasn't until I interviewed Richard that day,

sixty-five years later, that he found out the two men had been left to die in the darkness. How long had it taken them? What had they gone through? Did they die of starvation? Despair? Heart failure?

Richard was growing weepy again. "I always feared that was the case. Mr. Edison acted as if nothing had ever happened. He asked me if I had enjoyed my trip to his lab and the Ramapos. 'It's so beautiful that time of year,' he told me.

"We never spoke of the incident again."

By the time Nita and I returned to Rockland County from Fort Myers, the pieces of the puzzle were rapidly falling into place. But I knew I had a lot of legwork to do. I still had classes to teach at RCC.

Searching the public land records in the basement of the Rockland County Courthouse, I discovered that in 1765, one Peter Hasenclever uncovered a deposit of iron ore in the area. He built an earthen dam at one end of the swampy local waters, merging Cedar Pond into Lake Tiorati. He dug boreholes and pits, built a furnace for smelting, and even started a horse-drawn, narrow-guage railroad out of the mountains to the main road, to transport the material out.

Maps later drawn under the orders of General George Washington indicate the precise locations of the mines.

Over the next century, the mines and the land they were on were sold to various owners. In 1875 they were sold to one A. Lawrence Edmands. My research showed Edmands was a business partner of one Thomas Alva Edison.

I was then able to track down who the dead brothers were that Richard had referred to as Phil and Mo. Cryptic identification paperwork found in their pockets suggested a last name. They matched the name of the director and cameraman of *Pioneer Ramble*, listed in the supporting documents of the Library of Congress Paper Print Collection.

A search through Jacksonville newspaper files uncovered articles written about the curious disappearance of the two men in the motion picture world in the spring of 1920. But by then the people of Jacksonville were over the glamour of the industry and were about to rid themselves of it owing to the nuisance factor. Disappearances by film people working on the fringes of the industry were commonplace. There was no follow-up search or investigation. Weren't all the filmmakers fleeing town anyway? Heading west to Hollywood? It had been a perfect time for a kidnapping.

CHAPTER 44

The Pits:
POST PUBLICATION, 1986
ABBY'S WOODS
22 YEARS BEFORE THE MURDER

My parents' life would undergo great change again when my father published *The Pits* in 1986, two years before I was born.

The fact of a discovery of two corpses in a suburb of Manhattan and their association with Thomas Edison, plus information about the burgeoning pornographic movie industry of 1920, made it a moderate bestseller for my father. It sold well, but not as well as his Patrick Thomas potboilers had. *The Pits* was optioned by an independent Hollywood producer, but the option was never exercised and the film was never made. Some say it was because of pressure from Edison's heirs.

That he had fictionalized it and put a Rockland Community College professor in the lead role intrigued a wide range of readers and lots of local readers, and my father's writing started receiving a lot more attention and critical acclaim.

I would be born two years later, in the summer of 1988.

With all the time my father spent doing research in the Harriman State Park foothills, he became enamored of its beauty. The option money from Hollywood enabled him to buy some property as close to his initial investigation of *The Pits* as possible, because it was so beautiful and remote-ish.

An isolated vacant ten-acre lot just across the street from the park's boundaries, it became his place of solace, taking breaks, camping out overnight both with my mother and alone, and then eventually with me, between his arduous stints producing and writing and traveling.

Over time, the land had come to mean a lot to my father. It would, coincidentally, be where they found the body of the young woman my father would be accused of killing.

CHAPTER 45

FRIDAY AFTERNOON, OCTOBER 31, 2008
8 DAYS AFTER THE MURDER

Later that day, when he arrived back from Tremer's office in Manhattan, Abby drove to the Chief's office.

In the parking lot he was directed to park behind the building again. The paint crew was working. He looked for Nick among the workers, but didn't see him.

When he entered the Chief's office, he was visibly upset. "You wanted to see me?"

"Sit down, Abby." The Chief handed my father a folder, saying, "You know what these are?"

"No idea."

"It's an autopsy report and a ballistics report."

"Autopsy?"

"On Huck."

"Go on."

"According to our findings, Huck was shot with this."

The Chief opened his drawer and pulled out a plastic evidence bag with my father's pistol in it.

"That's mine?"

The Chief stared at him.

My father continued. "That's not possible."

"Oh, really? Why not?"

"For one thing, that pistol was at home in my drawer when Huck was shot. I know because I didn't bring it with me into the woods." Even as he said it, he was beginning to have doubts. Could he be sure of anything anymore?

"You know, Abby. These ballistics tests are very accurate these days. This is not some voodoo science. This is the real thing." He pulled out two more plastic evidence bags, extending first one and then the other. "This is the bullet found in Huck. And this is the bullet from the forensic testing. They're a match."

"This is preposterous." Abby stood and paced the floor. "So what are you saying?"

"What I'm saying is you'd better get a good defense lawyer because you're about to get charged with filing a false police report, for starters. And if that woman's body is ever found, maybe we'll charge you with murder.

"We find that body, and it's all over for you. Son-in-law or not, I'll charge you and see that you're prosecuted to the full extent of the law.

"I'll do what I can for you. But you're likely gonna go down for this,

just like anybody else, if we find a body with ballistics evidence as strong as this."

My father shook his head. "Something's not right. This doesn't make any sense at all. Think about it."

"I haven't stopped thinking about it, Abby. And I don't like what I'm thinking. And neither would you."

"This is some kind of frame-up."

The Chief turned away from him. "Did I ever tell you about how I got started in this business?"

"Why do I get this feeling you're about to tell me?"

"I was a prison guard. At Sing Sing across the river. I spent a lot of time on death row before I came to the Clarkstown Police Department."

"Yeah, I know that. So?"

"And you know what surprised me more than anything?"

"What's that?"

"Out of the dozens of guys on death row, not one of them was guilty. *Not one.* They were all 'framed.' Every single one."

"That's very funny."

"I'm not laughing, Abby."

"Neither am I. The questions are who? and why?"

"*Who* and *why* what?"

"Who is trying to frame me, and why are they trying to frame me?"

"This isn't one of your mystery novels, Abby. This is the real thing. You'd better hope we don't find a body."

"Can I see him?"

"See who?"

"Huck."

"He's over in the morgue in Summit Park. You're gonna have to wait a few days."

"Why?"

"Because I said so, that's why."

CHAPTER 46

JANUARY 30, 1968
NFL DRAFT DAY
BELMONT PLAZA HOTEL, MANHATTAN
40 YEARS BEFORE THE MURDER

When my father was drafted by the New York Giants in the first round of the 1968 NFL draft season, they announced it at a press conference at the Belmont Plaza Hotel in New York City.

As Abby looked out over the crowd of flashing strobes, television news-camera lights, and reporters asking rapid-fire questions, he saw something he never expected to see. He was used to the press conference format from both sides of the events. He had been interviewed by reporters dozens of times while playing for the Seminoles, and in the off-season he had been behind the camera, asking questions of others.

But on that day, surrounded by a smiling group of draft rookies, he looked out into the crowd to see Nick, Ossie, and Doc sitting proudly in the back row. And next to his friends was his father, with an odd look on his face. Abby gave a nervous little wave.

It had been Doc's idea to pull some strings to get them into the press conference. Ossie suggested that they bring along Mr. Traphagen. Nick, at first excited about attending, resisted inviting him. "I don't know if Abby and his father are getting along," he told the two other friends.

"We're picking him up," Doc said. "They can work it out in the wash some other time."

"Yeah, this day calls for a celebration."

And so his father was there that day to share in the festivities. What was my father thinking when they announced his name? What was his own father thinking? Was he remembering stories of his ancestors and what the Traphagen family had been through to reach this point in history? What would *his father's father*, Horst Traphagen, have made of all of this? From street urchins to brickmakers to ice fishers to farmers to golf course groundskeepers. Maybe now the Traphagen name would finally mean something in the world.

After, in the press room, my father's father, Abram Traphagen I, hovered at the beer tap, dressed in his gardening uniform. He stood out like a fish out of water.

Abby approached him. His father had aged considerably in the four years since he had seen him. Was it the drinking, or something else? My father tried to contain his emotions as he extended his hand. "Thanks for coming, Dad."

"Your friends kidnapped me."

"Well, I can pay the ransom now."

"I hope they're paying you for all this." He gestured to the NFL executives assembled in the Belmont Plaza ballroom.

Doc laughed. "That's why they're called the pros, Mr. Traphagen."

"So now I get to see you play football on television?"

My father thought of all the games his father had never come to. "You can only watch the away games on television. The home games you can come and sit in the stadium and freeze like everyone else."

"We'll have to see about that." There was a silence before his father spoke again. "You can't stay at

Dellwood anymore, you know. They moved me into a smaller place after you left."

"Don't worry about it, Dad. I've got it all covered."

They all rode back to New City in Doc's car. The boys were joking it up, but there was little conversation between Abby and his father. They stopped for lunch at MacDonald's Steak House in New Jersey, just south of Pearl River and the New York State line. As the three friends grew more raucous, surrounded by animal trophies and Revolutionary War Pennsylvania long rifles hanging on the wall, there was a strange silence between the father and son at the dining table. The steaks were perfect.

Later, as they drove north on Route 304, Abby took in all the changes that had taken place since he had last been to New City. The new highway 304 bypass had followed the old, abandoned railroad bed. They turned left at Laurel Road and took Main Street into town. Where the old Schriever Apartments had once been was now a strip mall, complete with a movie theater. When they passed Third Street, the old private home that had once housed the State Troopers and then Whooley's Cab company was torn down and replaced with a Burger King. Abby looked up at the boardinghouse opposite St. Augustine's. Miss Singer's window was still there, but the front porch had been torn off and there was now a storefront in its place. Another few feet north and Abby looked toward the old Lombardi Construction Garage. In its place was the new, New City Library.

"What happened to the old library?" he asked.

"Too small. They're going to tear that building down to make more room for the firehouse. They moved the library here. There's talk of building a new one on the north side of town."

My father thought back to the cinder blocks his friends and he had painted their initials on. "Is the same librarian still there? Elsa Bartels?" He hadn't heard from her in two years. He had never sent her any of his writing.

They all looked to him and shrugged.

The library was not the only thing about New City that had changed in the four years while he was at FSU. Everything had changed. History had been erased.

They drove his father home to the country club to drop him off. Nick, when he came home for visits from college, was still staying at his own father's place at Dellwood. He would graduate later that spring and, with Coach D's help, start his new job as history teacher at Clarkstown Junior High in the fall of 1968.

As they passed through the Dellwood gates, Abby turned to his father. "I'll get you guys some tickets

and you can come down and watch the home games."
He was hoping it would lighten his father's mood.

"I'll see if I can get off work."

"They have you working Sundays now?"

"You never can tell."

"It was good seeing you, Dad. Maybe you can come down to my place in Manhattan some night when I move there after graduation and have dinner."

"We'll see."

They dropped off his father and Nick and then headed over to Ossie's house.

"I've still got your mom's suitcases," Abby said. "I can get them back to her."

Ossie laughed. "She's done without them for four years. Another four years won't hurt."

Doc drove Abby back down the Palisades and across the George Washington Bridge to his hotel. He would fly back to FSU the next day to finish his senior school year.

"Your father is very proud of you, Abby."

"Sure he is."

"Has a strange way of showing it. He was always quiet, though, right?"

"Quiet? I think *silent* might be a better word choice."

"When was the last time you spoke to him?"

"Sometime during my first freshman semester. He wrote to tell me not to come home during Christmas break because there was no longer a place to stay."

"You told me you had postseason practice, had to get ready for the Gator Bowl game after New Year's. You played against Oklahoma, right?"

"That's what I told everyone. I was a freshman. I could have gone home for a couple of days."

Doc thought about that in silence.

Then Abby continued. "It's just as well. I never wanted to come back here after I left town."

In front of the hotel Doc pulled up and shifted into park. They both looked out through the windshield, not at each other. "We're all proud of you, Ab. It's almost unbelievable, except to say that if anyone could have done it, it's you. There's just something about you. . ."

Yeah, my father thought. Something about me. "Thanks, Ezra."

Doc remained silent, and my father turned to him, saying, "What is it?"

"There's something you need to know," said Doc. "No one else knows. Not even my parents."

Abby wasn't quite sure what to think. "What is it, Ez?"

"I signed up for the army. I'm going to Vietnam."

"No."

"Yes. I didn't want to say anything to anyone, ruin your day. But I wanted you to know."

"You ruined my day."

"I mean the celebration with your father."

"I don't know what to say."

"I'll be okay. Going to the ninety-day wonder OCS. I'll be a second lieutenant in three months. Plus, with my premed, I'll probably be a medic of some kind."

"On the frontlines?"

"Someone has to do it."

They sat in silence, my father obviously upset, trying to cover it up.

"Hey, lighten up, Ab. I'll send you some postcards."

They both tried to laugh.

A cop knocked on Doc's window. "Move along. No standing."

My father and Doc shook hands. "Thanks for all you have done, Ezra."

"Maybe if I get leave, I can come to one of the games in the fall. Wouldn't that be cool? I'll bring your father and Coach."

"You guys have been brothers to me," my father said. "I'll never forget it."

They shook hands awkwardly, and my father stepped out of the car. He was convinced he would ever see his friend Ezra again.

CHAPTER 47

FRIDAY AFTERNOON,
OCTOBER 31, 2008
LOW TOR CRIME SCENE
8 DAYS AFTER THE MURDER

After that disturbing meeting with my grandfather about his handgun, my father went back to the crime scene for a third time since he left that morning in the rain. He walked through the area thoughtfully, retracing his steps and replaying the scene in his mind. He walked to where he had been crouching on the ground in his sleeping bag and had witnessed the murder of the woman and the shooting of Huck.

Something didn't feel right, but he could not place what it was. He began to doubt his own memory. Was he losing it? Was it the dementia Doc had warned him about? How much mental capacity would he lose? How soon? Would he be aware of it, or would it flow seamlessly into the unknown, leaving him no time or warning to reflect on the progress of the loss?

He sat on a boulder and put his head in his hands, hit with sudden excruciating pain in his skull. He doubled over, squeezing his head with the heels of his palms until the pain went away. He later told Doc that it felt like a combination of having his head crushed in a vise and being stabbed with needles at the same time. He recalled what Doc had told him about his symptoms. This was all part of it, but maybe not the worst part. He thought back to whether he noticed any loss of cognitive thinking. Memory? Could he sit down and start writing a new book today, or were those days over forever? Was this the dementia setting in? Could he, in fact, have hallucinated the entire murder scene, as my grandfather had suggested? But no. Hadn't he left the gun at home? Wasn't Huck dead? Hadn't there been the paint scraping?

He lay on the ground for two hours, reflecting on his past—growing up in New City, playing for Clarkstown High, Florida State, and the New York Giants. Hadn't he led a full life of nonstop excitement? Hadn't he had enough?

Finally, he felt capable of walking back to the Range Rover on The Hill. Every step he took was laced with caution. He went back to his cottage and stood in front of his bookshelf, running his fingertips along the spines of the books Miss Singer had given him. Then he looked at the multiple copies of the books he had written. He opened a few and tried to remember writing those passages, tried to remember doing the research, the endless revisions and corrections. It was all beginning to fade into the mists of an Asher Brown Durand painting.

CHAPTER 48

SATURDAY MORNING, NOVEMBER 1, 2008 9 DAYS AFTER THE MURDER DOC'S OFFICE

Early the next morning he went back for another checkup with Doc.

"How are you handling the treatment withdrawal?" Doc asked.

"You mean besides throwing up in front of people outside a restaurant? I'm sick as a dog and exhausted. Getting winded easier. Headaches. I was up on Low Tor yesterday, and it felt as if someone had driven a pick-ax into my skull. I'm not sure if there is memory loss or not. What would be normal for someone my age?"

Doc didn't like the way my father looked. But it wasn't related to the illness. It was his demons. "You went to Low Tor? You shouldn't be going anywhere alone. You're going to have to resign yourself to it, Abby. It's not going to get any better."

"Why prolong the agony? Why not just get it over with?"

"Everyone is different. It could be months."

"Or hours."

"Everyone who goes through this asks me that question. Is that what you were doing up there that night? Taking 'a long walk off a short pier'? Those are questions you have to answer for yourself, Abby. You could start out with, 'because there are people here who love you.' Is that enough? How about this one? 'You kill yourself and everyone who loves you dies at the same time.' "

"Okay. You can stop. I'm just feeling sorry for myself."

"You have a right to feel sorry for yourself. You're dying. Just try to live every day, old friend—"

"As if it's my last day on earth?"

There was silence between the men.

"There's something else that's bothering me," Abby said. "Something's just not right."

"What do you mean?"

"How long were you coroner?"

"Ten years. But that was years ago. I quit because

I couldn't stand the sight of dead bodies. I wanted to work with patients who were still living."

"Let me walk you through this and then tell me what you think."

"I feel like a character in one of your mysteries."

"You are a character in one of my mysteries."

"I don't know if I like the sound of that."

They both tried to smile, but they knew that Doc appearing in any new Abby Traphagen mystery novel was unlikely to happen by that point in the history of their friendship.

CHAPTER 49

MONDAY, 8:00 a.m.
NOVEMBER 3, 2008
11 DAYS AFTER THE MURDER

Early Monday morning, there was great excitement in the Lower Hudson River Valley Park Police. Radio transmissions were blaring. Officers were hustling out the door. Chief Schoonmaker, my grandfather, was putting on his ceremonial cap as he walked out. He turned to the dispatcher and handed her a note.

"Call all the media. We found the body. Here's the location. Tell them we'll have a press conference at noon-sharp, on-site."

CHAPTER 50

MONDAY, 10:00 a.m.
NOVEMBER 3, 2008
11 DAYS AFTER THE MURDER

On my father's remote wooded lot off Old Gate Hill Road, the scene was chaotic, as local police cars, the Rockland County sheriff's deputies and state troopers all converged on the wooded area south of Harriman Park.

Within moments of the Chief's arrival, the news media began to show up and started videotaping establishing shots of the scene. They were held back by yellow crime scene tape and the warnings of the officers.

My grandfather walked under the crime scene tape and disappeared down the path, out of view of the reporters, photographers, and videographers. A hundred yards through the woods, a few feet off a rugged trail, several forensics team members covered head-to-foot in hazard clothing surrounded a hole in the rocky soil taking pictures. Another knelt in the shallow grave brushing dirt off a decomposed body. Two uniformed officers from the Lower Hudson River Valley Park Police leaned on shovels. A third wielded a pickax.

My grandfather surveyed the site and then looked down into the shallow grave. "Okay. What have we got? This had better be good. The whole world is going to be watching this, and like I said on the phone, I want to make sure we get it right."

Detective Mays of the LHRVPP stepped forward. "We found evidence of a recent burial when we were searching the property. We dug a few feet down, and there she was."

As Chief Schoonmaker listened, he appeared skeptical. He looked around at the other officers. "There 'who' was?"

Detective Mays pointed to the ground, and as if reciting memorized lines, "A woman similar to the one Traphagen described, and who matches the composite our artist created for him. Body's decomposed, but it's a match for sure. Entry wound in the left temple, just like he described."

"What else? Bloody clothes? Bracelet? Tattoo?"

"No clothes at all. No bracelet. One thing, though."

"What's that?"

"Jailhouse tattoo. Initials on right shoulder: B.O.W.

"Like the tattoo he described that first day."

"Just like it. Badly decomposed, but you can still see it. We took pictures."

"This is his property? You're sure?"

"According to the county clerk. We're still trying to find the survey markers."

"And the search warrant? That's in order? We *cannot* afford to screw this up."

Mays pulled a folded paper from his inside jacket pocket. "The judge's ink is still wet."

"Okay. Let's get ready for the vultures. They're already here. We'll give them a few minutes to set up. Let's get something down on paper that I can read for now. And have your judge swear out a warrant for Traphagen's arrest."

"You're okay with that? I mean, he is. . ."

"I'm going to serve it myself. I want an autopsy and a ballistics report as soon as you can get one."

"Yes, sir."

CHAPTER 51

MONDAY NOON,
NOVEMBER 3, 2008
11 DAYS AFTER THE MURDER
ABBY'S REMOTE PROPERTY

A media circus swarmed around the entrance road to the burial site. Television remote trucks with their microwave masts towering thirty feet into the air were surrounded by technicians stringing out cables. Reporters stood holding microphones, taking notes, memorizing their lines.

A deputy was setting up a portable lectern that had a battery-powered mic, a speaker system, and an audio-breakout box to plug in radio and television microphones. Six television cameras formed a semicircle ten feet from the lectern, and still photographers vied for position. Newspaper reporters, including correspondents from the *Daily News*, the *New York Post*, and even *The New York Times* were there.

Chief Schoonmaker stepped to the lectern next to Detective Mays and grabbed the mic. "Okay, you guys rolling?" He paused, waiting for nods from the reporters and techies in front of him. "Here we go."

He read from a prepared statement. " 'The Lower Hudson River Valley Park Police, Homicide Division, in conjunction with the Rockland County sheriff's deputies and the New York State Police, acted on an anonymous tip phoned in last night. A search warrant was issued immediately, and at daybreak we began a search of the property we're now adjacent to. Within minutes of arriving, a freshly dug grave was discovered alongside an old timber road that you can just see about one hundred yards behind me through the trees. Upon digging, the remains of a body of a female was found, un-clothed. Caucasian, blond hair, blue eyes, late twenties. Cause of death appears to be a gunshot wound to the left temple. Initial estimates indicate that the woman died approximately ten to twelve days ago."

The Chief was interrupted by a reporter. "Are you saying this is the body of the woman who Abby Traphagen says he witnessed being murdered last Thursday morning?"

"We can't say with absolute certainty at this time, but it does appear to match the description he gave and the composite picture we derived from his description. There are other details which match that we are not revealing at this time."

"Is he a suspect in this case?"

"I can't tell you that for now. Right now, everyone is a suspect."

"Who owns this property?"

"We're trying to determine that even as we speak. Remember, we just got here a short time ago ourselves—"

The television reporter Ronnie Leeds interrupted him. "Our own GPS indicator was cross-referenced with the county clerk, and this appears to be Traphagen's property. Any comment on that?"

"Well, if you know that already, you can come to work with us."

There was suppressed laughter among the press corps. "We'll confirm ownership of the property at the appropriate time. That's it for now."

A cacophony of questions came at the Chief as he left the lectern. He ignored them all.

CHAPTER 52

MONDAY, 1:00 p.m.
NOVEMBER 3, 2008
MY FATHER'S HOUSE
11 DAYS AFTER THE MURDER

My father was in the kitchen, washing dishes, when the phone rang. He picked it up. "Yeah?"

"Abby, it's me, Ossie. Are you watching television?"

"No. I'm not sure I own a television. No, wait, there it is. Why?"

"Stop kidding. Turn on the news, and don't say anything to anyone until I get there."

"What are you talking about?"

"*Talk to no one.* Understand?"

Ossie hung up, and Abby picked up the remote control for the television and started channel surfing.

He could hear police sirens approaching down the

street. He looked out the window as the Chief's car and three cruisers pulled into his driveway. He left the room without seeing the remainder of the news report.

Abby stepped outside and down the steps of the porch. Chief Schoonmaker stepped toward him and pulled the search warrant and arrest warrants from his pocket. Officers approached him from two sides.

"Abby, I hate to do this, but I have no choice. I'm placing you under arrest for murder." He turned to Mays. "Go ahead and read him his rights."

Mays stepped forward with handcuffs. "You have the right to remain silent—"

The Miranda Card reading was interrupted with the arrival of the media caravan pulling into the driveway. My grandfather held up his hand in a halting gesture. They were suddenly surrounded by members of the press jostling for position.

By this time, my father's confusion had turned to anger. He pointed to the new arrivals. "Keep them off my property, Chief. I'll press charges for trespassing."

"Abby, they're the least of your worries at this point. I have that search warrant."

"For the pistol you took the other day?"

"That makes it official. And to search the property."

My father didn't, couldn't react.

My grandfather turned to the other officers. "Okay,

boys. Have a look."

He turned back to my father. "You're in deep shit, Abby. You got anything to say?"

"My 'deep shit' specialist is due to arrive at any moment. You can talk to him."

"You're gonna need a criminal lawyer, my friend. This ain't no book deal."

My father thought of the irony of that. "Could be before it's all over."

"What's that supposed to mean?"

"You're way out of line here, Chief."

"I'm not the one being arrested at the moment."

Before my father could answer, a uniformed deputy arrived from the tool barn wearing rubber gloves and carrying a shovel in his fingertips. "Check it out," the deputy said. "My guess is the dirt will match the burial site."

"What burial site? That's not my shovel. I don't even own a shovel. I want to dig something, I call my yardman. Hey, while you're at it, let these TV guys get some close-ups of your planted evidence. This is a joke."

"This is no joke. We found her, Abby. We found where you buried her."

My father became outraged. "Buried who?" He was quickly losing his temper. He shook his head in disbelief. "Well, isn't that convenient. You found the shovel in, what, forty-five seconds after you arrived? You've got to be kidding me. I could never get away with writing anything so contrived as this."

"Like I said, Abby. This isn't one of your mystery novels. This is for real."

Mays approached them. "Mr. Traphagen, I'll need your car keys for our search."

"Sure, let's see what we can find in there. This should be interesting. Let me guess. The girl's clothing and gloves with blood all over them. Just call me O.J. while you're at it."

Abby gave him the car keys and followed him to his car.

Mays and a crime scene investigator searched the car. In the wheel-well, next to the tire jack, they found a bloody nightgown and a bloody paper bag with the B.O. W. bracelet. There was, indeed, a set of bloody gloves.

"What is this, *Candid Camera*? This is a setup, right? Could it have been any easier for you? No one's going to believe this."

The Chief walked up behind him. "I think you're wrong about that, Abby."

He turned, indicating the press corps. "I think they're going to believe what they see here today. You were very careless. I would think someone like you, if you were going to do something like this, would have been more careful. But then maybe you're not as smart as the bad guys in your books."

My grandfather turned to the other officers. "Okay. Finish reading him his rights and put him in cuffs."

Mays walked to Abby, who submitted to being handcuffed as he was read his rights. Mays turned him to face the bank of media cameras. He and Trask slowly escorted Abby through the encroaching media pack toward a waiting police car.

My father shook his head at Mays's obvious delight in the humiliation. "Nice move, Mays. That's very smooth. Subtlety always was your strong suit."

Mays grabbed my father's shoulder and yanked him toward the patrol car.

CHAPTER 53

MONDAY 3:00 p.m.
NOVEMBER 3, 2008
11 DAYS AFTER THE MURDER
LHRVPP INTERROGATION ROOM

Later that day, Abby was seated, in an oversized jumpsuit, handcuffed, at an interrogation table with Ossie, opposite the Chief and Officer Mays.

My father was not the only one in disbelief. Ossie was pouring on the outrage. "Come on, Chief, let's get real about this. You can't be serious."

My grandfather turned to my father's attorney. "I couldn't be more serious, Ossie. We got a dead body in a freshly dug grave on his property. We have a murder weapon that so far, at least, matches the bullet that killed his own dog. That is, ballistics confirmation that the bullet that killed his dog matches that of a test from his pistol. We got bloody clothing and the girl's bracelet, as described by him that were found hidden in his car. That sounds like a case to me."

Ossie interjected, "Except for one important thing. No motivation. What's his motivation?"

The Chief leaned into Abby's face. "Motivation? No problem. Let's see. You wanted a little action. Your wife's been dead for two years. You bumped into a groupie at a book signing. You got too rough, who knows, maybe you couldn't get it up or something? So you got rougher, things went awry, and you needed to kill her. You got scared, figured her body would be found eventually. Decided you had to report it. You killed your own dog to throw us off the scent."

Abby and Ossie looked at each other over the absurd claims.

My father spoke. "That's right. So I buried the body on property that belongs to *me* and returned the shovel to *my* toolshed without cleaning off the dirt from *my* remote property, and then I hid her bloody clothes and bracelet and 'the O.J. Simpson-memorial-bloody-gloves' in *my* car to make it easier for you guys to find. Did I leave anything out yet?"

Ossie cautioned him. "Shut up, Abby."

"Then I put the alleged murder weapon back into *my* desk drawer without cleaning it or making any attempt to hide it or throwing it in the river before I told you about it, *myself*. Wow, I sure know how to cover my tracks. I'm surprised you ever found me." He tried to throw his hands up in disbelief, but was restrained by the handcuffs.

The Chief shook his head. "That's right, Abby. Save it for the jury."

Ossie cut him off. "Chief, this isn't going to a jury, and you know it. This is preposterous on the face of it. When's the bail hearing? I want my client out of here."

The Chief stood to leave. "Arraignment is tomorrow morning."

Abby started laughing. "Make sure you call the press and let them know the time and location. You don't want them to miss the perp-walk."

Ossie held out his hand to my father's wrist. "Shut up, Abby."

CHAPTER 54

MONDAY 4:00 p.m.
NOVEMBER 3, 2008
11 DAYS AFTER THE MURDER
DOWNTOWN NEW CITY

Late that afternoon, the Chief held a press conference on the front steps of the Rockland County Courthouse, outlining evidence against my father. The media types hovered around him, TV reporter Ronnie Leeds taking the lead.

The Chief tapped a few microphones and looked at the gathering. "You guys rolling? Those of you who were with us earlier know that we found the victim's body in a freshly dug grave on the suspect's property. Okay, we have acquired a weapon from the suspect and are waiting on ballistics to confirm that it's the same gun that shot the victim. We do know it is the same gun that shot his dog. We found bloody clothing and the victim's bracelet hidden in the suspect's car."

There was a barrage of questions, most of them going over information they had covered at the earlier press conference on the property site.

Across the street in The Elms tavern, Nick was seated at the bar, fairly drunk. The live news conference was being watched on television screens by everyone in the bar. Nick was trying to make sense of it all.

On screen, the news anchor continued. Over her shoulder was footage filmed earlier, during the arrest of my father at his cottage.

"Earlier today, the suspect, mystery writer and former pro football star Abby Traphagen, was led into the jail area of the Rockland County Courthouse, where he now awaits arraignment tomorrow morning."

News footage showed my father being led on a "perp walk" from the police car to the jail at the courthouse. He was mobbed by the media. It all seemed perfectly choreographed, almost as if the arresting officers had rehearsed it and filmed a few takes to get it right.

The anchor had more. "It was Traphagen himself who first reported witnessing the murder while camping out near High Tor eleven days ago. When police combed the area, no evidence of a crime could be found due to heavy rains. Now, with the discovery of a body, Chief Schoonmaker promises a full-scale investigation of the local hero."

At The Elms, Nick, in his drunken stupor, tried to piece it all together as he watched the television over the bar. What were they trying to do to his lifelong friend?

CHAPTER 55

TUESDAY MORNING,
NOVEMBER 4, 2008
12 DAYS AFTER THE MURDER

By Tuesday morning, my father had spent a night in jail, listening to a drunk scream in his face. It was a night filled with fear, not fear for his physical being, but rather fear for his emotional well-being, adding to his rapidly escalating self-doubt. Was what he was accused of indeed the work of a man losing his mental faculties? Why would he bury a body of a woman on his own property, thereby incriminating himself in an obvious way? None of it made sense, unless you were on the belief-system freight train, barreling uncontrolled down the mountainside.

My father appeared before the judge in the Rockland County Courthouse that morning. The courtroom was packed with many of the same people who had watched my father play football at Clarkstown, then at

Giants Stadium, and had later watched his television appearances and eventually attended his book signings. Most of them were in disbelief. Miss Bartels sat in the back row. She had arrived at 6 a.m. to get a seat.

Ossie approached the bench. "Your Honor, with all due respect, the evidence presented today is clearly, almost laughably, circumstantial. You have nothing to hold him on. He's a lifelong resident in this area. He's an international celebrity, recognized anywhere in the world. There is no flight risk, and I'll see to it that he remains in my custody."

The judge was prepared for this. "He'll have to surrender his passport."

"We understand, Your Honor. We have it with us today."

"The court sets the bond at one million dollars."

The courtroom erupted as Abby and Ossie shared a sigh of relief. They wouldn't be holding him without bail. He would be able to await trial without having to go back behind bars.

Later that day after arranging bail, Doc and Abby were sitting knee to knee, watching Ossie pace the floor of his office. He was trying to figure out a defense strategy, even though they both acknowledged that a criminal lawyer would have to be hired soon.

"I hope you realize how lucky you are," Ossie said.

"Lucky? I didn't do anything."

"You of all people should know that you don't have to do anything to be kept in jail for a very long time. Suppose the judge had decided to hold you without bail? And we're also lucky because I'm definitely not a criminal defense lawyer. I learned everything I used today from watching Perry Mason reruns. We're lucky the judge didn't laugh me out of his courtroom."

"Get me someone who does know about this stuff. Get me the best. I can afford it." My father stood impatiently in frustration. There was silence as Ossie and Doc eyed their friend. Finally, my father broke the silence. "Let's go get something to eat. I'm hungry."

At the steak house, Jack ushered the trio of Doc, Ossie, and my father into a back room for more privacy. As they walked through the crowded dining area into the more secluded side room, a hush fell over the restaurant.

Jack seated them and signaled a waiter as Ossie continued their earlier conversation.

"This is no laughing matter, Abby. This is very serious. So don't think it's going to be easy. Is there anything you want to share with your two oldest friends?"

"Yeah, the blackened tuna is always good here. We can share that."

"We're not laughing."

"Like what? You don't believe what the Chief said during your interrogation? A 'book-signing groupie?' Get real."

"I only believe what you say, Abby. But I don't know if you've told us everything. Doc also told me that symptoms of what you are suffering from might include disorientation, hallucinations. We need to figure out what's going on here."

"You mean did I really kill her? Are you serious? You know everything. Except what I don't know."

"What do you mean?"

"I've been back to that crime scene two or three times, and something about the whole thing bothers me. I can't put my finger on it. It's all just unbelievable—"

Doc broke in. "What's unbelievable is that you're still trying to figure out what happened all on your own. What's really unbelievable is that the Chief would do this to his own son-in-law, especially since he knows . . ." Doc caught himself and stopped, realizing he had just been caught betraying a confidence.

My father didn't miss it. "Since he knows what?"

Ossie chimed in. "Yeah. Since he knows what?"

My father persisted. "Knows *what*, Doc?"

Doc knew he had blown it. "Knows about . . . your health situation."

My father shot a glance at Ossie. "He knows? The Chief knows? How does he know? I asked you not to tell anyone, Doc."

Doc started tap-dancing. "I thought you meant anyone outside our immediate circle of friends. Your family. I thought you meant, keep it away from the public. What. . . What difference does it make? He's your father-in-law. He's family. We're all family. Aren't we?"

Abby thought back to a day more than fifty years earlier. The consequences of that day. He was silent as he started putting all the pieces together. He didn't want Doc to feel bad. Finally, he spoke. "I don't know. I don't know what difference it makes. If it even makes a difference. It's just different now. It gives everything a new perspective. I just didn't want anyone to know for a while. You know, the press and everything."

He sat there staring blankly at the menu. His mind raced. "Wait a minute. When did you tell him?"

Doc wasn't sure of the consequences. "When?"

"Yes, Doc, *when* did you tell him?"

"Last week. The day you first reported the murder.

Maybe the next day."

"What did you say? How did it come up?"

"He called me. He wanted to know if you had been under any stress lately. More than usual. He said you were acting really strange. Exhausted. Mentally and physically. So I told him. Why?"

"What was his reaction?"

"It was—I don't know. Shock at first. Then sorrow, I guess."

"Did he sound resigned to it?"

"Resigned?"

"Is there an echo in here? Yes, *resigned* to my death. Relieved? Did he accept it?"

"Actually, now that you mention it, he sounded more interested than concerned, I thought."

"What do you mean?"

"It was like I could hear him thinking out loud over the phone. He kept saying, 'Are you sure? Are you sure?' At first I thought he was in shock. In denial. Then I got the idea that he was thinking something else. Like he was planning the future. I didn't want to pry. I get to tell a lot of people that they are dying. I get to tell a lot of families that a loved one is dying. Sometimes it's like turning a switch. They go from grief one second to immediately thinking, how am I going to personally deal with this? How am I going to get my hands on their money? They change instantly from shock and sorrow to it being all about them. I just thought maybe it had something to do with Little Abby. Did you *not* want me to tell him? I thought telling family was okay."

My father was making a mental list of the possible ramifications. "No. That's okay. But now you owe me big time."

As the trio was leaving Jack's restaurant, they were surprised to see Nick get out of a cab and approach them. He was very drunk, sheepish, as he approached his old friends. "Abby, guys. How's it hangin' tonight?"

It was Nick's casual way of acknowledging that he hadn't been invited out to dinner with them.

My father turned to Doc and Ossie. "Thanks, guys. I'll catch up with you tomorrow. Ossie, I'll be in around ten in the morning to go over some stuff. I'm going to drive Nick home."

The two old friends said their goodbyes to Abby and Nick and headed across the parking lot. My father turned to Nick. "Hey, Nick. You doin' okay? You look a little under the weather. We were gonna invite you to join us here, but we couldn't find you. We figured you had a hot date or something. Let me give you a lift home?"

"Yeah, yeah. That would be great. I need to talk to you about something."

"Okay." My father tried to remember if he had any cash with him. They could always stop at an ATM machine, if necessary.

They walked across the parking lot. Nick struggled to continue, almost as if he were confused. "Something I saw on television."

"I probably can't help you out. I don't watch a lot of TV."

"No, no. On the news. I don't want you to help me out. I want to help you out."

"Fine. Let me drive you home."

Ossie called from across the parking lot. "Go straight home after you drop him off. You're under my supervision, now. Don't go wandering off. Think of it as house arrest without the ankle bracelet."

They pulled up to Nick's place, a rundown garage apartment up on North Main, near where Christie's Airport used to be. It was behind a farmhouse from the 1800s that had been a pig farm and horse-boarding stable for sixty years. Nick and my father got out of the car and headed down the driveway toward his place in the back. They walked through a yard filled with broken-down horse trailers and derelict tractors. Nick's apartment was above a garage attached to the horse stalls.

They climbed up a rickety staircase on the side of the garage, and Nick unlocked the door.

Inside was a low-ceilinged room filled with a raggedy-ass sofa and some bookshelves filled with history books. It was a scene straight out of a college dorm room.

My father sat on the edge of the sofa while Nick paced the floor, then pulled out two beers from the refrigerator. He handed one to my father.

"So what's up, Nick?"

"I was doing some thinking. I wanted to say thanks for standing up for me at the football practice the other day. I just want you to know I appreciate it. I need to learn to keep my mouth shut and let the coaches coach."

"That's what old friends are for, Nick. No problem. You fixed okay?"

"Now I'm embarrassed. As a matter of fact, I could use a couple of bucks until payday."

My father pulled two, one hundred-dollar bills from his wallet. "Here you go. It's not a loan. I owe you. Pay some rent. Use it to stay warm. It's going to be cold this winter. You need to think about laying off the booze a little. Your friends are starting to worry about you."

"I don't have many friends left, Abby. Just you and the guys down at the football field."

"What about Doc and Ossie?"

"Those guys left me behind a long time ago, and you know it."

"You just need to take it easy, Nick."

"I'm a little worried about you, man."

"Me? Worried about me? Why?"

"You're in some deep shit. I saw it on TV."

My father put on his James Cagney act. "Dey ain't got nuttin' on me."

Nick laughed and looked out the window. "Abby—"

"Is that what you meant about you had a question?"

"Yeah, man. Something I saw on the TV the other day. It made me think back to when I was on the painting crew."

"You mean with Ditto Wyngard? I saw him the other day."

"Yeah, he's an old drunk like me. In the club, A.A. When I'm sober, he hires me to work his paint crew."

"I remember you told me that."

"We were out pressure cleaning the Park Police department's building the other day. They're getting ready to paint it."

"What day was this?"

"The same day you were there visiting the Chief. I knew you were inside because I saw your Range Rover."

"Last Tuesday, a week ago?"

"Yeah, I think so. Some cop came out and moved the Chief's car and then your car so we wouldn't get blowback sprayed on them during the pressure cleaning. It gets all over the place, especially on windy days, like that one. It's hard to get off when it dries."

"I had actually looked for you earlier, but I didn't want to interrupt your business."

"I was moving the scaffolding around back by then, anyway. That's what Ditto has me do—no pressure cleaning, no painting. Hands aren't steady enough, you know what I mean? Just moving stuff around for him."

"So?"

"So the guy who moved your car around to the back of the building, you know, so we could begin pressure cleaning?"

My father closed his eyes, trying to remember the details of that day. He had started to look out the window, but my grandfather had told him to remain seated. "Yeah?"

"After he moved your Rover to the back of the

building, I saw him looking in your hatchback, moving stuff around. He put a bundle of stuff back by the tire. I didn't think much of it at the time. Figured he was doing you a favor, putting something away for you. But after all this stuff on TV, I started to thinking. Something don't look right. Thought I should mention it."

Abby's mind was racing. He reviewed the scene that day, all played back in fast motion, although this time from Nick's point-of-view.

"Are you gonna be okay, Ab?"

"Yeah, Nick. I'm gonna be fine. You gonna be okay?"

Nick held up the hundred-dollar bills. Yeah, I'm gonna be fine, too, thanks to you. I'm supposed to get paid from that painting job, soon. Ditto promised. He's been a little late the last few times. Business is up and down."

"Don't worry about it. No problem. Royalties are still coming in."

"Thanks for believing in me, Abby. That means a lot. And, hey, I found a couple of your paperbacks at the used bookstore a few weeks ago. I was looking for some Civil War stuff. I'm gonna re-read them real soon."

"Thanks, Nick. That means a lot to me."

"Maybe we can get together and discuss them someday. You know, like they do on those talk shows. Like we used to do in school."

"Like who used to do in school?"

"Very funny. I tried. I could just never think of anything to say, if it wasn't about the Civil War."

My father thought back to those high school days, more than forty years ago now. Where had the time gone? He thought back to how troubled, like himself, Nick had been during those years, and he remembered the cause of it. He thought of all the missed opportunities he had to be a closer friend to Nick, to be a better friend. Somehow, he felt, his friend had missed out on so much in life.

"That would be fun, Nick. You take care of yourself."

CHAPTER 56

TUESDAY NIGHT,
NOVEMBER 4, 2008
12 DAYS AFTER THE MURDER

My father pulled up to Doc's house. It was almost midnight. He walked to the front door and knocked. After a delay, the interior lights came on and Doc answered. My father's face showed concern, disbelief.

"Abby, you okay? You need to go to the hospital?"

"Sort of. We need to go to the morgue."

"That's not funny, Abby."

"I'm not joking. Get dressed and I'll explain on the way over there."

The county morgue was over in Summit Park, near Pomona, west of Route 45, on Sanitorium Road.

On the way over, Doc tried to make small talk. "Nick okay?"

"Yeah. He just needs to stop drinking."

"How's he getting along now that he's not

teaching?"

"Still working for Ditto. Pickup labor."

"Sounds like a tough life."

"Beats roofing."

Doc laughed. My father was referencing a summer job they all shared in high school. Although the pay was higher than any of the other guys in town were making, after two days in the heat, they all quit. All but Nick and my father, who were used to hard work. In later years, whenever one of them complained about their respective jobs, one of the guys would always ready to chime in, "Beats roofing."

The morgue was in a two-story wood frame hospital built on a 110-acre campus after World War I to care for victims of tuberculosis. Over the years it had served as a welfare home and office, a hospital, a nursing home, and a hospice. Doc was no stranger to the facility.

They pulled into the parking lot just off Sanitorium near Summit Park Road. Abby and Doc sat in Abby's car in the shadows of the hospital. Doc was very nervous. "I feel like I'm in one of your mysteries."

"Have you been talking to Ossie? You *are* in one of my mysteries."

"Very funny. I could lose my license to practice doing this."

"Good. You're old. You need to *retire*."

"Not with three alimony payments staring me in the faceevery month."

"Well, whose fault is that?"

"What is it you want me to do here tonight, exactly?"

"Go in through the main entrance of the hospital. Pretend you're making your rounds."

"At midnight?"

"You've never made your rounds at midnight?"

"Sure, plenty of times, but not lately."

"So, go in and let me in the side door. The morgue annex. Anyone going to be in there this time of night?"

"Not unless there's a rush autopsy. Should be empty. What are we doing?"

"This is where they keep murder victims in this county, right? I want to see the dead girl. And Huck. I want to see them."

"What are we looking for?"

"I don't know. Something. Anything."

Inside the hospital lobby, Doc walked past the night receptionist. He didn't know if it was a good thing or a bad thing that she recognized him.

"Hey, Doc. You're burning the midnight oil on a Tuesday night. I didn't think you had any patients here right now."

"Just left some paperwork behind when I was here the other day. I'm getting forgetful in my old age. I need it for first thing in the morning. If I can find it, I'll only be a minute."

"I'm going off shift in a few minutes. I'll tell Andy you're here, if he ever shows up. He's late, as usual."

"I probably won't even be here that long. But thanks."

Doc walked down the corridor to the morgue annex. At that time of night this part of the building was empty. He let himself in with his key. Inside, he stood in silence, listening, before he walked to the side exit door and let my father in.

"I'll go out the front way so the receptionist can see me leave," he said to Abby. "I'll meet you back here in a minute. Leave this door ajar."

"Okay, but hurry. I just want to take a few pictures and get out of here. I want you to take a look, too."

Doc left, returned to the main entrance, while Abby went to the drawers along the wall, moving quietly in the near darkness. He kept the light off, using only the light from a flashlight strapped to his head. He pulled open three empty drawers before he found the one with the murder victim. Her body was badly decomposed after almost two weeks. Clinically, and without emotion, he quickly took some pictures and then examined her head more closely. On her left temple, an entry wound. On her right temple, what appeared to be a ghastly, horrific exit wound. Although the wound had been cleaned by the coroner's staff, it was almost more than he could stomach. He closed the door silently.

He found Huck's body and did the same. Only this time he became emotional, stroking the dog's cold ears and scrunching his neck out of habit and affection.

He looked at the chest wound on Huck. Flipping him over, he found another disturbing exit wound. Something started to click in his brain. He took a few more flash pictures.

Doc appeared from the morgue's rear entrance door. He was nervous. "Don't know how much time we have. What have you got?"

My father was still examining Huck's body. "Look at this."

"What?" Doc pulled out a penlight and walked over to my father, shining the light in the dim room.

Abby indicated Huck's chest, then flipped the body over to show his back. "They shot him in his chest. Here's the exit wound.

"I would say that is correct."

"So, if there's an exit wound, how did they examine a bullet? I don't remember any word of anyone finding any bullets when we were there that morning—or mentioning it later. All I heard was that there was a match between my pistol's test bullet and what they 'found.' When did they find it?"

Doc turned and walked to the other drawers. "Let me take a look at the woman."

Abby slowly pulled out the drawer that contained the woman's cadaver. Doc pulled on latex gloves from a cardboard dispenser on the wall. "You say she was shot in her left temple?"

"Yes. The gun was flat up against her head."

Doc twisted the woman's head back and forth. "Take some close-ups, here . . . And here . . ." he said, indicating the entry and exit wounds.

"What are you seeing?" Abby asked.

Doc turned from Huck's body to the woman's body several times as he examined them closely in the small flashlight pools. "How many times did you say they shot her?"

"Just once. That's all it took."

"And Huck?"

"Once."

"You're absolutely certain?"

"I'm positive. Why?"

"Look at this. Huck's wounds provide the hypo-thesis, and her wounds seem to bear out my theory."

"What?"

"It appears that she might have been shot twice. Once at the crime scene, when you saw it happen. See these powder burns from the entry wound at close range?" He pointed to gray burns on the girl's temple and cheek. "Then look here. It appears that another bullet was fired into her with a smaller caliber gun, maybe a .25 caliber. Notice what looks like a second powder burn spray pattern. It's wider, indicating that she was shot from farther back, maybe two feet away. I don't think a .25-caliber bullet would leave such a large amount of damage that this gaping exit wound indicates. I would say a .38, based on my experience and research. I've seen lots of similar wounds, and I don't mean just in pictures. More than I want. Now let's go back and look at Huck."

Doc turned to Huck's body. "The same thing here. Shot twice. I'd bet on it. He rubbed Huck's chest, pushing the hair against the grain. "How far was he from the pistol when he was shot?"

"Eight, maybe ten feet."

"Too far away for powder burns like what we see here, unless there was a second bullet later. First, with a large caliber bullet, say, a .38. Out in the woods that night. Later, in the exact same spot on his chest, with a maybe a .25, but at very close range to match the entry wound exactly. See the powder burn patterns from the .25? Not from the .38."

Doc reached for a magnifying light that swiveled near the pullout drawer. "Now look here. The two bullet holes on her temple don't exactly coincide. Look at the edges. This is very sloppy, careless work. Like they're not expecting any real scrutiny. Probably done in a hurry. The original bullet caused severe blood trauma. The second shot, fired when she was already dead, maybe days later, doesn't exhibit the hemorrhaged tissues."

He pointed with his fingers to a minute difference. My father wasn't sure he even noticed it. "I think it confirms my hypothesis, but we'll need official confirmation from an expert. But the big thing that screws up their story? Both of these original gunshot wounds with the .38 on her and Huck were 'through-and-through.' The real spent slugs are probably still up on the crime scene, buried in the hillside. There's no way they could get a ballistics test on bullets they don't have. Do you recall seeing any of the crime scene guys making sweeps with a metal detector?"

"No. I had the feeling they weren't trying very hard to find anything once they tried to convince me I had imagined it all and dismissed me. It was like they were more concerned about getting out of the rain. But they confiscated my .25-caliber pistol for tests a few days later. The one they probably shot them with the second time."

"Right. They saved your .25s for the bogus ballistics match. After they shot her and Huck a second time. Right. Take some more photos and let's get out of here."

My father went in for extreme close-ups. Extreme close-ups that seemed to reinforce what Doc had hypothesized.

Would the photographic evidence even be admissible in a court? Even if admitted, would it be convincing enough to prove that the bodies had been tampered with postmortem? Would the case even go that far? Or would my father be dead by the time the case came to trial?

CHAPTER 57

WEDNESDAY MORNING, NOVEMBER 5, 2008 13 DAYS AFTER THE MURDER

The next morning, my father parked at the bottom of a slope that was adjacent to the police building. He worked his way up to the top but remained hidden behind a cluster of mountain laurel. Through binoculars, he verified the presence of security cameras on the corner of the building that might later corroborate Nick's story about the car tampering.

That's if the cameras were actually working and if he could get access to the tapes, and if they hadn't been erased.

Later that morning, my father pulled up along Demarest Avenue alongside Moore's Hardware Store. He had been going there with his own father since he was a kid, and he would have been helped by old Tom Moore, if Tom hadn't died the previous year at the age of almost one hundred. Now some pimply-faced kid who didn't recognize my father offered to help him. My father asked for shovels. The kid led him to a rack on the back wall. There was a selection of spades, hoes, cultivators, post-hole diggers, and Hickory Harvest shovels.

Within ten minutes my father left the store. On his cell phone was a photo of a yellow credit card receipt he had talked the kid into showing him, by paying him twenty bucks.

A half hour later my father was in his den off South Mountain Road examining the receipt he had received at the hardware store, trying to figure it all out, and then a phone call came that pushed him toward the solution.

A Manhattan number came up on the caller ID. It was Captain Tremer. My father picked up a legal pad and a pencil and picked up the phone. "Yeah?"

"You may want to come on down here and look at some stuff."

My father looked at the clock on the wall. "I'll be there in ninety minutes if the bridge traffic doesn't hold me up."

He arrived at Tremer's precinct in less than ninety minutes. The Captain spread some paperwork in front of him on the desk. "Okay, Abby, just to set the record straight, you didn't get any of this from me. You're a murder suspect now, right?"

"Thanks for reminding me."

"I've known you for too long, Abby. I just don't believe you would do anything like that. But I've got to cover my ass."

"Understood. What do you have?"

"First of all, I don't think anyone is going to respond to Hudson River Park Police about the composite drawing of the victim."

"Why not?"

"Because it never got sent out. At least not by them. We checked, and the only department that sent it out was ours, after you gave it to us. We sent it out to everyone but Orange and Rockland County jurisdictions, so none of the locals would know."

"What about the television stations?"

"You mean the local television stations covering a local murder that likely doesn't get broadcast anywhere else for more than one news cycle?"

"What are you saying?"

"As far as we can tell, it probably would have never been circulated beyond the local broadcasters, even if it had been sent out to the stations, which it was not. However, when we sent it out to law enforcement agencies around the country, like I say, except in Rockland and Orange counties, we got a response. It was from a lieutenant in down in Memphis who just came back from vacation. He would have responded sooner, but he's been out of town and didn't see it until this morning. He's an old-timer."

"Memphis? And?"

"An immediate positive ID. The guy is willing to talk to you as long as I'm in on the conference call."

"Why does he think we're calling?"

"A pending investigation. Which is what it is. Except—"

"Except I'm not a cop. I'm the suspect. I get it."

"Right. I told him you were an outside consultant on the case. That's it. He's been on a fishing trip the last couple of weeks. Doesn't know about your arrest, I don't think. But that could be subject to change at any minute. But there's more."

"What do you mean?"

"There's a big controversy around this woman. It's not a real popular subject down there. Very touchy. So go easy on this guy. Try to sound official. He'd just as soon hang up on you and forget the whole thing."

My father was confused, sitting there in silence, trying to piece it all together. Why had his own father-in-law not broadcast the composite picture as he had promised?

Tremer put his hands on the phone. "So, you want

me to call him?"

"Let's go." Abby picked up his reporter's notepad and pencil.

The captain picked up the phone and dialed.

A harried voice on the other end of the line answered. "Homicide. Lieutenant Holcombe. How can I help you?"

"Lieutenant Holcombe? Captain Tremer calling back from Yankee-land P.D. Can you talk? I have that consultant I told you about sitting here next to me. You're on speakerphone."

"Yeah, but I gotta make it quick. And totally off the record."

"Say hello to Abby Traphagen."

"The guy on TV who writes those books?"

My father rolled his eyes at Tremer. "Yeah."

"Hey, I read some of them a few years back. Not bad. At least they don't make cops look stupid."

"Thanks."

"So you're a consultant for them? I thought those guys up there knew everything there was to know about everything. At least that's what he told me."

Captain Tremer laughed and broke in. "You're watching too many cop shows on TV."

"You're probably right. Gotta figure out some way to solve all our cases, right? So anyway, I was telling

Captain Tremer, we never got any composite from the Lower Hudson office. The first time we got it was from the know–it–all guy sitting next to you. I was out fishing on a lake in Arkansas for a couple of weeks and didn't see any TV news. None of my guys mentioned anything about a composite. Too busy with local stuff. And I didn't see the photo until I got back from vacation this morning and it was brought to my attention by one of my longtime senior guys. He recognized her right away, showed it to me without bringing it up to the rest of the department."

My father looked to Tremer. Tremer knew what was coming. My father didn't.

"So you knew her? How? An open case? Missing persons?"

"You might say she was a local celebrity around here a while back, say fifteen years ago, and it's not likely I would forget her face. Although the composite wasn't real good at reminding me at first. She was older now, of course. Our younger guys would not have recognized her even if they had taken the time to look. There was just something familiar about the picture, and then I caught on."

"Caught on to what?"

"She became notorious a while back, like I say, maybe . . . fifteen years ago. She'd be about thirty now, right? When she was about fifteen, she started hanging out with cops on the beat here in Memphis. You know the kinda girl I'm talking about?"

My father looked at Tremer. "Not really."

"She would fall in love with men in blue. She looked and acted a lot older than fifteen. She would seduce our guys in their police cars while they were on duty, in uniform. Tallied them up one by one, like she was keeping score. Of course, our guys didn't tell anyone; no one ever said anything outside the ranks. No bragging rights there—young girl, and all. Pretty soon the number of guys involved with her reached critical mass. At first it was kind of an inside joke until some whistle-blower didn't see the humor. He had a fifteen year-old daughter of his own. Got a guilty conscience.

"But when the story broke and it was investigated by Internal Affairs, it was discovered that she had screwed over thirty-one of the cops on the police force, all while they were on duty, in uniform, and in their cruisers. You see a pattern here? Local news got a hold of it, and all hell broke loose."

My father and Tremer exchanged glances. My father raised his eyebrows.

Lieutenant Holcombe continued as my father took notes. "She kept a list. Badge numbers. Named names, dates, locations. Her testimony and her notes were all corroborated with their schedule sheets. Only one way she coulda known all that. She accuses one, two, three guys, maybe they could have gotten away with it. But she corroborated all their schedules. Like I say, dates, times, locations. Over thirty guys. There was a big I.A. investigation. A couple of guys came clean, turned state's evidence, testified against the rest. The guys were all fired, more than thirty of them. Lost their pensions. A lot of families broke up, and a lot of careers were destroyed. They were gonna charge them all with statutory rape, you know, her being just fifteen and all, until it was discovered that she had done the same thing out in the Northwest two years earlier, when she was thirteen, and our prosecutor decided . . . Well, I don't know what she decided. Maybe she felt she didn't have a strong case. This girl, apparently, was just obsessed over men in blue.

"Remember her name?"

"Everyone in Memphis knew her name for a while. Wallace, Beatrice Ophelia."

"B.O.W."

"Yeah. She had a homemade tattoo on her shoulder. Right shoulder, I think. The local press referred to her affectionately as Bow-Wow."

"What happened to her?"

"You mean after she screwed up the lives of over

thirty cops and their families?"

"Yeah."

"Don't get me wrong. She's fifteen years old at the time, or whatever. She's definitely the victim. Someone under age can't have 'consensual sex.' At least not in Tennessee. She didn't force these guys to have sex with her. They should have known better. She did one first, then another, then another over a period of about three months. No one said anything until the numbers got up there to twenty-five or so. It gets lonely out there on patrol. There's an old expression, 'a hard dick has no conscience.' "

"So I've heard."

"She disappeared into the Mississippi River mists one night soon thereafter. Some folks were convinced that she was murdered by some of Memphis's own cops. It wouldn't have surprised me."

There was a pause in the phone conversation. Silence from all three men.

Lieutenant Holcombe broke the silence. "So she's dead, eh?"

"Very dead."

"Again, I'm not surprised. Sounds like she finally might have screwed the wrong cop."

"What do you mean?"

"Some guys don't like anybody messing with their

pensions. Messing with family stability. Telling tales out of school. Not a smart thing to do."

"Yeah. Well, let me ask you something. Wait—"

My father took the phone off speaker and covered the headset while he spoke to the captain. "Can we ask him to embargo this information for forty-eight hours?"

Captain Tremer shook his head. Was he getting deeper into this than he wanted to? "We can try."

My father put the phone back on speaker. "Lieutenant. Would it be possible for you to sit on this for a few days?"

"I can sit on it for the rest of my life. The only request I ever got about this was from you guys, and consider this my official response: 'I'm done here.' I don't know anyone from, let's see here, Lower Hudson River Valley Park Police, and I don't care if she's dead. She helped ruin the lives of a bunch of my friends. I'm not saying they were without blame. They were committing a crime, and they knew it at the time. There but by the grace of God, go I, or whatever that expression is."

"Thanks, Lieutenant."

"No problem. Hey, Traphagen, can you put me in your next book? Wait, never mind. Forget I asked that." He laughed at his own joke. Abby did not.

They hung up. Abby and the captain exchanged looks. Abby was speechless.

Captain Tremer thought for a moment and then pushed his intercom button. "Sergeant, get me the Rockland County District Attorney's Office on the phone. I want to talk to D.A. Sansone, personally. Tell him it's me and tell him it's confidential."

The captain hung up and looked at Abby. My father sat there in silence trying to absorb it all. His look seemed to be saying a lot of things. But most of all it said, *Now what?*

CHAPTER 58

*WEDNESDAY,
NOVEMBER 5, 2008
13 DAYS AFTER THE MURDER*

During the nights after his arrest my father had nightmares. In each one, he relived the night of the crime. He saw a close-up of a .38-caliber handgun put to girl's head. A close-up of a .38 muzzle flash that dropped Huck.

Back at the crime scene on Low Tor for the fourth time, Abby swept the leafy, rocky terrain with a metal detector. In the area of where the girl's head was, he passed the device back and forth, back and forth while running the scenario in his head over and over, testing possible trajectories the bullet might have followed against a checklist and a diagram he had drawn the night before, which he kept in his shirt pocket. He swept the detector over and over again in ever-widening concentric circles. Had he considered a ricochet factor? It could be anywhere. Had it rolled, tumbled, washed away in the rain? Finally, although not exactly where he would have thought, the detector beeped, and he bent to scrape the dirt. Using a hand trowel, he dug up a slug flattened by the rock beneath it.

Finding Huck's bullet was more difficult. He again had to calculate the trajectory, reliving the murder of his beloved friend in his mind as he fought back the tears in his eyes. When my parents brought Huck home that first day, fifteen years earlier, who could ever have imagined what his final days would be like, how it all would end for him. He deserved better.

A needle in a haystack? That would have been a lot easier to find. But he found the bullet after four hours of trudging in tiny steps, even on his hands and knees. He finally found it by reenacting the shooting in his mind. He set up a camera tripod to the approximate height of the pistol that was fired. He tied a string around the tripod head and, pulling the string taught behind him, walked off several trajectory paths, remembering Huck's last-second lunge. One trajectory led to a fallen oak. There, he found the .38 slug. It all seemed so obvious in retrospect. Abby was exhausted, panting for breath. His arms were tired from sweeping. He would have to rest before he could attempt to walk down from Low Tor to his car on The Hill.

CHAPTER 59

WEDNESDAY EVENING, NOVEMBER 5, 2008 13 DAYS AFTER THE MURDER

For this next part of the story I can provide a lot more detail than in these past pages. Why, you might ask? Because I was present, hiding upstairs in my bedroom at the Chief's house, just as I had been when my father knocked on his door at five a.m. on the morning of the murder two weeks earlier. Now, as I stood at the door at the top of the stairs and listened, I was dizzy with confusion, trying to figure it all out. At times, it was difficult to keep up. I lacked the full context of what they were talking about.

After my last visit to my grandfather's, where I was on the morning of the murder, I had spent almost two weeks with my friends down in the Village, watching the TV news, reading newspaper accounts, hating my father, sad or glad that he was finally going to get what was coming to him. Hadn't he hurt enough people? I decided to return to my grandfather's house for a few days. I didn't bother to tell him I was stopping for a visit. Unbeknownst to my father, I had my own key and an open invitation. But on this night, neither my father nor my grandfather knew I was in the house.

A half-hour after sunset, my grandfather pulled into the driveway and started walking toward the front steps. At that very moment my father pulled up into the driveway, as if he had been waiting for the Chief's return, maybe even following him. My father was obviously trying to contain himself. Anger maybe?

My grandfather walked him up the steps to the front door, but before he unlocked it, he cautioned my father.

"You know it's highly irregular to have a murder suspect stop by for a social visit at the house of the chief investigator."

"I'm a highly irregular guy with a highly irregular story."

My grandfather admitted him into the house. "Coffee?"

"Sure."

My grandfather filled the Mr. Coffee urn from the tap. "So what's on your mind? I've got work to do."

"I've been thinking about this. Why was someone trying to frame me?"

"Like I said, there are no guilty men on death row. They were all framed."

My father paced the kitchen, preparing for the confrontation he knew was about to explode.

"Unless *you* already knew who the murderers were?"

My grandfather stopped putting coffee grounds into the paper filter and turned to my father with a questioning look. "What do you mean?"

"Unless *you knew* who the murderers were and you needed a scapegoat?"

"You're not making sense."

"I found out who the woman was."

"Oh, really? You mean the woman *you* murdered?"

"Her name was Beatrice Ophelia Wallace."

"Brilliant observation, Sherlock. I suppose you used your mystery writer's resources. The Internet and all that stuff. So what? You know the name of the woman you killed. No surprises here. How long did you know her?"

"The surprise is, I didn't murder her. You did."

"You say I killed her? I was home in bed. Remember when you knocked on my door at five a.m.?"

"So someone you know murdered her. Same

difference."

"Abby, are you okay? I mean you've been acting weird, or should I say *weirder*, lately."

"No one from your office ever sent out the composite picture of the woman so you could find out who she was."

The Chief appeared unnerved, even confused. "Really? I'll have to get back to you on that one. Someone dropped the ball. No big deal. We're really busy these days."

"What was the real reason for that little oversight? Because you already knew who she was."

"Oh, really? How so?"

"It seems she had an interesting background."

"Meaning what?"

He spoke as if it were a matter of routine, commonplace. "Meaning she had a weakness for men in uniform. A somewhat cunning weakness."

"You'll have to give me more, Abby. I'm not used to reading your mysteries. And my psychic powers are a little rusty from lack of use."

"I think that woman was shot by two of your own park police officers because she screwed them while they were on duty and they found out she was about to cause trouble. Maybe she screwed more than just those two.

"Maybe she screwed a lot of your guys. I think maybe they all conspired to kill her because she was going to blow the whistle. It would have ruined their lives, their marriages, their pensions. Just like she had done before, years ago in Memphis, and up in the Northwest before that. Of course your guys didn't know that about her when they accepted her advances in their patrol cars. So they take her out to Low Tor and kill her, thinking they'll have time to dump the body over the Tor, maybe. Finding the body would almost certainly be highly unlikely, at least until after the winter thaw. Even if it were to be found, they'd be called in to investigate it themselves and be able to cover it up.

"But Huck spooked them. They thought there might be a witness nearby. What they didn't count on was me being a witness."

The Chief was nonplussed.

My father continued. "Maybe everyone is involved. Maybe even the lab guy who fabricated autopsy reports and ballistics reports. Maybe even you."

"You have a very vivid imagination, Abby."

"You drove me home to take a shower and change clothes the other day."

"Yeah, what about it? You were drenched, shivering."

"It was a diversion. A way to keep me away for a little while. When I was in the shower, you called your men and told them there was a witness to their shooting and to get out to the crime scene and get rid of the evidence, *pronto*. Or maybe, when the killers saw Huck, they suspected there had been a witness. So they hid on The Hill near the chain and waited and they saw me leaving during the storm. Then they went back in, pulled out the body—

"And then you all realized, all of a sudden, that you needed a suspect for what I had told you I witnessed. A scapegoat. A readily convenient scapegoat."

The Chief was silent a long moment. "You're good, Abby. Very good. You should write mystery novels. Except you should market them as fantasies. Just like what you're describing here."

"And then, not too long after, Doc told you that I was dying. Bingo! You had your scapegoat."

What was my father talking about? Dying? Was he dying?

"You could blame it on someone who was going to be dead soon. End of investigation. A very convenient solution. And so you never sent out an APB with the girl's composite."

"That doesn't prove anything. Like I say, probably just an oversight by a busy staff member."

"Not very convincing. You guys aren't that busy. No. You didn't have to send it out. You really didn't care who she was. But you knew her intimately, shall we say. And you couldn't take the risk that anyone could identify her. She would just be another anonymous missing person who disappeared forever."

The Chief looked around the room. As usual, he was stoic, unperturbed, calculating, a trait I had always admired in him until this moment. He was deciding what to do. Upstairs, I was confused. Was my father implying that my grandfather was involved in all this?

"Someone has to take the rap for this, Abby, and that someone just might have to be you. You should have left this alone. Let us handle it. Delay it all until after you're gone. But now, you're correct. You're gonna have to take the fall.

"We got a clean search warrant. The gun, the panties, the bracelet, all your souvenirs were found in your car and the body buried in your woods with your shovel. You left some souvenirs inside her, too."

"What do you mean?"

"The woman was raped before she was killed. I'd be willing to bet that a sperm sample will match."

"No one's gonna believe that."

"We'll see."

"What, you got someone to fix the autopsy? He's

going to testify my semen was in her?"

"You're gonna take the fall for this, Abby. There aren't any other options left here."

"That's the only thing I don't understand. Why are you telling me this? Why do you think I would agree to do that? Not cry frame-up, and fight back?"

"Why? Very simple. Because if you agree, I'll let you see your son before you die."

My father suddenly became enraged. At that point I stepped back from the bedroom door. What did my grandfather mean by what he had just said? Was he planning to kill my father? My confusion grew. Was my father dying of natural causes?

"You know where he is? Where he's been all this time?"

"I know his cell phone number by heart. I talk to him every other day. I'm his grandpa. He trusts me."

"Why would you do that to me?"

"That's the way he wanted it. And that's the way I wanted it, too. For what you did to my daughter. You killed my daughter. She drank herself to death thanks to you."

The enormity of the situation began to sink in. "What if I refuse?"

"Things could get real ugly. I predict you might even get shot trying to escape."

"Let me get this straight. If I do confess to the crime so I can see my son one last time, you're figuring I'm thinking, what difference does it make to me, anyway? You'll have your murderer, and I'll be dead in thirty, sixty days. At least I got to see my son one last time. Right?"

"Good. You're paying attention. Who's to know or even care that you didn't really do it? She was a drifter."

"And if I don't play along?"

"You'll never see your son before you die. I'll make sure of it."

"So I give up my reputation for the chance to see my son one last time."

"No one really cares about your reputation, Abby. It's all just one big ego trip for you, isn't it?"

"You want my son to think I'm a murderer."

"He already knows you're a murderer. You killed his mother. Let's not quibble. We're just talking numbers now."

Upstairs, I leaned against the wall and sank to the floor. I couldn't put all the pieces together.

When my father didn't answer, my grandfather continued. "It's a simple formula, really. Confess or not confess, it all has the same ending. For you. What's a visit from him worth to you? Like Doc told me, you'll be dead in another month or so."

"Why are you doing this to me?"

"I don't have a choice. You know how many lives this would ruin if the truth came out? How many retirement plans? How many divorces? How many college educations would come to a halt?"

"Even you, too?"

There was a silence, and then, "An old man needs comfort from time to time. So what?"

"What if I say no?"

"You can do this the hard way or the easy way. Saying no? That would be the hard way. You need to decide right now, Abby. Right now. We've got enough evidence to convict you anyway. The gun, the clothes, the bracelet, the shovel, the body in the grave on your remote property with your DNA inside her."

"But you *planted* all of that. You're saying even the lab guy was in on this, too?"

"We might even be able to dig up a few witnesses who will say they saw you with the woman. I already told you. Every murderer who's ever been arrested cries 'frame-up!' You'll just be another pebble in a vast, rushing riverbed of whining, crybaby murderers.

"Look, let me spell it out for you. You got caught up in one of your own stories. Things got out of hand. You've been living life in the fast lane for the past forty years or more. Thought you knew all the tricks. Thought you could get away with it. Commit the perfect crime."

"People will ask, why did I tell you about it? Why would I not just dump her over the Tor and be done with it?"

"Who's going to ask that? No one cares. Even if they did, so what? Maybe you got cold feet. You were afraid someone might find her body. You might need a smoke screen to separate you from your crime. What difference does it make anyway?"

Then my father shifted gears. "And you had to find a scapegoat. A patsy."

"If you say so, Abby. You're the smart guy."

By this time the coffee was ready and my grandfather poured two mugs. My concentration was whiplashing around inside my head, trying to catch up, fill in the blanks.

As the Chief extended one of the mugs toward my father, my father was thinking back to events of fifty-two years earlier. My father dropped the bomb. "Like you did with Ruth Singer."

It was as if my father had gut-punched him. The Chief's attempt to recover from my father's accusation was feeble. "I'm lost. What do you mean? What does a murder from fifty years ago have to do with this?"

I was lost, as well. What did my father mean? Who was Ruth Singer? I tried to recall if I knew that name. I was obviously confused. Had I missed something? I didn't know what he was talking about. Was he accusing my grandfather of something else, as well?

"You framed that poor young veteran for Miss Singer's death. He was no more guilty of her death than I am of this one. But you needed some scapegoat to protect your bigshot Dellwood friends. A Mr. Wellman, if memory serves me, and his limo driver, Rudolph, or Rudy."

There was a long silence from my grandfather. I couldn't see his face from the top of the stairs, but I could imagine it. It was all starting to make sense to him now: my father's lifelong aloofness toward him. The confusion and questions I had been told about by my mother, caused when *Sweetclover* was first published.

I could hear him pull out a chair as he sat down at the table. "So you knew about it when you wrote that book?"

"Yes."

"Who told you? Did your worthless, drunken father make a deathbed confession about dumping her body?"

"My father? I guess you would know he would never

confess to anything like that. We didn't speak for years before his death. No, Nick and I were under the Dells bridge that afternoon, just hanging out, when they pushed her off."

"She fell."

"That was Wellman's story. And you believed him."

"He was a very important man. He did a lot for this town. A lot for me. So, if you knew what happened, why didn't you tell anyone?"

"I was there at Sweetclover, later that night with Nick, when our fathers and Rudy dumped her body into the creek. Our fathers were complicit. And so were you."

"I knew there was something you were holding back all these years."

"You mean the fact that my own father, and my wife's father, covered up a murder? Some poor, helpless young woman, unable to protect herself from the big shots?"

"She knew what she was getting into running around with that crowd."

My father and grandfather kept throwing out pieces of the puzzle, but I didn't know where the pieces fit. I couldn't see a final picture.

"She was just some innocent young teacher. She had her whole life and career in front of her. She might have even become a novelist. That's what she aspired to be."

"Like you? Is that all that counts with you?"

There was silence in the room as both men reflected on the damage created by the disappearance and death of Ruth Singer, how it ruined my father's childhood as he witnessed what evil his own father was capable of committing.

"Why did you cover it up? Were you paid off? Impressed by the wealth and influence of the Dellwood crowd? Pressured to cover it up by other sources at play? For political reasons? Threatened by losing your job? Were you looking for just a quick, easy fix? Did they threaten to kill you? What did they promise you? A job after retirement? Is that it? *This job*?"

"Yes, well, it was all a long time ago, Abby. No one cares anymore."

My father raised his voice. "*I care!* I saw what my father did. She was so sweet. So innocent."

Of course, not having read *Sweetclover* myself at that time, I was still trying to figure out what it all meant. Who was Ruth Singer and what did she mean to my father?

It was too late in the game for my father to dwell on it any further. He thought back to the countless times he had looked at his father and measured his hatred

473

for the man. At that moment I realized I didn't want to feel that way about my own father anymore. Could he have done what he was accused of doing to this Memphis woman? For the very first time since the news broke, I knew he could never have done it.

My father tried to regain the upper hand in the negotiating. "You're overlooking one very important consideration with your big scheme to frame me."

"What's that?"

"My son will think I'm a murderer for the rest of his life. He'll have to live with the same feelings I've had to. I don't want that to be his memory of me."

"I told you, he *already thinks* you're a murderer. And you know what? So do *I*. You murdered his mother. You killed my daughter with your drinking and philandering. Same as if you had shot her. The kid's smart enough to see that."

There was silence again. It was as if I could hear them thinking.

"So, Abby, what's it going to be? The easy way or the hard way?"

"Let me think about it."

Another three seconds passed before my grandfather spoke. "Time's up. What's your decision?"

"Where is he? When can I see him?"

"All in good time. Let's just let this unfold a little bit more. Surrender peacefully. Plead guilty at the trial. Let the press chew on it for a few more days. Get the public used to the idea that one of their football heroes turned writer is a murderer. What's this? A celebrity murderer? Old news. A guy who's going to be dead in a few months anyway. Like I say, who cares?"

"So I was right. That morning you drove me to my house to shower and change. You called your boys then, didn't you? They rushed out and cleaned up their mess before we got there, right?"

My grandfather waited before answering, reflecting back to that morning. "You were right. They suspected there might be a witness when they saw the dog. They waited and saw you run out of the path in the rain. They went back and cleaned up the mess after they saw you disappear, running down the hill."

He stirred his coffee in the silence as he thought about it all, then laughed at my father. "You should be a detective. Ever thought about that?"

"Yeah, I thought about it. A lot lately, as a matter of fact."

"What do you mean?"

"Like I have a witness who says he saw Mays and his boys putting stuff in my Range Rover the day he borrowed my keys."

There was a long silence as my grandfather thought back to that day. "A witness? Who?" Then he laughed in recognition. "Oh, you mean Nick on the paint crew? No one's going to believe the town drunk."

"No, but they might believe those security cameras on the building."

My grandfather was starting to become rattled. He laughed again to disguise his feelings. "We turned the cameras off that day, covered them with plastic bags to keep the spray off them."

My father continued. "There were minute paint chips from Mays's SUV. I found them on a tree branch in the woods. They'll match samples from his car.

"So? Sure he was there in his own vehicle. He was doing crime scene follow-up later that day. That's when the paint was scraped off his SUV. No one is going to believe you. You have no official chain of evidence anyway."

"How about autopsy photos of the girl and Huck?"

"What are you talking about?"

"You know, where you, or one of your men, shot her a second time, after she was dead, with my gun? And the same thing with Huck? So you would have some ballistics evidence. There were no slugs inside the girl or Huck when you brought them in. Through-and-through, I think they call it. I've seen both bodies, taken pictures. I found the missing .38 slugs on the murder site."

He pulled them out of his pocket to show my grandfather, who took them in his hand and scoffed. "Like I say, you have no official chain of evidence. They could be from anywhere."

"Anywhere, right. But you know they're the ones. And then there's the shovel. Sure, Sandra had a grape hoe and a spade for her small garden, but I never even owned a shovel. All my yard work is done by hired guys. They'll testify to that. They've been coming around for twenty years. So I went to Tom Moore's hardware store. Kid showed me shovels like it. He pulled out a receipt. A Hickory Harvest shovel was bought by Mays less than a week ago on his credit card, before it was *discovered* in my barn, covered in dirt from my vacant lot from when they buried her."

"I see you've done your homework. But then you always were the bookworm. It really makes no difference in the long run, because you're going to take the fall either way. The choice is yours. You want to see your son again or don't you? It doesn't make a difference to me. But knowing you, I think you're going to want to see him one last time."

There was silence from both. What were they

thinking? They were both thinking about my mother and me, but in different ways.

Finally, my father shook his head. He stood to leave. "Okay, I think I've heard enough."

The Chief put down his mug and slapped his thighs with his palms. "I know. Me, too. This is getting tiring. I've heard enough, too. So what's your decision? See your son before you die, or not. You don't want to go that other route. Get shot trying to escape? Either way, I've got a murder case to prosecute. You're going down."

There was a silent stare-down between the two. Then my grandfather stood, and even at that distance up the stairs I could hear him pull his service revolver from its leather holster. "How about this? You came to visit me tonight, try to talk things through. You thought I was being unreasonable and started to threaten me. When I wouldn't listen to you . . ." He must have aimed the service pistol at my father. "Well, you get the idea."

I was just about to step out of the bedroom, run down the stairs, and confront both my father and grandfather, stop the imminent shooting. But what my father said then stopped me. He stood and faced my grandfather. "Like I say, I've heard enough. And I think they've heard enough, too."

"They? They, who?"

When my father didn't answer right away, my grandfather caught on immediately. I could tell by the sound of what he said that he could not believe how stupid he had just been. He lowered his pistol, re-holstered it, and in defeat, sat heavily on a kitchen chair that he pulled from under the table. "You always were a smart-ass."

My father pulled out a microphone and a wireless transmitter from under his jacket. He spoke into the lavalier mic. "Hey, guys. Is this where I get to do my Tony Bennett impersonation?"

Outside, in a van on the Chief's street, a surveillance crew from the Rockland D.A.'s office was listening as they taped Abby's conversation with my grandfather. D.A. Enrique Sansone was there himself, along with the Clarkstown Police Department Chief and Captain Tremer from Manhattan.

My grandfather put both hands on the table. "You're going to hurt a lot of families this way."

"Maybe you should have thought about that sooner."

"Now you never get to see Little Abby. I'll make sure of it."

From the second-floor stairway near where I sat, I could hear footsteps rushing up the front porch. I waited, remained in hiding at the top of the stairs, frightened and confused, grasping the banister as I tried to sort out the questions racing in my mind.

I heard the snap of handcuffs. I heard my grandfather being read his rights.

When the house emptied, I waited another ten minutes to make sure everyone was gone. I was confused. Still angry at my father, but paralyzed with doubt and disbelief over my grandfather's role in placing me as a pawn in his murder cover-up.

I ran from my grandfather's house near Camp Jawonio to my father's cottage on South Mountain Road, retracing the steps I had taken that night when I fled two years earlier. I had to talk to my father. I was confused by it all. Who was Ruth Singer? So many blanks to fill in.

When I arrived almost an hour later, no one was there. I collapsed on the sofa in front of the cold fireplace and fell into a deep sleep.

My father didn't come home that night.

CHAPTER 60

THURSDAY,
NOVEMBER 6, 2008
14 DAYS AFTER THE MURDER

The next day, I woke up and hitchhiked into New City to The Elms, hoping to find Nick. He was sitting in the bar when I walked in. He looked up at me from his beer and started crying. He hadn't seen me since my mother's funeral. He knew what my return would do to my father. Then he called Ossie.

Ossie drove Nick and me to Good Samaritan Hospital in Suffern. The stress of the day before had weakened my father. In his hospital bed, my father looked tired and drained. When he saw me, his face transformed.

Someone once told me that you can't know what loving a child is like until you actually become a parent. I guess the look on his face at that moment is what they were talking about. I had never seen him share any emotion, but at that moment, like Nick, his face screwed up into silent sobbing. I had never seen him weak. I had only ever seen his public persona. Local hero. Now he looked drained, almost unrecognizable.

A wave of remorse filled my chest and throat. It had been two years since we'd seen each other.

CHAPTER 61

FRIDAY,
NOVEMBER 7, 2008
15 DAYS AFTER THE MURDER
ROCKLAND COUNTY COURTHOUSE

The following morning, my grandfather, Chief Walter Schoonmaker, and four of his officers from the Lower Hudson River Valley Park Police, Sergeant Victor Mays, Officer Charles Trask, and two others were charged with the first-degree murder of thirty-year-old Beatrice Ophelia Wallace and conspiracy to obstruct justice. Another cop, the guy who was going to fix the autopsy, made a plea deal: his testimony in exchange for a lighter sentence.

While my grandfather was in the county jail with the others that first week, held there without bail as he awaited the trial, he called in his attorney and signed over a quit-claim deed of his house and several acres of property adjacent to Camp Jawonio, to me, his sole heir.

Did this mean I was sentenced to a life in New City?

CHAPTER 62

THURSDAY,
NOVEMBER 13, 2008
21 DAYS AFTER THE MURDER

In the days that followed, I moved back into the house where I had grown up and spent every waking hour at my father's side. I watched him failing on a daily basis, and it broke my heart. He never took his eyes off me. I wanted to somehow recapture the two years I had spent away from him, but of course you can never do that. My thoughts were filled with deep regret.

We had long discussions about my mother, about Huck, and about how he felt he had been a terrible father. I didn't know how to answer him.

I made gourmet meals I had learned to cook down in the Village.

He filled me in on the details I have related on these pages.

We made plans to visit some sites he wanted me to

see.

CHAPTER 63

DECEMBER 2008,-MAY 1956
52 YEARS BEFORE THE MURDER

In 1988, five years after the death of my father's father, two years after the death of Nick's father, and not long after I was born, my father had published his novel *Sweetclover*.

Now, twenty years had passed since its publication.

Although originally touted as a work of fiction, many who had grown up in New City during that era immediately recognized the story as a thinly disguised version of what had happened to Miss Singer. It became obvious that the narrator and his young friend were, of course, young Abby and Nick, fictionalized into the characters of Caleb and Aron.

With all the speculation, my father and Nick never admitted that it was a true story, always insisting that it was a work of fiction, that my father had made up the whole thing, exploiting the facts of a real murder, blending them into his novelized version.

After reading the book, my grandfather Schoonmaker wasn't sure what my father was up to. Could he possibly know something about what really happened to Miss Singer? The cover-up? How was that possible? Was Abby messing with his father-in-law's head? Was he trying to make a point? Was he suggesting that my grandfather had been involved in a conspiracy of some kind? A convenient rush to judgement?

My father had hated my grandfather, the Chief, ever since the disappearance of Miss Singer in May 1956. My grandfather could sense the animosity, but he never figured it out. Perhaps it was typical son-in-law stuff. But after publication of *Sweetclover* their relationship was never the same, and the unspoken conflict between them intensified when my mother died.

Everyone in town supposed that Abby was a typical author who was inspired by a true story and added some speculation and imagination while writing another potboiler.

And so my father, world-famous football star, television celebrity, best-selling author, probably had a skeleton, maybe literally and figuratively, in his own closet. A skeleton, I came to realize, that might have tormented him all of his life, reminding him every day of the roots from which he had risen, from where he had tried so hard every day to escape; a skeleton that would drive him and deter him, would influence every decision he ever made, including marrying a woman he loved, who also happened to be the daughter of a man he had come to hate.

For many years my father hated his New City roots. He hated his father. He hated his own wife's father. He hated his own past. It drove him obsessively to succeed, just as it had the opposite effect on his friend Nick, who was driven to obsessive drinking. It made my father a difficult man, a man no one ever really understood, especially me. Did the guilt and shame he carried excuse his actions with me growing up or the way he treated my mother? Probably not, but perhaps they serve to mitigate what others might see as horrid behavior.

In 1956, investigators had never found Miss Singer's body for a reason. In 2008, when my father was close to death, he confirmed that *Sweetclover* was more a memoir than a work of fiction.

For the last twenty years of my father's life, he took the book royalties, paid the taxes, and passed the rest of it on to a secured account he shared with Nick, sending him monthly disbursements. Nick's ex-wives and their divorce attorneys knew nothing about the fund. It was my father's hope that it would ameliorate the pain he and Nick had suffered together over the years.

As far as the disappearance of the real Ruth Singer, few knew the real story until years later. Her parents had put up reward money, and the Chief had questioned everyone, or had he? The veteran was blamed. According to Chief Schoonmaker, he confessed. Anyway, the veteran, a dung cleaner, was dead, hanged himself in the jail cell. Case closed. Local police were at a loss to find the body. They searched the reservoir downstream behind where Clarkstown High School is and all points south, as Lake DeForest was filling up in those days. Bodies couldn't drift north against the current, could they? Some in town wondered whether Chief Schoonmaker knew who Ruth Singer's real killer was. Was he protecting someone? Hiding all the secrets?

I'll let one of my father's last pieces of writing explain. Upon first hearing about the possible terminal nature of his illness from Doc, my father wrote a short manuscript addendum to *Sweetclover.* It was in the envelope he had given Ossie, that day after his final diagnosis, to pass on to me. In the event that he and I had not reconciled prior to his death, he wanted me, and the world, to know what really happened to Ruth Singer.

According to my father's *Addendum to Sweetclover*, it was on a late-spring afternoon that the real events of Ruth Singer's disappearance occurred, facts that had originally inspired my father to write *Sweetclover*. Of course when my father published the novel in 1988, anyone but those who lived in New City would have thought it was just another work of fiction. Locals knew it was inspired by specific events. What they didn't know was that the novel intentionally pointed readers away from the real killer through misdirection, following Chief Schoonmaker's official investigation that framed an innocent man, instead of toward the truth.

During his last days, my father shared that manuscript with me, describing what really happened to Miss Singer, my father, and Nick on her last day.

It might be difficult for some to understand why my father hid the truth all those years. Others would eventually realize that the fictionalized version was meant to protect his own father and Nick's father while they were still alive. It also served to protect his wife's father, my grandfather, from criminal charges of obstruction of justice.

In this addendum manuscript, my father tells the

real story in his own voice, as he and his friend Nick Tremontana actually witnessed it. It could be considered a *confessional.*

Sweetclover

Addendum, by Abram Traphagen II, Autumn 2008. To be made public after my death.

Along the western edge of the original Zukor's Country Club there is a stone and wooden bridge across the upper Hackensack headwaters that runs through the Dells. Some old-timers call the north-flowing waterway Crumm's Creek.

For cars to get from what is now called North Little Tor Road to the west side of Zukor's Country Club and Golf Course in the 1920's, you had to cross over Crumm's Creek and the deep sandstone ravine known as the Dells, using this stone and wood bridge.

The bridge was originally conceived and built by production designers from Adolph Zukor's Paramount Pictures movie crews. Zukor wanted it to look like a faraway place, a fantasy retreat for his friends and visitors.

My father and my grandfather had caddied for

Zukor during the 1920s, starting each April, when the weather started to turn warm and the course was opened for members.

Nick Tremontana and I had continued that caddy tradition into the '50s after Bernie Nemeroff purchased the land in the late 1940s for what he called the Dellwood Country Club. He named it after the mysterious ravine. Nemeroff and his cronies would come into town from Manhattan on the weekends.

During weekday afternoons Nick and I would explore our domain, wading, fishing, trapping. We would hang out, listening to the music of the water cascading over the rocks, being young boys, while we searched for crayfish beneath the sandstone walls of the Dells, surrounded by Native American markings from the *Lenape* dating back hundreds of years. Those signs spoke to us of a faraway time.

That afternoon, under the stone bridge that led to Zukor's Country Club from Little Tor Road, Nick and I watched the trees cast long afternoon shadows across the rushing water. This stream eventually forms the Upper Hackensack headwaters that flow into Lake Lucille and eventually Lake DeForest. As the sun fell slowly, the springtime waters from recent heavy rains rushed and roared beneath our feet in celebration of the season.

Above us, a car approached from the west. It was a beige Lincoln Continental, we would soon discover. It stopped above, and a door opened. Voices were heard. One woman and one man at first. The woman was Miss Singer, our schoolteacher. I would have recognized her voice anywhere. What was she doing here? I wondered. We knew from our Peeping Tom days—exploits I would later describe in *Sweetclover*—that she spent weekend nights at the club. But this was a Friday afternoon, a school day.

The man's voice was unknown to me. "You can't just get out of the car here."

"I can, and I am getting out here."

Yes, it was Miss Singer, the real teacher I later fictionalized as Adina Perlman.

"What's the point?" the man asked.

"The point is I don't know what to do."

"I already told you what to do. I know a doctor who can fix this."

"I don't want to 'fix this.' I want to keep it. And don't call my baby an *it*."

"Keeping the baby is not an option."

"That's not your decision."

"Well, if like you say, I am the father, then of course I have a say in the matter. Blame it on that rat-shit guy you're seeing, if you're going to keep it."

"He's just a friend. You're trying to hide everything."

"I have a wife and a family, and you're not going to intrude on that."

"Well, you've started a second family with me, and you'll have to take that into consideration."

"Rudy, can you get out of the car and help me convince Miss Singer to get back into the car? We'll go to the clubhouse, have a drink, and straighten this all out."

We heard a second man's voice that I didn't recognize at first. "Yes, sir."

"Ruth, we have to talk about this. You're being unreasonable."

"I'm three months' pregnant with your child."

"You might have a tough time proving that. How do I know it's not the dung cleaner?"

"I don't have to prove it to anyone. You're the only one who could possibly be the father."

"Get in the car."

"No."

"Rudy, we need to convince Miss Singer she needs to get in the car."

"I'm not getting into the car."

"Ruth, Rudy here, is not someone you want to argue with or ignore. Trust me. It could become very unpleasant."

There was a scraping of shoes on the concrete bridge roadbed. The sound of a brief struggle?

"No, I'm not—"

Not three feet from where Nick and I sat crouching beneath the bridge, hiding in fear, speechless, Miss Singer's body slammed into the shallow stream with a splash and a thud. There was no scream, no sharp exhalation of breath during her thirty-foot fall. We were sprayed with stream water and a mist of blood as her head hit a protruding rock. The angle of the bridge piling arched her back, snapping it, and locked her between the concrete and the stream boulder.

Her eyes were still open, staring at us, but she was dead, her neck twisted at an odd angle. Blood seeped quickly from her nose and ears and became diluted in the racing stream.

We stared at her, and I was holding back the tears. We froze in horror, sure we were about to be discovered. Discovered as witnesses, but witnesses to what? What exactly had happened? Was she pushed off the bridge? Did she jump? Was it an accident as a result of her resistance?

We crouched back into the shadows of the bridge silently. Above us we heard voices again.

"What a stupid, stupid—"

"I didn't touch her, Mr. Wellman."

"No, of course not, Rudy. She made a motion. An evasive motion. We were only trying to convince her to get into the car so we could drive her to safety. She resisted, tried to dart away, lost her balance near the low wall."

"Yes, sir. That's what I thought, too."

"Rudy, drive me back to the club. Have Mr. Tremontana and Mr. Traphagen come back here with their pickup truck after dark. Tell them to bring flashlights and climb down there and get her body. We'll have to figure out what to do with it. This is all so unfortunate."

"Yes, sir. You might want to consider putting the body over by Sweetclover, under the Sweetclover Bridge."

"Sweetclover? Why is that, Rudy? That's in plain sight."

"It won't be after this weekend. The area is being flooded for the new reservoir. The road's been closed. Water's about a foot above normal now. They can wrap her in a tarp. Weigh her down with chains and a couple of concrete blocks from the maintenance building. Another few days, raining like it has been, and that entire area and all the nearby land will be underwater. It will be inaccessible with the reservoir covering it all up."

"I heard something about that new reservoir. No one will see her?"

"No. Roads have already been closed off from future traffic, forever."

"Why that's a brilliant idea, Rudy. Why don't you accompany the men tonight to make sure they do the job correctly?"

"Yes, sir."

"That's really a good idea. No swimming or diving in the new reservoir, I hear, so her body will never be found.

Unless. . . ."

"Unless what, sir?"

"Will they ever drain the reservoir?"'

"Those people down in Jersey are always thirsty sir, but not thirsty enough to drain this new reservoir."

"Rudy, you always did make me laugh. Here. Take this. And thank you."

"Oh, that's not necessary, sir."

"Rudy, it's my pleasure. Buy something nice for your wife."

"Thank you, sir."

"Before we head back to the clubhouse, why don't we make sure that the west entrance gate is locked. We don't want anyone driving by here and glancing down below."

Two doors slammed and the car backed up to where it had come in through the west gate off Little Tor Road.

Nick and I sat there in silence, looking at the body of Ruth Singer, both too frightened to move. I wept openly, shaking in fear at the sight of my beloved, who lay before me, her skull crushed, her neck snapped in a final indignity.

Minutes later we caught a glimpse of the beige limo as it drove east toward the clubhouse. Another gate to lock up behind them.

I sat there looking at her body. "Miss Singer?"

Nick shook his head in anger, disbelief, and fear. "She's dead."

"I can't believe this happened. We have to tell the police."

"Are you crazy? They'll try to blame it on us. Or our fathers"

"We didn't do anything. Our fathers didn't do anything."

"What difference does that make? You don't know anything. Those rich guys control everything."

"What are we going to do?" I asked.

"I don't know about you, but I'm going over to

Sweetclover. Wait for them. See if they really do what that guy Rudy said to do."

I reached over and closed Miss Singer's eyes. I couldn't bear to look into them any longer. Her face was still warm.

Nick watched me. "Come on. We've got to get over there and hide before they get there. We'll stop at Centenary Store and get something to eat to bring with us."

To be on the safe side, we pedaled our bikes out the west gate to Little Tor Road and then north to South Mountain Road. Centenary Store was just a few minutes farther east, and we stopped for cold drinks, some pretzels and Devil Dogs. Then we continued east to Ridge Road and south toward Sweetclover.

A hundred yards south of the Sweetclover Bridge, we hid our bikes in the underbrush and slowly crept forward.

The water level had come up faster than what Rudy, the limo driver, had described. Under the bridge, the water had risen two feet, with the spring rains causing a current faster than we had ever seen, just like we had noticed at the Zukor bridge.

Above, the bridge roadbed was empty, the access having been blocked off forever, in preparation for the rising reservoir waters. Our fathers would have to move barricades to drive their pickup truck to the bridge.

"How long do you think we'll have to wait?" I wondered aloud.

"It will be dark in another hour. No one can see down here anyway. Who knows?" Nick was angry.

The darker it became after sunset, the more emboldened we became, and we crawled forward in the dusk, closer to the bridge, remaining concealed behind bushes and underbrush. We huddled and ate our snacks. How would our fathers behave?

Nick turned to me. "I'll never forget the first time I ever saw her. She was just so beautiful."

I thought back to the day before school opened that year, meeting her for the first time on the porch of the boardinghouse, that day she stole my heart.

At Sweetclover Bridge, we waited another two hours before the rainstorm began, and we were pelted with the cold drops before the headlights from the pickup truck pierced through the darkness where we crouched, hiding. My father's truck stopped on the bridge, and the driver turned off the headlights.

By that time we had crawled through the darkness to within fifty feet of the concrete and rock structure.

Wearing black rain slickers, our fathers and Rudy

got out and looked around.

In the darkness and heavy rain we could see our fathers take the body out of the back of the pickup truck. It had been wrapped in a heavy canvas tarp and tied with a rope.

I was sure they were going to carry Miss Singer's body to the embankment and ease her down the slope. Instead, they unceremoniously dumped her over the low stone wall into the streambed below. In the few days since the dam had been closed at the south end of what would become the reservoir, not only had the water risen two feet, but the streambed had widened to four times its width as we had known it. Sweetclover valley was being filled in.

Then, as Rudy looked on, our fathers reached back into the bed of the pickup, pulled out a length of heavy chain and threw that over the side, followed by four cinder blocks.

We couldn't tell whether the chain and blocks had landed on Miss Singer's body. They didn't seem to care. I didn't even want to think about it. The rain drenched us, and we shivered, watching our fathers do their work.

We could hear Rudy giving orders. "Wrap her up good. We don't want her floating to the surface."

Our fathers walked down the embankment and

drew Miss Singer's body back from where it had drifted downstream a few feet. They encircled her canvas-wrapped body with the chain and secured it to the cinder blocks. They placed it all on the upstream side of the concrete-base piling of the bridge. The weight of the chains and concrete blocks, aided by the natural flow of the water, would pin Miss Singer's body to the concrete support.

In ten minutes, it was over. The truck drove south and they stopped to put the road barricades back in place. Where we crouched in the underbrush, just a few feet in front of us, were the remains of our Ruth Singer.

Has the fifty years of flowing water moved the body from its final resting place against the bridge abutment? Has the stream always flowed with urgency since the day we witnessed what happened? Or have droughts slowed the waters to a gentle caress? What could be left? What would we find if we looked?

I would later fictionalize Miss Singer as Adina Perlman in my novel, *Sweetclover*, twenty years ago. This is the real story of the real Miss Ruth Singer's disappearance.

As we pedaled our way out of there that night over fifty years ago, drenched and freezing from the spring rain, we turned to glance at our upper Hackensack River as it flowed south into what was rapidly becoming the new reservoir, Lake DeForest.

CHAPTER 64

LAKE DEFOREST RESERVOIR
NOVEMBER 28, 2008
FIVE WEEKS AFTER THE MURDER
52 YEARS AFTER MISS SINGER'S DEATH

Just before he died, my father also admitted to the Rockland County Sheriff's Office that *Sweetclover* was, indeed, based mostly on fact. He related to them his eyewitness account from fifty-two years earlier of what happened to Miss Singer that day. My father's statement to the sheriff was similar to the letter he had given to Ossie for me to read after his death. Nick's subsequent testimony corroborated what my father told them.

District Attorney Sansone decided not to proceed with any further charges. He considered charging my grandfather with "aiding and abetting" and "obstruction of justice" in the accidental death of Ruth Singer in 1956, but decided it would serve no further cause. Nevertheless, Chief Schoonmaker will likely die in Adirondack Correctional Facility, where he faces his eighties all by himself.

In the days leading up to Christmas week in 2008, a diving team from the crime scene unit pulled up to the edge of the Lake DeForest reservoir, and using an old map and GPS, corroborated the area of the Sweetclover Bridge overpass.

D.A. Sansone was there, accompanied by two deputies from the Sheriff's Office. Sansone was also a local boy, a few years behind my father and Nick at New City Grammar and Clarkstown High and had grown up listening to the speculation. One of the surviving Water Department crew members, who had been there in the days when the reservoir was being flooded, stood on the bank. He was eighty-five. I was there with my father, along with Nick, Ossie, and Doc.

The librarian, Elsa Bartels, and our retired principal, Murray Cannon, now both ninety years old, were invited to attend on that day. As word got out around town, these two would become minor celebrities, as everyone knew that they were the inspiration for Miss Van Houten and Jeff Cameron in the novel. Two of Miss Singer's teaching colleagues had retired in the area, and they showed up, watching tearfully, in disbelief, from the bank. Visions of the classroom in the old school on the hill flooded their memories along with the sound of generations of children's footsteps echoing on the hardwood hallway floors.

Two members of Clarkstown Police Department flanked my grandfather, who was in handcuffs. He didn't meet my eyes. He looked askance, hatred filling his face. It was D.A. Sansone who had "requested" that my grandfather be present, forcing him to face a crime to which he had been an accessory so many years earlier.

Wearing heavy wetsuits against the cold, the divers motored out to the area in a yellow rubber Zephyr, and within ten minutes found the skeletal remains of Ruth Singer, wrapped in chains and her canvas blanket, and anchored to cinder blocks. The mystery of the missing schoolteacher from New City Grammar School was finally laid to rest.

Many of the leading characters in *Sweetclover*, based on real people, were long dead. My father's father, Nick's father, the man later revealed to be the father of Miss Singer's unborn child, and Rudy, the limo driver, had all died years earlier, taking their secrets to the grave.

As for the two eyewitnesses to Miss Singer's death at the Zukor/Dells Bridge, just nine years old when it occurred, they were now in their early sixties, and they stood by, remembering that night as they shivered in the bushes near the Sweetclover Bridge.

One was trying to drink himself to death. One was dying of brain cancer.

After Miss Singer's remains were placed in the coroner's van, the small crowd gathered there looked at one another in silence. Sansone walked over and put his palm on my father's shoulder as a way of saying "thank you."

My grandfather exclaimed his innocence. "I'm telling you guys, I knew nothing about this. Nothing."

Nick turned and faced him directly. "You were complicit. They paid you off."

The deputy holding my grandfather's elbow had to pull him away as he screamed over his shoulder. "I kept your fathers out of jail. I kept them out. Remember that. You should be grateful."

As we walked away from the site, my father wrapped his arm around Nick's shoulders and mine, and as he had done on the day of Miss Singer's death, he wept openly. Was it for her or her memory? Was it that he knew his life was over and that his New City days were coming to an end? Was it for all the time lost between the two of us? I'll never know. Doc and Ossie followed us through the chain-link gate to where Ossie's big Cadillac SUV was parked.

Nick turned to my father. "We should have told everyone."

My father answered, never looking at him. "They were our fathers. We were frightened kids."

"Still," Nick said. "Think of how infinitely different our lives would have been, if we had told."

My father didn't answer. He was thinking about that, but an answer wouldn't come.

That night, Nick Tremontana stopped drinking for the first time in almost fifty years.

CHAPTER 65

THE FINAL DAYS

One of the final walks we took together was to High Tor. I didn't think it was a good idea, but I finally relented. I had to. My father wanted to climb Hi Tor with me for what we both knew would be the last time.

Instead of parking at The Hill on Little Tor Road and walking past the Low Tor crime scene to get there, we parked in the pull-off where Short Clove Road meets 9W, and we climbed the more arduous trail from the southeast. I wasn't sure he was going to make it, but he soldiered through. He was out of breath the entire trip but determined to make his final ascent. Nothing, he told me, would stop him. It had been unseasonably warm late in December and most of the snow had melted. On this day it was turning frigid again, making hiking conditions both arduous and dangerous.

From time to time he looked back over his shoulder to the trail behind us, as if waiting for Huck to catch up, as he had on so many climbs in the past. He looked once more, as if he couldn't help himself, convinced that if he looked, Huck would appear behind us. When he knew I caught him looking, I put my arm around his shoulder. "I know. I keep thinking he's following us, too."

"He is."

"He is."

"We'll never have a friend like that again."

"I know."

At the top of High Tor, he looked across the Hudson, almost expecting it to stop and reverse its flow, as it had for centuries before for the *Lenni Lenape*. But as with so many of our lives' experiences, our timing was off.

Then he turned and looked down at New City. "So many stories. So many stories."

He looked to me, as if imploring me to carry on his tradition of New City storytelling. "I spent so much of my boyhood up here, just gazing in all directions, taking it all in. I could never get enough."

It would take me a while before I understood and appreciated what he meant.

From the summit, we overlooked the valley to the south.

"You have some more reading to do. I gave it to Ossie to share with you."

"I know, Dad. You've both told me." Had he

forgotten already?

"I've made mistakes . . . "

"Dad. Don't. You don't have to."

We sat down and leaned against some boulders. He closed his eyes, lost in thought.

"I wish you could see all the things I have seen in my life. Gone to all the places I've been. I wish I could go back and visit all those places and take you with me this time. I could point out . . . So you could see."

They were words I would contemplate many times in the days ahead. I reached out and held his hand. "It's okay, Dad."

"No. No it's not. I never spent enough time with you."

"You had to work, Dad. I understand."

"I didn't have to work. We had plenty of money. I could have quit at any time. Quit TV. Quit writing. Spent more time with you. More time with your mother. I was selfish."

"No, Dad. You did what you wanted to do."

"Did I ever tell you about the first time I met your mother when she was all grown up? I mean, I knew her when she was a little girl. I mean that day I met her at Clarkstown High, the day I was a guest speaker and she was this teacher who approached me?"

I had heard the story from my mother's perspective,

but never from his.

"She came up to me and started talking, and I was swept off of my feet. She was telling me all these things about New City history, and I couldn't believe she knew so much about it. How could she? She asked if I could come speak to her group at the Rockland Historical Society. She was so smart and so beautiful. I wondered, who was she, and how did she know all this stuff? I had never met anyone like her, but of course I had known her as a kid. I just didn't recognize her. I hadn't seen her in almost fifteen years, and she had grown into a woman. I fell in love with her at that moment and decided I wanted to move back to New City just to be near her. And then when she told me her name, I was . . . astonished. I recognized her right away. I felt so foolish.

"I asked her to marry me on Low Tor. Did you know that?"

I did not. But now it all made sense.

He opened his eyes and looked at me. I could almost see the strength draining out of his body.

"I see her every time I look at your face. She's alive inside of you. Never forget that. All the best of her lives in you."

He touched my face, cupping my jaw in his palm. "I really loved your mother. I did stupid things. But I did love her. It's important that you know that."

A cold breeze was starting to pick up from the north, blustering its way down the Lower Hudson Valley, cooling the mild December day. In the wind we could hear the voices of the *Lenape* and Bryant whispering to us, competing for our attention. They wouldn't stop. He turned and faced New City. "So many stories,"

Doc wanted my father to check into the hospital when it became worse, but he refused, so they brought in hospice care those last few weeks, as he continued to waste away before my eyes.

"So much we've missed together" was all he kept saying over and over in those final days.

"I was never around to take care of you when you were a kid, and now here you are, taking care of me."

"Dad, that's not true. It's not true."

"Will you read my books?"

It was a plea he had been waiting to make, afraid to make, afraid of what my answer might be.

"Of course I will, Dad."

Two weeks later, a few days into the new year, just after dusk, a light dusting of snow fell outside the living room window of our house. The fire was blazing in the fireplace. I looked over at my father and he was smiling at me as he turned from the window. "Let's go outside, toss a ball around."

I looked for a football, but couldn't find one. I bundled him up and helped him walk down the front steps in the porch light. The light mounted on the barn illuminating the driveway backlit the powdery flakes as they fell silently. Behind him, through window, the glow of the fireplace cast an umber aura upon his shoulders. He reached down into the inch of snow that had fallen and grabbed a handful and rolled it into a golf ball-size snowball. He compressed it in his bare hands.

"You remember the day Mom took that picture with the four of us?

"Of course." I looked to the porch, Huck and my mother ready to join us. I could barely even make out their memories through the snowfall.

"I've never stopped thinking about that day. It may have been the highlight of my life. My *happiest* day."

He also looked around the yard, as if expecting my mother and Huck to come join us outside, take another photograph, start another snowball fight. He waited, perhaps still not ready to accept the reality of it all.

After a moment of silence he looked up at me and smiled. "I'm ready," he said, throwing the snowball at my chest in defeat. It hit my heart.

The next day my father was gone.

CHAPTER 66

NEW CITY
JANUARY 3, 2009

It made television news, of course, my father's death. One of the sports channels even did a highlights reel that lasted more than fifteen minutes and included 16mm footage Coach Morrow had given them from my father's Clarkstown days and the infamous Nyack game that November 9, 1963.

The memorial service was held at Germonds Church and the funeral took place right outside in the adjacent, centuries-old cemetery. There were more than four hundred people there, and they had to park their cars across Route 304 in the Albertus Magnus High School parking lot and walk up the hill.

It seemed as if almost everyone my father had ever known had shown up. Of course Ossie, Doc, and Nick were there. Nick had been sober for over a month. The librarian, Elsa Bartels and Murray Cannon, the principal from New City Grammar School were invited.

The RCC teacher who was the model for his fictional character, Ivan Heskestad, and the two cavers. Captain Tremer from Manhattan. More than twenty past team members of the New York Giants; teammates and coaches from the Clarkstown Rams of 1963.

I looked around at all the lives my father had touched.

His camera crew from Florida, Cliff and MaryAnn flew in. They had since married and were still living in Tallahassee. They brought two special guests with them, Junior Wiley and his wife, Rebecca. By that time they were forty-eight-year-old grandparents.

I introduced myself to Junior Wiley, and we had a brief conversation before the press corps that had shown up for my father's funeral caught on to who this black man and his white wife were. The older, seasoned reporters rushed to him and began firing questions, drawing on faded recollections of headlines past.

Robbie was there as well, the woman who had been my father's production assistant and who was now a producer my father had an ongoing affair with for more than five years. She avoided me at first, spending a long time talking to Junior. She would eventually come over and talk to me. She seemed distant, awkward. Was it remorse? She looked at me and said,

"I loved your father very much. It wasn't just a fling for me. He taught me so much. I hope you will come to understand what a wonderful man he was."

"I'm trying."

She smiled, "Someday you will." She turned and walked away.

Before Junior Wiley left, we exchanged e-mail addresses. Junior would later write to me.

> After the shrimper dropped us off in Texas, another fishing boat out of Mexico took us to the Yucatan. When we showed up, we didn't know anyone and no one knew who we were. We lived in complete anonymity for years. We both worked in the kitchen of a beachfront resort for the first ten years and then we got a promotion when an American company came in and took over. My wife was made head of housekeeping and I became a bartender. I eventually worked my way up to running the bar.
>
> My parents used to sneak down here to visit us twice a year. Now they have moved down here.
>
> One night a few years back, a guy who went to FSU came up to me and kept looking at me in a weird way. He recognized me and confronted me. I denied it, but he wouldn't let it go. I finally convinced him, begged him

really, not to tell anyone. He agreed, but for the past few years it's been difficult. Our little girl has grown up thinking we were Mexican. We never spoke English in the house. Just Spanish. Ever since then we've been waiting for the press to converge. I guess the guy from FSU kept his promise. It hasn't been an exciting life out of the limelight, but it's been a good life. I have no regrets.

"Rebecca's brother and father are dead, so we felt it was safe to show up for your dad's funeral. We wanted to pay our respects to your father. He kept his word. You should know that about your father. He kept his word and it saved our lives. That's not an exaggeration.

At the end of the ceremony Elsa Bartels came up to me and handed me an envelope.

"Your father wrote this when he came back to play football for the Giants. It was the first writing of his that he ever shared with me."

I started to open the thin envelope. "Not very long. Is it a short story?"'

"No, it's a poem. He wrote it after he had been away at school for four years. His heart had never healed after seeing what happened to Miss Singer, and later what had happened to his hometown. Keep it.

Someday maybe we'll talk about him." She turned and walked away before I could answer.

Later I would read his poem. I believe it to be his very first piece of writing about New City. Or perhaps the first piece that has survived.

It is indeed a poem, an ode to New City that he wrote upon returning to his boyhood town in 1968. He called it "The Woods."

The Woods
by
Abram Traphagen II

On my trip home I returned to the woods,
And to the field in the woods where the ballgames
were played.
I stood on the embedded rock that was
Used as the pitcher's mound and pitched a stone
<u>*toward*</u> *home.*
Thinking back, I lowered myself
To where my eyes were at ground level
And my chin rested on my palms, and my belly
Felt the wet, damp ground. The ground between bases
Is now weed-filled, where once many a boy's
Worn sneaker trampled down the line to the bare,
Hard-packed earth. The outfield is now covered

LOW TOR

With sumac and tiny, wild maples.

Many battles were fought and wars won in
These woods with wooden-stick rifles with their
Vocal-chord shots, and sights and triggers of bent nails.
Weapons were hid in the hollow tree trunks,
To be used, then captured by the enemy,
And hidden again in a pile of leaves.

Many a sea-battle was fought here on the
Swampy lake on inner-tube rafts that sent us
Home with wet, muddy clothes. The stream with its
Frogs and crayfish always lured our shoes into
Getting wet, and I remember still the
Squishing sound they made, walking home at dusk.

The heavy, strong, wild grape-vines provided
Each young Tarzan a brief flight into space.
Always the bigger boys would swing first,
To test the vines' strength for the younger brothers.

In summer the woods provided us with
A dark place to hide- -green tented. In the
Autumn, a reddish glow was cast by the
Leaves, that later, having dropped to the ground,
Made a crispy path on which to walk.

In winter, the trees' black skeletons
Would stand out against a white landscape
and gray sky.

Most woods, once used, are passed on to younger
Brothers of another generation.
So they might stage new battles and conquests,
And get their shoes wet. But not this one.
This one will be forever mine, for
Someday soon, a bulldozer and chain-saw
Will attack and conquer, and the trees will fall,
The stream be diverted, and the lake filled.
All that will be left of my beloved woods
Will be forty-nine, three-bedroom houses
In what the ads will call
a nice, quiet, suburb.

I showed the poem to Nick, Ossie, and Doc on three separate nights. They read it in turn, closing their eyes afterward, and all said the same thing. "Yes. We did that." And "Yes, the woods are now gone." They each stared out toward their own horizon and were silent for a moment. Nick, the historian, was the most vocal. "New City was a very special place to grow up, once upon a time."

EPILOGUE

Some would say I've done a lot in the eight years since my father's passing, and some would say I've done nothing. They would both be right. As the sole heir to my father's surprisingly large estate, plus the Chief's, I will never have to *work* a day in my life, in the traditional sense of the word.

Instead, I stopped running and hiding and moved into the two-hundred-year-old cottage where I grew up. Just the ghosts of my mother, my father, and Huck live there with me now.

I didn't get to see the last sheets of paper from the folder my father gave to Ossie until after my father died. I'm not sure why he wanted it that way, but he did. It's three sheets, and it's called "Letter from Huck."

Hi Brother,
If you're reading this letter, it means that
Dad has probably died. He found this letter

after I typed it, but he tucked it away and then gave it to Uncle Ossie to hold for you, and I didn't know how to get in touch with you for two years, anyway.

I know you're probably surprised to receive a typewritten letter from a fifteen-year-old, blue-tick coonhound, so let me explain.

All those years I spent at Dad's feet while he toiled away at the keyboard was a great learning experience for me. I watched him and I learned that those tap-tap-tap noises he was making with his fingers actually *meant* something. They corresponded with what followed. It all came to me when I heard him tapping and then he stopped to read aloud what he had just tapped out. I put two and two together and realized that each tap was a tiny part of what he was thinking or trying to say. Simple cause and effect, right?

When he wasn't around, I taught myself how to type on his keyboard. This was not easy, given the fact that my nails haven't been trimmed since Mom left us two years ago, and the chair isn't really set at the right height for me. So this took a lot of tapping and backspacing and correcting, almost one letter at a time, with the ergonomics working against me the entire time. Hey, if Christie Brown can do it one letter at a time, so can I.

[Author's note: I had to look up what Huck meant by that.]

I wanted to write this letter for a long time. It's been over two years since Mom died. I can't tell you how much that hurt me. She took such good care of all "her boys," as she called you and Dad and me. I will never get over her death. And then, when you disappeared just days later, it made everything a whole lot worse. I really don't understand why you left and never came back. All I know is how it made me feel and how it made Dad feel and what it eventually did to him.

If Mom's dying wasn't enough to end his world, your leaving right afterward certainly did. I witnessed it all. He was a broken man after that. Instead of working at the keyboard all the time, we would spend most days just sitting in the rocking chair on the front porch together, me on the doormat next to the rocker or sitting on his lap in the wintertime. He wouldn't even rock much, just sit staring out toward the barn. Sometimes he would just walk around in the barn or climb up in the hayloft and dangle his legs over the edge, leaning back against the hay bale. I curled up next to him and didn't ask any questions.

At night he let me hop up on the bed, something I was never allowed to do when Mom was alive, if you remember. He'd pull me to him and I would sleep in the crook of his shoulder, just like you and I used to do when Mom wasn't looking. Many times he would cry, and I would try to snuggle closer, but it didn't seem to help his throbbing shoulders.

So I wanted to write this letter to you in the hopes that it would get to you soon, or at least before Dad died. Why can't you come back home? I really miss you, and Dad is lost without you and Mom.

I keep thinking about the day Mom and Dad found me in the woods, abandoned by my family, because I was the runt of the litter. I hadn't eaten in days and I could hardly walk. I was literally starving to death. When they brought me home wrapped in Dad's winter coat, I looked up and saw the wonderment on your face and it made me feel alive. I'd never seen a happier face. And then I looked over at Mom and Dad and I saw two other happy faces, and I knew I was home at last. I'd never felt such love.

That first day, you held me close to you all day and night. You didn't even get mad at me when I started trembling and peed on the sofa next to you. I remember Dad said, "No one has ever taught him any manners, poor little guy." I tried to learn better manners fast.

The next fourteen years were the happiest of my life. I never wanted for anything, and you and Mom and Dad were always there to help me, no matter what. I could never understand the love you all had for me. I never did anything to deserve it. You all just gave it to me. I've had a better life than many humans.

I really miss you so much, bro. Can't you come home and work out your differences with Dad? I know he really misses you. He acts like his life is over without you. I'm really worried about him. You're the only thing he's got in his life. Everything else has seemed to lose its importance.

You need to come home so we can toss the Frisbee around. I miss those days and our long walks in the woods and our climbs up High Tor. We need another snowball fight.

So please consider. Dad is broken and I'm not sure it can be fixed.

I hope the printer is not out of paper and I can remember how to work it.

I think I just heard Dad pull in the driveway. I have to print this right away and hide it before he comes in.

It's so lonely here without you. Please come home. Please come home.

Your loving brother,

Huck.

P.S. Was I supposed to indent new paragraphs?

Next to Huck's name was a paw print, as if he had taken his foot and inked it with a stamp pad and then pressed his paw on the page, like a librarian stamping a due date at the back of a library book.

I don't know why my father wrote this letter in Huck's voice. Was he actually trying to make me feel worse than I already did? Cry even harder? Was he being manipulative? Cruel? Trying to exercise his artist's prerogatives? Maybe he wrote it to assuage some of his own guilt. Maybe he was trying to make me laugh. I'll never know, but the loss of Huck two years after the death of my mother, and then, in those early days of 2009, the death of my father, was all too much for me to take.

If, as my father suggested, I should *"grieve not, but find strength in what remains behind,"* would I be able to do that? Would I find the strength? I had to find out.

The day after the funeral, I went to work. I started by rereading the paperwork my father had given to Ossie. I opened the thumb drive. On it was a journal my father had kept from the time he left New City in the summer of 1964 up to the day of his diagnosis. It was mostly transcribed from handwritten notes to a WORD® document. It was all there. Of particular interest were the entries he made starting the night after I ran away. The common theme seemed to be, *Missed opportunities between a father and a son*, an age-old story. Does it *always* have to be that way?

I reimagined my father's boyhood adventures. With Nick and Ossie and Doc. I attended Clarkstown High School North Rams football games every Saturday during the 2009–2016 seasons, watching Doc walk the sidelines in search of sprained ankles or concussions or torn ACLs. I talked to the bus driver who drove the high school kids home on the late bus to Centenary after practice every autumn evening back in the early 1960s. What had my father been like in those days? Was there something different about him that separated him from all the rest when he was that age?

My father had concluded that his only way out of town required *reading* his way out of town. And that's what he had done. I concluded that the only entrée into the town of my father required reading my way *into* New City and thereby into my father's brain, just as he had entered and occupied his beloved Miss Singer's brain in the late 1950s.

So I read all of Miss Singer's forty-four books, and like my father, I became a different person forty-four times.

As I read, I noticed that the pages were filled with endless marginalia. Some of it was written by an adult in using the old-fashioned Palmer Method. One of the books had a bookmark with an inscription Miss Singer had apparently handwritten and laminated together with a dried lilac, most likely from her boardinghouse backyard earlier that spring:

> *When you are old and grey and full of sleep,*
> *And nodding by the fire, take down this book,*
> *And slowly read, and dream of the soft look*
> *Your eyes had once, and of their shadows deep;*

I looked it up. It was from a poem by William Butler Yeats. The handwriting matched the marginalia.

But a lot of the margin notes were also written in the penmanship of what we would now call a middle schooler. My father documented each of his discoveries as his young fingers turned the pages and his eyes widened with each revelation of worlds heretofore unknown to him. Each discovery, each epiphany, was checked or underlined or asterisked with a blue ballpoint pen, now smudged or faded and bleeding into the facing page. And as he took notes over fifty years before, so did I in the days and weeks and months after his death I followed in the footsteps of Miss Singer and my father.

What did his marginalia tell me? My father was more insightful as a ten-to-twelve-year-old sixth to eighth grader than I was as a man in my twenties. Did this reflect the decline in reading ability we hear so much about? Probably. It was difficult for this twenty-something to read some of this mid-century prose. My father's sixth-, seventh-, and eighth-grade reading skills and comprehension far surpassed my own as an adult.

Was the marginalia a Rorschach test of some kind? I think it was. For following the marginalia was like being an eyewitness to my father's intellectual and spiritual awakening.

I visited Elsa Bartels again and spoke with her at length. I told her that I had read all the recommendations she had given to my father, suggested reluctantly to him back then due to the adult nature of some of the writing. Now, she shrugged it all off, even the *Lolita* stuff. Had he, in fact, given her copies of his own novels, as he had written them? Yes. She had a signed copy of each one that she showed me. The inscriptions were filled with his thankfulness. Her fingertips touched the faded ink as she looked down at the pages

And then I read all the books my father wrote. It was a painful, emotionally draining experience, as if he were sitting there behind me, talking to me over my shoulder. I recognized the voice, but the words were all new to me. Every page, every sentence, every word made me sob until I had to put the books down hundreds of times over. And when I finished the collection, I started all over from the beginning, just as he had done.

I saw all the documentaries he made during his days at Florida State, working-out his brain instead of his body when he was supposed to be in the training room. I was surprised they were all preserved by the State Archive of Florida on a website called Florida Memory Project. I stayed in touch with Junior Wiley.

I spent countless hours talking to all my father's friends. Ossie and Doc were informative, but I had no idea of some of the things Nick would reveal about what it was like growing up with angry, drunken, brutal fathers. How can people treat their children that way?

I spent the next eight years writing this book, trying to make sense of it all.

My father knew that his own father was complicit in the murder of Miss Singer, a woman he loved and idolized. He knew that his wife's father was implicated in that same murder. What impact did that have on his relationship with his father-in-law? With his own wife? Did it cause him to doubt his marital choice? My mother could not have known about any of this, but she's the one who ultimately paid the price for all of it, her magnificent brain pickled in alcohol into oblivion as a way of self-medicating for her pain over my father's infidelity. And what of her own grand dreams that she had given up to serve my father?

What happened to all those stories he made up in his head but never got out? Don't they count as *matter*? Where are they? *Where is this matter?*

Can the same be said for anyone who dies? Or does the matter only matter when there is something important to be said?

I want to access it all before it is lost forever, but I don't know how to go about it.

When all is said and done, my father was a complicated man.

Now that I know what happened to him, what drove him to obsession, what prevented him from becoming even more successful, maybe I can begin to forgive him for what he did to my mother, and to me—forgive him for the boyhood I never had.

On that last adventure on High Tor, there was so much going on. It was as if he were saying farewell to his old friends, Natty Bumpo, Chingachgook, and Uncas; my mother. He was finally in agreement with William Cullen Bryant, willing to at least contemplate if not accept the consolation he offered in "*Thanatopsis*." He knew he was being summoned to join *the caravan* to that *mysterious realm* with its *silent halls.* He was now ready to *lie down with pleasant dreams.* He knew, at least, that he would be joining old friends on his trip.

One of the last questions I asked my father was on that final day on High Tor. The air was chilled and filled with silence for a long time as he gazed out at the Tappan Zee and then turned to face Lake DeForest. It was a question that had been on my mind for the last few weeks. "When you took your last hike, why didn't you stay up here at the summit, if this place meant so much to you? Why, instead, did you decide to spend your last days on Low Tor?"

He reflected a moment, but somehow I got the feeling that he had prepared, maybe even rehearsed his answer.

"*High Tor* belongs to Maxwell Anderson."

THE END

AUTHOR'S NOTE:

I have not lived in New City for the past fifty-five years, but the truth is, I have never really left my hometown. I'm not sure leaving New City can be done. New City was that kind of place.

My question has always been, "Is the lasting impact of a child's hometown as strong for others as it has been for me?" I don't know the answer and those I've asked have not really been forthcoming. Maybe they don't want to address the question. Or maybe it's just not important to them.

In addition to my parents who dedicated their lives to shaping and influencing our lives through positive examples, part of my childhood foundation was my paternal grandmother, Elsa Bartels Eberling, to whom this book is dedicated. Her influence cannot be overstated. In addition to hunting for books with my father for her in the New City and Spring Valley libraries every week, she had a bookshelf in her own living room that was a constant source of enlightenment for us. She showed us her favorites, told us why we should read them. The story of her showing me the *Sunday New York Times Book Review* of *To Kill a Mockingbird* is based on an actual series of events that I remember vividly. I kept the review for many years. She taught me how to quilt, her thimble-covered fingertips racing along the patterns she had cut from a cardboard template she had crafted.

She also took in a boarder in 1955-56. She was my fourth grade teacher, Barbara Copeland, and all the boys in class were in love with her.

In 1958, when I was twelve and Brother Ray was ten, my father walked us around New City producing a photo essay for his sister, Frances Eberling Rogers, to use for a slide presentation to accompany a historical lecture she was asked to give.

That walk with my father and brother was one of the most memorable days of my life. My father took slides of the old railroad station where he had taken the train to N.Y.U every day and met the woman who would become his bride and my mother. We went to the grammar school on the hill where his father, uncle, and he had attended. My older sister, Bonnie and I had attended through sixth grade and Ray through fourth grade. We walked the streets of New City, and with every step he shared local history and lore with us. The Methodist Church on Maple Avenue, Doc Goebel's animal hospital that had been the original New City Grammar School, and later Forester's Hall and St. Augustine's Church. The current St. Augustine's was also originally the second Forester's Hall. We walked on to New City Park Church, New City Park Lake, Greenberg's Pond, the Irion mansion, the Demarest Kill, and the Dutch Garden where we bumped into the Fishberg twins. He took my picture at the old spring head that flowed through watercress in the run behind the courthouse. We walked past the Eberling family homestead atop New Hempstead curve. We stood in front of the Courthouse and two war memorials, The Elms, Jerry's Tavern, the site of the Eberling Shoe Factory where the Court House Annex now stands. We visited the two original sites of Eberling's Market on Main Street and the new site on Maple Avenue. Shriever Apartments on South Main. They all showed up on his slides and his stories are forever embedded in the brain pans of my brother and me. It was an unforgettable day. Later, he showed us actual photos taken inside the shoe factory and the old school houses decades before.

I've spent countless hours retracing our footsteps along the Demarest Kill behind Irion's mansion. During my forty-plus years as a professional documentary filmmaker, making well over 3,000 film and television segments, I never once pushed the button on my 16mm film or video camera without thinking of that day walking the streets of New City with my father and brother. It was a watershed event in my life, that winter day of 1958

Many elements of LOW TOR are based on fact, including the story of a young woman with an attraction to men in police uniforms. It happened in Memphis in the early 1970s. I went to visit my high school friend, Vinny Burns, there in the summer of 1973 and we made three music videos for legendary music producer, Steve Cropper. The police sex scandal was unfolding when I arrived. When I first heard the bewildering story I came up with so many questions. One question could be, could her actions be a motive for her murder? I hung on to that story thread for over forty years. The young woman would eventually admit to sleeping with over 100 Memphis policemen while they were on duty. When I first started writing LOW TOR, I Googled this incident and read several articles about that case. Now, many of the articles have mysteriously disappeared. Try this: {https://www.memphisdailynews.com/news/2017/jul/15/july-14-20-2017-this-week-in-memphis-history/}

Low Tor started out as a screenplay I wrote about 2005, set in New City, specifically for Burt Reynolds. I had interviewed him as a college newspaper reporter in 1967, thanks to a tip from my mother. Later, as a TV news reporter I had the chance to interview him several more times. I later worked for him for about twelve years at *The Burt Reynolds Institute for Film and Theatre* in Jupiter. He had appeared in my award-winning documentary about our Shakespeare professor at Palm Beach Junior College, *Goodnight, Sweet Prince, a Tribute to Watson B. Duncan, III.* Duncan had discovered Burt Reynolds in 1956 and cast him in a play. It was the start of his career. Duncan had encouraged me to become an English major.

Mr. Reynolds and I spent many nights together with some of Florida's greatest actors doing scene study, rehearsals, work shops. He would direct, and I would film. We would consult about camera placement, movement, lenses. He knew camera. He was one of the greatest teachers I've ever worked with; passionate, patient, encouraging. Those were magic years.

I wrote the *Low Tor* main character of Abby Traphagen specifically for Reynolds, and the other characters were written for his friends, Ossie Davis as his attorney, Charles Nelson Reilly for Doc, Charles Durning for Chief Schoonmaker, and Alfie Wise for

Vince Tramontana. I thought by offering his friends parts in the ensemble cast, he was sure to say "Yes." Can you imagine what it would have been like for me to return to my hometown of New City to direct a Burt Reynolds movie? He turned down the script with some important advice. "Don't show me a script. Show me an *offer*." He said it in friendship, but that's how things work in that world. He would eventually perform a cameo role in my children's environmental feature film, *Turkles*.

When all of Mr. Reynolds' friends passed away or became too old for the physicality the roles demanded, I decided to turn the *Low Tor* story into another New City mystery novel. But, of course, the plot was too thin. What to do? Round out the character of the novelist, Abby Traphagen, with stories about his past, to understand how his character developed. Make his estranged son, Abby III, the narrator of the novel, talking about his father.

I tried to give it some interesting New City history, for more background, but not as much as what I did with *Demarest Kill*.

As far as the Traphagen documentaries he filmed while a student at FSU? They pretty much mirror the documentaries I made while working as a freelance producer for Florida PBS. Yes, I really did interview a surviving ninety year-old employee of Thomas Edison on the Edison estate in Ft. Myers. And yes, I really did get almost lost in the middle of a cave in the middle of the night in the middle of a cow pasture in Ocala, Florida, in early 1965.

There are so many rich, New City stories to tell. Is anyone interested without there being a mystery-genre plot attached? I don't know.

For interested readers, I hope to have my next New City novel ready by the end of 2019. It's a comedy-drama, set in New City Park during the summer of 1963. It's called *The Glorious Summer of Our Content*. No murders this time like in *Low Tor* and *Demarest Kill*. It's about three generations of an extended Norwegian family all living together and how historic world events beginning in late 1963 and in the following decades, impact the lives of each family member. Think of *Life With Father* meets *I Remember Mama*, set in the summer I refer to as "the calm before the storm."

Also coming up is a novel that begins and ends in New City over a fifty year period, but much of which takes place in south Florida. It's called *Jimmy Vanderbeek's Last Refrain*. And yes, there is a murder in this one.

Frank Eberling

THE GLORIOUS SUMMER OF OUR CONTENT

a novel by
Frank Eberling
©2019

Now is the winter of our discontent
Made glorious summer

        RICHARD III, WILLIAM SHAKESPEARE

With apologies to William Shakespeare, John Steinbeck, Charles Dickens, Herman Melville. Oh, and Leo Edwards, Max Shulman, Mark Twain, Robert McCloskey.

CHAPTER 1

Call me *Iver*.

Or call me by my friends' nickname for me, "Ivy."

It was the *best* of times, it *was* the best of times. It was the age of happiness and discovery, it was the age of innocence and *naivete* and excitement, it was the epoch of optimism, it was the age of belief in the future, it was the season of brightness, it was the season of open horizons, it was the spring of smiles, it was the summer of hope, it was the age of belief, the age of foolishness. We had everything before us, we were all going to Heaven.

It was *the glorious summer of our content.*

In the summer of 1963, all was well with the world. Or, at least my world.

I was living in a perfect place in time, in the embrace of a perfect home and extended family; a life filled with love and music and laughter and wisdom. It was all so tangible, I could reach out and touch it and cradle it in my hands while it shaped me. Why didn't I take the time to listen? To notice? To observe? To *pay attention?*

Looking back, from today's perspective, it is often difficult to imagine that such a family and such a place existed. Was it all conjured up by a Hollywood screenwriter to exemplify what an ideal life could actually be? Weren't we living in an Ozzie and Harriet meets Norman Rockwell world? Please tell me it all wasn't a dream. Never mind.

Don't bother. I know it wasn't a dream. I know it wasn't a dream that I was a third-generation Norwegian boy growing up in New City Park in a house my grandfather had built with his own, tired, gnarled shipbuilder's hands for my father to grow up in and eventually inhabit with my mother and my three siblings and me.

I know it wasn't a dream that there was an identical house that mirrored ours across a patio he had also built for my aunt when she married, where she could raise her own family, my three cousins.

I know it wasn't a dream that my grandfather and his Norwegian immigrant friends and neighbors, newly settled in New City Park after World War I, had created the New City Park Club and had converted an old mill pond on the Demarest Kill into the best swimming club in the entire world, and I know it wasn't a dream that I was privileged to be a lifeguard there for three summers in the early 1960s.

It would be a few more years before *we tripped the light fandango, turned cartwheels 'cross the floor*[1], but if I had been paying attention, would I have noticed that change was in the air? Would I have noticed that the world was about to trip and stumble and career out of control, never to regain its firm footing, while we stood by and vaguely sensed something was happening, but were, somehow, oblivious to it all?

It was indeed, earth-shattering. Our lives and our world were never to be the same again. As Ernest Hemingway said, "It was the end of something."

And so looking back at that final summer of 1963, after all we have been through in the ensuing sixty years, I still cannot believe it was real.

[1]From *A Whiter Shade of Pale*, Lyrics by Gary Brooker, Keith Reid' and Matthew Fisher

JIMMY VANDERBEEK'S LAST REFRAIN

a novel by
Frank Eberling
©2019

Jimmy Vanderbeek picked up his Martin guitar and walked out onto the screened-in porch of the cottage and watched the late afternoon sun trying to dance its way through the nearby tree branches.

The small, weekend house on Lake Lucille off South Mountain Road in New City was surrounded by huge maple trees, and a light breeze signaled the approach of the fall season as he sat down on the porch swing hanging from chains bolted to the rafters.

He tried to assess his situation. His ten year-old son was enrolled at Clarkstown Middle, had started school two weeks ago, and seemed happy with his new environment and friends.

He, himself, had some new songs he wanted to write and his notepad was filled with scratches and scraps of lyrics he had been inspired to write in the four weeks since he had returned home to New City after forty years. Although writing about upstate New York was quite a different exercise than writing about south Florida, where he had been living during those ensuing years.

He would have to listen for new rhythms, discover new inspiration, revisit his boyhood walks in the woods. Make himself aware of different voices. He didn't think it would be that difficult if he didn't run out of time. Time was really the issue.

He had real money in his pocket for the first time in many years, after trying to survive on the salary as a high school music teacher in Palm Beach County for the past ten years. That and playing weekend gigs at a million local waterfront bars in Florida for audiences who wanted to hear Jimmy Buffett songs instead of his stuff. Once in a while there was even a royalty check in the mail from a song or two he had written twenty-thirty years ago. Some had even been recorded by name artists in the past. Names that no one remembered or recognized these days.

Yes, life was good. If you didn't count his health issues and the body of the dead woman sprawling across the bed in the room behind him. It looked like a suicide to him. Would it to others?

He started strumming his guitar, waiting for the police and ambulance to arrive. He started playing a song he had recorded thirty years ago that had reached #120 on the Billboard Charts, "bubbling under the Hot 100," before disappearing forever.

Just as Jimmy got to his last refrain, he could hear the wailing sirens of the approaching vehicles as they maneuvered the twists and turns of the narrow New City mountainside road on their way to answering his 911 call.

Demarest Kill

a novel by
Frank Eberling
©2016

SUMMARY

When an investigator from the District Attorney's Office in New City, New York, arrives at the scene of a brutal murder on the stream bank of the DEMAREST KILL in The Dutch Garden, he discovers the victim is his high school sweetheart and lifelong love.

Shocked and heartbroken, his search to find the killer takes him back in time over forty years to when they first met; their glorious childhood and teen years; their falling in love; and their inevitable break-up.

As he relives the boyhood he was so desperately trying to forget, he is forced to confront the mistakes of his past. When he is implicated and becomes a suspect himself, he struggles to defend himself before an investigative team of lifelong friends.

The DEMAREST KILL takes the reader back to a perfect time in a perfect place in a perfect world, to tell a tale of reminiscence,f obsessive love, regret, and reconciliation, in a New City, New York that no longer exists.

WHAT READERS ARE SAYING

"I grew up in New City during this era. Every page took my breath away with a closely observed reminiscence. He nailed it."
"Heartbreaking. It made me homesick for the old days."
"A mystery of a place as well as of characters."
"It defies the conventions of a standard mystery to focus on an unforgettable love story."
"Not just another Sixties' story. Far from it.

ensueño

a novel by
Frank Eberling
©1982–2014

PROLOGUE

Where were you on the night of June 20, 1986?

You probably don't remember. If you're like most people, you may not even remember 1986. But I remember what I was doing on the shortest night, before the longest day of that year. I remember because I was kidnapped.

Kidnapping can take on many forms. Usually, it implies that a child has been stolen from parents. In my case it takes on an entirely different meaning.

Even though I was over thirty years old, you might say I was still a "kid." And I was definitely "napping."

As far as being stolen from my parents, I prefer to think they were stolen from me.

And what I was doing the night that I was kidnapped and what happened as a result?

I remember it quite vividly, because that night was the flash-point that ignited changes in my life that had been in the making for quite some time, without my knowledge.

Now, when I think of my "kidnapping," it's almost like it was......*a dream.*

CHAPTER 1

I sit, typing, filling up a canary yellow second-sheet with my story. The words flow from me and spill onto the page as effortlessly as if I had taken a razor and sliced the veins in my wrists and allowed the blood to flow onto the keys.

As I type in the darkened room, I feel his hand fall on my shoulder. It is a touch of comfort, approval, love perhaps. He keeps his hand on my shoulder for a moment, then taps his cupped fingers twice, slowly, and walks away.

I finish the sentence on the page before I turn. But, by then he is gone. I walk to the door and as I step over the threshold he disappears into the darkness before I can call his name. I am too late.

Then like a drowning victim filled with gasses, I ever-so-slowly rise to the surface and awaken from my dream.

JUNE 20, 1986:

The full moon in June cast a long shadow on Lake Worth as it rose over the Flagler Museum on the Island of Palm Beach. From across the water on the West Palm Beach side of the Intracoastal, I lay aboard my forty-foot Morgan sailboat, half dozing from my dream. There was not a breeze in the air, and as I stared dreamily over the water toward that mysterious, palm-laden island paradise, I kept waiting for the familiar lapping sound of the water against my boat's wooden hull. But the sound wasn't there. The water was as flat and still as a table top. As black and motionless as death.

I had been thinking a lot about death lately. How it comes so unexpectedly and leaves you with such mixed feelings: sorrow, regret, an empty longing than can never be filled; pain, and sometimes, even relief. At least those were the feelings I had felt about my late wife, Nikki: dead at the age of thirty.

I was trying not to think of the events of the last two months: all the changes I had gone through; the emotional turmoil, the "going through the motions" of work at school; ignoring my students and waiting for the school day to end.

Trying to forget about those Spring days was not possible, even now that it was early Summer and school was out and I had nothing to do but sit on my sailboat in the almost empty downtown marina and decide what to do with my life.

Coming into a lot of money suddenly is not all it's cracked up to be. Not when you were as confused as I had been lately.

So I just sat there in my sling chair on the shortest night of the year and stared out at Flagler's "Whitehall" and wondered what life had been like for the railroad tycoon eighty years before in the big white palace across my watery front yard. And still, there was no lapping sound against my hull. Not so much as a ripple.

Half asleep, I climbed down into the hold and pulled another beer from the box and rolled the icy bottle against my forehead. The cold felt good against my sunburned skin. One more beer in this heat and I would be asleep again before I knew it. Another chance to dream.

A yacht sounding its horn went by out in the Intracoastal as it motored north toward the Palm Beach Inlet. The bell on the drawbridge rang, announcing its intent before the red lights started blinking and the black and white gates swung down and the steel roadway cracked open and pointed toward the black sky like a trap door. In a moment, the passing boat's wake would reach me and I would feel the lapping of waves I had been waiting for all night.

As I climbed up the gangway, the gentle rocking began, and I had to grab onto the rail to steady myself as I pulled up the ladder. And then it stopped and I was once again alone on the hot, motionless water.

There were only a handful of boats roped to the three T-docks in the Downtown Marina. Four months earlier, at the height of the tourist season in February, over one hundred boats had been moored, and the make-shift city afloat, made up of the finest boats from the North, had been a bustling winter community of its own. But now, the boats were all in their home berths in Newport, Providence, Baltimore, Annapolis and Martha's Vineyard, and I was here to sweat out the summer with the few remaining permanent residents.

I don't know how long I had been dozing when the rippling sound began somewhere out in the channel. I was so used to hearing the water break in my sleep I didn't think much about it until I remembered there was no breeze and no boat to cause it.

And then I could hear the coarse breathing, of what

could only be a person, swimming closer to the end of the dock where I was moored. I sat up in my sling chair and squinted my eyes into the moonlit darkness. Behind me, no one was about on the few boats nearby. Whoever was swimming toward me was coming from out in the channel. Unusual. No one swims in the fouled Intracoastal, at least not on purpose, especially at night.

And then I saw it wasn't a *whoever,* it was a woman. She had dark hair and a dark tan to match, but even in the bright moonlight I had trouble making out her features until she was holding onto the rope attached to my dive platform. As she pulled herself up hand-over-hand over the transom, gasping for air, I could see what looked like a pure white two-piece bikini. But then as she walked over to where I was sitting, spellbound in my chair, I could see it wasn't a bathing suit after all, just pure white skin with dark tan lines. I glanced down to the glistening black patch between her legs and then up to her white breasts and dark nipples and then to her face. When she opened her mouth to speak, her teeth were so beautifully white, I almost didn't hear what she said in a breathless, urgent whisper.

"I know who killed your wife."

Sweet City Blues

a novel by
Frank Eberling
©1982, 2013

SUMMARY

"Ever had your life changed by a movie character?
Sixteen year-old Charlie McGill did.
Too bad it was the Paul Newman
character in the movie
HUD. "

In the late 1970s, a Country/Western disc jockey drives around Sweet City, Florida, in the same 1958 pink Cadillac Paul Newman drove in the classic movie, *HUD.*

A small-town celebrity, 'Goodtime Charlie McGill' spends his mornings on the radio airwaves and his afternoons and evenings chasing women and living the life of a philandering derelict. Now, it's all about to catch up with him when he finds himself in a life-threatening jam.

A bittersweet, melancholy comedy for all lovers of Florida stories and Country Music. At times it will have you laughing out loud and a moment later you'll be holding back the tears, but you won't soon forget Goodtime Charlie McGill.

SWEET CITY BLUES is a rollicking tale of life in a small country town when sex was, you know, good, clean fun.

"My nomination for the next Florida-novel-that-should-be-turned-into-a-film. You'll agree."

"Like Country & Western Music? You'll love this story."

"Can a clueless, profligate, knucklehead be the hero of a story? You be the judge."

"Hilarious...A Florida not often seen by outsiders. This is a rare treat."

"An instant Florida classic.

Snowbirds

a novel by
Frank Eberling
©2019

SUMMARY

On a cold miserable winter day in Manhattan, three diverse married couples from varying age groups and interests, all hop in their cars and drive to Florida for a short getaway from the miserable weather.

The trendy, mid-Twenties couple, head south to Cocoanut Beach to make a big cocaine score.

The suburban-looking middle-aged couple also head to the same town to attend a giant swingers' convention.

The retired mid-sixties couple are headed there to attend a national shuffle-board tournament where the husband is defending his championship ranking.

All three couples have identical luggage, a red plaid suitcase, and when they check into the hotel and their bags are intentionally switched, all three couples descend into 72 hours of panic.

Meanwhile, three long-time unemployed losers from Detroit in their mid-Twenties also arrive in town, in pursuit a giant beer party. They're just killing time, spending their last few dollars, before they have to return to pick up their next unemployment check. Totally without direction or ambition, all three score huge financial windfalls within a matter of hours of arriving at Cocoanut Beach.

Between the three couples from New York and the three knuckle-heads from Detroit, these **SNOWBIRDS** make sure that South Florida, and screwball comedies will never be the same.

f /stop

a novel by
Frank Eberling
©1976–2019

SUMMARY

f/stop:
An aperture setting on a camera lens
which determines how much light
is allowed in to pass through and expose the film.

In 1976, the Florida Department of Law Enforcement announced that over a dozen organized crime families had moved into Palm Beach County from the Northeast and were conducting business as usual in illegal gambling, prostitution, drug running and pornography. None of the local television news programs reported this announcement.

Jacob Alexander Gardner has seen just about everything.

As a ten-year old he witnessed a gruesome murder in a corner newspaper store in Manhattan.

As a thirty year-old television news shooter, he's spent years filming conflicts in Vietnam and the Mid-East.

He's chased crooked politicians bad guys all over town, and now he's burned out.

Leaving his estranged wife, he suddenly packs up in the middle of the night to get away from it all. He heads to Key West, for some well-deserved rest and umbrella drinks.

But while driving through West Palm Beach on I-95, he finds himself caught in the final moments of a high-speed car chase that culminates in a shootout. Instinctively, he films it all, and none of the local affiliates have can match his footage.

Hired to fill in temporarily at a West Palm Beach television station, he soon settles in to a new routine as a local news shooter.

But then one night while filming a sports feature at the local *Jai Alai fronton*, he sees someone from his past and his whole world careens out of control as he becomes implicated in Florida mob-related activities.

f/stop is look back at South Florida in the mid–1970s, just as millions of new residents were pouring in from the north, seeking a better, quieter life. What they often found was neighbors from back home.

f/stop is based on many of the events witnessed by Frank Eberling as a television news cameraman over almost a decade. He would spend another thirty-five years as a television writer, producer, director, cinematographer. This novel represents some of his earliest work in long-form fiction.

ABOUT THE AUTHOR

Frank Eberling is a fifth generation New City native.

After graduating from Clarkstown High School in 1964, he moved south to attend the University of Florida. He taught high school English for five years before becoming a television news cinematographer and news reporter at Channel 12 in West Palm Beach for eight years.

Following a stint as a television entertainment magazine producer, he became an Emmy Award-winning documentary filmmaker for almost forty years, producing over 3,000 television segments.

In addition, he taught filmmaking at Palm Beach State College for twenty-six years and at *Burt Reynolds' Institute for Film & Theatre* for ten years.

He has written thirty screenplays and stageplays, six novels, and has written and directed two feature-length narrative films in Palm Beach County.

He is currently developing a slate of micro-budget feature films with Florida themes for Florida actors.

He lives in Florida.

Frank Eberling

Made in the USA
Middletown, DE
18 March 2019